$15°°

12/14

D1081948

WITHDRAWN

THE CAINE FILE

Angela Ciccolo

Marion Carnegie Library
206 S. Market St
Marion, IL 62959

No longer property of
Marion Carnegie Library

Copyright © 2014 by Angela Ciccolo

All rights reserved. No part of this book may be reproduced or transmitted in any form or by any means, electronic or mechanical, including photocopying, recording or by any information storage and retrieval system, without written permission of Publisher, except where permitted by law. For information address: Carthage Road, Ashburn, Virginia.

Carthage Road

ISBN-10: 0615971938
ISBN-13: 978-0615971933 (Custom Universal)

Library of Congress Control Number: 2014933611
Carthage Road, Ashburn, VA

Disclaimer

This is a work of fiction. Names, characters, businesses, places, events, and incidents are either the products of the author's imagination or used in a fictitious manner. Any resemblance to actual persons, living or dead, or actual events is purely coincidental.

The Roman Ritual and rite of exorcism are authentic, spiritual prayers designed to free a possessed person from evil spirits in the name of Jesus Christ. The prayers described here in *The Caine File* are presented in an abridged form, with no intention to minimize their effectiveness or to disparage their legitimate, authorized use under appropriate circumstances.

For My Family

Prologue

Leesburg, Virginia
1983

Today was Michael Avery's day off. It was Monday, summer, and he felt like a million bucks because he didn't have to go to work, see his asshole of a boss, and deal with all the stupid idiots he worked with. Even better, his kids had gone up to Maine to visit their grandparents for two weeks and his wife had to work. He had the house all to himself.

Michael had planned his day with precision. He had a 9:30 a.m. tee time at the Goose Creek Golf Club. Later he would head into town for a bite to eat. Then he would take a long nap and do absolutely nothing. That's right. Absolutely nothing. He closed his eyes, enjoying the silence, when his solitude was interrupted by the persistent ringing of his bedside telephone.

Only his wife, Michele, would call him at 8:04 on a Monday morning. He knew she was pissed off because she had to go into work and he was off for the day. *I should just let it ring,* he thought. But maybe that wouldn't be such a good idea. There might be something wrong with his kids, or it could be his brother calling him about his four-year-old nephew's chemotherapy treatments.

"Hello," he growled into the phone.

"Hey, Mike, I hope I didn't wake you up." It was Michele. Damn it. She'd just left the house ten minutes earlier. He'd just talked to her. What could she possibly want?

"I was asleep, honey." He did not want to have this conversation right now.

"Well, I didn't want to bother you, but I wanted to remind you that today is trash and recycling day."

Damn. She was always coming up with something for him to do. This new recycling thing was a bitch. You had to separate glass, metal, and paper, and you had to put all that shit out with your regular trash, and if they found it mixed in with your garbage, you got a fucking ticket.

"Honey, are you listening to me?" Michele was jabbering away. He hadn't heard a word she'd said.

"Sweetie, I'm just falling back asleep here. What do you want?" Michael reached over to look at the clock. He would have to get up anyway to make his tee time.

"I need you to get the trash out his week. It stinks something awful. I went to get in my car and I could hardly stand being in the garage, it smells so bad."

"OK, I'll take care of it." Mike hung up. He was sure Michele was still talking, but if he didn't get her off the phone, she'd have a list of chores a mile long for him to do—crazy stuff like cleaning out the junk drawer in the kitchen or taking the dog to the vet. Anyway, his armed forces memorabilia collection was in the garage. If the uniforms and papers he stored there absorbed the garbage odors, he wouldn't be able to sell any of his stuff at the upcoming collector's show in Manassas.

Michael scrambled out of bed and went into the bathroom. He slipped on a pair of ratty green flip-flops and pulled a plaid robe around him. He didn't want to give his neighbors a show. That would be all he'd hear about for weeks if he dared to go out in his underwear and someone saw him.

He walked boldly through the front door, awake now, leaving it unlocked behind him. He made his way across the backyard to the detached garage. Phew. Michele was right. The stench was just plain nasty. He would get on the kids as soon as they got back. They must not have taken out the trash for weeks before their vacation for it to smell this bad. He'd reminded them at least six times to take it out and they'd said they had.

The early morning light shone through the windows of the double-door garage. His car was parked where he'd left it two weeks ago. They'd used Michele's minivan to drive the kids up to Maine. He didn't see the trash cans around, but it did smell bad. Probably a possum or cat or something had gotten locked in and then gone on to meet eternity in his garage. Damn it.

Michael moved forward, wishing there were a little more light in the garage. His memorabilia would need to be aired out. The smell was overpowering, nauseating. He grabbed his daughter Sarah's bike and moved it out of the way, and then fell away from what he saw. *Jesus.* Michael Avery ran, puking on the garage floor and then on himself, screaming now, "Call 911! Call 911! Somebody call 911 right now!" He flew into his kitchen and called the emergency response number. The sheriff's office sent a deputy right over because the dispatcher could not make out what Michael Avery was saying about the skin, the skin.

***

The Leesburg sheriff's office lab technicians completed their work and were in the process of returning their tools to the police lab van. A lone photographer was snapping pictures of the exterior of the garage. Michael Avery watched from his kitchen window. The detective, Roger Luby, was headed to the kitchen door. Michele Avery had rushed home and was pacing in the background, smoking cigarette after cigarette, even though she'd paid five hundred dollars for the Smoke Enders program and hadn't smoked in over a year.

Detective Luby entered the door. "Mr. Avery, I just want to go over this one more time."

"Sure, Detective." Michael motioned for him to sit down at the kitchen table. He was still in his underwear. He could see the medical examiner's van pulling away. He sensed the detective was as skittish as he was.

Luby referred to his notepad as he spoke. "Now, you say you've been on vacation for two weeks?"

"That's right. We took the kids to Maine. We left them with their grandparents for the rest of the summer. We do it almost every year."

"And did you leave your garage unlocked?"

Michael held his head in his hands. His wife continued pacing behind him. "Like I said before, I really don't remember. I don't usually lock it. We go in and out a lot for the kids' bikes and stuff."

"Ma'am, do you know whether the door was locked or unlocked when you left?"

"Listen, goddamn it," she snapped, "I don't remember if I locked it or not, and I sure as hell don't know what that has to do with that thing in my garage." She was crying now.

"Ma'am, I know this has been an extremely stressful—"

"Stressful?" Michele yelled. "You're calling it *stressful?* There is some psycho killer on the loose who's skinned God-knows-who in my garage—that's right, in *my* garage—and he left the skin right there in a neat pile, and you think that's *stressful?*"

Luby looked to Michael for sympathy but got none. Michael held his head in his hands and did not respond. Luby was tired of Michele Avery and her hysteria. "Ma'am, I'm just trying to see if there is anything you might remember that would be helpful."

Michele snapped again, "That's right, Detective. I'm just going to forget some six-foot-three guy walking around Leesburg without any skin on his body. Yeah. I would probably remember that. Oh yeah, and I would probably remember some blood-soaked psycho killer walking around the cul-de-sac with a machete."

Luby returned to his notes. "I want to ask you about all those boots out there in the case in the garage. What kind of collection is that?"

Michael snapped back to reality. Michele rolled her eyes and released an exasperated sigh.

"That's my war boots collection," Michael said. Luby never ceased to be amazed at the peculiar collecting habits of seemingly normal individuals. "I have boots from armed conflicts from all over the world—Vietnam, the Civil War, the Spanish American War," Michael went on. "World Wars I and II, of course. I even just got some boots in from the conflict in Afghanistan. They still had blood on them. It's very collectible memorabilia. I have uniforms, papers. All that kind of stuff. I keep it out there. Michele doesn't like it in the house."

This interview was certainly becoming counterproductive. Luby thought back to his recently completed detective's class on ending unproductive interview sessions. He looked up at Michael Avery with genuine understanding, because he knew Avery had to live with Michele and she would probably never calm down about this. Not ever. They would have to move.

A loud knock at the back door caused all three to jump. A deputy sheriff, young, no more than twenty-five or so, appeared. The young man was ashen and pale; having seen more than he signed on for when he'd joined the police force.

"Sir, the medical examiner wants to have a quick word with you before he follows the remains to the morgue." The young deputy stepped outside and sat down on the steps.

Luby went outside. Willard Randolph, the longtime coroner, was waiting for him. Luby guessed Randolph was nearly sixty-five years old, and he looked every bit his age. Randolph's gravelly voice matched his demeanor. He was smoking a stubby cigar and leaned his left elbow against the hood of the medical examiner's van while he puffed on the cigar in his right hand.

"Well, Detective, I'm headed back to the morgue now. Got anything useful to tell me?"

Luby shook his head. "Have you learned anything? I mean, Willard, have you ever seen anything like this before?" He pulled out a cigarette and lit it, then leaned back against the dusty van. Willard could be obnoxious sometimes. He was a real old-timer.

"Well," Willard drawled, "that's a compound question. Let me take the first part first." Willard could be methodical. It was part of his nature. Luby was different. He worked in response to instinct and emotion. He didn't always reach the right conclusion, but most of the time he did. That was important for him, because in police work, quick actions were often required. Sometimes, though, this led him to stick to his conclusions even when the evidence showed otherwise. He was working to be more like Willard Randolph and to let the facts lead him to conclusions. Maybe by the time he was Willard's age, he would be like that too, but now it didn't seem that there was enough time for such a luxury. There was a killer on the loose. A very sick individual. And most of the victim's body was missing.

"Are you even listening, Luby?" Randolph had little patience for anyone who couldn't keep up with him. "I have learned that the victim was male, Caucasian, and approximately six feet, two inches tall, with brown hair and type O-positive blood. He was alive at the time of the event. Obviously, he is very likely dead now, yet there is no sign of any other remains. You don't happen to have any missing persons' reports of skinless six-foot men, do you?" Randolph laughed, blowing a smoke ring.

Luby did not react. He'd seen more than he wanted to today, and this was something he hoped never to see again. Randolph continued, "Your second question was whether I have ever seen anything like this before. My answer is no. I have never *seen* anything like this before." Randolph methodically closed the back doors of the van and got into the driver's seat, holding his cigar firmly between his front teeth. He continued to talk to Luby through the open window. Luby swore he could smell formaldehyde fumes mixing in with the cigar smoke.

"I have, however, *heard* of this type of thing before. You should send down to the closed files to read about it. Back in 1943, I was away at the University when it happened." Randolph was an old-school Virginian, part of that class who called the University of Virginia "the University" as if it were the nation's only institution of higher learning.

"Over at The Oaks, they found a boy skinned. They never found his body, just the skin. That was a strange autumn. He was a colored boy. Seemed like he'd drowned in the back pond there. There were other murders, but they never found the culprits. Then the killing just stopped. One happened in Middleburg, one in Upperville, and the last here in Leesburg. My brother sent the clippings down to me at the University at the time."

Randolph looked Luby in the eyes. Luby was a relative newcomer to Loudoun County, having been born and raised in Arlington. There was a lot of local history he didn't know. The locals were always ribbing him because he didn't know which team won the 1975 football game between Loudoun Valley and Broad Run High School. He didn't remember the old winding roads or the milk train that used to run through the county to deliver produce to Washington, DC.

Randolph started the van. "What's that file called, Willard?" Luby asked.

"Can't remember any names. I just remember they said there wasn't any trace of blood near the skin."

"That's true here too, isn't it?" Luby stepped back, away from the truck.

"That's right. There's no blood in that garage, either."

Luby laughed as he considered an unlikely scenario. "So what we're dealing with here is some sixty or seventy-year-old serial killer."

Randolph grinned and threw the stub of the cigar onto the street. "That would be something, wouldn't it?"

He drove off, leaving Luby standing in the cul-de-sac. It was going to be a long summer.

CHAPTER ONE

Washington, DC
April 2003

Etienne Napoleon Charleroi made his way quickly through the corridors of the Rayburn House Office Building to the House Subcommittee on Intelligence hearing room. He never ceased to be amazed at the number of people who stopped to greet him or who wanted to shake his hand. Sean, his insufferable executive assistant and master in the art of ass kissing, discreetly handed him a note and whispered a few reminders about today's testimony.

Charleroi considered himself a man of the people. Every handshake was a potential vote, every gesture a historic moment to be remembered by those he met. He'd eliminated his pretentious first name years ago and shortened his middle name to Leon, just so it was easier to pronounce by news anchors and his colleagues. At one time there had even been talk that he might run for vice-president of the United States.

As a popular former member of Congress, Leon Charleroi enjoyed easy access to the building. The testimony of his partners today was crucial to paving the way for an initial public offering of his growing technology company, Aspirion Sector. Charleroi entered the hearing room from the witness holding area, shook a few hands, and seated himself behind a name tent on the table before him, which he shared with several other men who worked for him.

The subcommittee chairman, Brian Browning, nodded warmly at Charleroi and called the hearing to order. "Swear in the witnesses," growled Browning. A nearby court reporter administered an oath and then instructed the witnesses to be seated. Charleroi surveyed a list of questions he would surely be asked when it was his turn. Ordinarily he would have been only mildly interested in what Jared Talbot had to say, but today his financial future would depend on it. Talbot was the former director of interactive counterintelligence for the National Logistical Intelligence Bureau, the NLIB, referred to as the LIBBY in the intelligence community. Talbot looked like the stereotypical tech geek. He was pale, wore thick glasses, was unquestionably hyperactive, and could be socially awkward. He was also undeniably brilliant. Talbot could have made millions in the private sector years earlier. Word was that he'd stayed with the federal government so long because he got a kick out of being associated with top-secret work and the perks of meeting members of Congress and the executive branch. Charleroi had been able to lure Talbot away from the LIBBY for a seven-figure salary and stock options. The little twerp had earned almost four million dollars thanks to Charleroi. They both stood to double their fortunes if this testimony went well.

Talbert had testified many times. This time, however, he was uncharacteristically overdressed in a smart, salmon-colored tie and tailored sport coat. A laptop computer was positioned on a podium to his left, and several flat-screen television monitors were positioned throughout the room for easy viewing by the spectators. The audience was small and restricted to select members of the intelligence community.

"Ladies and gentlemen," began Talbot with a dramatic flourish. "I am happy to greet all of you. Good afternoon, Chairman Browning and Vice-Chairman Axelrod. For the record, I am Jared Talbot, former director of the National Logistical Intelligence Bureau, and currently the principal technology officer for Aspirion Sector." Aspirion's logo appeared on the screen. "I am here today to share an exciting development with you."

Charleroi grinned. Having a contract with the government's intelligence agencies was more lucrative than playing legislator. The war on terror gave his company multiple opportunities to share its research and to entice government procurement officers. As a former member of Congress, Charleroi had been able to engineer the hearing. Aspirion tended to focus on human intelligence solutions, James Bond–like gadgets that staff and members of Congress enjoyed seeing and paying for.

Talbot reminded Charleroi of a Willy Wonka type, a Pied Piper of technology. Their new device would go on display today. Wowing members of the subcommittee could lead to millions for his firm. He looked back and nodded at his assistant technology director, chief financial officer, and chief of information technology, who were seated in the audience behind him.

A congressional staffer in the rear of the room groaned. Talbot's exciting revelations sometimes digressed into a discussion of physics or biomedical engineering, which went over almost everyone's head. Charleroi's team had spent hours preparing Talbot for today and for this display. Talbot continued animatedly as he began his presentation. "The idea for our latest innovation in the field of counterintelligence was inspired by the Hollywood film star Jackie Chan."

Two interns began to giggle as a picture of Jackie Chan flashed across the screen. A short film clip accompanied Talbot's excited delivery. "You see, in the movie *The Tuxedo*, Jackie Chan utilizes a mechanically engineered suit designed by government intelligence agencies to permit the wearer to perform any number of difficult stunts and nearly impossible physical maneuvers." Committee members began to chuckle. "After seeing this movie, I was inspired to create such a suit." Charleroi looked at Vice-Chairman Axelrod, who tried to suppress a yawn.

"I wanted to create a method for our intelligence agents to obtain visual data at close range." Talbot stood dramatically, moving from behind the table to stand before the committee members. The members of the Capitol Police looked at Talbot nervously and moved in closer. Vice-Chairman Axelrod waved them off.

"I present for your approval, ladies and gentleman, Aspirion Sector's Cybervisionwear." As Talbot touched the top button of his jacket, images of the committee members appeared on the projector screen. Several committee members laughed and nodded with approval. "That's right, ladies and gentlemen. You're on television; you're being recorded right now courtesy of Cybervisionwear. This suit is programmed using a patent-pending optic net. This 'seeing-eye suit' is imbedded with microscopic cameras undetectable to counterintelligence surveillance equipment."

Talbot continued as images appeared on the screen. "The advantage of this approach is self-evident. Agents may enter a targeted area of interest and generate photographic evidence without detection." He paused and gestured to his colleague standing on the other side of the room. "In addition, the X-ray option is able to detect hidden weapons; to review data within desks, clothing, or behind other barriers; and to read that information clearly."

On cue, Emilio Gonzalez, Aspirion's intern, stepped up to the front of the room. Talbot continued. "By straightening my lapel, just like this"—Talbot paused and stroked his lapel, removing an imaginary speck of lint—"I am able to see exactly what is inside Mr. Gonzalez's breast pocket." Projected on the screen was a document folded into four quadrants and lodged in Emilio's pocket. Talbot's voice rose excitedly. "I can zoom in here"—Talbot now brushed off his lapel—"and voilà!" The image unfolded as if animated. It was upside down, but the words in Spanish were clearly visible. Talbot touched a button on his lapel. "I have now just forwarded this information to my staff at Aspirion's headquarters, where intelligence analysts will manipulate and translate the image into English." The committee members nodded appreciatively.

Charleroi smiled to himself. He was going to make a fortune.

***

Kathy Marsh relished entering the hearing for the House Subcommittee on Intelligence. Kevin Washington, the Capitol Police officer she'd screwed last week, smiled and opened the door for her.

"Thanks, Kev."

The man returned her smile. "Any time, any time."

Kathy held a folder tightly to her chest. Congressman Browning sat on the dais with three of his colleagues, two on the left and one on his right. Nameless staffers sat behind each congressman. The committee vice-chair, Axelrod, sat with his eyes closed, but he was listening. Former congressman Charleroi was at the witness table. He had been out of office for several years, but it was as if he'd never left. His company, Aspirion Sector, had developed the technology that was being displayed at today's hearing.

Mr. Talbot sat across from the committee members next to Charleroi, nodding and smiling like an idiot. His perky assistant sat in the row behind him, looking proud and confident that their stock price would rise just in time for the company's initial public offering and after winning a fat government contract.

Kathy smiled at Tad Dunnigan, Congressman Browning's chief of staff. Tad was taking her out for a drink after work and they were going to talk about her raise. She grinned to herself. She was going to do whatever it took to get that raise. The office secretary, Stephanie, had been right. It had only taken lightening her hair a few shades to get Tad's attention. Kathy wasn't certain, but she thought that even Congressman Browning had been friendlier lately.

She walked down the left side of the aisle and made her way between the staffers and behind the witnesses. She bent behind Charleroi, tapping his arm to get his attention. Congressman Floyd from Missouri was asking the witness about digital mapping technology, and Talbot was babbling away like he was on geek-school radio. Kathy knelt beside Charleroi and whispered in his ear.

"Congressman Charleroi, you have a message from John Hunt." She handed him a pink message slip. "He told me I should find you and give this to you immediately."

Charleroi looked at the message and then at the clock. He whispered to Kathy to give Browning a message that they needed to take a recess. Kathy made her way to the members on the dais and whispered the message into Browning's ear as Floyd and Talbot continued their discussion. Browning responded immediately. He was, after all, Charleroi's man.

Charleroi looked down at the message and then at the clock. Browning interrupted Talbot midsentence. "Ladies and gentlemen, let's take a thirty-minute recess."

Charleroi did not wait for anyone. He went briskly to Browning's office. Tad ran behind him, trying to catch up. He worked for Browning, but everyone knew that Charleroi was really still the boss.

***

Charleroi breezed through the front door of Congressman Browning's private office, past the receptionist. He barked a stern order: "See that I'm not disturbed, Lois. I have an important call to make." Browning, a representative from Kentucky, allowed Charleroi to use his office whenever he needed it. Browning had benefited from their friendship to the tune of several million dollars through their business deals. For all intents and purposes, Browning's office was Charleroi's office.

Charleroi punched in the number rapidly. He knew John Hunt's number by heart. The two men had been friends since the age of four, having grown up in New Orleans society back in the '40s and '50s. Their mothers had been the best of friends, and so they too had become friends and remained friends even now, with five wives and many more children between them. Both had pursued legal careers after college. After law school, Charleroi had entered politics while Hunt joined his grandfather's successful private practice and lobbying firm. He was Charleroi's personal counsel for all sensitive matters. Charleroi couldn't remember John ever having described anything as urgent. Something important must have happened.

The phone rang twice. Gloria, John Hunt's longtime personal assistant, answered. "Mr. Hunt's office, how may I help you?"

Charleroi hesitated. "Hello, Gloria, this is Leon Charleroi. I was hoping to speak to John." He pulled his Blackberry from his breast pocket and began to type an e-mail to a colleague from Minnesota regarding the pending cybersecurity legislation. Since founding Aspirion, Charleroi had not only made a ton of money but had also parlayed his access to lawmakers into a successful and lucrative second career. The funny part was he didn't really know anything about technology. He left all that to the geeks. His job was to open doors and get them access to funders and appropriations. The techies took care of all the gadgets and software.

"Mr. Charleroi, how are you, sir?" Gloria sounded genuinely pleased to speak to him. She had not changed a bit over the thirty-some years he had known her. She was always at work and didn't seem to have a personal life.

"I'm just fine, Gloria. I hope you're doing well. John left a message for me to call and he said it was urgent. Is everything OK?"

"Mr. Charleroi, hold on, please. I told Mr. Hunt I would try to patch you into his cell phone. He's on the way to the airport. Hold on."

Charleroi put his Blackberry aside and rummaged through Browning's desk for a pen. Gloria returned to the line. "Mr. Charleroi, sir, I only got his voice mail, but he did ask me to tell you that if you called and he didn't get to speak to you, I was to let you know he would speak to you when he sees you this evening."

"This evening?" Charleroi didn't know John was planning a trip to Washington.

"He said he'd talk to you in person when he got there."

Charleroi was puzzled. "Gloria, do you have any idea what he was calling about?"

"No, sir, I don't. All I know is that he canceled all his afternoon appointments and had me book him on the first flight to Washington. He should get there around three thirty."

"Thanks, Gloria. If he calls you, tell him that I want to speak to him. I'll make sure he gets put through directly to me."

Charleroi put down the phone and looked out the window, frustrated that he would have to wait until later to find out what was up. He stood, buttoned his jacket, and prepared to return to the hearing.

***

Charleroi's attention wandered. Talbot, his principal technology officer, answered any number of questions about Cybervisionwear's technical specifications. Several members asked for the device to be directed at their desktops, which resulted in delighted expressions of wonder as Talbot described in detail the information at each member's desk.

When the hearing adjourned, Charleroi bolted from the room and made his way through the hallway. Browning's assistant, Stephanie and chief of staff, Tad, walked by his side, each trying to put in a pitch for why they would like to work for Aspirion when they finished their current positions on the Hill. Charleroi looked at his Blackberry and saw that Lois had sent him a text telling him that John Hunt had arrived and was waiting for him in Browning's office. Charleroi walked faster.

"Lois, I don't want to be disturbed," Charleroi commanded as he went into the office, slamming the door behind him in Stephanie and Tad's faces. This was going to be a very private meeting.

John Hunt stood by the large window, taking in the remarkable view. The office was impressive, one of the benefits of Browning's long tenure and rank as member of the House leadership.

"Hey, man! How've you been, you rascal?" Hunt grabbed Charleroi and hugged him with genuine affection. Charleroi smiled. John Hunt was his oldest friend and the only person he really trusted. He couldn't wait any longer to find out what was so important that John had interrupted his golf game to come see him. He was certain that whatever it was must be related to Sam's paternity. Such an unexpected visit could only mean one thing. In the words of talk show host Maury Povich, "He was *not* the father."

"Leon, I want you to sit down so I can talk to you about some things." Hunt gestured toward the couch.

Charleroi bristled. "I don't want to sit down, John. I just need you to tell me what's up."

Hunt moved back across the room and sat down across from his longtime friend. "You're going to tell me he's not my kid, aren't you?" Charleroi asked. He grabbed a crystal ashtray from the coffee table and threw it against the far wall, knocking down several of Congressman Browning's many plaques. Lois and Tad rushed in.

"Sir, is anything wrong?" Tad asked, giving his best caring look and seeming genuinely concerned. He moved across the room to pick up the plaques.

"What didn't you understand?" Charleroi barked. "I told you I didn't want to be disturbed!"

"But we heard…" stammered Lois.

"Get out!" Charleroi yelled. The embarrassed aides slumped back through the door, confused. Charleroi hoped they wouldn't call security to report the disturbance. "Look, Leon. It's not what you think. He isn't sick, either."

"Thank God," cried Charleroi. "I love that kid." He teared up. Charleroi took his children very seriously.

Hunt handed him a box of facial tissues from Browning's credenza. "Leon, we did the investigations and tests you asked us to do. I understand that you wanted to take steps to verify paternity in the event you decided to move forward with divorce proceedings."

Charleroi nodded but did not speak. Hunt cleared his throat. "We've been conducting surveillance of Marissa for about eleven months now. Your concerns were warranted. We've documented thirty-six separate sexual encounters with men and women Marissa slept with within hours of meeting them. Some encounters involved three or more persons."

Charleroi tensed as Hunt continued. "We've documented sixteen separate purchases of illegal drugs, including four cocaine, two LSD, six heroin, and four recent purchases of methamphetamines. Marissa has accumulated over ninety-six thousand dollars in credit card debt, most in the form of cash advances to purchase drugs."

Charleroi shook his head. His worst suspicions were coming true. She would ruin him and the sterling reputation he had worked to build. At this rate she would bankrupt him. He needed to end the relationship now, before Aspirion went public. Hundreds of millions of dollars were at stake.

"In addition, Leon, my investigators documented four car accidents. In two instances she hit parked vehicles and left the scene without notification. The other two incidents involved collisions. In one instance she was not at fault. She was rear-ended. In the other, damage to the other vehicle, a motorcycle, was significant. The owner accepted a large amount of cash from your wife—as best as we can estimate, over forty-eight hundred dollars. In addition, the motorcycle owner accepted some drugs, although we cannot verify what she offered and what was accepted. Lately she has been seeking out fortune-tellers and mediums. We intercepted some of her e-mail and discovered she's hooked up with some con men online. I'm sure she'll start shelling out to them too." Hunt pulled a thick report from his briefcase and dropped it onto the coffee table. "We also have reason to suspect that Marissa falsified her identity when she came to this country."

Hunt rose and crossed the room, then turned back to look at his old friend. Charleroi recognized the look on John's face. He was about to give Charleroi some really bad news. "At your request, Leon, we performed DNA tests on your son Sam to determine paternity." Charleroi remained still, looking down at the floor with his head in his hands. "We received the results approximately eight weeks after the samples from you and Sam were submitted in a double-blind study for analysis at two different labs."

Charleroi looked up, waiting for the news he dreaded would come.

"Leon, the results confirmed unequivocally that you are Sam's father."

Charleroi breathed in deeply, as if he had not heard the news correctly. "John, I don't understand. According to what you just said, you've known for nearly two months that I was his father. Why didn't you tell me?"

John looked out the window. "Frankly, Leon, we were concerned that the results were not correct."

"What do you mean you were concerned about the results? You said you did two double-blind studies and they both came back saying I was the father. What else could you need?"

"Based on some puzzling test results, we sent additional samples for a second double-blind study, once again to two different labs, different from the labs we used the first time. The most recent results came back in the mail two days ago. That's when I decided I needed to talk to you."

Charleroi rose from his seat. "Stop bullshitting me, John. Get to the point." He tensed, expecting the worst. It must be something bad. Maybe cancer. Maybe some unpredictable genetic defect that would manifest itself at any time.

"As I said, each of the tests that came back was consistent in that all had the same results regarding paternity. The results are 99.9999989 percent accurate and demonstrate with certainly that you are Sam's father."

"John," Leon whispered hoarsely, "I just don't get it. What is it that I am missing here?"

"Leon, listen. All the tests results showed that Marissa is not Sam's mother."

Charleroi burst out laughing. He reached for a flask of whisky inside the bottom left drawer of Browning's desk and poured a healthy glass for himself. Browning's office manager had worked for Charleroi for many years. He encouraged her to stock Browning's desk with his favorite snacks and drinks, especially since Charleroi was a frequent visitor. "John, you're absolutely full of shit. The results have to be wrong, for God's sake. You were there with your wife, Liz, when Marissa went into labor. You went with us to the hospital. Marissa was as big as a house. I even made a video as Sam was being born, and Liz was pissed because she said I shouldn't videotape a woman giving birth. We laughed about it." He took a long drink. "You must be dealing with a messed-up lab. No wonder all those folks keep writing to Browning about how labs messed up their DNA test results. They are probably all innocent." He drank deeply and laughed so hard he began to cough.

"Leon, I need for you to listen to what I'm saying. We didn't know what to think." Hunt sat down on the couch, and Charleroi poured another glass of whisky. "At first I thought maybe someone had switched the kids at the hospital. I could see it happening." Charleroi cleared his throat and finished off his whisky. "Then we considered whether Marissa had actually carried Sam. We wondered if maybe she had used a surrogate. But I told the labs that a surrogate was not a possibility. I told them I was present at Sam's birth."

Charleroi continued to nurse his drink. He paced the length of Browning's office and shook his head in disbelief as Hunt spoke.

"Yesterday I met with a representative of the lab myself. He explained to me that your son is fine, and that you are fine. Your wife, however, is rather unique genetically."

Charleroi stopped short. "Are you trying to tell me that she's really a man or something, like one of those hermaphrodites? Are you telling me I married a transvestite?"

Hunt laughed. "No, she's not a man. She hasn't had a sex change, and she's not a hermaphrodite. What I'm trying to say is that she's Sam's mother, but she's not his mother. She is a chimera."

Charleroi sat quietly, absorbing news he did not fully understand. "I don't know what you're saying, John. Are you saying she's some kind of freak or something? It sounds like you're saying she's a fucking alien."

"I'll explain it to you like it was explained to me. Even before we enter the world, we spend nine months in the womb. Some of us have a twin, but sometimes that twin doesn't make it. Most of the time the mother doesn't even know she is carrying twins. For some unexplained reason, one of the twins gets absorbed into the other, essentially is cannibalized by the other."

"I've read something about this before. Maybe I didn't read it, maybe it was on *Ripley's Believe It or Not!*. There was a Chinese man who had an extra head growing out of the side of his neck. The head used to move its mouth like it was talking. And there was another story about a man with teeth in his stomach. The program said it came from his twin."

"It's just like that, Leon. What essentially happened is that Marissa's twin was absorbed into her system. Apparently she did not pass on her own DNA, but the DNA from her absorbed twin."

"I don't understand. Are you saying that her twin is inside her, and it's the twin who got pregnant and had Sam? That's pretty freaky."

John laughed. "When you put it like that, you're right, it does sound like a freak show, but think about this." He gave Charleroi his full attention. "It's like this. All the eggs a woman will ever have are formed early in the fetus' development. For some reason, Marissa is passing on her twin's eggs rather than her own. Her twin didn't make it, but in a sense she was more successful from an evolutionary standpoint because she is passing along her DNA and Marissa is not."

"So what you're really saying is that Marissa isn't Sam's mother after all. She's his aunt."

John looked up. "That's right. Genetically she's his aunt."

"Well, thank God for that. That bitch doesn't have a motherly bone in her body." Charleroi smiled. "Let's go get a drink, buddy."

CHAPTER TWO

Leesburg, Virginia

The headlights of the BMW sedan cut through the darkness of the private, tree-lined road. "Damn, girl. You didn't tell us you were a fucking debutante," Reggie said excitedly as he looked at the driver, who drove steadily toward the antebellum mansion in the distance. Reggie passed around "candy" to the car's occupants. Now that they had reached their destination, it was probably OK to give them the Ecstasy. He was going to pass tonight. He wanted to remain alert.

"Man, we're in the middle of fucking nowhere," a voice called out from the backseat.

The driver turned, surveyed him, and sneered back as she turned up her nose. "Shut the fuck up, you shit bag." Both burst into laughter. A lone raccoon scurried across the road in front of the car.

"Shut the hell up, Doug!" cried Reggie. "You almost made her run over that fucking dog."

An older woman's voice joined in, also from the backseat. "I don't think that was a dog. It looks like one of those fucking striped things."

"Like…?" Reggie finished her sentence. "Like a fucking zebra?" The driver, Doug, and Reggie burst into riotous laughter.

The older woman was perturbed. "That's not funny. You know what I mean, like one of those black-and-white things." She flicked the ashes of her cigarette as she talked.

"Like a panda bear?" the driver chortled. The house loomed in the distance less than fifty yards away. An ornate mechanical gate swung open to welcome the vehicle.

"Yeah," the woman replied. "A fucking panda bear." She laughed and rolled her eyes. Reggie had had more to drink than he usually did on these occasions. He was buzzed, but not so much that he didn't appreciate all that this rich lady might be able to do for him.

Reggie nodded appreciatively toward the driver. "Nice crib." One of his contacts from southern Maryland had told him to look at this woman's postings on an on-line chat room because she was a "seeker," trying to reach the spirit world for kicks. Some of what he read in her postings told him that she probably had this kind of dough. Most of what she wrote online was about how much money she spent partying and about trying to communicate with the dead. Some felt the need to exaggerate their looks and what they had on the online forum; others minimized everything. When her page advertised she'd be at Nathan's Saturday night, he made his way there with Doug and Sandy. They'd been partying all night in Georgetown, trying to make their contact with her seem casual and unexpected. When the conversation turned toward deeper subjects, she was hooked. They made her feel like she knew them, because they had done their homework on her habits and interests. They connected with her on almost every level because they knew what to say. Reggie also knew from experience that it was always easy to get someone hooked when they had been drinking all night. As he drank with this woman at the bar, her Jimmy Choos and tailored clothing caught his eyes. He estimated the shoes had cost her almost two grand. If she could afford shoes like that, she was someone he wanted to get to know better.

It was early Sunday morning now, and cold. He drew his coat around him as he, Doug, and Sandy, the woman in the backseat, got out of the car, arguing about whether Ginger on *Gilligan's Island* would sleep with the professor or the skipper first.

The driver shivered, pulling a black leather wrap snugly around her. She pointed the remote key lock to secure the crimson, custom vehicle. Reggie had seen many a BMW, but nothing like this one. He would have to ask her more about it in the house. The gravel crunched beneath Reggie's feet as he slowly followed her to the side door. Some of the Ecstasy must have come off on his hands and made its way into his system. It was the only explanation for the intensifying colors and sounds of everything he was seeing and hearing now. The drug always affected him quickly. Others seemed to ease into it over hours, if not days.

A security booth was situated to the left of the driveway. The driver waved to it as they made their way inside. A lone security guard looked at the group and waved as they passed him and proceeded up the three steps to the door. Reggie would have to keep himself together. He needed to make a connection with this woman so he could move in closer to her and her bank account.

"I'm serious now," Reggie said to the driver. "This is your place?"

The woman unlocked the side door and led them into a spacious, custom kitchen. Glittering copper pots and pans hung from a rack positioned above a large kitchen island. They shone at him as if smiling, like some goofy cartoon. "It's my husband's place."

"Husband?" He needed to make it sound like that would complicate their relationship. "Well, girl, maybe we can work around that."

The rich bitch laughed. Doug and Sandy entered behind them. The driver opened a wood-paneled Sub-Zero refrigerator and retrieved a carafe of fresh-squeezed orange juice.

"Get some glasses out of the cabinets behind you," she ordered Sandy. To Doug she barked, "And you, pretty boy, get the vodka out of the cabinet next to the sink." She turned to Reggie next. "There are some chips and popcorn and stuff like that in the pantry. Make yourself useful and get it out for us." She nodded to a door on the other side of the kitchen. Obviously this bitch was accustomed to giving orders. Reggie walked to the pantry and reached for the well-worn doorknob. His senses were drawn from the kitchen to the hallway. The swishing sound he heard reminded him of a beating heart. It called to him. The sounds of Sandy and Doug arguing about *Gilligan's Island* faded away as he moved to the hallway and into a large, ostentatious formal dining room.

Sandy and Doug always talked about *Gilligan's Island* when they sensed paranormal activity. It was their code and it meant a spiritual entity was present. It was all based on Sandy's claims that she had once contacted the spirit of Alan Hale Jr., who'd played the Skipper on the '60s-era TV show. Sandy claimed to have connected with Hale in the '70s at his lobster restaurant in Los Angeles. Whenever she felt a nearby spirit, she mentioned Hale's character. Reggie entered the dining room. The walls were a deep purple color, almost black, the color of a ripe eggplant. Silver accents adorned the room. Mirrored panels spaced at intervals along the walls made the room seem much larger than it was. His image was reflected from every angle. His senses were heightened and more aroused now. His lean body stood at attention, adrenaline rushing. A presence was here.

An antique mahogany sideboard was to his left. There beside it stood a man. An African. A warrior. His hair was a mass of matted gray curls and kinks, and he was clothed in filthy, coarse burlap pants and shirt. He stood in a pool of water that seemed to grow, seeping toward the carpet in the middle of the room. As his luminescent image became more defined, Reggie became aware of a putrid scent—rotting meat punctuated by sulfur. The man was there with him, but his reflection did not appear in any mirror. The warrior faced Reggie with angry eyes, fists clenched at his side. Slowly the figure opened his mouth, not merely to speak, but to argue. This dialogue was without words, but rather with a growling, guttural, alien sound that held no meaning for Reggie but was disturbing in its tone and intensity.

The giant continued his speech, angrily waving his arms as if to castigate Reggie. Still no recognizable words came from his lips, only the horrible sound and accompanying stench. Then the figure changed, distorting his size and appearance. The warrior glared at Reggie and breathed deeply, audibly, as if the air was being forced from his lungs into the room. As the figure blew, first from his nostrils and then from his open mouth, the stench intensified. And although he continued to breathe in and out more and more rapidly, the strange sounds of unknown words continued to emanate from deep inside him.

Reggie was a logical man. He knew he had to be high. This was good stuff. The image was now a woman, and a fat one at that, with bulging blisters pulsating from her chest. The woman transformed into a skeleton that grinned, pointing at him. Reggie reasoned that the drinks and Ecstasy he'd had tonight were making this experience particularly real. He had not had as much to drink as the others. They got high regularly to open themselves to other realities. He tried to process what he was seeing. Maybe this was why they took the LSD and shit—to intensify the experience. He'd seen things before when he was high, but the added feature of the smells and the strange language made his flesh crawl, like when someone scraped their fingers along a chalkboard. Maybe this was what they had been waiting for.

Reggie had sensed a presence early in the evening, long before he entered the house. In fact, he knew he was onto something when he first spotted Marissa Charleroi at the bar. The essence of it clung to her like a fading psychic perfume. Doug and Sandy had felt it too. The silent, knowing glances among them signaled their recognition that the encounter that had eluded them for some time had become a reality again. The Internet made it easier to find other believers like them, believers in a world of spirits that most people no longer believed existed.

It was easy to understand why Sandy and Doug had become involved in Reggie's spiritual church, The Gate. Each hoped to reconnect with a lost loved one. Sandy hoped to find her missing daughter, who'd disappeared years earlier at a shopping mall during a moment of parental inattentiveness. When Sandy and Reggie had first met online, she told him she had simply turned around to look at some plastic storage bins, and when she looked back, the girl had vanished. Relentless hysteria and a complete nervous breakdown consumed her life with her then-husband, other children, and relatives who never really cared for her and could not forgive her. They could not understand how this precious daughter of hers had vanished. Some blamed Sandy, saying she'd killed the girl herself.

After a period of decades, Sandy had eventually regained a semblance of a life. Her Social Security disability payments gave her a small but steady source of income, which she donated to mediums and other fortunetellers in an effort to find her child, whom she presumed to be long dead. Sandy had nurtured her senses during the grieving process and was masterful at distinguishing true seers from the carnival-variety soothsayers who hoped to make names for themselves on late-night television, preying on the emotions of the grieving. Reggie believed Sandy had some kind of gift, because when money was tight, she claimed the spirits gave her winning lottery numbers. When she played the numbers as directed, she never failed to win some type of prize.

Doug had come to him in a similar fashion, having spent the better part of his adolescence and young adulthood in mental health facilities for killing his paternal grandfather at age eleven. Doug had been diagnosed as a paranoid schizophrenic with auditory and visual hallucinations and was a skilled manipulator. Upon reaching age twenty-one, he convinced the court that he was cured, and by age twenty-five was released from the mental facility where he had spent the previous decade. He drifted in and out of jobs, jail, and mental hospitals. Reggie was convinced in Doug's abilities because Doug told him things only Reggie and people who'd grown up with him would know—things like long-forgotten arguments or favorite childhood items of clothing. Doug claimed to be in constant contact with his grandfather, who told him things. Doug said he liked to be around Reggie and Sandy because he felt like he belonged somewhere when he was with them.

Reggie himself claimed to see the spirit world around him, and over the years he had cultivated a substantial, devoted following up and down the East Coast as a spectral guide and medium. Reggie openly refused to accept money for his readings, which led to his cachet. This did not stop him, however, from accepting donations. Those he helped eagerly let him stay at their homes, pool houses, and guest cottages without charge until he moved on. Reggie never needed money for food or new clothes. Someone was always there to pick up the tab.

Before Reggie started The Gate, he'd dabbled as a web designer for an Internet startup company. Then he'd sold some stock options and stepped away from steady jobs and income. He used his nest egg to maintain his freedom and flexibility for his passion and to build an attractive website devoted to the paranormal.

Since his childhood, Reggie had been searching for conversation with the spirit world. His fascination started on his ninth birthday when his grandmother gave him a Ouija board. He never did get through, but he quickly realized that there were millions of seekers out there who just wanted to be led. He started The Gate when he was thirty-one and used the donations to build a loosely organized enterprise. Although most of his followers believed him to be a nonmaterialistic wandering savant, he estimated that his holdings exceeded $9 million. If he could bring along this woman, Marissa, he would be all the richer. All she said she wanted was to talk to her long-dead sister, whom she had tried to reach on her own. Reggie had gotten rich giving rich bitches like this what they wanted. He kept Doug and Sandy along for the special effects, and because they really believed in this stuff and could come up with odd bits here and there that were convincing enough to make seekers feel like all this was real.

Reggie laughed about this rich woman because she probably thought that their meeting in the bar was a chance encounter. Chance didn't work well for Reggie, so he'd done some more research, and he'd get a big donation from her if he played this right.

"Reggie, man, hurry up," called Doug from the kitchen.

At the same time, a competing voice called out. It was the rich woman. "It's down the hall on the left, past the dining room."

Reggie ignored them both, watching the phantasm. The African figure was back and had calmed down now, and was gesturing as if telling an important story. Still no words, only the guttural sound. The figure put both hands over his eyes and shook his head from side to side as if a vision played out before him that was so horrible he could not comprehend it. The figure then bent at the waist as if praying and began to convulse. Reggie stepped away instinctively. The phantasm grabbed its stomach, looking up at Reggie as if pleading for help. It was as if something inside the warrior was churning its way up from his distended stomach and through his throat to escape. The figure sprang like a coil, raising his arms to the ceiling as if imploring God to save him, and then opened his lips to release a thick black cloud that hung suspended for a brief period. Then in one motion it rushed to the ceiling with a crashing, thunderous roar, shaking the entire house with a rumbling bolt of fire. Reggie's knees buckled. He bent over and began to heave onto the carpet as the stench consumed him. A putrid, sulfurous cloud permeated the room. Anxious footsteps approached from behind him. He could hear the rich bitch coming, her heels clicking down the hardwood floors of the hallway.

"What are you doing? Oh my God!" she screamed as she absorbed the scene around her. "That's an Oriental rug. It's a fucking antique, you bastard!"

Doug pushed her aside, bending down to tend to Reggie. "Get the fuck out of my house!" the bitch screamed, running to the hallway. "Security!" Her shrill voice filled the house. Sandy ran to join Reggie and Doug, joyous, as the vomit continued to spew from Reggie's mouth like a fountain.

"What happened?" Doug probed excitedly. Sandy ran around the room, skipping and dancing like an eight-year-old girl.

"I can feel it. I can feel it!" she screamed.

"Security, I need you in the dining room immediately!" Marissa cried. "I need your help!"

Two men in blue sport coats with white shirts, ties, and ear buds burst into the dining room. "Mrs. Charleroi, what's going on here?" The older of the two men twisted his face in disgust and uncertainty as he approached the vomiting man.

"You can see it well as I can, damn it! I don't know what's wrong with him, but that son of a bitch is messing up my rug. I want him and his fucking friends out of here now."

The older man growled at his assistant, "Call 911, and get the sheriff's office to run a squad car over here right now. He could have HIV or the Ebola virus for all I know."

The rich bitch paced back and forth, arms crossed over her chest and tears flowing in anger, confusion, and pain. "Get them out of here, and get this damned mess cleaned up."

Reggie could sense that the presence was strong. Sandy began to rock slowly, her arms wrapped around her body for comfort. There was no doubt, a bona fide presence was here. Doug pushed Marissa out of the way. "Man, can't you see he's sick? Call an ambulance or something."

More men began entering the room. The smell of sulfur intensified, burning Reggie's nose and eyes. Sandy began to chant. Another guard, the one from the booth, grabbed a struggling Doug by the arm, saying, "I could tell they were stoned by the way were talking when they walked by my booth." Another jerked Reggie from his knees and dragged him back toward the kitchen. The remaining guard pulled Sandy from the floor as she fought, screaming and cursing.

"Mom, what's going on here? What's that smell?"

A preteen boy, headphones bracketing his neck, an MP3 player in hand, stood in the doorway to the kitchen. Wearing sweatpants and a white T-shirt, he waved the air with his hand to clear the stench.

"Sam, don't worry about it. Everything is under fucking control." The woman grabbed linen napkins from the sideboard and began to throw them onto the vomit. "This shit will eat right through my carpet. Get me some paper towels now."

The boy watched his mother place the napkins onto the pool of black vomit, which looked like thick, oily mucus. "Hey, Darrell," the boy said to the security supervisor, going into the kitchen. He watched as the intruders were hustled out into the cold.

The guard didn't answer the boy. His attention was fully on his Blackberry as he sent a text.

"Hey, did you feel that earthquake or something?" the boy persisted. "Did we get hit by lightning? What's going on?"

Darrell rolled his eyes. "Just some friends of your mother's, son." He looked out the window. "The sheriff will be here in a minute to make a report and try to suck up to your dad. Too bad he's not here." He smiled wryly. "When I see the sheriff, I'll ask him about what happened. I felt it too."

The boy walked to the refrigerator and looked inside, gazing at the contents. He did not make a selection. He could hear his mother yelling in the other room for paper towels. He rolled his eyes and shook his head. "Mom, would you please stop yelling? You're giving me a headache." He went to the window. "Looks like the sheriff is here."

A series of blue lights streaked up the winding driveway through the woods. The other guard made his way to the kitchen, holding a struggling woman who was screaming obscenities. Both men were needed to restrain her. What she was saying didn't make any sense, but she was saying it over and over: "*Zhorig, Zhorig, Zhorig.*"

It was 3:24 a.m. His mother continued to scream. The boy could tell she was drunk again and hysterical. He made a mental note to call his dad in the morning to tell him, although he was sure Darrell had already texted him to tell him everything.

Four muscular deputies burst into the kitchen. The boy recognized Sheriff Luby among them. He heard his mother yelling about the paper towels. He would get them from the pantry.

In the confusion, someone had locked the dog in the pantry. It bolted from the narrow space as the boy opened the door. The dog ran from the kitchen and the scene, tail between its legs. The boy didn't want to hear any more. He put on his headphones and headed back upstairs, leaving the paper towels behind.

CHAPTER THREE

Darrell Hawk was tired. The double shifts were killing him, and all because Al Snyder was on vacation. His late-night catnap had been interrupted by the early-morning scene. Besides, he had forgotten to ask Sheriff Luby about the earthquake. Maybe he should survey the house for damage. The foundation might have been cracked. He turned on the radio to listen to the local news on WTOP. He listened to the traffic, weather, and sports reports and waited for news, which was reported about every ten minutes.

"This morning residents of Leesburg, Virginia, reported a jolting experience. Shortly after three a.m., a substantial earthquake registering 6.2 on the Richter scale awakened many residents from their beds. The epicenter of the quake appears to be just outside Leesburg. Representatives of the US Geologic Survey are en route to take measurements and to examine a curious fault line."

An older woman's voice followed, giving her description of the event. "We were in bed, oh my. I thought we were having a terrorist attack or something. My dog just could not stand still."

"In other news…"

It would make sense to have someone come out and look at the foundation, Darrell thought. He'd get approval from Mr. Charleroi later.

***

Sheriff Luby sat at his desk drinking a cold cup of coffee. He was exhausted. He had been sound asleep when the call came in about a disturbance at The Oaks. Two of the three arrested were meth addicts and had long records. The third was the preacher from some kind of made-up church. The woman had an outstanding warrant in the District of Columbia for writing bad checks and would need to be transferred there. Sooner would be better than later, as far as he was concerned. She was the nastiest of the three by far.

His desk was a mess. He had so many reports to write. The primary election was coming up and there were several challengers who thought they could do a better job than he could. There were at least two pending lawsuits against his department. One was a car accident case, and the other was a claim that one of his deputies was filming women prisoners in the showers and posting the videos on the Internet.

Luby was startled by a commotion in the hallway. He could hear excited voices and see a frantic discussion between his deputies. A siren howled in the background. *It is too early for this kind of mess,* he thought. He set his coffee cup down on his desk and went to find out what was going on. It wasn't even seven a.m.

Mike Hollis grabbed Luby's arm and pulled him in the direction of the stairwell. "Come on, Luby, we got to get down to the holding cells. We got a problem."

Luby looked up. Hollis was not an excitable fellow. He got most excited over what he was going to have for lunch, as far as Luby knew. He had never seen Hollis so agitated. Luby followed him toward the cellblock.

"Slow down, Mike. What's going on?"

Luby could barely finish his question. Hollis was breathing heavily. "We got two suicides. One of the men and the woman we bought in from The Oaks hung themselves. The other one...the other one..." He looked close to tears.

"Hollis, what is it?" Luby was angry. The fact that two inmates had been able to kill themselves while he was in the building would not look good. Not good at all. He had never seen Hollis like this. "What about the other one?" Luby ran to keep up.

"I can't explain it, boss. I just got to show you. I ain't never seen anything like this at all. Lord, have mercy."

As they reached the ground floor, Luby and Hollis pushed their way past two paramedic teams. Two new female deputies were crying. One was vomiting in the corner.

One of the deputies opened the door to the cellblock. Hollis pushed everyone out of the way and stopped in front of cell number four. "Look," Hollis said, pointing urgently.

Luby felt sick. He's seen this before. Jesus Christ Almighty. A pile of human skin lay in the center of the cell. There was no body. There was no blood. There was no explanation.

***

Luby returned to his office and pulled the blinds that shielded his desk from the sun. He dropped a file onto his desk and selected a small key from his key chain. He ran his palm over the front of the drawer and located the lock with his fingertips, then inserted the key. Inside was a selection of files. He reached to the back of the drawer and removed a thick red folder labeled "John Doe. 1983. X-ref. 1943?".

Luby did not open the folder. In the past, he'd reviewed the contents from cover to cover at least once a year. This represented the third case of its kind that he knew of. The first was the Harold Gamble file, which he'd read several years ago when he was working on the 1983 case. He'd sent it back to closed files and had never been able to relocate it. If he found it again, he would make a copy. The second case was the John Doe file from 1983 when he'd first joined the force.

Luby picked up the phone. "Liz?" He knew his assistant was probably at her desk, logging in the mail as she normally did at this time of the day.

"Yes, Sheriff, what do you need?"

Luby ran his hand over the side of the folder. "I need for you to copy a very sensitive file."

"Can't the copy service do it?" Liz sounded perturbed. Copying was beneath her. She enjoyed passing on her work to someone else whenever she could. "I'm trying to finish that report you need for the County Council meeting next week."

Luby rolled his eyes. Liz was so predictable. "It's very sensitive. I need for you to do it." He placed their call on speakerphone and went to the window. He could see the lockup and the press gathering to take his statement. "Get Kerry the intern to do it if you can't."

"You mean Kristy."

"I need Krissy or Kristy or Katie or whatever the hell her name is to do a memo on these files and the info I gave you as soon as you got in this morning. I need her to get the Gamble file out of closed files and compare it to the one I'm going to give you. I want to know any common features between the two files. You know, witnesses, locations, methods."

"OK, I'm on it. I'll get the file right now."

Luby continued to look out the window. Liz entered his office. "Where's the file?" she asked. Luby nodded toward his desk. She looked at the folder on his desk and sneered, "Geez, you didn't tell me I would be copying a phonebook."

Luby ignored her. "Find the intern and send her in."

***

It was nearly ten a.m. when the criminal justice intern rapped on the glass door separating Luby's private office space from the rest of the Leesburg police station.

"I found the file you were looking for, Chief," she said. Luby looked up, not recognizing the girl, but finally remembering he'd asked Liz to have her to locate the Gamble file in the basement storage room this morning, as soon as he'd learned of the jail suicides.

The girl sat down as if she actually wanted to discuss the file with him. "I had a hard time finding it because it wasn't with the chronological files."

Luby was in his morning fog, made worse by a pounding headache and a hangover. The girl would not stop talking. Her voice reminded him of a jackhammer. "Just put the file down. Thanks," he said.

"Yes, this one was hard to find. It had slipped down back behind the file drawer. You wouldn't believe what I had to go through to get it."

Luby watched the girl's mouth open and close. He tuned her out and stared out the open window.

"The amazing thing is that there were actual fingerprints in the record. All these carbon copies are yellow, but the fingerprint card was in an envelope like it was brand new."

Luby took a sip of coffee from the mug in his hand. As usual, by the time he got to drink his coffee, it was cold. He took a deep breath and tried to focus on what the girl was saying.

"Well, I thought finding the fingerprints was the most amazing thing, so I asked Sergeant Cox what I should do, and he said the protocol was to run the prints against the national fingerprint database to find out if we could identify a common suspect."

Luby laughed out loud. "What's your name again?"

The girl paused, looking offended. As if Luby could remember her name, especially with all that had been going on around the jail. "I'm Kristy."

"Well, Kristy, I need for you to read through the file and write me a memo on the salient facts of the investigation. I want to know the names of the suspects, and the race, age, and sex of the victim. I need you to learn as much as you can about this file and then brief me on it."

He took another sip of coffee and stared at the girl, who was writing feverishly on a legal pad. "But do you want me to run the prints?" she asked. "That's what the protocol says. It says I should run the prints."

She spoke so rapidly, Luby had a difficult time understanding her. "Hell, you should follow the protocol," he said, walking past her. "And I'll even tell you this. If these prints match anyone, you are to call me at any time of the day or night. Is that understood?"

Luby didn't wait for a response but headed to the bathroom. He was going to be sick.

CHAPTER FOUR

Leesburg, Virginia
Six Months Later

Vaughn was asleep on the couch in his mother's living room when his cell phone vibrated in his front pocket. He was so fucked up from the night before he didn't even bother pulling it out to see who was calling. He loved his mother and all that, but he wished he had his own place again. Ever since Monica had kicked him out, he had nowhere else to go. Bad things really did happen in threes. The first bad thing was his leg, mangled from the IED his truck hit in Iraq. He was lucky, though. Two members of his company had been killed. But his leg throbbed all the time, and there were never enough pills to cover the pain. After spending six months in Walter Reed for rehabilitation and surgery, he was walking again. Sometimes it hurt like hell, and the Vicodin didn't take off the edge like it used to. The headaches were bad, so bad he felt like the pain was screaming at him.

The second bad thing to happen was his wife, Monica. He didn't think about it much at the time, but she had only visited him three or four times during his hospital stay. She told him the kids were running her ragged, and that between work and everything else it was hard for her to make the trip into DC. Right when he was supposed to be released, she showed up and told him she was moving to Delaware to be with some chick she'd met online. It was bad enough having his wife leave him, but having her leave him for another woman made him more curious than anything. If she'd left him for a man, he thought he would have been angry. His kids didn't seem to notice. It was like they had forgotten all about him.

In the hospital, he fell in and out of consciousness, seeing his friends killed over and over. And then he was so doped up from his injuries that he had conversations with that Iraqi boy from the village where he'd been hurt. The weird part was he didn't even know if he was awake or asleep sometimes when he was having these discussions. It was all so real, and in a strange way it was comforting for him to talk to the boy.

The dreams and voices were with him all the time. He heard them like they were right there in the room with him. Sometimes at night he swore that boy from the village near Kirkuk was there talking to him in perfect English. He didn't remember how the boy knew so much about him, although Vaughn did remember they'd had conversations for a long time, and he'd told the boy a lot about himself as he went in and out of his drug haze. He never did learn how the boy knew English, or how the child made it to the hospital after Vaughn's accident with the IED. It was strange, though, the boy would just show up in places, like when he was walking in Red Rock Park in Leesburg, or getting coffee at the Dunkin' Donuts. They would talk for hours. The boy never explained how he'd made his way to the United States to Vaughn's mother's house. Vaughn's reasoning told him that it must be all the drugs he was taking. Otherwise it didn't make sense.

He tried to talk to Monica about it once, but she never wanted to discuss the boy. His mother never seemed to be around when the boy showed up. The doctor said it was all a normal part of post-traumatic stress disorder and that it would go away in time.

Vaughn's leg really hurt him today, and that made him think about the third bad thing that had happened. Just as he was released from the hospital with a medical discharge and was ready to return to work, the cable company had sent him a notice that they were downsizing and didn't need him anymore. Vaughn hired a lawyer to try to get him reinstated because of his veteran's status, but the lawyer must have disappeared somewhere into a sinkhole because he wasn't returning his calls. Vaughn was tired of talking to the guy's paralegal because she didn't seem to know anything. He knew a hearing was scheduled, but not for two more months.

The phone vibrated again. He looked at the incoming number but didn't immediately recognize it. The phone stopped for a few seconds and then vibrated again. Whoever it was wanted to get in touch with him badly. There were three missed calls from the same number, all within minutes of each other.

"Hello," he answered casually, thinking maybe it was Monica calling from her new number to ask for money for the kids, or maybe it was a bill collector.

"Hey, Vaughn, this is Sonny. How you been?"

Maybe things were looking up. Sonny was the recently retired foreman of the landscaping crew at The Oaks. He and Vaughn's mother were some kind of cousins. From time to time, Sonny had work for Vaughn, which had sustained him during his teenage years. He could sure use it now.

Vaughn sat up. "Hey, man, how you doing?"

"Well, well, I finally got you. I been calling you and calling you. Where you at?"

Vaughn yawned. "I'm just at Momma's, you know, hanging out until I find something." He tried his best to sound upbeat.

Sonny cleared his throat. He sounded like he was eating while they were talking. "I got a job for you, but I need you right now."

"OK." Vaughn stood and made his way to the bathroom as he talked.

"Be in the parking lot of the Balch Library in fifteen minutes. Don't be late."

"What kind of—" he started to say, but the line went dead. *Shit,* he thought. What was up with that?

After relieving himself, he knocked on his mother's bedroom door. She was probably long gone, since it was nearly eleven a.m. He peeked in but she wasn't there. He decided if he brushed his teeth, he could get away with wearing the sweats he had been sleeping in. Sonny wouldn't mind.

As he was leaving the house, he saw that his mother had left him a letter to mail. It was tucked in corner of the mirror in the hallway. Since Vaughn was a boy, she'd left letters for him in this exact spot and it was his job to mail them. Today was the twenty-fourth of the month. Time to pay the electric bill.

***

Vaughn reached the Balch Library parking lot and backed his car into a spot near the west rear entrance of the building. Several cars were there, but not Sonny's Buick. This would be the first time he was earlier than that son of a bitch, who was always on time for everything. Vaughn didn't know how an eighty-five-year-old man could have so much energy.

A Lincoln Town Car glided into the space to his right. Before he knew it, a white man in his sixties wearing an expensive tailored suit, opened the door and sat in the backseat on the passenger's side. Vaughn hadn't seen Leon Charleroi in several years, but he recognized him immediately.

"Drive," Charleroi ordered with authority that made Vaughn feel he was driving Miss Daisy. He remained silent, and without another thought, he pulled out of the parking lot and drove with no destination in mind. Neither man spoke for several minutes. Vaughn headed onto Route 7 West and then turned onto Route 9 before Charleroi said another word.

"Vaughn, Sonny told me I could get you to do a job for me. He said you were looking for work. I didn't even know you were back. You should have let me know."

Vaughn looked in his rearview mirror. His passenger seemed to be enjoying the ride and was looking out the window beside him. "He told me you've been working as a sound engineer for the cable company," Charleroi said. "Is that right? I haven't had the chance to talk to you or see you for such a long time."

"*Was* a sound engineer," replied Vaughn. "I got downsized last month."

"That's too bad, son. You should have told me. I could have done something about it." Charleroi tried to catch Vaughn's gaze in the mirror and slid forward in the seat. Leon Charleroi was a funny man. Vaughn's mother seemed to know him well. Charleroi had been helping out his family as long as he could remember. His mother was very protective of the Charlerois. She never talked about them to anyone outside the family. Few knew of her connections to this powerful and wealthy man. Vaughn had seen Charleroi a lot more before Charleroi married his current wife. That was when his mother still worked at The Oaks. If Vaughn had been using his head, he would have called the man to see if he could have kept his National Guard Unit from being sent to Iraq.

Vaughn listened as Charleroi spoke. "I want you to take a look at the video security system in my house. I want to make sure that the cameras and the sound system are working properly. There are some strange noises and voices showing up in the recordings and pictures. I think the film is recording over itself but not fully erasing the old pictures before it records again."

"Why don't you just call the security company?" Vaughn asked. "It's their responsibility. You should have them fix it." He continued driving past the village of Waterford, heading into the small hamlet of Hillsboro.

"Like I said, I need for you to look at the camera and the sound system and some of the tapes. I need to know if they've been altered. My wife and I are going to be divorced soon. I think she's been trying to turn off the recordings and taking some valuable items out of the house." Charleroi moved in close and looked at Vaughn intently. "I've known you for most of your life. I think I can trust you to tell me what you find without spreading rumors or going to the press."

"I don't understand." Vaughn looked quizzically at Charleroi in the rearview mirror.

"I don't want you to think there's something wrong with me, but I hear all kinds of shrieking and scratching on the tapes. I want you to take a look and let me know what you see, and whether you think the sound or tapes have been altered. She may be trying to get some kind of advantage in the custody negotiations. You know, maybe trying to erase some of the film of what she's been doing."

Vaughn slowed to twenty-five miles per hour. Hillsboro was a speed trap and everyone knew it. "I'll see what I can do."

Charleroi lowered his voice. "I don't want to take the tapes to anyone I don't know well. I'll be able to file the divorce papers soon. I can't have anything mess it up. We both have hired detectives to find out anything they can. I don't want you to talk to anyone about this, not Sonny or anyone else. I don't want them to think I'm losing it." He cleared his throat. "I mean, in some of the tapes I hear my boy, Sam. He sounds like he's crying or screaming in the background. He's never said anything, and I don't think he'd ever speak against his mother, but I don't know what's going on. I'm afraid he might be being abused somehow. I don't know. I don't know if it's her or one of those men she's been bringing around."

Vaughn was sympathetic. He knew how ex-wives could be. He expected Monica to hit him up for more money any day. She had lied and told her lawyer Vaughn was talking to himself and addicted to painkillers. She probably just wanted to sit on her ass in Delaware and collect child support and his disability payments when they finally came through. In a way he was glad he wasn't working because he didn't want to give her anything.

Vaughn drove. They were headed in the direction of Charles Town, West Virginia.

"Sonny said your mother is looking for work too, is that correct?"

Vaughn looked back into the mirror. His eyes met his passenger's. "Yes, that's right." Vaughn's mother had been looking for something just a few hours a week to keep her busy. Money was tight since he'd moved in. His disability checks hadn't come through yet.

Charleroi cleared his throat. "I know she knows the house. My wife isn't up to doing much of anything but screwing around. She could use the help watching our son at night when she goes out."

Vaughn glanced in the mirror. Traffic was light. There were no oncoming vehicles, and no one was behind him. His mother had retired from The Oaks just when Charleroi's new wife moved in. His mother had stopped talking to Charleroi then. She said the new wife was trashy. That had been several years ago.

"Why don't you help watch your son yourself?'

"I can't. We're in the middle of this divorce. I need to be living outside the home for a year to make it final when the papers get filed in a couple of months. When I'm there at The Oaks, she's not, so I can spend time with my son without her. I can't spend the night there. I know she wants full custody. If I move back in, even for a night, the clock starts all over again. I won't have the requisite number of months of separation. I need to make sure I do this by the book."

Vaughn shrugged. "That's messed up."

"My wife's assistant placed an advertisement that will run in the Loudoun *Times* on Wednesday. She's looking for help with Sam. He's been sick and seeing doctors. We're not sure what's wrong. I've had so much going on too, with this divorce thing and with my new company."

Charleroi ranted about his wife for miles as Vaughn made his way from Virginia across the West Virginia state line. "All she had to do was to ask me. I know people. In my position I like to be careful whom I let into my personal life. I want someone in the house I can trust."

Vaughn chuckled to himself. Nothing with these guys was ever left to chance.

Charleroi slid a business card onto the front seat. "Here's the number to the residence. Have your mother call. I'll let the housekeeper know to set up an interview with my wife. I'm still on good terms with the housekeeper, if you know what I mean. I'm still paying the bills, after all."

"OK." Vaughn looked back at Charleroi, who reached into his breast pocket for a pair of dark glasses.

"Let me out at the 7-Eleven up the road there."

Vaughn turned into the parking lot and stopped the car. Charleroi stepped out. "I can drive you back to Leesburg after you go in the store if you want," Vaughn called through his open window.

"No worries." Charleroi smiled and dropped a fat envelope onto the passenger's seat. "Just let me know what you find out from the tapes as soon as you can. My lawyer friend advised me to have someone make an anonymous call to child protective services, and I probably will. I just need to know as much as I can about what's going on there before I do."

"How will I get in touch with you if I need to follow up on something?"

"Don't worry about it," Charleroi said without even looking in Vaughn's direction. "I know how to find you. I'll call you in a few days."

Vaughn watched as silver Range Rover pulled in. Charleroi opened the back door and jumped in, and they sped off in the direction of Leesburg. Vaughn looked down and opened the envelope. He counted out fifteen, twenty, twenty-five twenty-dollar bills. He smiled and pulled over to get some gas. This would be a good time to fill his tank.

CHAPTER FIVE

Leesburg, Virginia

Mae Etta had a good feeling. This job was certainly going to be hers. After all, she'd been down on her knees every day and every night, praying for work. God had to be tired of hearing her worn-out old prayer: *God, please help me find a job close to my home.* Mae Etta imagined she was just like that woman in the parable who kept whining and asking for justice until the unjust judge broke down and gave her what she wanted. If she had to pester God, and beg God, and nag God, and be the squeaky wheel that wore on God's last nerve, that was exactly what she intended to do to get what she needed.

She didn't know how she'd gotten by this long. Social Security barely paid for her mortgage and food, and since Jimmy passed away, she'd had to squeeze by on half his portion, which barely paid for her prescriptions. Her meager savings were long depleted, and Vaughn was home now but out of work. God knew that if she ever looked at another package of ramen noodles she would just throw up. They cost eight cents a package at the Shop Rite and she had been eating them for breakfast, lunch, and dinner as long as she could remember.

She spread the newspaper open on her kitchen table and looked at the note Vaughn had left for her. There was the advertisement in the classified section of the Loudoun *Times,* just like he'd said it would be. The ad was simple.

Special someone needed for light housekeeping. Must have reliable transportation. 703-555-2090. H. Victor.

Mae Etta recognized the name Victor immediately. Hattie Victor was the head housekeeper at The Oaks. Anyone in Loudoun County or in the DC metropolitan area could put two and two together and recognize the job was for the Charlerois. The job must be to work for that damned Marissa Charleroi, who couldn't keep help because she didn't know how to treat people. Marissa was the much younger wife of former congressman Leon Charleroi, who'd left Congress to found an Internet company. Mae Etta recalled an earlier article in the *Times* describing how Congressman Charleroi had visited Loudoun County for a fundraiser and been instantly charmed by its beauty and proximity to Washington. He and his first wife, Suzanne, had acquired one of the area's oldest, most distinguished estates, known as The Oaks, shortly after he was elected to Congress. Mae Etta read the Loudon *Times* each week and knew from the society column that Charleroi divided his time among a condominium in DC, his home in Louisiana, and The Oaks.

Mae Etta remembered the first Mrs. Charleroi as a matronly, philanthropically minded sort who spent most of her weekends when Congress was in session at The Oaks while her husband traveled to Baton Rouge to meet with constituents. Mae Etta worked in the kitchen then, and sometimes Suzanne Charleroi would come and sit in the kitchen and talk about her problems like she was an ordinary woman. Mae Etta remembered seeing her once at Farmer John's produce market, buying fresh fruit and vegetables and talking with everyone there, and pausing to admire every small child in the vicinity. Suzanne just liked people and did good things for everyone. She'd lost a lot of her phony old friends when she protested against efforts to display the confederate battle flag in the local library, but she'd made new ones who wanted to make Virginia a better place to live for everyone, regardless of their color.

Charleroi had divorced Suzanne when she was fighting breast cancer, and she died unexpectedly before she'd gotten the chance to change her will. Her husband inherited her money. He'd sent their two sons to boarding school in Connecticut while he romanced women near and far. Mae Etta laughed. There wasn't a woman she'd met who hadn't been charmed by him. It was rumored he'd fathered several illegitimate children. Mae Etta knew these rumors to be true.

Charleroi quickly married a strange but rich woman, heiress Agnes Firestead Burleigh just weeks after his divorce from Suzanne who died days after she learned her ex-husband had a new wife. Ms. Agnes did not like to socialize. In those days, they used to say Ms. Agnes had bad nerves. Mae Etta now knew the woman had suffered from agoraphobia. After their divorce, the second Mrs. Charleroi acquired an in-town residence and began a long, slow process of reinventing herself as a contributing editor for a travel guide on the South. Once Agnes was no longer married to Charleroi and living at The Oaks, she became outgoing and successful, unlike so many of the other invisible ex-congressional spouses. If Mae Etta remembered correctly, Charleroi had divorced her just before he established his new technology company, Aspirion Sector, using her money. Agnes Charleroi got a half a million dollars and that was it, based on a prenuptial agreement. By then he had already taken up with a new younger woman.

Mae Etta understood that the new Mrs. Charleroi, Marissa, preferred to stay out of Washington and out of the path of her predecessor. Marissa apparently found it easier to party in private with her Euro-trash friends, far from the disapproving eyes of the conservative rat pack her husband hung around with in Washington and the few bitter friends of her husband's previous wives.

Mae Etta was fond of Charleroi and his drama-filled life, and she missed working in the house where she'd grown up. Charleroi had been nice and they had been close, but not as close as they had been right after Vaughn was born. That Marissa changed him, and when she finally married him, Mae Etta quit.

Charleroi's affair with Marissa Cruz had been regular fodder for the tabloids as lawyers fought over Agnes Firestead Burleigh's prenuptial agreement. Agnes ignored her lawyer's advice to fight Charleroi over the company he founded. Mae Etta knew she gave up her fight to keep her husband after learning that Marissa Cruz was pregnant with the congressman's child. Agnes herself could not have children. Mae Etta would never forget the congressman's tearful plea for forgiveness from the pulpit of a Baptist church, televised live on the Fox network. The voters seemed to love it and reelected him by an overwhelming margin. Marissa lost that baby and several others until their son, Sam, was born when Marissa was older but still acting like a teenager.

Mae Etta had read in a *Vanity Fair* she'd found at the library that the congressman had first met Marissa when she was working as a staffer on the Armed Services Subcommittee while his first wife was cloistered far away in Louisiana, fighting breast cancer. Marissa Cruz had been born into poverty in the slums of Cuba and arrived in Washington after a harrowing flotilla ride and convenient marriage to a vacationing American widower who was visiting Florida and happened to work for the Capitol Police. According to the article, Marissa had taken a job working as an office assistant for a house member from Texas and drew the attention and admiration of those around her when she talked about freedom and how bad Cuba was. Mae Etta had seen photos of Marissa Cruz and did not consider her the least bit attractive. Marissa Cruz had been compared to Wallis Simpson in that she was intriguing, mysterious, and a witty conversationalist. Rumor had it that Congressman Charleroi "comforted" her after the death of her husband, who was killed making a routine traffic stop. Mae Etta remembered seeing a picture of Marissa Cruz being escorted to the funeral by Congressman Charleroi, who always liked being in the spotlight. Mae Etta still couldn't understand why someone would ever wear so much makeup to a funeral.

Based on what she had seen and read of the woman, Mae Etta could understand why the latest Mrs. Charleroi didn't care to go down to Baton Rouge every weekend with her husband. The way she heard it, a party started every weekend at The Oaks as soon as he left. And anyway, most of Charleroi's friends could smell trash from a mile way. The Baton Rouge crowd would eat Marissa Cruz alive if given the chance. Mae Etta guessed that Marissa Cruz might be trashy, but that didn't mean she was stupid. Recently, though, she imagined, Mr. Charleroi wasn't traveling much anywhere. As the CEO of Aspirion, he was on television almost every day as a commentator, trying to explain the war and the fighting in the Middle East. Mae Etta shook her head.

All those boys dying over there nearly every day. It was a dirty shame. And Vaughn getting all messed up…She had lost more respect for Charleroi when it seemed that he just wanted to make money off the whole thing. She'd tried to call him when Vaughn's unit was called up, but he had never returned her message.

She considered herself lucky that her boy had come back in one piece, at least physically. He did seem different now. Quieter, except at night, when she would hear him talking in his sleep, holding full conversations.

Mae Etta knew that there didn't seem to be any more important dinners being held at The Oaks like there used to be. She'd heard from her friend Cuda Taylor, that Charleroi had stopped sleeping there. Maybe offering Mae Etta this job and giving Vaughn the extra work was Charleroi's way of making amends. It wasn't like him to cross her, not with all she knew about him. Charleroi was way too smart for that.

Mae Etta knew The Oaks like the back of her wrinkled hand. She could navigate the grounds blindfolded. She could maneuver through every hallway of the main house, identifying each room by the particular sounds of the creaking floorboards, which were as distinct as the voices of her family and friends. She knew the history behind the nicks and indentations in the chair rail, banisters, and railings. Just by closing her eyes, she could recall weddings, spring cotillions, wakes, and funerals.

She lifted a cup of coffee with extra cream and sweetener to her lips and savored the thought of returning to the place where she'd been born and raised. God was going to give her that job, and even better than that, he was going to give her a job at her home. The Oaks would always be her home, no matter who lived there and no matter where she laid her head down to sleep at night.

Mae Etta had been born and raised at The Oaks with the children of other sharecroppers in the '30s, long before Loudoun County was subdivided into estate-sized lots for mini mansions and suburban housing developments. She was pleased when she saw at least a few colored people moving into those big houses, although she didn't know what kind of jobs they had that let them afford home prices that were now exceeding one million dollars.

She laughed to herself. Back when she was a girl, her mother and almost everyone else—except for poor whites, who used the n-word—had called them "colored." She could almost hear her mother's voice now, telling her to hold her head up high because she was a direct descendent of the slaves who built The Oaks. Her mother used to say, "Remember, Mae Etta, your people—colored people—built this house with their blood, sweat, and tears. It's more yours than anyone else's, and don't you ever forget that." Mae Etta had to laugh. No one ever used the word "colored" anymore. She grinned as she took another sip of coffee. Her mother would have slapped her silly if Mae Etta had ever said she was black. Now she was "African American," but she didn't really agree with that because all the Africans she had ever met did not consider her to be one of them. The Oaks had been her home and would always be.

Most of the plantation had been sold off in the early 1960s to pay debts. She grinned again at her political incorrectness. "Plantation" wasn't a word people used much anymore either. Her family and the other remaining blacks had been forced off the land as it was sold little by little. Many ended up in the hamlets of Purcellville, Hamilton, and Upperville. Some ended up in Leesburg, like her and Jimmy. The remaining manor house, stable, and dependencies on one hundred acres remained a beautiful and impressive estate. Whenever she had a chance to drive by or walk the grounds during the annual home and garden tour, she always did, because The Oaks was her home.

Jimmy had thought she was crazy for wanting to go back there and refused to go with her. He never understood her devotion to the land. He never understood her relationship to the manor house. He never understood her desire to reconnect with the place she was born and raised.

The green numbers on the clock on her kitchen stove glowed in the dim morning light around her. The time read 9:02 a.m. That meant it was actually 8:57; Mae Etta set the clock five minutes fast because she didn't like to be late. She reached across the table to pick up the telephone and dialed in nervous anticipation. The phone rang once, twice, three times before it was answered by a Hispanic woman who spoke with a heavy accent.

"Charleroi residence, may I help you?' The woman spoke softly and Mae Etta did her best to understand her.

"Yes," replied Mae Etta. "I'd like to speak with Ms. Hattie. I'm calling about the job at The Oaks." Mae Etta tugged at her left earring as she always did when she was nervous.

"Is this Ms. Rock?"

"Yes, it is," Mae Etta answered confidently. *That's good. She's expecting my call.* She was pleased at the thought.

"Hold on, please. I want you to speak to Mrs. Charleroi directly," said the woman, and the telephone silence was filled with generic music that reminded Mae Etta of the tunes the bank or electric company played when they put you on hold. After a few selections of stalwartly patriotic band music, the Hispanic woman returned to the phone. "Please keep holding. She will be with you in a minute or two, OK?"

"Thank y—" replied Mae Etta, but she didn't get to finish her sentence before she was back on hold. Her coffee was cooling down but she continued to drink it. She was excited. She just knew this job was going to come through. She was tapping her toes to a John Phillips Sousa march when Mrs. Charleroi picked up the line and greeted her.

"Hello," the woman said. She sounded unusually tired, like she'd woken up from a restless sleep. Marissa had a strong accent and a gravelly voice. Mae Etta's first thought was that Marissa sounded like a man. She wasn't going to waste time, though. She would get right to the point.

"Good morning, ma'am. My name is Mae Etta Rock and I'm calling about the job you have there at The Oaks."

"I'm sorry," the tired voice replied. "I didn't get your last name."

"It's Rock, ma'am. Like Rock of Ages, rock garden, rock and roll. Mae Etta Rock." Mae Etta was used to people asking her about her name. It was so simple, but people seemed to have a hard time getting it, at least the first time they heard it. People often asked Vaughn if he was related to the comedian Chris Rock. When Vaughn was trying to show off to new folks and especially to women, he would give a little speech about how he thought they were related because Rock was a very uncommon last name. Then he'd say an older relative had once told him that they were indeed related as distant cousins. After hearing Vaughn's story, people always smiled and treated him better.

The woman laughed politely on the other end of the phone. Mae Etta could sense a phoniness about it. Laughter was usually good, but this laughter sounded forced and snobby. Mae Etta didn't care, though. She needed a job and she could be phony with the best of them.

"Well, Ms. Rock. I certainly won't forget that one. My husband and I live at The Oaks. Do you know where that is?"

Here was Mae Etta's chance to get the job for sure. "Yes, ma'am, I know The Oaks. I was born on the land there. Me and my family lived there until most of the farm was sold off. I know that place like the back of my hand. Do you still have those orange Formica shelves in the kitchen pantry?"

Mrs. Charleroi laughed again, this time more genuinely, like she was surprised. "Yes, we do. Those shelves are the ugliest things I've ever seen, but I've never replaced them because when the pantry door is closed and they're covered with shelf paper, you can't see them." She spoke precisely, pronouncing each word carefully—almost too carefully.

"Yes, ma'am. Orange was Mrs. Hartwell's favorite color. She owned The Oaks when I grew up there. She had it everywhere." Marissa laughed again. *Maybe she's coming around,* thought Mae Etta.

"Well, that explains all the orange around here. When the painters were peeling back old wallpaper, everything underneath was orange." Marissa pronounced the word "orange" with three syllables—orr-and-juh. *I'm going to need to listen real good if I'm going to ever understand a word she's saying,* thought Mae Etta. She almost laughed aloud when she thought about Marissa's pronunciation.

"Mrs. Hartwell was what you might call eccentric, ma'am," Mae Etta said, but then she stopped herself. There was no need to go into the former owner's peculiarities, or to tell Mrs. Charleroi how Mrs. Hartwell had said the orange color kept her safe from the devil. Mrs. Hartwell had had some strange ideas about the devil and spirits and demons. She said the orange color kept her safe, but everybody knew you couldn't keep the devil away with a paintbrush and some orange sherbet. When Charleroi and his first wife bought The Oaks, they could barely make the mortgage payments. Suzanne had left Mrs. Hartwell's décor in place because she found it charming. Mae Etta was glad that Marissa had spruced the place up a bit and laughed nervously. When she got to know Mrs. Charleroi better, she'd tell her about Mrs. Hartwell, but she needed to get the job first.

"Well, Mae Etta Rock, I think that you should come by to discuss the job. Somehow I feel that you would be able to help us. Can you come this afternoon?"

Mae Etta almost leapt from her seat. "I sure will, Mrs. Charleroi, and I'll bring references with me. Is two o'clock good for you?"

Marissa paused. "I'm sorry. I have appointment for my son then. Do you think you could come by later, like around five or five thirty?"

"I'll see you then, Mrs. Charleroi." Mae Etta hung up the phone and did a little dance around her the kitchen. "Thank you, Lord!" she cried aloud. She'd bring references, but she wouldn't tell Mrs. Charleroi she was nearly seventy years old. White folks couldn't ever tell her age. She could easily pass for sixty. After all, age was only a number, and she was going home again at last.

CHAPTER SIX

Mae Etta warmed up her Oldsmobile for nearly five minutes before she backed out of the driveway. She kept the car washed, waxed, and in excellent condition. A man on the radio was talking about reverse mortgages. Maybe she could get one of those to help her pay some of her bills. Maybe she could ask Leon Charleroi to help her. He'd always said to call her if she ever needed anything, but she hadn't taken him up on his offer for many years.

House prices were skyrocketing in Leesburg. Why, ten or fifteen years ago, you couldn't have given her little frame house away. But she knew that after her neighbor Mabel Washington had passed away, Mabel's family sold her house for nearly $180,000. That was two years ago, and Mae Etta knew she could get more now. Jimmy had always taken good care of their house. It was bigger than Mabel's, and besides that, she had the best garden around.

It was exactly 4:30 p.m. and overcast. It would be getting dark soon, and it would take her exactly ten minutes to drive to The Oaks. She wanted to be early. As she made her way to Route 15, she turned right and headed north, her heart beating in anticipation. Her mother understood, though. Her mother had had "the gift," just like Mae Etta did. The gift let her see right through people, right into their hearts and souls. It let her judge their motives. It let her distinguish good from evil. It gave her security and well-being. Mae Etta believed it was her connection to God. The gift protected her from harm. It was like a presence or force that had saved her from certain trouble on many an occasion.

There was the time way back in 1957 when she'd met Alonzo Lee over at the Mount Zion church because his daughter was missing and the entire community was looking for her. She remembered brushing past him, and Mae Etta knew right then and there in a heated flash of insight that he was the one who'd killed the girl. Two sheriff's deputies and their cadaver-sniffing dog discovered the girl's body in a shallow grave inside the shed in the alley behind where Alonzo Lee stayed with his mother, wife, and other relatives. Those deputies were joined by eight or nine others who beat Alonzo Lee up so bad that his face swelled up like a giant plum. Mae Etta heard him laughing as they beat him, like he was enjoying it the harder and more fiercely they hit him. Strange, staccato laughter, like the wild hyenas on Mutual of Omaha's *Wild Kingdom.* She saw Lee swagger as the deputies dragged him from the shed, hands cuffed behind him, eyes full of frenzy, mouth foaming as he thrashed like a rabid dog. It took the strength of eleven men to subdue him and secure him in the wagon. His laughter remained with her. It was inhuman and otherworldly.

Mae Etta looked from her car to the wooden fence and remembered the exact place she was standing when the deputies dragged Alonzo Lee to the patrol wagon. Everyone in the neighborhood was there, standing speechless at a respectable distance because getting involved might bring arrest, a beating, and maybe death. They had all heard the beating and the laughter. Lee looked right at Mae Etta as he passed her, his face covered in blood and dirt. He looked right at her and smiled, but it wasn't his face she'd seen. It was the Bone Man's skeletal grin.

Alonzo died in the electric chair, by all accounts a meek and quiet man, so different from whatever had taken hold of him that day in Leesburg.

Mae Etta hadn't thought of that day in many years. It was not the first time she had seen the Bone Man. She had first started seeing him when she was about nine years old. He didn't scare her. Being able to see him was her protection. But when she did see him, it always meant that something bad was going to happen. The first time she saw him was the day Harold Gamble drowned in the sheep pond in the back thirty of The Oaks. Harold was her age, but he didn't go to school with the rest of the children. He was strong but a little slow, and he'd suffered from seizures since the day he was born. He mostly helped the women shell peas, and the men carry bricks or tools. The summer Harold died he had been obsessed with following the "lights," which everyone else called fireflies or lightning bugs. Harold would turn up missing over and over again, and usually she and the other children would go looking for him. They would find him in trees across town, or singing in the hayloft in the south paddock barn, or—more than a dozen times—in the kitchen pantry.

On the day Harold died, Mae Etta had been washing windows in the rear hallway of the main house. The ammonia water made her eyes sting and gave her a powerful headache. Her hands were itchy, sucked dry of moisture, even when wet. After washing windows, her fingers remained stained for many a day with ink from the newspapers she used to wipe away the streaks on the glass. Mae Etta was rubbing her eyes with her apron when she looked out the window and saw Harold skipping along like there was no tomorrow and holding the hand of a tall man who was so thin he didn't seem real. Just then, like he knew he was being watched, the man looked back over his shoulder right up at her and smiled. She gasped and backed away from the window. The man wasn't a man at all, just a skeleton, all bones and teeth—a bone man. He grinned at her and waved like he was one of her friends. That was the last thing she remembered before she backed up into her bucket and tumbled down the stairs into unconsciousness.

Mae Etta woke up in her mother's bed, feverish and confused. She spent the next three days in bed, rising in and out of a sweaty fever, not eating or drinking. When the fever left her and she awoke, her mother and her cousin Pearl and older sister Beta were sitting right beside her bed, looking at her like she was someone new, like they'd never seen her before. Her mother cradled her in her arms that day and praised God that her baby was going to make it.

Later that week, when she was stronger and taking broth, Mae Etta's friend Cuda visited her and said Mae Etta was scaring everyone because she kept talking about Harold and the Bone Man. After Cuda left, her mother told her that Harold had died, drowned in the pond on the same day Mae Etta had fallen, and that all during her sickness she'd cried out his name and mumbled on and on about the Bone Man.

Mae Etta never forgot what her mother told her that day as she sat beside her bed and read the Scriptures to her. "Mae Etta," she said, "I know the Bone Man, baby. Not everyone can see him. Not everyone has the gift." She dabbed Mae Etta's forehead gently with a cool face-cloth and hummed softly. "If you ever see him again, you stop what you're doing right then and there and say the Lord's Prayer and ask to be delivered from evil. Then you come and find me, girl, because when the Bone Man's in town, it means something bad is going to happen."

The next time Mae Etta saw the Bone Man was that day with Alonzo Lee, and then she didn't see him again until she was grown up and married to her Jimmy and her mother was long dead. They were at a dance and Jimmy kept wandering off. When she found him, he was in a dark corner sitting way too close to a pretty, familiar girl who was talking to him in hushed tones. Jimmy didn't see her as she approached, but the girl did, and she didn't smile but seemed defiant. Jimmy rose and introduced the young woman as Viola Davies. Mae Etta reached out to shake her hand, but then she tried to pull away, feeling like she'd touched a hot stove. The hand she'd touched was not a hand but rather bony fingers surrounded by rotting flesh. The thing she'd greeted was not a woman but the Bone Man, grinning and shaking his head. Mae Etta gasped and excused herself, then retreated to the other side of the ballroom, reciting the Lord's Prayer under her breath with every quick step.

She knew then with certainty that Viola had been sleeping with Jimmy and that Viola was pregnant with Jimmy's child. She didn't look at Jimmy the same after that. They never discussed it, but he must have known she knew. He knew she had the gift and had wanted to spite her, she supposed. There was never enough money after that. Whatever Jimmy earned went to Viola and the baby, Regina, who lived on the other side of town. Viola dumped Jimmy after she took up with Martin Smalls who owned Smalls Funeral Home, but Jimmy paid again

49

Marion Carnegie Library
206 S. Market St
Marion, IL 62959

and again. Money for Regina's school, clothes, and everything Regina needed at the beauty parlor or the store. Mae Etta's own daughter, Trina, got nothing from him. Everything went to Regina and Viola. It made Trina bitter and made Mae Etta bitter too.

There was the time that her boy, Vaughn, was wounded in a blaze of mortar fire in Iraq but she knew before the call came to her, because she'd woken in a cold sweat, dreaming that every hair on his head was on fire. Vaughn had come back home to her, but he was never the same. He'd lost his job and been locked up for walking around town talking to himself. She didn't see the Bone Man with her eyes that time, only the yellow haze of him in her dreams that warned her something was horribly wrong.

Of course, there were many more times that she did not recall that day as she made her way to The Oaks. Mae Etta laughed aloud as she wondered what someone like Mrs. Charleroi would say if she really knew the history of The Oaks and about the Bone Man. As she turned left onto the long driveway and made her way to the house, she noticed what appeared to be a construction site. Like most historic houses, the original kitchen dependency to The Oaks was housed in a separate building to the left rear of the mansion. Mae Etta saw blue tarp and construction material covering what appeared to be a work in progress, a breezeway adjoining the main house to the kitchen dependency. Why couldn't these folks leave anything like it was?

Mae Etta was distracted and tense as she heard the distinctive roar of a mountain lion. The Oldsmobile's engine died along with the radio. "Lord, have mercy," whispered Mae Etta as her racing heart beat faster and faster. She breathed deeply to steady herself, closed her eyes, and said aloud, "Just a little engine trouble." She turned the key and pulled it from the ignition. The radio continued to play, first music, then static, then the distinctive roar of the lion again, this time from the radio.

Mae Etta recited Scripture: "The devil prowls about like a roaring lion, waiting to see what he will devour." Suddenly there was a scratching across the driver's side door, first softly and then with such intensity that her car began to shake. Mae Etta gasped but could not pull her eyes away from the thing facing her. There rising from the ground was a hideous, bleeding figure shrouded in black rags. It surveyed Mae Etta with piercing red eyes and jagged teeth, shaking its head from side to side. The thing licked a monstrous pink tongue along the window and then grinned at her. The demon mouthed words that were unmistakable, and punctuated by subtle puffs of nauseating, putrid vapors.

"Welcome back," it groaned, and then in an instant it disappeared into the mist.

Mae Etta shook but steadied herself in prayer. She calmly placed the key back into the ignition and drove to the car port, not taking her eyes off the blue tarp and the construction site. She reached in her glove compartment for a large crucifix, which she slid into her handbag. She was going to need it. She was going to make it this time. She intended to die of old age in her bed, not here and not like this.

As she left her vehicle, she let the door slam behind her, announcing her arrival. On the door she glimpsed what appeared to be hundreds of deep scratches in the steely exterior. The smell of sulfur penetrated the air. Mae Etta recited the Twenty-Third Psalm and the Lord's Prayer and marched toward the door, looking neither to the left nor the right.

Someone was following her on the gravel path to the house. She could hear the gravel crunch behind her, the steps quicker than her own. Whomever it was would soon pass her. She froze as the steps seemed directly in pace with her own. Suddenly a chill passed through her like a cold, damp shadow. It was the Bone Man, only when he looked back at her this time, he did not smile. Something was wrong at The Oaks. More wrong than it had been in a very long time. But Mae Etta was older now, and she hoped she was up to facing it this time.

Mae Etta grabbed her chest. It had been some time since she'd seen the Bone Man. She continued on the gravel path, making her way to the side door, the service entrance. She peered through the window and saw a young woman sitting at the kitchen island, smoking a cigarette and talking angrily on a cell phone. Mae Etta recognized the woman as Marissa Charleroi. "Lord Jesus," she whispered to herself. "She looks horrible."

Mae Etta rapped anxiously, eager to get inside and away from the Bone Man. Marissa's conversation spilled through the closed door. "I don't give a flying fuck who is going to be at that dinner. You need to get your ass out here. It's been bad today."

Mae Etta knocked more anxiously. Marissa looked directly at her and abruptly ended her conversation. "Look, I have to go now." She rose and opened the door for Mae Etta, taking a long drag on her cigarette and studying the older woman from head to toe.

"Who in the hell are you?" she asked, trying to assume a confident demeanor even though she was drunk as hell and probably knew she had just been overheard at her worst.

"Hello, ma'am. It's me, Mae Etta Rock." Mae Etta smiled and followed Mrs. Charleroi into the kitchen. Mae Etta hardly recognized the place. Decorated in soft yellows with gleaming cherry cabinets and caramel-colored countertops, the room was warm and inviting. Marissa retrieved an ice-filled glass from the countertop. She smelled of sweat and alcohol. Her face was puffy, and deep wrinkles creased her brow. It was hard to believe this was the same woman Mae Etta had spoken to this morning.

The interior architecture of The Oaks had not changed much, observed Mae Etta as she followed Marissa from the kitchen down the hallway. The chair rail she remembered was still in place, and the center staircase was intact. She looked up at the ceiling and saw a few cracks that she remembered from the old days. Apparently the latest Mrs. Charleroi hadn't gotten around to fixing the ceilings yet, which seemed strange because Mae Etta had counted three surveillance cameras mounted in several corners since she'd entered the house. Many of the original light fixtures remained, including the gold-and-crystal chandelier that adorned the center of the marble ballroom. Marissa Charleroi and her husband had apparently spent hundreds of thousands of dollars on decorating. Plush leather chairs and sofas, soft

Oriental rugs, mirrors, statues, porcelain lamps, and occasional tables decorated the spacious manor house.

"I wanted to tear up the floors, but my husband wouldn't have it. He says they're original." Marissa watched Mae Etta as she examined the floors. The wide planks in the hallway retained their characteristic tilt. They creaked as the two women walked along the corridor.

"Mrs. Charleroi, these floors were old when I was a girl. My mama said they are the soul of the house. You can listen to the floors no matter where you are and tell who's coming just by the sound." Mae Etta couldn't tell if Marissa was paying attention or not.

Two men were seated in straight-backed chairs in the hallway ahead. One was reading a newspaper; the other was talking animatedly on his cell phone. They paused and nodded as the two women passed by.

"They're part of the security detail. The security center is the library, which is just about the only place I could keep them out of my way." Marissa nodded toward the right corner of the ceiling. "There are freaking security cameras everywhere." She raised her glass in a mock toast to the camera. "I can't have any peace, if you know what I mean. My husband put them here."

She continued down the hallway with an unsteady gait and turned directly to address the nearest camera. "My ass-wipe of a husband is watching me. He thinks I'm going to take his fucking money. And he's right!"

The man on the cell phone shook his head in disgust and continued his conversation. Marissa stopped abruptly and turned to face Mae Etta, surveying her again like she'd never seen her before, let alone walked with her through the house. They stood before the chapel doors. "That's right. I remember now—you're the one who said you were born here." It was as if she'd just heard what Mae Etta had said about the floors.

Marissa opened the chapel doors wide for Mae Etta to see. "We haven't done much in here." She staggered slightly, sloshing a good portion of her drink onto the floor. Mae Etta stepped inside, but Marissa did not follow. Mae Etta walked down the aisle past three well-worn pews on each side. The room was dark and the air stale. Rolls of abandoned blueprints lay on the altar. Mae Etta crossed herself. *An abomination,* she thought as she quickly removed the blueprints from the altar. She turned back to Marissa who stood in the doorway, watching but too drunk to ask serious questions. Mae Etta returned to the hallway and pulled the double doors closed behind her. "Can't leave anything on the altar, Mrs. Charleroi, that's sacrilegious."

Marissa did not respond but smiled and took another gulp of her drink, laughing. "Sweetie, you don't know the half of it." She turned and headed for the main parlor. As they walked along, cold air rushed past them, causing Mae Etta to shiver and to pull her jacket closer.

"You see, we haven't gotten much sleep lately," Marissa explained. "Nights aren't good around here."

Click, click, click, click. Both women looked up at the ceiling. Something seemed to be running above their heads. Something inside the ceiling. The chandelier swayed gently. The lights flickered slightly, then returned to their natural brilliance.

Click, click, click, click. They looked at the left wall. Framed pictures documenting Mr. Charleroi's illustrious career began to shake. One fell to the ground, the glass cracking. Mae Etta retrieved it and placed on the table with some other photos. Inside the frame was a picture of a smiling Congressman Charleroi shaking hands with Pope John Paul II.

Marissa tilted her head and ran her left hand through her bleach-blonde hair, exposing graying roots seeking freedom. "My husband says it's squirrels," she said, taking another drink and shaking her head in mock disbelief.

Not squirrels. Not squirrels at all, Mae Etta thought

"My husband says this is an old house and squirrels come in when the weather gets cold. That's what we tell Sam, anyway. He's our son."

"Too big, too heavy, too fast for a squirrel." Mae Etta continued to watch the ceiling as what sounded like footsteps seemed to run toward the kitchen. Marissa put her drink down on a corner mahogany table where several gold-framed family pictures were arranged in a semicircle.

Marissa fingered the gold crucifix around her neck. "At first I thought it was someone running upstairs. I didn't know who it could be, though. Everyone in the house was downstairs at the time."

Mae Etta gasped as a large brown Rottweiler moved toward them, growling as it too watched the ceiling.

"Down, Ziggy." Marissa reached down to pat the growling animal, which stared beyond Marissa and Mae Etta at an area on the ceiling behind her. Mae Etta saw nothing there. Marissa looked up at the ceiling as she knelt to pat the growling animal.

"You're not afraid of dogs, are you? The security company brings him around in the evenings." The animal ignored Marissa and stared at the ceiling without moving.

"No, ma'am, I'm not afraid of dogs."

"I don't know what's gotten into him. Sometimes Ziggy is like this around new people."

"I don't think it's me he's worried about, ma'am."

Ziggy stood at attention and barked ferociously at the ceiling. *Thump, thump, thump, thump.* The thing in the celling seemed heavier and to be running back toward them and then away from them, sounding more like a team of draft horses pulling a sled across the floorboards on unshod hooves. Ziggy followed suit, chasing the unseen thing.

"He belongs to the security company. I'm going to ask them not to bring him anymore. I can't stand his running around." Marissa shuddered as the dog ran off toward the kitchen. "My son is reading in the parlor. I want you to meet him."

"I have a son too," offered Mae Etta. "'Course, he's all grown up now." She tried to read Marissa. She couldn't decide if she trusted her or not.

Marissa looked at Mae Etta squarely for the first time. "Like I was saying, we haven't been getting much rest around here. The squirrels are driving me crazy with their scratching. They scratch all day and all night."

Mae Etta did not respond to this. "My son is a shy child, Ms. Rock," Marissa went on. "He hasn't been sleeping well. We had to take him out of school." She shifted from one foot to the other like a nervous child. "A tutor comes around three times a week for his lessons. I don't want him to fall behind."

"Children sometimes go through phases, Mrs. Charleroi. I've minded a lot of children in my time. Most of the time something is bothering them and they just need reassurance and love." Mae Etta looked at the younger woman, trying to gauge her reaction.

"He has these night terrors, Ms. Rock. He wakes up in the middle of the night screaming. It makes it difficult for me to sleep. I haven't had a decent night's sleep in weeks."

"What about your husband, Mrs. Charleroi? What does he say?"

Marissa tensed. "That fucking weasel. He stopped sleeping here months ago. He came out a few weeks ago to help and ended up napping all day. He said he was tired. He doesn't know what tired is." Marissa could not hide her anger. Raising the subject of her husband had set her off. The alcohol spoke for her. "He's sleeping somewhere in DC and I'm stuck in Hicksville with the fucking Amityville Horror and he won't bring his ass out here." She started to cry. "That's what this is really about. I just need someone who can be here at night with Sam when he wakes up. I just need to be out of this place and around normal folks for once."

Mae Etta was surprised. She hadn't expected a night job. Marissa continued, "There's really nothing you'd have to do at all. All the housework and cooking gets done during the day. I just need someone to mind Sam while I'm out. I need to get some rest, and I can't do it here."

Mae Etta was concerned. She did not want to be responsible for a sick child. What if he got really bad? What was wrong with him?

"The security detail is here twenty-four-seven. There are always three of them here, so you'd never be alone."

Mae Etta was more concerned about the boy and his health. "Have you taken your son to the doctor, Mrs. Charleroi?"

Marissa's anger returned. "Yeah, I've taken him to a doctor. He recommended hospitalizing him at the Psychiatric Institute of Leesburg last week, especially since he started scratching himself again."

Mae Etta didn't like how this sounded. "What do you mean, scratching himself?"

"If you had been listening to a word I've been saying…" Marissa rolled her eyes and called out to the parlor, "Karen, give me another scotch."

"Yes, ma'am," a voice called back. Soon a Hispanic woman appeared with a drink and a napkin.

"This is my new housekeeper, Karen. She's filling in for Hattie Victor. Hattie had a stroke and hasn't been back to work. Karen, Ms. Rock is going to be helping in the evenings."

Karen nodded but did not speak or smile. The dark circles and bags under her eyes told Mae Etta that Karen wasn't sleeping either. Mae Etta frowned at Marissa and watched Karen make her way back to the parlor.

Marissa Charleroi slurred her words. "She has to get back to Sam. I don't like to leave him alone anymore. She's the only help I have left. The rest of the staff quit." She took another gulp of her drink. "Sam has these night terrors, Ms. Rock. Something strange began to happen a few weeks ago. He wakes up in the morning with scratches all over his stomach and back." She ran her free hand nervously through her hair and sloshed most of her drink onto the plank floors. Mae Etta made a mental note of the spot. She wasn't going to slip and fall on her first day of the job. A broken hip was the last thing she needed.

"Mrs. Charleroi, did you ask him how he got the scratches?" Mae Etta was too old to go through this mess.

"The doctor says he's probably acting out because me and his dad are going through this separation. He says it's quite common for children, especially bright ones like Sam, to act out in these situations. Sam denies doing it. He said the Skeleton Man did it to him." Marissa watched Mae Etta. Mae Etta was careful not to move, smile, or speak.

"You see the security cameras." Marissa looked up at the ceiling. "They record everything. I think the fucking government should pay for all the cracks I have up here." She was crying again and not making any sense. Mae Etta didn't know what she was talking about. The cracks in the ceiling weren't new. They had been there for as long as she could remember. "We even have a fucking camera in his room. I've looked at the film. There's never anyone in Sam's room but him. He seems to have these convulsions, and sometimes it looks like he's fighting with someone. Anyway, my husband won't let me have him admitted and says he'll grow out of it. That bastard. He's even accused me of doing it to Sam. Can you believe that?"

Mae Etta had known Charleroi for a long time. It was just like him to put his family last. She supposed he did not understand the seriousness of the situation. She glanced past Marissa to where the boy was sitting on a couch. Even from where Mae Etta stood, she could see the fatigue in him. The pallor. He did not look well. He was drawing on a pad of paper. "Look, Ms. Rock," Marissa said. "I need for you to start as soon as possible. Even tonight if you can. I'm willing to pay you $140 a night for four nights a week."

Mae Etta reached into her purse. "I have my references right here," she said and handed Marissa a crisp white envelope.

"That's fine." Marissa tossed the envelope on the table without looking at it. Mae Etta was even more concerned. What kind of mother would leave a complete stranger to look after her child without even checking the person out? Marissa sure was lucky Mae Etta was not a serial killer.

Mrs. Charleroi did not enter the parlor. "I suppose I should show you around." She looked at Mae Etta out of groggy, bloodshot eyes, having forgotten they'd spent the last twenty minutes going through the house.

"You're not going to be driving anywhere tonight, Mrs. Charleroi," Mae Etta said. Marissa continued to sip her drink.

"I'm not drunk, if that's what you mean. Anyway, Karen is going to drive me. She's going to take me to Reston. I have a reservation at the

Ritz Carlton in case anything comes up. I just need some sleep. I'll be back in the morning."

Mae Etta didn't like the way this was going. She certainly wasn't prepared to spend the night. Both women paused as the thumping in the ceiling resumed, first almost imperceptibly and then with greater intensity. Marissa looked at the walls and screamed, "Why don't you just fucking stop it before I kill you!" She flung her glass at the wall. Karen reappeared from the parlor, as did the taller of the security two security men.

"I'll stay," whispered Mae Etta. "I'll stay." She had to stay. She had to keep that child safe as long as she could. Not only from the Bone Man, but also from his mother and father.

***

Mae Etta wandered to the kitchen with Sam in tow. *This boy is really sick,* she thought as she surveyed the deep circles under his eyes, made darker in contrast to his parchment-colored skin. He entered the kitchen and sat impassively at the kitchen island. His fingernails were raw and red, bitten down to the quick.

"What would you like me to make you?" she asked. "I can fix you anything you want."

Hawk, the security guard, sat at the kitchen table, reading the sports page. "Ma'am, he doesn't eat much," he offered without looking up.

"That's too bad. A boy his age needs to eat. He needs his strength, especially because he's sick. Ms. Charleroi said Hattie Victor had a stroke. When did that happen? I expected to see Hattie here."

"She's on sick leave. She had a stroke or something. I can't say I've seen him eat much of anything these past few weeks. I guess being sick takes away your appetite." They both looked at the boy, who seemed oblivious to them both.

"Well, it's getting late," Mae Etta said. "He needs to eat and get ready for bed."

Hawk looked at her intensely. "Did his mother tell you what's been going on?"

Mae Etta shook her head. "No. She told me he had been sick and was out of school. That's about all."

Hawk watched the boy try to juggle oranges and apples from the bowl on the center of the table. Outside, the fall night was pitch black and quiet, almost as quiet as Mae Etta ever remembered at The Oaks. "This has been going on for about a six months, but it's been really bad for the past two weeks, Ms. Rock. Everything happens at night. If I wasn't here to see some of the things myself, I wouldn't believe it. She's got some other folks helping out too. Friends of her husband from way back. One's a priest. He's come to help out some nights. I'm getting paid overtime and a bonus to be here. Everyone else said no. The guy before me has been on disability for two weeks after being here just a few nights. Heard he went nuts."

Mae Etta felt the hairs on her neck rise. She didn't want to hear this kind of talk right now. Especially not in front of the boy. She hoped Charleroi hadn't gotten his old friend Father Gaul involved. She'd always felt uncomfortable around him and didn't like the way she'd seen him interact with children. It made her uneasy. "How about some waffles? I can make them with whipped cream and berries. We can turn the clock around and have breakfast for dinner. How does that sound?" She forced herself to smile.

The boy grinner ever so slightly, raising his eyebrows with approval. Mae Etta got a mixing bowl and then went to the cupboard for some Bisquick and the waffle iron. The orange shelves were still there, reminding her of her childhood.

"You sure know your way around here," Hawk said. "It's like you've been here before."

Mae Etta added her ingredients and stirred the mixture with a well-worn wooden spoon. The boy walked to the window and looked out into the darkness. Mae Etta did not look at Hawk but focused her attention on her work as she spoke. "I grew up in this house. I was born and raised here at The Oaks."

The boy perked up and spoke. "I know a friend of yours."

Mae Etta continued to stir. "That sounds nice. Who would that be now?"

The boy looked worn out, as if he'd run a very long race. Mae Etta smiled at him. "I suppose you could tell me who it is, couldn't you?" Mae Etta was intent on endearing herself to the child one way or another. She intended to keep this job and to keep him safe for as long as she could. As for whom she and the boy might know in common, the only one she knew who might know the boy was her cousin Sonny who worked the grounds until he retired a few months ago. And then there was Charleroi. The boy had to be talking about one of them.

"He said he'd stop by and surprise you sometime." The boy picked up the oranges again, only this time he began to juggle with the ease of an experienced circus performer. Mae Etta and Hawk watched transfixed as the oranges danced in the air, even though the boy's hands remained folded neatly on the kitchen island. The oranges moved faster and faster in an increasingly smaller circle, then plummeted onto the countertop. One rolled off the edge onto the floor and came to rest by the refrigerator.

Mae Etta prayed silently as she turned to Hawk while continuing to stir. "When did all this start, Hawk?"

Hawk was on his cell phone. "We've had another incident."

Mae Etta waited as Hawk related the details. When he hung up, she persisted, "I said, when did this all start?" She poured the batter into the grooves of the waffle iron.

"Ma'am, I'm supposed to report anything strange as soon as I see it." Hawk looked over his shoulder at the boy and out the window. He ran his hand across his forehead, sweeping the sweat beading there into his hair. "I can tell you when it started. It was the same day we had that earthquake a few months ago. I don't know about you, but I need this job. But I can't deal with—and excuse my language now—this weird shit. I'm going to trade with one of the other guys for the rest of the night."

Hawk grabbed his coat from the back of the kitchen chair and strode toward the door. The boy watched him with intense fascination and whispered, "You can go now, Hawk. Our friend is coming. Harold is coming."

Mae Etta watched Hawk walk through the moonlight to the booth. Then she turned her attention back to the boy. Creamy batter oozed from the sides of the waffle iron onto the counter. "When exactly did you last see Harold?" she asked.

The boy just stared at her. "I think the waffles are done, Ms. Rock."

"Yes, honey, they are about done, but just tell me. When did you see Harold Gamble last?"

"I see him a lot."

Mae Etta remained calm as she stuck a fork into the perfectly formed waffle and dropped it onto a waiting plate. Steam rose from the waffle iron and hung there between her and the boy. "Was it inside the house or outside?"

"It was outside. I always see him outside."

Mae Etta's heart jumped. "He was looking in the window at us earlier," the boy said. "He asked to come in, and I said I'd have to get permission first."

Mae Etta moved around the kitchen island and grabbed the boy firmly by the shoulders. She looked deep into his eyes. "Look, honey. I don't want you to get in trouble with your mom now, and I know you wouldn't want to get in trouble with me either, would you?" The boy shook his head. "Good. It's just..." Her mouth was suddenly and completely dry, and she could barely speak. "It's just that if Harold ever asks to come inside, you need to tell him no, all right?"

"Why? He's my friend."

Mae Etta needed to get through to him. She didn't have patience for this. "You have to do as I say now. Just don't let him in. Do you understand?" The boy nodded. "I mean it. No matter what he says or does, you have to promise me you won't let him in." She let her words sink in. "Do you understand?" The boy nodded again. Mae Etta handed him the plate of waffles, then sprayed them generously with whipped cream and added banana slices and syrup.

The ringing phone scared her, causing her to jump and grab her chest. It was the security booth. They were sending a replacement agent for Mr. Hawk, but he would not arrive for about an hour. The guard explained that the other men didn't want to be in the house right now.

CHAPTER SEVEN

St. Paul, Minnesota

Father Robert Malveaux enjoyed teaching criminal law as a visiting professor at the University of St. Thomas School of Law in St. Paul. The experience was exactly what he needed to keep him engaged and interested in his work, given the difficult past few years he'd experienced. He especially enjoyed the part-time night students. They were somewhat older than the day class and more grounded in the real world of bills, jobs, and relationships. As he entered the lecture hall, the fifty-or-so-odd students seemed not to notice. One student in the back row had his head down on the desk, taking a catnap. Several had extra-large cups of coffee to keep them awake during the two-hour class.

He supposed he was a bit of an anomaly to them. There were very few priests teaching these days, and certainly not many black ones. He laughed to himself. At least he didn't have to worry about tenure. Malveaux placed his lecture notes on the podium and cleared his throat. As if by magic, the room came to attention.

"Yes, Mr. Gupta?" Malveaux looked up from underneath his glasses. There was a time when he hadn't needed them to read. These days he did. He remembered when he was their age. It seemed like decades ago. And it was.

Mr. Gupta waved a newspaper and smacked the back of his hand on a large black-and-white photo displayed prominently on the page. Malveaux could not see who or what was in the picture, even with his glasses.

"What is it, Mr. Gupta? What has you all worked up tonight?" The class laughed and craned their necks to look at Syed Gupta, who was in the back row. Gupta was a regular feature of the class. At least once a week he would make a sweeping pronouncement about the criminal justice system and the hypocrisy of American values.

Malveaux sympathized with Gupta to a certain degree. Gupta had come to the United States on a student visa. As an active, vocal Muslim, he was swept up in the frenzy following the September 11 attacks when his name appeared on the Terrorist Watch List. It took considerable effort for Gupta to demonstrate that he was not the individual the list hoped to guard against, but rather someone who shared the suspect's name. Gupta had missed two semesters and was more than a year behind his classmates.

As the students sat transfixed, listening to Gupta rant about the day's most recent injustice against a detained Muslim clergyman, they hardly noticed a tall man quietly enter from the left side of the room and slide into a seat in the back row of the lecture hall. The red-faced man looked directly at Malveaux and nodded without smiling. He removed his coat and a beige scarf from around his neck, revealing a clerical collar and the black pants and garb of a Catholic priest.

Malveaux tuned out Gupta's rampage, focusing on the visitor. What was Donald O'Reilly doing in his lecture? Robert Malveaux noticed O'Reilly's square jaw had not changed since their days in the seminary. Few people knew that Robert Malveaux had delayed his final priestly vows for several years after graduating from Our Lady of the Grove Seminary. He'd finished his studies with O'Reilly in 1978, then turned instead to a career in law and suffered through two serious but failed relationships. Malveaux then returned to the church and made his final vows. Over the years, Donald had resurfaced from time to time to lay a guilt trip on him, claiming he had broken the vow of celibacy, of all things. He was trying to remember the last time he saw Donald when Arnold Fairchild angrily responded to Gupta's tirade. Arnold Fairchild was a conservative Catholic member of the Federalist Society and worked on the staff of a Tea Party congressman. Malveaux had never heard Fairchild lose his composure as he did tonight.

"I get so sick of your bullshit, Gupta. Every week you come in here and try to convince us that some Muslim cleric has been railroaded. Why don't you just face it that the people you're defending have as their sole mission the destruction of the United States of America? You people have no idea what it means to be free. You should just shut up and go back to where you came from."

Members of the class cried out in indignation at Fairchild's outburst. Gupta responded, enraged, "Fairchild, you and your child-molesting, hate-mongering Catholics need to step aside and respect the views of people of color. We will be in charge sooner that you think."

There were groans and shouts of approval all at the same time. Malveaux wondered where he fit into Gupta's calculus, being black and Catholic at the same time.

"Mr. Gupta." Malveaux inserted himself into the debate. "I would love to continue this dialogue, being both a person of color and a Catholic, but we need to get our lesson started."

Malveaux could see O'Reilly in the rear of the lecture hall, trying to contain his laughter. "You are going to have to leave this discussion on free speech and freedom of association for your Constitutional Law class. We have a lot of ground to cover and this is going to be on your exam, so I recommend we get on with it."

Fairchild and Gupta glared at each other across the hall. Fairchild opened his laptop and muttered a string of obscenities under his breath. Gupta raised his coffee cup into the air like a trophy, nodding and smiling at all those who would look at him. Malveaux cleared his throat and began his lecture. Surprisingly, Donald O'Reilly opened a spiral notebook and began to write along with the students. This was going to be a ninety-minute lecture. He hoped O'Reilly didn't expect him to truncate what he had to say just because he had a visitor from his old seminary days.

"On tonight's syllabus is the subject of forensic evidence." Malveaux looked at his roster to pick his first victim. He preferred the Socratic method, feeling it best prepared students for litigation practice, although few of these students were destined to appear in a courtroom before a judge. Most would end up in corporate America. But why spare them? He would call on his two most vocal students first. "Mr. Gupta. Let's see how much you remember about the readings for tonight. What can you tell the class about the law with respect to DNA evidence in the state of Minnesota?"

Gupta sat his coffee cup on the desk and stood to address the class. "Professor Malveaux, DNA evidence was first considered by the Minnesota Supreme Court in the case of *Minnesota v. Schwartz*." He shifted from foot to foot as he spoke.

"Good. Now that I know you did the reading, I want to spend some time on the extra material that was part of your reading assignment. Let's walk through the facts of that case."

"OK. *District of Columbia v. Johnson* was the case highlighted in the reading material. It concerned the prosecution of the murder of Simon Marcants. In presenting evidence, the prosecutors introduced forensic evidence in an attempt to link Johnson to the brutal murder of Simon Marcants in the Georgetown neighborhood of the District of Columbia."

"Be specific, Gupta. What kind of evidence?"

"Blood, sir."

"Gupta, you're going to have to learn to stop rocking back and forth when you talk, and you need to spit out what you have to say. My clothes are going out of style just waiting for you to give me the facts of this case. What about the blood was significant?" The class laughed at his corny joke.

"Well, Professor, police technicians found Simon Marcants's blood, but they also found tissue and skin cells underneath his fingernails, indicating there had been a struggle with his killer."

Malveaux shook his head and exhaled heavily. "Gupta, just because Simon Marcants had skin cells and tissue underneath his fingernails doesn't prove that the tissue belonged to his killer, does it?" Malveaux paced back and forth at the front of the classroom.

"Man, that's too obvious," someone called out.

Malveaux didn't catch who made the comment, but he looked up and said, "That's exactly right. We must observe the obvious, but always be on the lookout for the less obvious explanation."

The class sighed and laughed. Malveaux laughed too. This was his mantra, the "less obvious explanation." Things were not always what they seemed to be. He had fooled them all the first day of class when he came into the room wearing a tracksuit. When he went to the podium, no one expected the black man in the tracksuit to be Father Robert Malveaux. Since then he had reminded the class to remember that things were not always as they seemed, and to be on the lookout for clues that others might miss.

"Thank you, Mr. Gupta. Mr. Fairchild, let me ask you about the obvious in this case. Was it reasonable to assume the blood and tissue under Simon Marcants's fingernails came from his attacker?"

Fairchild stood and looked confidently at Malveaux. "Yes, it was a reasonable explanation." Fairchild never called Malveaux professor. Malveaux didn't necessarily think it was a race thing that made Fairchild so arrogant. It was rather a matter of pride.

"Why was it was a reasonable explanation, Mr. Fairchild?"

Fairchild gestured with his hands as he spoke, like he was giving some great political speech. "It was reasonable because the crime scene showed signs of a struggle."

"Be specific, Fairchild. You and Gupta have something in common after all. Neither one of you can give me a concise answer to my question."

The class seemed amused. Fairchild continued. "Well, first of all, Simon Marcants's room was in disarray. A cupboard had been overturned, and drawers had been rummaged through in the kitchen. Several lamps were broken and a glass coffee table was shattered."

"Go on, Fairchild, you're getting there."

Fairchild continued with renewed confidence. "There was a trail of blood leading from Simon Marcants's body through the kitchen and out the back door. When Mr. Johnson was apprehended, he was covered with blood that matched that on the floor of Marcants's kitchen."

"What other evidence was recovered at the scene?"

"A large bowie knife and an ice pick. The autopsy showed that Marcants died from a puncture wound to the chest, probably consistent with the ice pick, which had apparently been wiped clean."

Malveaux was satisfied that the class was back on track, at least for this night. "OK, enough from both of you. Where is Ms. Washington?"

Ms. Washington stood. She was a heavyset older black woman with glasses. Her hair was twisted in an elaborate hairstyle and she was somewhat unsure of herself. She was not unattractive, but Malveaux felt she had certainly let herself go. Malveaux was sure others would think it was strange that he still desired women and spent time gauging their attractiveness. His profession and vows did not let him act on his feelings.

Ms. Washington steadied herself on the edge of her desk with one of her fists. She remained hunched over, as if her back was in pain. She raised her head only to respond. "Professor Malveaux, what happened is that the DC police booked Johnson on suspicion of murder in the first degree. Johnson had a long criminal record of violent assaults, which had resulted in three separate felony prison sentences. He was found wandering in the neighborhood high on bad Ecstasy."

"Good, Ms. Washington. When Johnson was arrested, what occurred?"

Ms. Washington looked down at her notes and then back at Malveaux. "Police officers found Johnson in a park near the Key Bridge. All agreed he was covered in blood."

"What did Johnson say when they took him into custody?"

Ms. Washington turned a page in her casebook. "He said, 'I told that hairy woman to get off of me.'"

The class burst out in laughter.

"Say that again, Ms. Washington. What exactly did he say?"

Ms. Washington tried to control her own laughter but couldn't help it. "He said, 'I told that hairy woman to get the hell off me.'" Even Malveaux laughed this time, as did O'Reilly in the back row.

"Ms. Washington, what did they observe about Johnson?" Malveaux asked. She hesitated. "Remember, it is the facts that will set your client free. What else did they notice about Mr. Johnson?"

Ms. Washington continued to flip through her notes. Malveaux didn't want to embarrass her. She'd done well. He would move onto someone else.

"Mr. Simms. What else did the police officers notice about Mr. Johnson?"

Simms stood. "They said he had a black eye, bruises on his forearms consistent with a struggle, and blood on his shoes. They also found blood on the ground around him." He sat down.

"Not so fast, Mr. Simms. Tell us, what did the police officers testify to at trial?"

Simms stood again and looked around to the class as if he was addressing the audience in a great theatrical performance. "The police officers testified that Johnson was found in the park covered with blood. His statements about the hairy woman were admitted into evidence as an excited utterance."

"What did the police officers say about the hairy woman?"

Simms was laughing too by this time. "They said there were a few transvestite prostitutes in the park, but none of them looked like a hairy woman to them. None of the prostitutes were covered with blood, either."

Everyone was laughing now again now.

"What else did Johnson say about the woman?"

Simms obviously knew his facts cold. "He said she was bloody and that she fell on him and kicked him."

"What did the forensics expert testify to before the grand jury?" Malveaux checked off the names Washington, Gupta, Fairchild, and Simms on his roster. He would not need to call on them again for a few weeks.

"The forensics expert testified that he took samples of blood from Mr. Johnson's parka, and that the blood matched the blood found on the floor of Simon Marcants's kitchen. Based on this evidence, a grand jury returned an indictment of first-degree murder."

"Mr. Simms, why don't you finish the case for us?"

"Very well," said a smug Simms. "Johnson was assigned a public defender, who did a check of all municipal activity in the area for a six-hour period after the crime."

"What was he looking for?"

"He was looking for the bloody, hairy woman. You know, like at a hospital or in a police report of something. The bloody, hairy woman was that classic 'other guy' who did it."

"When you say 'other guy,' what do you mean?"

Simms continued in all his glory. "Well, it is common for those charged with crimes to claim that the crime was actually committed by some other guy. The other guy usually doesn't have a name. He appears, commits the crime, and then disappears."

"Good, Simms. Take a seat. I'll take over from here." Malveaux put on his glasses and dimmed the lights. A large projector screen descended from the ceiling. Malveaux clicked through actual photos of the crime scene as he spoke.

"This is a famous case. Not only because it exposed weaknesses in the investigation techniques of the DC metropolitan police department, but also because it presented an excellent reminder to investigators and law students to look beyond obvious explanations of the evidence and how it all ties together. It always reminds me that we should question what we consider to be well-accepted facts."

Malveaux turned his neck to look at the screen behind him. A small rectangular light illuminated the lectern. "In a collateral matter, the case also exposed the weaknesses in the reliance on expert witness testimony and the methods of investigation as a precursor to *Daubert*. You will recall that the *Daubert* case requires expert witnesses to prove that the methods they utilize are those methods that are commonly recognized and accepted by experts in their field using those same scientific techniques."

Malveaux cleared his throat. There was something about this lecture hall that always made his throat scratchy. Maybe this was a sick building. "Johnson always maintained that he did not kill Simon Marcants. But when the Ecstasy wore off, he didn't remember anything about a hairy woman. He remained steadfast through all interrogations that he did not kill Marcants. As you know from the case study, the fact that the blood found on Johnson's parka matched the blood on the floor of Marcants's kitchen was a key factor in the prosecution's belief that it had an airtight case."

Malveaux flipped through several slides that showed a green parka covered with dried blood, and another shot of the linoleum tile in Marcants's kitchen, smeared with streaks of blood. Malveaux zoomed in on the photo to focus on what was otherwise an unremarkable screen door.

"As I always say, you must look for those clues that are not obvious. If you look closely, you will see a small tear in the lower right-hand corner of the screen door." He used his laser pointer to highlight the areas he was describing. "In the mesh of the screen door, police technicians discovered hair and fibers that were also found on Johnson's parka. Interestingly, the fibers did not match the fur lining of Johnson's parka hood." Malveaux zoomed in on the parka. "Every indication—Johnson's highly drug-induced state, the blood on his parka, and the blood on Marcants's floor—pointed to a sure guilty verdict for Johnson. Also damaging was the revelation that Johnson performed handyman services for Marcants over an approximately two-year period, and the two parted ways over a disputed disappearance of some valuable silver coins during the time Johnson was repairing the ceiling of Marcants's kitchen." Malveaux zoomed to another slide picturing receipts made out to Johnson and bearing Marcants's signature. "When the public defender surveyed the police activity in Georgetown, he found no evidence of a hairy woman. In fact, none of the people he spoke to remembered seeing such a character. But several men unloading kegs at the nearby liquor store saw Johnson panhandling that evening prior to the murder. None recalled seeing any blood on him at the time."

Malveaux switched to another scene, which showed several college-aged students with backpacks walking past the park where Johnson was arrested. "Several students came forward to say they saw Johnson that evening lying in the park, motionless and seemingly intoxicated.

Two calls, not to the police but to other municipal authorities, were worth noting, however. One came from Holly Goodland, who lived on 35th Street." Malveaux clicked on a narrow row house painted colonial blue. "Ms. Goodland placed a call to animal control and reported she was afraid to take out her trash because a deer was running erratically through the alley." He clicked a picture of a trash-strewn alley. "Animal control arrived on the scene but didn't find a deer."

"The second call came from Ms. Hortense Harris." Malveaux clicked to show an older African American woman wearing glasses and a knit cap. "Ms. Harris, then over ninety years old, was one of the few remaining original African American homeowners in Georgetown. Her house was located on 35th Street in a block you've probably seen if you know the area. It's the steep street with cobblestones. Her home was located across the alley from Marcants's. When police investigators interviewed Ms. Harris, she had no information about the crime and could not recall the present date or year. Unconvinced that she would provide any meaningful assistance, officers began to leave when Ms. Harris asked if they had finally come to get rid of the deer." Malveaux clicked to show a slide of Harris's backyard. Near her rear porch was a buck covered with blood, his neck twisted in agony, legs splayed. "Harris told the police officers that she had called animal control over and over but they would not send anyone to take the deer away."

Malveaux clicked to show a courtroom artist's depiction of Johnson at trial. "Let's just move on the finish this case before our break. We all know that the forensic expert was John Michael Tompkins. Tompkins was a well-known expert, a fixture in the criminal law courts of the District of Columbia. Tompkins had impressive credentials, including a bachelor's of science degree from DePauw University in Indiana, and a master's degree and doctorate from Indiana University in the field of forensic pathology. Tomkins had testified over 380 times in court and always been accepted as an expert witness without dispute." He clicked the screen to show a fat man wearing a tight-fitting suit and with so much dark, thick hair that he appeared to be wearing a toupee. Tompkins wore wire-rimmed glasses and was pointing authoritatively at a chart.

"Now, class, this is a matter of trial practice that will benefit you in the future. You must never accept findings just because someone tells you they're true and just because they are given by a so-called expert. You must always be prepared to go back over facts and assumptions and evidence that others have accepted as the gospel truth."

Malveaux cleared his throat and took another sip of water. "When it was time to qualify Tompkins as an expert witness at trial, the public defender listened patiently to Tompkins' credentials but would not accept him as an expert and offered an objection for the record. The trial judge was mortified, but at that point he excused the jury from the courtroom for a discussion outside their presence." Malveaux laughed out loud. "Folks, this isn't in the casebook, but I can tell you the judge was pissed off at that public defender and threatened him with sanctions for questioning Tompkins' credentials. The trial court judge pointed out to the young, inexperienced lawyer that he had presided over at least fifty cases where Tompkins had testified at trial and had been qualified as an expert. It was at that point that the young public defender said he had researched Tompkins's credentials and found that Tompkins had not graduated from DePauw University, and did not have a PhD from Indiana University in forensic pathology. The judge noted the serious nature of the charges but indicated to all present that he would take up the matter later. He also inquired about the defense expert's testimony and asked if the expert would testify that the blood on Marcants's floor matched the blood on the parka.

"The public defender, who was no more than thirty at the time, answered in the affirmative, that the blood indeed did match. The judge said he'd heard enough and would resume Tompkins' testimony." Malveaux paused. "Remember, class, you should always be truthful with the court." He shook his finger at them in mock admonition. Two women giggled.

"When asked at trial, Tompkins testified that blood and flesh were found under Simon Marcants's fingernails, and that the blood and tissue were identical to the blood found on Johnson's parka. Then, on cross-examination, something very interesting happened. The public defender rose and asked Tompkins if the blood on Marcants's kitchen floor and the blood on Johnson's parka were the same. Tompkins, angry that his testimony had been questioned, replied flippantly, 'Young man, obviously you didn't hear me before when I told you they matched.' The jurors looked from Tompkins to the public defender because they had all grasped this important point. That was when the public defender asked if Tompkins was familiar with the term 'DNA.' Tompkins said that he was, and went on to explain in great detail to the jury how every living thing had a genetic fingerprint, so to speak, called DNA, and how no two living things shared the same DNA."

Malveaux took another sip of water. "At that point the prosecutors stood and voiced an objection, stating that DNA evidence was not yet established as reliable scientific evidence, and asked the court to strike references to DNA. The court, ever on the prosecution's side, agreed and instructed the jury to disregard any and all testimony related to DNA evidence. The young public defender noted his exception to the ruling and asked Tompkins only one more question, which seemed obvious in its simplicity, but was the actual crux of the matter. He asked Tompkins if the blood found on Marcants's kitchen floor and on Johnson's parka was human blood.

"Well, you can imagine that this question caused a chain reaction in the jury. They began laughing, and Johnson put his head down on the defense table. The judge struck the question *sua sponte*, of his own accord, and recessed the case for lunch."

At that point a student called out from the darkened room, "Professor Malveaux, you talk like you were there. Did you sit in on this trial?"

Malveaux pushed a button on the lectern and a new scene appeared on the screen. "Yes. I was there." He had their attention now. "After the lunch recess, the prosecution rested, and the public defender called the police officers who'd responded to Holly Goodland's call. Then he called the officers who'd interviewed Ms. Harris to describe the dead deer they found in her backyard. After the judge made a flip remark, something to the effect of 'What did Bambi have to do with this case?,' which naturally caused the jury to break out into laughter, the defender called his last witness, a forensic pathologist, Elliott

Francis. He asked Mr. Francis if he had examined the forensic evidence in question, and Francis said he had. And then he asked Francis if the blood on the parka matched the blood on Marcants's floor, and Francis replied that the blood did match. Then the defender asked if the blood on the kitchen floor and on the parka was Johnson's blood. Francis replied that it was not. Then the public defender asked if the blood was Marcants's and Francis replied that it was not. Finally the public defender asked the crucial question: Was the blood human blood? And Francis turned to the jury—and you really had to be there to see the dramatic look he gave them as he shook his head—and said, 'No, it was not.'

"You can imagine that everyone in the courtroom was transfixed at that point. The judge was listening intently. The jury was listening intently. Johnson was listening intently. Francis continued his testimony. 'The blood on the parka and the blood on the kitchen floor is the same blood, but it is not human blood. The blood is deer blood.'"

Malveaux sipped more water and watched his class as they seemed caught up in his story. "Francis went on to explain blood typing and the differences in the cell structure of human blood and the blood of other mammals. He said he had examined tissue samples from the puncture wound to Marcants's chest and found tissue from the antler of a male deer. He confidently explained that the puncture wound was consistent with the puncture from the antler of a buck. He said the evidence of the struggle on the first floor of Marcants's home likely resulted from a mortally wounded deer attacking Marcants in a frenzy rather than from an attack by Johnson. "Needless to say, by looking for the less obvious explanation, the public defender was able to dispel facts that everyone had assumed—that the blood on the floor and the parka belonged to Marcants—and to show there was another logical explanation. However, when the public defender asked Francis to describe the DNA and its role in his reaching this conclusion, the prosecution objected, and the evidence was never heard in the courtroom. When Johnson was acquitted, no one ever challenged the judge's ruling on DNA. That didn't occur until the 90's, which was many years later.

"Now," said Malveaux, certain that he had their attention, "you may have guessed by now that the public defender was me." He clicked to one last photo, a younger, thinner version of himself with a long braids. The class burst out into sustained applause and laughter. "Johnson was acquitted, like I said, and died about six months later of a drug overdose. Tompkins, who had lied about his credentials, paid a steep fine and served some time in jail for tax evasion. He hadn't been reporting his income."

"This case was at the very beginning of a trend to introduce new techniques and science to criminal legal practice. DNA was not accepted then as evidence as it is now, as a tool for clearing those wrongfully accused of crimes. But remember, you must be prepared to challenge even DNA evidence, which is not in and of itself foolproof."

Simms raised his hand. "But Professor, I thought that everyone had their own unique DNA. Isn't there is a 99.9 percent chance that a DNA match is reliable physical evidence?"

Malveaux picked up the cup of water and took another sip, hoping he was not coming down with a cold. "You're right. That's why after the break we will discuss ways to refute DNA evidence, and we will discuss the chimera problem."

"Was the chimera material in our reading? I don't remember coming across it." Simms was anal and seemed to be panicking that there was something he was supposed to read and hadn't.

"No. This material is in a handout. Come get one during the break. It's really cutting edge. We'll take a ten-minute break while I head down to get some coffee."

Malveaux abruptly left the lecture hall for his office. Maybe he had a cough drop or some gum for his throat. He also wanted to avoid talking with Donald O'Reilly, who had risen from his seat in the back row and headed toward the stairs to confront him.

Malveaux darted into the stairwell. He did not feel like talking to O'Reilly right now and seemed to be getting the worst headache he'd had in years. O'Reilly would head to the cafeteria to intercept him, but he had no intention of getting coffee right now.

Malveaux took the stairs two at a time so that no one would catch him. He unlocked his office, turned on the light, and closed the door behind him. The space was decorated—or not decorated, as the case might be—with the typical flare of an academician. There were stacks of papers everywhere, and not one inch of his desk could be seen. The bookshelves were bursting at the seams with volumes and papers and knickknacks. Several framed certificates and diplomas hung on the walls, including his undergraduate diploma from Our Lady of the Grove Seminary, his law school diploma from Loyola University, and his certificates of admission to the District of Columbia bar, the United States District Court, and the United States Supreme Court.

The message indicator light was blinking on his phone. He would listen to the message later; right now he needed to find an aspirin and a cough drop and just put his head down for a few minutes. Malveaux plopped himself down into his desk chair and unlocked his side drawer, where he kept a bottle of mineral water. His upper center desk drawer was unlocked. There he found a few cough drops and some aspirin. He popped the aspirin into his mouth and unscrewed the water bottle, washing down the pills. Malveaux tore open the cough drops and popped one into his mouth. He'd just put his head down on the desk when his phone rang. He wouldn't answer it now. Right now he needed a break.

***

Malveaux returned to the lecture hall with several cough drops in his pocket. The students were engaged in conversation around the hall. A few were sitting alone, reading the newspaper, and one seemed to be writing out checks to pay bills. One woman had her head down on the desk to catch up on her rest. He didn't see O'Reilly in the back row. That was a good sign. But then again, maybe he'd spoken too soon. As he tapped on the microphone to get their attention, O'Reilly entered the rear of the lecture hall without looking at him.

"Johnson always maintained that he did not kill Simon Marcants." Malveaux looked around the lecture hall, trying to avoid O'Reilly's gaze. O'Reilly stared at him intensely, taking a note here and there. Malveaux continued the rest of his lecture, more or less on autopilot. After teaching the same class year in, year out, he pretty much knew the drill and could anticipate the questions the students would ask.

After explaining how the expert's testimony exonerated Johnson, he dismissed the class, reminding them he'd be out for two weeks and wouldn't see them in class until after Thanksgiving. He assigned them 340 pages to read during his absence. A groan filled the hall as the students packed up and left quickly. No one stopped to talk with Malveaux, although Gupta turned to wish him a happy Thanksgiving. Malveaux did not look up as he stuffed his course outline into a thin manila founder.

O'Reilly stood barely three feet away. Malveaux could hear him breathing and smell the institutional soap that all priests used. Malveaux removed his glasses and placed them into a red cylindrical case, which he also secreted in his briefcase. Then he looked squarely at O'Reilly and said, "What is it, Donald? What do you want?"

O'Reilly did not smile. "That's just like you, Malveaux. No pleasantries, no hellos. Always right down to business."

Malveaux met O'Reilly's gaze. As Malveaux observed the man more closely, he could see the priest was aging badly. O'Reilly looked thin and his skin was blotchy. His hairline was receding, and his bloodshot eyes made Malveaux wonder whether the man was suffering from some eye disease. O'Reilly coughed violently and persistently, raising a tissue to his lips and expelling a large amount of mucus and blood. Malveaux grew concerned. This was no ordinary cough. O'Reilly was sick.

"You don't sound so good." Malveaux watched O'Reilly throw the wad of bloody tissues into the wastebasket.

O'Reilly looked at Malveaux and smiled wanly, lowering his droopy lids over his bloodshot eyes. "Last time I checked, AIDS was not an especially contagious disease. You won't get it from just being around me."

Malveaux froze. "Oh, it's OK," O'Reilly continued. "I have good days and bad days. Lately I've had a lot more good days than I deserve."

Malveaux's dismissive attitude turned to compassion. "Do you want to sit down? Do you want to go sit in my office? We can talk there."

O'Reilly shook his head. "Let's go over to the Grotto. I really feel like a drink. I need to unwind a little bit."

Malveaux was concerned as O'Reilly continued to cough violently. "It sounds like you have pneumonia or something. Are you sure you should be drinking?"

O'Reilly laughed as he pulled more tissues from his pocket. "Yeah, I probably do have pneumonia. I'll go to the hospital later. I need to talk to you first, though. It won't take long."

"What does your order have to say about that?" Malveaux arranged a wool scarf around his neck and buttoned his overcoat as he waited for O'Reilly to stop coughing.

"They don't know and I don't intend for them to find out. It's none of their fucking business."

Malveaux looked at O'Reilly as if he were seeing him for the first time. He'd known O'Reilly for nearly thirty years and he'd never once heard him curse.

"You heard me right," said O'Reilly as he pulled on a pair of black leather gloves. "Those hypocritical bastards wouldn't know compassion if it jumped up and bit them on the ass."

"Damn. It sounds like you finally got some sense in your head after all these years."

O'Reilly smiled. "Facing death does funny things to a man, Malveaux. You shouldn't feel sorry for me. I know I look like shit, but this disease has been a blessing for me. It's given me the chance to see my life for what it really is and to really get close to God."

"That's deep," replied Malveaux as they exited the lecture hall. Gupta was in the hallway, talking excitedly on his cell phone. He nodded and smiled, acknowledging Malveaux and O'Reilly as they passed by on their way to the Grotto.

Most of Malveaux's students hung out at the Grotto at least two or three times a week. The bar had gone through many reincarnations over the years. A cross between a true Irish pub and a St. Paul dive, the food was predictably bad and the beer was perpetually cheap. Recently the owner had tried to establish the Grotto as the "in" place for the university crowd, especially the graduate students, and introduced a series funky microbrews. The trend didn't last, though. Now he was back to serving Miller Lite and Pabst Blue Ribbon and the Grotto was making a comeback. Those beers were cheaper and the students didn't have any real money. Malveaux figured if he lived long enough, he'd see Schlitz come back too.

O'Reilly and Malveaux sat in a corner booth. Most of the tables were full, but Malveaux was a regular. There was always room for him.

Mac, the big-bellied waiter, made his way to the table with a pitcher of Bud Lite. He spilled a fair amount of the contents onto the red-and-white-checkered oilcloth and used his dirty apron to wipe up the mess.

"You should be home now, Father, out of the storm that's coming, I say," Mac said to Malveaux. He nodded at O'Reilly. "Looks like you could use a shot of whiskey yourself."

Mac was a strange figure. His Scottish accent seemed out of place in an Irish pub. During an all-night drinking binge after his first serious girlfriend left him, Malveaux had become good friends with Mac. Both men agreed that a bunch of drunk Americans couldn't really tell the difference in the accents. Sometimes when customers were really drunk, Mac convinced them he was from Boston.

Now Mac sat down at the table with Malveaux and O'Reilly. Mac and Bud Lite had nursed Malveaux through bad times. He liked to talk to Mac about his failed relationships with women. Mac's favorite saying was "a pint is a steady friend." O'Reilly, on the other hand, had weaned Malveaux off Scotch and gin and even attended a series of Alcoholics Anonymous meetings with him in the early '80s.

O'Reilly began to cough, and he pulled an inhaler and four bottles of pills from his pocket. Mac looked at him with concern and stood abruptly. It was obvious to Mac and anyone who was observant that O'Reilly was gravely ill. He needed to be in a first-rate teaching hospital, not hanging out in a drafty bar in the middle of St. Paul during the chill of a late fall evening.

"I'll get you some water to go with that," Mac said. "And I'll get you a spot of tea too, Father." O'Reilly didn't answer, but when his coughing jag ended, he found water and hot tea waiting for him. O'Reilly took two short puffs on the inhaler and began to breathe easier.

"Donald, why didn't you tell me?" Malveaux looked at O'Reilly but avoided his eyes. O'Reilly always saw too much. If he looked him in the eyes, Malveaux would be sucked into a bad place. O'Reilly, meanwhile, looked like someone was walking over his grave. He removed one pill from each of the containers and arranged them in patterns as he talked.

"I guess it's not something I wanted to talk about. I try to put it out of my mind. That's the only way for me to make it from day to day."

Malveaux changed the subject. He would probe more, but only later. "How are your parents?"

Malveaux began to sip his beer. Mac returned with a dish of peanuts, more hot water with lemon, and a teapot. He placed them down silently and disappeared behind two swinging doors.

"They're the same. I've been living at home the past year or so. It's been good—it's given me time to reconnect. You know, make amends."

Malveaux nodded. It was so strange. O'Reilly's voice was the same, it just didn't fit the old man he was looking at across the table. The disease had taken a toll. O'Reilly seemed to be aging as they sat across from each other. When they'd met nearly thirty years ago, they'd become instant friends. More recently, arguments had caused them to drift apart. Malveaux had actually picked up the phone to call O'Reilly several times, but he'd never followed through. Now he regretted failing to call and check in. After all, their last fight had been his fault.

O'Reilly raised his glass of water, popped the four pills, and garbled, "Carpe diem." Then he threw his head back and swallowed hard. Malveaux could hardly believe his oldest friend in the world was dying. He knew O'Reilly knew he was dying too. Intellectually everyone knew they were dying a slow death, but O'Reilly's mortality was just out there, flashing in front of everyone like the bar's neon sign. It was almost too much to take.

They were opposites in every way. O'Reilly came from a prosperous Irish Catholic family from Boston. His father was a millionaire construction contractor. His mother was a homemaker, mother of eight, and consummate volunteer. Malveaux could still remember the names of O'Reilly's seven brothers and sisters: Declan, Sinead, Shannon, Jane, Jean, Patricia, and Francis. O'Reilly had entered the seminary at age fourteen and never left. His family was especially proud that one of their sons had entered the priesthood.

"Look, Robert, I'd like to catch up with you, really. I've missed talking to you." There was so much Malveaux wanted to know, like how O'Reilly had contracted AIDS and whether or not there was anything he wanted Malveaux to do for him.

"I know that you have been dealing with a lot yourself with all the cases."

Malveaux nodded but did not speak. Teaching at the law school was only a part of his current duties, and certainly only the enjoyable part. For the past eleven years or so, he had been involved in reviewing and making recommendations to various archdioceses around the country on litigation regarding child sex abuse within the church. The work was gut wrenching and left him wide awake, wondering what he was doing in the church. He was lucky—he was basically able to fly under the radar. He'd become such an expert in these cases that many in the church called him "bishop" out of respect, as he led North American church leaders from a culture of sticking their heads in the sand and denying the gravity of the problem to confronting it, kicking out the perpetrators, and working to come to terms with victims and the damage suffered on account of years of lies and cover-ups.

O'Reilly coughed hard and spit into a dirty handkerchief. "Robert, I wanted to speak to you directly about this. I didn't want to write to you or even call your office to let you know I was coming."

Malveaux was intrigued, but he understood the need for discretion in these situations. "I entered the seminary very young, as you know," O'Reilly said. Malveaux nodded. This conversation was beginning to feel like a bit of a confession. "I always admired you because you had the strength to leave." O'Reilly took a long sip of tea and looked down into the cup as he talked. "When you came back, I was upset with you for a long time. I thought you'd made a big mistake."

Malveaux laughed. "You weren't the only one who thought I'd made a big mistake. I still think that some days."

"I always knew you were an intuitive person, Robert. You seemed to see things about people, like you could look inside them and know them. You were like an older brother to me. You treated me like a friend and you never asked for anything from me."

Malveaux listened. O'Reilly was correct. He did have a gift, a sense of things. It had helped him through the years, certainly through these molestation cases and in helping the victims. The gift had helped him in other ways as well.

"Do you remember Father Charles?"

Malveaux froze. It had been years since he'd thought about Father Charles. Charles was part of the reason he'd left the church after seminary. Malveaux didn't trust him. He could never put his finger on it, but there was something about the man that made his flesh crawl.

"I remember Charles. I didn't care for him. You know that."

"He raped me, Robert."

Malveaux looked at O'Reilly, enraged. "He what?"

O'Reilly repeated, "He raped me. Not just once. He did it over period of years. It started when I was fifteen."

"Donald, why didn't you say something? Why didn't you report it? Oh my God. This is horrible." "He said he'd embarrass my family. He said he'd kill me. I was too scared to do anything. I thought there was something wrong with me."

Malveaux put his hand on O'Reilly's arm. "What can I do, Donald? This has to be reported. You know I have to report it." Malveaux was required to report any new victims who came to his attention, either through direct outreach or through his investigations.

"Robert, I'm just asking you to wait until after I'm gone. I don't want to face my family with this. I can't. Not now." O'Reilly's parents were elderly and infirm. They would hardly be able to absorb the news.

O'Reilly pulled a silver key from his pocket and pushed it across the table toward Malveaux. "I collected some evidence. Letters he sent me, and gifts. I have them in a safe deposit box in the Bank of America near South Station. You'll receive the contents as a bequest from my will. All I'm asking for you to do is make sure he's punished. Do whatever you can."

Malveaux took the key and added it to his keychain. "Where's Charles now?" Malveaux knew from his work that many victims tracked their abusers over the years. Donald would likely know where Charles was.

"He's in a retirement community in central Virginia." O'Reilly stood. "I have to go now, Robert. You need to watch that guy who works in your office. He's one of them, you know."

Malveaux knew Donald was talking about Sean Hennigan, his assistant. He couldn't stand Hennigan and didn't trust him. Hennigan read his mail and was intimately involved with each investigation. Malveaux had asked to have him reassigned, but to no avail. Hennigan's presence alone made him know that someone in the church hierarchy was protecting the perpetrators of a great and evil abuse of the innocent.

"Let me walk with you. Where are you staying?" He could tell his friend was tired.

"I have a flight headed out in a couple of hours. I'm headed to the airport."

"Let me ride with you, then."

O'Reilly nodded, and Malveaux grabbed his coat and hat, following his dying friend to the exit.

CHAPTER EIGHT

The cleric, Hennigan, opened the door and presented himself squarely in front of Malveaux's massive desk. Malveaux was deep in thought and did not look up from his papers. He gripped a yellow marker in his left hand and continued to highlight passages of text. He had to come up to speed on this new case—the Charleroi case—quickly. There was something about the witness statements that did not make sense to him.

Malveaux studied the statements again. The first statement, marked "Security Officer Number 1," was succinct.

> *I arrived at the bedroom of the juvenile, S., at approximately 22:15 based on a disturbance heard and observed from the security monitor. The monitors had been working irregularly, and the function of this particular monitor had been restored after a two-week period. It was unusual that there was activity at that late hour. It had been shorting in and out.*
>
> *I called for backup and ran up to the second-floor bedroom. I attempted to open the door and burned my hand on the doorknob, which was hot. Suspecting fire, I asked my partner to call the fire department. The door was locked. I could hear voices from the room but did not recognize all of them. I was not able to open the door, which was jammed. I kicked in the door.*
>
> *I found the suspect (Fr. Gaul) engaged in a physical altercation with the juvenile and with Marissa Charleroi. The babysitter, Ms. Rock, was in the room and was also struggling with Gaul. Officer Hawk entered the room and we pulled them apart. The juvenile was*

screaming and pointing at Gaul and yelling that he had molested him. Mrs. Charleroi and Ms. Rock were hysterical. We escorted Gaul from the room and read him his rights. Despite the warning, he continued to speak, insisting he had not done anything wrong and that the boy was dangerous. Ms. Rock and the other man in the room presumably left the scene before giving statements.

We placed the suspect in custody of the Loudoun County sheriff's office and sought additional support. We then traveled to Loudon Hospital for treatment of first-degree burns on my right hand.

Malveaux continued to flip through the pages and read through the statement for the second officer.

Revised

Responder was the second officer on the scene after receiving a call for backup. I heard an altercation in the second floor bedroom of [illegible]. I entered the room and vomited from the strong smell. I joined my partner and assisted him in pulling away the suspect, Father Gaul, from Mrs. Charleroi and the juvenile, S. There was another man in the corner. The amount of blood, and what appeared to be pounds of feces on the bed, caused me to vomit again. We removed Gaul into the hallway and S. made several explicit declarations that Gaul had touched him sexually. Mrs. Charleroi was out of control and screaming "no," and was instructed to back away.

As the firefighters entered the home on the lower level, I returned to get the statements and to clarify who else was in the room. At this time I fell, and woke up with the paramedics several minutes later.

I heard Gaul being Mirandized by the sheriff's office. He was yelling that the boy and family were in danger. Heard assessment that suspect was unstable. Mrs. Charleroi refused to give a statement. Sheriff's office contacted Loudoun Social Services. I called Leon Charleroi per instructions to report the incident.

Hennigan cleared his throat, trying to get the older man's attention. "Father Malveaux?"

Malveaux did not look up from his reading and did not respond. He turned the page of the transcript and continued highlighting line after line of text. Hennigan got on his last nerve. He was always interrupting him, bringing so-called "important matters" to his attention. The man was obsequious, always coming around like a poor relative who needed gas money. Malveaux put his index finger to his lips and whispered, "Shhhh." He did not look at Hennigan; he just wanted him to go away.

Malveaux had inherited Hennigan when he was appointed to oversee litigation for the Conference of North American Bishops regarding the child sex abuse scandal. Hennigan was not the type Malveaux would typically have working in his office, especially now. Hennigan's file was three-quarters of an inch thick. He had been a model seminarian and was rated highly by his superiors. There were, however, three separate complaints from parishioners in three separate parishes complaining of Hennigan's interaction with their young sons in the '70s. Hennigan had been transferred from parish to parish again and again and had undergone "treatment" for sexual disorders. This current post was administrative and did not place him in contact with minors. Assigning him to assist Malveaux was like asking a starving man to guard a box of doughnuts because it fed his need for salacious information about the victims of the various abuse scandals. Malveaux didn't feel comfortable having him around, and he especially didn't like that the little prick had friends in high places to shield him.

Hennigan spoke excitedly. "Father Malveaux, there is an urgent message for you from Washington, DC." Malveaux did not look up from the transcript or acknowledge him. There had been many messages from Washington and even Rome over the years. He did not get excited about them anymore, especially given all he'd learned about the hierarchy since he had been charged with shepherding the North American church through the present sex abuse crisis. It didn't help that he had Hennigan in his office every three minutes looking over his shoulder and typing his correspondence. Hennigan's presence made it difficult to keep secrets.

Malveaux folded down the upper right-hand corner of the transcript to mark his place, then closed it. He silently removed his glasses and placed them on the desk. Rubbing his eyes with his left hand, he slowly looked up at Hennigan, who was holding out an envelope that bore some kind of seal. If Malveaux didn't know better, he'd think Hennigan was drooling. "I received a call from Washington. They said your immediate response is required."

Malveaux did not speak and did not open the letter. He waved dismissively at Hennigan and said, "That's all, Sean." He suspected Hennigan was a bit of a racist. The man didn't relate well to minorities from what he could see. Malveaux suspected Hennigan found it difficult to accept directions from a black man in the holy Roman Catholic Church.

"Don't you want to open the letter so I can forward your answer? I understand your response is needed today."

"That's all," said Malveaux, standing to face Hennigan. "Leave the letter; I'll phone in my response myself."

"All right," murmured Hennigan. Malveaux could tell he was disappointed not to learn the contents of the letter.

The light on his second phone extension came on. Sean Hennigan was probably calling one of his friends right this very minute to find out what the letter was about. Robert Malveaux walked to his closet and removed his overcoat and hat. "I've got to get out of here," he said to himself, and slipped out of his private exit with the letter in hand.

***

Robert Malveaux walked from the warmth of his study into the frosty cold of St. Paul. His discussion with Donald O'Reilly days earlier weighed him down like a millstone around his neck. He wore a simple cloth coat, a burgundy scarf, and a Milwaukee Bucks knit cap. The snow and ice crunched beneath his boots. There were iron gates in the distance, and he could see a sanitation crew collecting recycling materials. He approached a large keypad and entered a security code. The rear gates of the compound slowly opened and he found himself in the rear alley near the service entrance. As he walked through the gates, the door swung shut behind him.

"How are you doing, Father Robert?" called out a young man picking up trash from the alley. Todd Arnold did odd jobs around the complex. He was dependable and always seemed genuinely glad to be alive. Todd was a recovering heroin addict and was doing well despite complications from hepatitis C. Malveaux and some law students from the public interest clinic had helped Arnold obtain housing and his GED.

"I'm good, Todd," said Malveaux, who went over and shook his hand warmly. "I just need to get out for a while and stretch my legs." He tried to be pleasant despite his tension. "Sometimes I just need to get away, if you know what I mean." He nodded back toward the church compound.

Todd put down the green trash bag he was holding. It was amazing how many cans and bottles and papers and littered the alley. Two large rats darted from bushes behind them and ran into the gated compound. Their movements caught the men's attention.

"Looks like you'll have to do something about that, Todd. Get some cats or something. Those are some big rats." Malveaux laughed and shook his head.

"You could just send Hennigan out to get them. They would be good little friends for him," replied Todd with a laugh. Father Malveaux and Todd shared a common dislike for Hennigan. Malveaux suspected Hennigan thought he was superior to Todd—and just about everyone else. The weasel had tried to get Todd fired at every opportunity.

Todd spat on the ground and looked at Malveaux from under the brim of the dirty baseball cap he wore. "Father, I don't know how you put up with it all. You seem like such a regular guy, watching football and having a beer every now and then. You're not like the rest of them."

Malveaux grinned. "Damn straight."

"Father, you just gotta break free sometimes, know what I mean? You're too tense. You gotta chill."

Malveaux just nodded and continued down the alley past Todd. He didn't even look back as he shouted, "See you later."

"Yeah, man, see you later," Todd answered.

Malveaux continued down the alley until he came to St. Catherine Street. A city bus belched out exhaust as a woman ran alongside it, trying to get the driver's attention. Malveaux turned left and headed toward Providence Park. Todd did have a point, he thought, as he waited at the corner for the red traffic signal to turn to green. What the world was he doing here in St. Paul dealing with all these problems?

Across the street he saw a woman with two young children. The kids were bundled up tightly with scarves, hats, and heavy coats. The woman carried two plastic grocery bags in one hand and was holding the hand of the younger child as they walked along the sidewalk, heads down to avoid the gusty wind. Looking at them reminded Malveaux of his own childhood nearly fifty years ago. His mother had immigrated to the United States from Haiti by traveling on a dangerously overloaded fishing boat. She made her way to New Jersey to work for a prominent couple from Port au Prince and soon found herself pregnant with her first child—Robert's brother, Pierre—and then eight years' later with him. She never spoke about their father, but Malveaux remembered hearing her cry sometimes in a corner of the bedroom they shared when she thought he was asleep. Malveaux never heard from him and did not even know his name. He sometimes fantasized that the men on the street corners or behind the counter of the butcher shop were his father. They were kind and smiled at him and sometimes handed him treats of rock candy. Certainly his life would have been different if his father had been present in their lives. Their family would have been complete, he supposed, but maybe not.

He was lucky to have had a mother who cared for him, if only for a brief period of years. How lucky he was to have had someone to fuss over him and love him unconditionally. He treasured those memories dearly. They were a poor family, but she was kind and loved him and Pierre. She sang them songs and smiled and prayed over him and his brother in their beds at night. Sometimes she told tales of her childhood. Tales of the green-and-blue waters of Haiti in the village where she lived with her grandmother and brothers and sisters, a village where no one disrespected her because they feared her grandmère and her seeing eye.

His mother always became solemn when she spoke of her grandmère. He remembered her tales of the old woman, who by his mother's description was more than eighty years old, even when she was a child. He did not remember if Grandmère was his mother's grandmother or great-grandmother, just that she was very well known. By merely gazing into your eyes, she was said to be able to predict your future with absolute certainty, and the manner of your death. Robert had begged his mother many times to tell him what Grandmère had seen when she looked into her eyes, but she would never say much, only that he too would inherit "the gift." At the time, Malveaux could not understand what she meant. He only laughed and felt special, as all children should.

Robert dreamed of running through the coffee fields with his mother and eating the berries from the bushes until the juice burst from the sides of his mouth. He dreamed of his grandmère, whom he'd never met but could imagine. She would look into his eyes and tell him his future while feeding him banana bread and cakes layered with happiness and joy. He was always happy and laughing in his dreams. Grandmère would laugh with pleasure when she saw him and nod approvingly. She only used one word in his dreams. "The eye," she would say. He never mentioned this to his mother, but as he grew, he understood that "the gift" and "the eye" were one and the same.

Through his work in the church, he had traveled to Haiti many times. One day he hoped to visit the village where his mother came from. Perhaps he would find an ancient man or woman who'd known her as a child, or known his grandmother. He would like someday to talk to someone who shared "the gift." In his entire life, he had never met anyone who truly understood it. He hadn't thought about it in years, but he felt sorry that he had never been close enough to anyone who might understand if he explained it. His friends and coworkers always said he was amazingly intuitive; nowadays some said he had "high emotional intelligence." But his instincts, his marvelous instincts, gave him guidance, and the guidance was too real to be ignored.

Malveaux vividly remembered the first time he understood his gift. He could have been no more than four years old, and he was at home in bed with a fever and chills. His brother, Pierre, was charged with his care while his mother worked. That day he passed from consciousness to unconsciousness over many hours. When his mother returned, she placed her cold hands on his burning forehead. When he opened his eyes to look at her, he could not explain what he saw, only that everything was discordant and amber colored, like a sepia-toned photograph, only luminescent. He looked deep into her eyes and somehow felt her life streaming from her; the grains of her soul seeping from a broken hourglass, one grain at a time. He vividly remembered his words to her: "Mother, you are not well." She froze and then laughed away his words. Mere months later, she died of a fast-growing cancer. She was not prepared, even though Robert suspected she knew somewhere in the deep and secret places inside her that her death was coming. One day she complained of a headache; the next day she was gone. Years later he ordered her death certificate, which listed her death as a drug overdose and the cancer as a secondary cause. He supposed the pain she felt had caused her to self-medicate. He did not blame her.

Malveaux and his brother lived in their one-bedroom apartment for nearly a month without electricity and little food until Social Services found them and placed them in the children's home run by the Sisters of Mercy. Pierre ran away as soon as he was able and eventually joined the Army. Malveaux did not see him again for years and only after Pierre had been wounded in a military training exercise. Malveaux ended up staying with the sisters and caught their attention when he showed competence in the study of Latin. The words seemed comforting and familiar to him. They reminded him of the Creole French his mother had whispered to him at night. He supposed that was how he came to the priesthood. He had no other family, nowhere to go, and knew no other life.

He tried his best not to use the gift, but sometimes it intruded in his life. It was a burden in so many ways. Looking at a man, he could see depravity, death, tragedy, bravery, or great fortune. More lately, the gift had become more and more intrusive. He supposed that was why he could not even bear to look at Hennigan, who did not appear to him as a man but rather as a rotting, mobile corpse with stinking flesh. Malveaux knew Hennigan loathed him and perhaps was even a little afraid of him. That was a good thing.

***

Malveaux entered the CVS drugstore on the corner and walked back to the pharmacy.

"Hello, Father. How's it going?" A short, youthful Vietnamese man appeared behind the counter. Tran was one of the first people Malveaux had met when he arrived in St. Paul. He saw Tran weekly at Mass, and each time he went to the pharmacy to fill his prescription for high-blood-pressure medication. Tran was always there. He must have worked every single shift the pharmacy was open.

"Hi, Tran. What's going on?" said Malveaux as he reached for a box of animal crackers in a display beside the counter.

"I'm good, Father. God is good. I am so blessed." Tran smiled. He was short, maybe five feet tall. He had an infectious grin and never complained. Tran had fled to the United States during the fall of Saigon, making his way to a refugee center in the Midwest without a dime in his pocket. Through determination, he'd put himself through school and reunited his family, bringing at least thirteen people to the St. Paul and Milwaukee area while working several jobs to save money to purchase a small restaurant which was run by his wife, brother, and children. He worked at the pharmacy for the health insurance benefits and toiled in his spare time at their café.

Malveaux appreciated Tran because he was a true friend. Tran treated Malveaux as he would treat any friend. Tran didn't come to him to confess his sins. He didn't talk to him about God more than he would have to anyone else. Tran let the priest be himself.

"Hey, Tran. I just need to get a refill. I've got a trip coming up and I need to make sure I don't run out."

"You need to put those cookies down and lose some weight. You don't take care of yourself."

Malveaux laughed. "You know I just eat what they give me over there."

"They need some cooking lessons about how to fix good food," replied Tran as he typed Malveaux's name into the computer. He slid the pen across the counter. "You know the drill. Sign here. Now put those cookies back or your insurance company will pay for your bad eating habits."

Malveaux chuckled as he put the cookies down and signed his name.

"Where you going this time?" asked Tran as he counted out the small green pills and dropped them into a bottle.

"Tran, can you give me some bigger pills than that? If I drop one of those on the floor, I won't be able to find it without a magnifying glass."

Tran sauntered over to the counter and affixed a black-and-white label to the prescription bottle. "You need to drop some weight and then you won't need these pills." He handed Malveaux the pills across the counter. He looked into the priest's face and then frowned with concern. "There is something wrong. What is wrong? Something is bothering you, I can tell. Why are they making you travel now before Thanksgiving? The law school has finals now. What's wrong with them?"

Malveaux took the package and looked at Tran for several seconds, but did not speak. Then he slid the pills into his pocket and wiggled his hands into his gloves. "I'll talk to you when I get back. Give my best to your family." He reached into the other coat pocket and handed the wisp of a man a crumpled letter. "Throw this away for me, OK?"

Tran took the crumpled paper and threw it into the trash bin beneath the counter without looking at it. He threw papers away for Malveaux regularly. He knew the man didn't want his assistant rummaging through and reading his trash.

"You going back to Washington?" Tran called to Malveaux as he walked away, but Malveaux did not answer. He knew this trip to

Washington would bring him more bad news for his cases. Something really big must have happened, and he knew just by touching the letter that something was very, very wrong.

CHAPTER NINE

Washington, DC

Reagan National Airport was deserted. Several bleary-eyed travelers were making their way down the corridor ahead of Malveaux. The terminal was decorated for the Christmas holidays even though Thanksgiving hadn't yet been celebrated. He didn't feel like it was the holiday season though with so much work to do. He maneuvered around an elderly couple, making his way through security and the Starbucks kiosk to the escalators leading to the new baggage claim area. As he approached the carousel, he could see his suitcase circling on the conveyor belt. He waited for the nondescript black American Tourister bag to make its way toward him. A seasoned traveler, Malveaux had tied a bright yellow ribbon to the handle, making it easier to distinguish his bag from all the others that looked just like it. Several other passengers stood poised on the very edge of the conveyor belt, ready to push aside anyone who would get in their way. A young girl stood in front of him. Like the others, she was practically riding the belt with the luggage.

"Excuse me," he said as he reached in to grab his bag. He pulled at the handle with one fluid motion and walked through the throng toward the taxi stand. After all, this was his eighteenth trip to Washington in as many months and he knew the drill.

He'd gone no more than twenty yards when he heard a voice calling from behind. "Robert Malveaux? Father Malveaux, is that you?"

Malveaux recognized the voice immediately and kept walking. He didn't feel like talking to David Levin. Levin was likable enough, he just didn't feel like dealing with him now. Levin worked for *The Secret*, a new tabloid with a strong online presence. The magazine had gained national recognition for reporting on the altar boy scandal.

Malveaux was a regular reader of *The Secret*, although he'd never admit it to anyone. Tran usually set aside a copy for him at the drugstore. He'd return to his office, read what the paper had to say, and return it to Tran for disposal. He didn't trust anyone with anything, even his trash. There was just too much at stake. The funny thing about *The Secret* was that it had gotten word of the altar boy scandal before any other major newspaper, and its articles on the scandal were right on point. It was almost as if the "unidentified source" was an insider, because the paper reported facts and circumstances that only those with insider knowledge would have access to.

The altar boy scandal gained notoriety because it happened in the nation's capital and involved children in all wards of the city. The victims and their families were outraged to learn that several predator priests had been transferred to some of D.C.'s neediest neighborhoods and had continued to prey on innocent children. Their anger increased when a leaked memo revealed that the minority victims were offered a mere fraction of the monetary compensation offered to those in more affluent sections of the city. People across the city and the region demanded equal compensation for all victims and Malveaux had been called in to investigate and resolve the disparities.

Malveaux had been investigating the priest sex abuse cases for a number of years. When his conclusions and analysis from the investigation of the altar boy scandal began to appear in *The Secret*, he knew that someone with access to his sensitive files was leaking reports to the media. Several insiders accused him of leaking the information himself, leading to great distrust between him and the church hierarchy. It was no surprise to anyone who knew him that he felt strongly about the scandal and believed the public deserved to know the truth about predator priests. He had personally advised the council investigating the larger issue of priestly sex abuse to come clean and turn the perpetrators over to the authorities. His warnings had come years before people began connecting the dots and realizing the events in New

Orleans and Washington, DC, were all part of a larger, more serious problem for the church.

Malveaux stopped short, blocked by Levin. Levin was probably still mad at him. Last year Malveaux had inserted several detailed but misleading and inconsequential facts into several of his reports to determine the source of the leaks. These details were deleted from final reports. As predicted, the false, salacious details turned up less than two weeks later in a story penned by Levin, who was almost fired from the paper as a result. Once Malveaux knew his reports were being leaked to the media by a highly placed source, he felt confident that other church leaders supported his position and began to grow more persistent in his call for reform and justice. His strong recommendations and ideas began to show up regularly in *The Secret*. These stories were now being picked up by the mainstream media within a day or two.

Malveaux was no longer angry that his reports were being leaked. He realized that a strong coalition in the church had no intention of following his recommendations to protect the flock. Someone he had not yet identified, someone in a high place, was doing a great service by leaking his reports to the media, but this didn't stop Levin from stalking Malveaux with amazing regularity. The fact that Levin was there to meet him meant something big was happening.

As Malveaux reached out to touch Levin's hand, he fell back, grabbing his head. Everything around him faded to amber. As he struggled to retain his balance, he realized he was slipping to the floor.

***

Malveaux awoke in the rear of an ambulance and slowly opened his eyes. He reasoned he was suffering from some kind of vascular event. The ambulance veered sharply to the right and came to a halt. Medical personnel retrieved him. Malveaux could hear Levin telling someone how Malveaux had passed out at the airport.

Malveaux could feel himself being lifted from the ambulance onto a gurney. He peered beneath his eyelids at a set of double doors and recognized the Georgetown University seal. The ambulance must have taken the Key Bridge into the District and arrived at Georgetown University Hospital's emergency room, which was just off of Reservoir Road.

"You can't come back into this area, sir," an older woman cautioned Levin as she pulled Malveaux's overcoat up onto the gurney so it did not drag on the ground.

"But I brought him here. I've got his briefcase. He's here to meet with Cardinal Lowell." Levin held Malveaux's briefcase tightly.

"I don't care if he's here to meet the Pope, you ain't coming back here." With that, the emergency room attendant snatched the briefcase from Levin's hand and placed it at Malveaux's feet at the end of the gurney. She let the door swing back into Levin's face. Malveaux smiled slyly and relaxed. He was feeling better already and would "wake up" shortly.

CHAPTER TEN

A solitary man unlocked the nursing records storage room on the third floor of the hospital and slid silently behind the rows of shelving, using only a flashlight to illuminate his path. It was 3:30 a.m. and there was little chance he would be disturbed. He had ensured the nurses would be occupied elsewhere thanks to the fire he'd set in the room of an elderly patient.

The man scoured the rows, finally finding the object of his search. He pulled the slim file from the brown envelope, placed it in a folder, and moved hastily from the storage room.

He approached the X-ray viewing box located on the wall by the nursing station. A flip of a switch caused the box to illuminate, making the image on film, a human uterus, clear and distinct. Additional medical reports were inside the sleeve holding the X-rays. The man placed the documents onto a nearby table and used his cell phone to photograph them. With military precision, he then photographed the image on the viewing box. Satisfied with the results, he pulled the documents from the table and stuffed them and the X-rays back into their original envelope and pushed them into his waistband. He pulled his shirt down over the envelope and pulled his coat around him. He turned off the viewing box and moved away from the unattended nursing station in the confusion of the moment. He pulled his cell phone from his pocket and dialed a number.

"Yes?" a worried voice answered.

"Your Eminence, she fits the bill," the man whispered.

"Are you sure?" the very weary voice replied.

"Yes, I'm sure. There is no mistake. We need to watch this closely. She's not the boy's mother. I can see the vestiges of her absorbed twin in her womb."

The man walked confidently toward the bank of elevators and pushed the down button. Within seconds, the doors open before him. He recognized the women in the elevator as cafeteria workers, originally from Nigeria. "Good night, Father," one offered with a smile.

"Good night, dear," the man replied as he exited and the doors closed behind him.

CHAPTER ELEVEN

Malveaux had no problem convincing the overwhelmed hospital staff that he was ready to be released. Routine tests and X-rays performed by the hospital showed no irregularities that would justify keeping him even a few more hours. The CT scan confirmed a prior minor vascular event, and he was advised to see his doctor to consider whether he was a good candidate for a pacemaker. The hospital staff seemed relieved that they would have another available bed. Malveaux signed his discharge papers, promised he would take his high-blood-pressure medication more regularly, and agreed to make an appointment with his regular physician when he returned to St. Paul in a day or two.

Malveaux dressed, retrieved his briefcase from the bedside table, and made his way to the lobby, where a few taxi drivers were waiting outside. One looked asleep behind the wheel. It was nearly three forty-five p.m. and the rush-hour traffic had begun to clog the narrow streets of Georgetown. Malveaux fixed his gaze on the iconic and familiar sites of the capital. He ignored the ramblings of the taxi driver, who tried to engage him in a discussion about his finances of the District government and how racial profiling had increased since the September 11 attacks.

They arrived at the cardinal's residence in northeast Washington at 4:17 p.m.. Malveaux had lost an entire day. He would have to work into the night and tomorrow to make up the time so he could get back to St. Paul. Malveaux paid the driver, collected a receipt, and climbed the stairs. The door opened before he could reach out to ring the bell.

"Father Malveaux. What are you doing here? You're supposed to be in the hospital." Geraldine Monroe grabbed Malveaux and hugged him around the waist. She was a tiny bit of a woman who barely reached his midsection. He did not know the politically correct term for her medical condition. Mentally Geraldine was a sharp as a tack, not from academic pursuits but because she had solid common sense and an intuitive nature, even though Malveaux believed her medical records classified her as "developmentally delayed." Geraldine had worked in the cardinal's residence for over thirty five years as a housekeeper and would likely continue to do so until the day she died.

She took him by the hand and led him inside the residence.

Malveaux supposed Geraldine was the perfect housekeeper. She did not steal, she did not miss work, and she didn't ask for raises or better working conditions. She seldom complained. Although her hair was now streaked with gray, and she moved more slowly than she had in earlier years, she remained a loyal and dedicated servant.

Malveaux had known Geraldine for twenty-eight years, since the days when he'd been assigned as a young priest to Washington. In those days Geraldine had been working at the cardinal's residence for about seven years and traveled by bus to her home in nearby Mount Rainier, Maryland. One night after leaving the cardinal's residence, she had been brutally raped by a throng of young men. Malveaux and another priest, Malcom Brody traveled to Providence Hospital to meet Geraldine the next morning and escort her to the boarding house where she lived. The young woman shared her version of the attack through uncontrolled sobs as they traveled to her home. En route, Malveaux recalled Geraldine became increasingly agitated as they drew closer to Mount Rainier. Brody grabbed her and attempted to restrain her in the backseat as Malveaux sped toward Maryland.

This insensitive move on his colleague's part further damaged the young woman's fragile and scarred psyche. Geraldine's crying and hysterical screaming made it almost impossible to drive. He vividly recalled pulling the car over and trying to calm her as she fought them with the strength of a man nearly twice her size.

He would never forget staring into Geraldine's eyes in an effort to soothe her. He placed his hands firmly on the rear of the seat and commanded her to stop, promising her she would be OK. "You don't have to go back there. We'll take you to the cardinal's house."

Geraldine ceased writhing and scratching his colleague, who bolted from the backseat, pulling a handkerchief from his pocket. Geraldine stared back at him that night, soaked with fresh blood and nervous perspiration. Malveaux saw there not a hysterical beast but rather an intelligent injured soul, trapped in a physical condition that prevented her from fully expressing her deep hurt and loss of dignity. In fact, Malveaux had never forgotten the deep intelligence he saw that day. The fear and anger he saw fade from her eyes reminded him of the anger, fear, and uncertainty he faced every day as a black man in the holy, catholic, and apostolic church.

He distinctly remembered Brody saying, "I'm telling you. She's possessed, it's unnatural. There's no way she could be that strong."

Malveaux did not respond to the man who was clearly alarmed. Instead he said, "Geraldine, why don't you come and sit in the front seat with me?"

Geraldine paused, looked at Malveaux squarely in the eye, and to his great surprise leapt over into the front seat like an Olympic gymnast. Malveaux gestured for his companion to get back in the car and they drove silently to the cardinal's residence, where he was forced to advocate for Geraldine's change of residence as a humanitarian gesture. His colleague, Brody attempted to convince the cardinal that Geraldine was possessed, but Malveaux interrupted, insisting that the woman was scared and merely reacting to the horrible, demeaning attack. Malveaux remembered the cardinal's comment like it was yesterday.

"Well then, Malveaux, why don't you believe in what the Gospels teach?"

Malveaux considered the cardinal's question bizarre and irrational. It was 1976 and no one believed that stuff anymore. In the seminary he remembered studying psychology and learning discrete symptoms that in earlier days were attributed to demonic possession. These symptoms were in fact manifestations of biochemical imbalances, he believed.

Malveaux cleared his throat and offered his opinion with clinical precision. "Your Eminence, she was raped and assaulted. She was reacting to the trauma and her strength was a simple adrenaline rush. There are no such things as demons, and they sure weren't riding with me in your car through the streets of Washington, DC."

The cardinal pursed his lips with disapproval and replied, "Perhaps, perhaps." He nodded at Geraldine, who stood behind Malveaux like a child hiding from grownups. "I'll make room for her in the attic here at the residence. She can stay here from now on. Malveaux you can work on that can't you?" Malveaux nodded. The cardinal left the room and his acolytes followed, uncertain how to react because they'd never seen anyone stand up to the man before.

Malveaux located a suitable room for Geraldine in the spacious, comfortable attic, and the next day he packed and moved her meager belongings from the boarding house to the cardinal's residence. As Geraldine's pregnancy became apparent, he arranged for her to have a leave of absence and moved her to St. Anne's Infant and Maternity Home. He supervised the adoption of her child, a girl, and made sure her baby had a real home, something she herself had never had, as the key to a better life. Since that day, Geraldine had been Malveaux's most loyal friend, and he had yet to see his first demon.

Now Malveaux watched Geraldine lift his briefcase and move toward the stairway. "Gerry, sweetie," he called after her, "there's no need to take my briefcase upstairs. I'm going to work down here this evening and see if I can make up any of the meetings I missed today. I'll be taking the last flight out tomorrow evening back to St. Paul."

Geraldine did not look back but responded, "You're staying. The cardinal says you're staying longer."

Malveaux didn't think he had been mistaken with his travel arrangements. He'd asked Hennigan to make a return reservation for him the next evening. Yet he knew Geraldine had been eavesdropping on the cardinal for years. Malveaux imagined that the cardinal took little notice of Geraldine and probably underestimated her intelligence. She probably knew his schedule and what was going on better than he did.

A prim, sour-faced woman stood into the hallway inspecting Malveaux, and she greeted him with a contemptuous grin. "The cardinal will see you now, Father. Follow me." The woman's sharp heels shattered the silent hallway. Malveaux could not place her accent; she was from Eastern Europe, possibly Russia or even the Czech Republic. "I'm quite pleased to see you're well, Father. We were so concerned when we heard you had been hospitalized."

Malveaux fell behind her in the hallway, keeping his distance. He did not recognize the woman, but he couldn't shake the notion that he knew her or had seen her somewhere before.

"That's curious," he replied. "How did you learn I was hospitalized?"

The woman did not pause as she opened the door of the study and gestured to Malveaux to take a seat. She gathered a stack of newspapers on the nearby desk and said matter-of-factly, "I suppose the cardinal mentioned it. I'm sure someone from the hospital called him. Since we lost some meeting time, he asked me to rearrange your flight. I talked to Hennigan in your office, and he's rescheduled your meetings in St. Paul for the next several days so you can be here instead."

"Thank you." Malveaux examined an extraordinary landscape painting hanging over an ornate marble fireplace. He couldn't bear to look at the woman. There was something about her that unsettled him.

"Cardinal Lowell will be with you momentarily. I'll get you some coffee if you wish."

Malveaux looked at the woman but avoided her eyes. She seemed to do the same.

"No, thank you. I'm fine."

"Very well." She nodded, closing the door behind her.

Malveaux rose and walked toward the bookshelves where dozens of leather-bound books were organized neatly. He imagined some were quite rare.

He turned as the study door opened and the cardinal entered the room with two attendants. Malveaux did not recognize either attendant. He greeted Cardinal Lowell, kissing his ring as a sign of respect and obedience.

"I've been in meetings all this morning," Lowell said. "I'm glad to see you so well. I feared you wouldn't make it over here today."

The attendants grabbed the cardinal's overcoat and placed a cup of coffee on the table next to a luxurious leather recliner.

"Will you have a cup of coffee with me, then?" Lowell smiled as one of the attendants brought him sugar and cream.

"No, Your Eminence, I'm fine," answered Malveaux as he took a seat directly opposite the elderly man. Cardinal Lowell turned to the two attendants, who had seated themselves on a nearby couch and were preparing to take notes. "You may leave us, gentlemen. I wish to speak to Father Malveaux in private."

The two young attendants glanced at each other and left the room. Malveaux initiated the conversation. He had a good idea of why he was here.

"Your Eminence, I imagine you asked me here to discuss the Charleroi case. I know that it is a sensitive matter for you, and I'm gratified to know that you will consider some type of settlement. I think it would be best to conclude the matter while you are still in residence here, especially since the Washington altar boy scandal has hit the press."

Cardinal Lowell sipped his coffee and put his cup down. Malveaux continued, "I read the transcripts myself. I'm sure you're aware of the allegations made against Father Gaul. I know you appreciate the gravity of the situation and the damage it will do to the church. "We're going to get the Charleroi case out of the way," Lowell interrupted. "In fact, the Charlerois will be here in about forty-five minutes. I've made an appointment for you to speak with them today rather than tomorrow at the law firm as we had originally scheduled." The cardinal sipped his coffee. "I have another pressing matter today. There's so much to be done for advent. Christmas is just a few weeks away. Why don't we get together later? That way you can fill me in on the meeting."

One of the cardinal's assistants opened the door, and Malveaux saw that he was not being given a choice. He followed the assistant out of the office.

"Father Malveaux, your appointment with the Charlerois will begin in about a half an hour or so," the assistant whispered. "Geraldine moved your briefcase to the conference room. You'll have enough time to prepare before you meet them. Charleroi had a late meeting in DC. We were able to send a car to pick up his wife. She's not in in any condition to be driving into the city. This makes it more convenient for them."

"Fine. That's fine." He was prepared for the meeting, even if it was going to take place earlier. Maybe he would be able to get an earlier flight home tomorrow after all.

Malveaux waited with his briefcase in the cardinal's ornate conference room. He sighed and rubbed his temples, closing his eyes while trying to escape the details of the assault, if only for a moment or two. This was the thirty-seventh such case he had dealt with. He had become more cynical with each court filing. The cases were not concentrated in any particular geographic area. He had traveled as far away as Alaska and as close as small towns near St. Paul. Some good had come out of his work, he supposed. Each archdiocese had now adopted policies and procedures for immediately reporting claims of abuse. He had advocated for stiff criminal penalties for the accused when convicted. Resistance had been strong from many quarters. There were some who felt he was being too harsh, and that the shortage of priests made it important to save and "rehabilitate" as many of the accused as possible. Others argued that as a "forgiving" institution, the absolution of sins was all that was required. This particular argument always made Malveaux irate. Yes, everyone sinned. No one would ever be wholly blameless, but he could not rationalize giving a pass to men who'd abused the trust of countless innocents, forever changing their lives and futures and often destroying the victims' normal psychological and sexual development.

He took a long sip of mineral water from a bottle of Perrier on the conference room table and looked toward the window. His brother had told him years ago that the priesthood attracted sexual deviants. He laughed now, remembering how he had defended the institution. In his experience he'd met many men, most flawed, some more than others. Many were dedicated to God, but few he could think of approached the type of holiness he'd envisioned when he'd first entered the church and taken his vows those many years ago.

His brother had said these men were evil. Malveaux had often wondered about evil and what it really was. Was it simply human failing, or was it something more? Certainly what he was seeing now was human failure, accentuated by a lack of control, deviancy, child abuse, sin—all these things. Certainly these crimes did qualify as pure evil. He believed Hitler was evil and Idi Amin was evil. Pol Pot was evil. The North Korean regime that denied the most basic rights to millions of individual souls, a regime his own government refused to stand up to, was evil. All human behavior. All human failing. It really didn't matter. On a large scale involving nations and millions or on a small scale involving just one victim, it was all wrong. All unforgivable because there was no repentance.

Malveaux laughed. He imagined the whole of history could be rewritten by substituting the word "devil" with the word "evil" and the result would likely be the same. This led him to suppose that if he didn't need the devil to explain evil, then maybe he didn't need God to explain goodness.

He stood up and stretched, deciding to take his pills before the Charlerois arrived. He was being too cynical. He hadn't talked to God in a long time. This whole business was messing with his mind and his faith. Not a good thing for a priest in the Catholic Church.

One of the cardinal's assistants opened the door to the conference room, followed closely by Marissa Charleroi. She sat down, smoothing her navy-blue skirt beneath her and folding her hands in her lap. She did not make eye contact. Malveaux scarcely recognized her from the photos he'd Googled online. He had looked forward to meeting the former glamour girl, but this woman bore no resemblance to the striking woman who was a favorite of the paparazzi. Dark circles ringed her eyes and her raven hair was greasy and punctuated by gray roots running the extent of the part in her hair.

Charleroi arrived several minutes later. He nodded at Malveaux but did not speak. He looked pale and worn, as if he hadn't slept in days. His clothes were wrinkled, like they'd done double duty as pajamas. The fresh stubble on his cheeks was hardly the image Malveaux expected of a multimillionaire technology baron and former member of Congress.

Malveaux arranged the papers on the conference table while the assistant asked if they wanted coffee or water. All declined. Malveaux waited for the couple to settle into their seats. He hated these interviews. The accusations. The crying. The uncertainty. Which category would this discussion fall into? From his experience, Malveaux knew the interviews fell into several distinct categories. Some victims and their families wanted an apology and recognition that they had been wronged. They sought assurances that the abuser would be removed from the priesthood and branded with a scarlet letter. Other victims viewed the opportunity as a once-in-a-lifetime chance to cash in. These victims, had, for the most part, deeply buried scars. They had suffered and moved onto other addictions and dysfunctional relationships and wanted as much money as they could get.

There was also a third group. A group who never came forward. Some because they respected the authority of the church and somehow believed they had invited the abuse, and others who were too ashamed and wanted to forget, but still bore the scars of their victimization. Some of these victims came to the attention of the authorities based on eyewitness accounts from other victims. Occasionally it was through the confessions of a remorseful priest.

Malveaux hadn't seen anyone like the Charlerois before. They clearly did not want to be anywhere near him, yet they had demanded this interview for weeks. It was rumored that Leon Charleroi had reported abuse in the home in order to gain an advantage in his custody dispute with his soon-to-be-ex-wife, but tried to back away from the claims when the police became involved. Malveaux was anxious to hear their demands, especially since the accused, Father Gaul, was a prominent figure in his investigation of the DC altar boy cases. Sam Charleroi hadn't been an altar boy, but had come in contact with the priest through the cleric's life-long relationship with Leon Charleroi.

Malveaux was astonished the pair had come alone and not with legal counsel. Charleroi hadn't made any demands for immediate justice. From the reports, both he and his wife had made several attempts to secure the release of Father Gaul and have him return to their home. A court order prohibiting any contact between Gaul and minor children had kept the man out of their lives.

"Hello, Mr. Charleroi." Malveaux held out his hand and grasped Charleroi's. Mrs. Charleroi nodded. "I'm glad you could finally make it in. We'll try to get through this as best we can."

Neither returned his gaze. Charleroi paused, then spoke, but did not look at his wife or Malveaux. "Hello, Father. Afraid neither one of us got very much sleep last night. We are exhausted." He looked down in his lap. Marissa stared at her hands and did not speak.

Marissa looked up at him. Her eyes were rimmed with puffy dark circles. She had been crying, and had paid absolutely no attention to her personal hygiene. All this from a woman who had graced the covers of *The Washingtonian* and *People.* Something was wrong here.

Malveaux could hear a strong steady wind blowing outside. They sat in silence for a moment. At last Charleroi spoke. "This has all been very unfortunate for me and for my family." He looked squarely at Malveaux. "My wife and I have discussed this at length. We do not want to pursue any kind of civil action in this matter. We have agreed to accept the $2.4 million Cardinal Lowell offered this morning. As we discussed with him, we want the money to be used for Father Gaul's defense. We would like for you, for the church, to consider this matter closed. We don't want this business to affect Father Gaul in any negative way whatsoever. I assume Mr. Delmonte has filled you in on this."

Malveaux was speechless. What kind of family was this? "Mr. Delmonte?"

Marissa joined in. "Mr. Delmonte has been working with us from Cardinal Lowell's office. We told him last week what we wanted. We want to see Father Gaul released as soon as possible."

"I'm sorry, but I want to make sure I understand you. You want to drop this matter?" Malveaux couldn't believe it. Lowell had never mentioned he'd made the Charlerois a two-million-dollar offer, or that they wanted to use it to help Father Gaul and not their child. And the cardinal had never mentioned Mr. Delmonte.

"Yes," Marissa Charleroi and Leon Charleroi answered in unison.

"And you are quite sure about this? Will you be willing to sign a release of all claims?" Marissa looked at Charleroi, who spoke for the couple. "Yes, but I want to know where Mr. Delmonte is. He knows all about it. If you're the one who'll be preparing the papers for us, I'll make sure they're signed right away. You can bring the papers out to the house. I'll take care of it."

"Well, you both would need to sign," Malveaux said. Marissa nodded. "And what about your son? Do you think this is what he would want? In the future, he might want to raise this matter. He might want compensation, therapy, or even an apology." Malveaux frowned. There was so much evidence against Father Gaul, it did not make sense to just let him off the hook like this.

"I don't think so," Charleroi said. "We all want to put this behind us." He and Marissa stood.

Malveaux reached in his pocket and handed them each his business card. "Here's where you can reach me."

Marissa put the card in her pocket without looking at it. She pulled a knit cap from her pocket and put it over her greasy hair. "I need to get back," she mumbled. "My sitter hasn't shown up for the past week or so and I'm not getting enough sleep. I need to get back home and find out if she's coming back to work or if I need to get rid of her. I don't want to, though. She's really good with Sam."

She left without acknowledging either man. Charleroi shook Malveaux's hand and followed her.

The meeting had lasted exactly eleven minutes.

CHAPTER TWELVE

After the meeting with the Charlerois, Malveaux rummaged around in his briefcase and seized a faded yellow Post-it note. He dialed the number written there and hoped someone was still in the office in St. Paul and that his staff had not gone home early for the day since he was away. It was ten minutes past five p.m. Eastern Standard Time. The phone rang four times and as Malveaux expected, he reached the answering machine but did not leave a message. He disconnected his call and punched in the extension for the cardinal's office. He was surprised when Mary Lawrence, Lowell's assistant, picked up the line. Come to think of it, he hadn't seen her in the office when he'd come in.

"Hi, Mary, this is Robert Malveaux. How are you?"

Mary paused, and when she spoke, her voice was stilted. Perhaps someone was in the room with her, or was listening in on their call. "I'm doing pretty well. I'm back on family medical leave, answering phones remotely three days a week now. I'm having chemotherapy treatments again."

Malveaux was surprised but quickly recovered. "I didn't know, Mary. You sound good. Just stay positive and keep at it. I'm sure it will all work out fine." They made small talk about the weather back in Minnesota, an upcoming conference, the holidays, and his recent health scare. Finally he said, "I need to talk to Cardinal Lowell."

"Yes, of course," answered Mary. "I suppose your meeting with the Charlerois will be starting soon."

"The meeting is over," Malveaux grumbled.

"I don't understand. You were scheduled to start at five. You're finished already?"

"Yes, that's right, we're finished. They came here a little early. I need to speak to Lowell right away." He was becoming uncharacteristically impatient.

"I'll connect you, but you may have to hold awhile. He's on an important call. I'm getting ready to shut down the switchboard for the day. At least if you hold on, you should be able to get through to him. You know he has never gotten into the whole e-mail thing. God bless."

Malveaux expected to be on hold for a long time. Lowell loved making people wait, especially people he didn't like, and Malveaux was certain he was at the top of the cardinal's list. He was genuinely surprised when the cardinal picked up the phone after only six minutes.

"Your Eminence, thank you for taking my call," Malveaux began, though in his mind, there wasn't really anything eminent about Cardinal Lowell as far as he had ever been able to tell.

"Yes, Father. I was expecting your call," growled Lowell. Malveaux wasn't surprised. Whenever rich and powerful people were involved, the top men were always involved too. "I just got off the phone with Charleroi. He said—and these are my words, Malveaux, not his—that you were not prepared for their meeting and that you didn't want to settle the case the way they wanted."

Malveaux expected as much. "Cardinal Lowell, that's a bit unfair, don't you think? I had no idea you'd been in settlement discussions with them. I had no idea they wanted Gaul released. It doesn't make sense. I am totally exasperated." Malveaux paused, but Lowell did not speak. "I have never had a situation like this. Something just doesn't make sense. I understand they are rich and powerful people, but I don't understand why they aren't more concerned about their child and instead are so worried about Father Gaul. Their son was emphatic that Father Gaul touched him inappropriately. Even the security team who was there said so in their report. I can't understand why the parents are so concerned about Father Gaul's well-being and getting him out of jail. Quite frankly, they should be more concerned about their own child."

Lowell did not reply. An uncomfortable silence passed. Finally Lowell spoke slowly, pronouncing each syllable of every word. "Yes, you are right. They are—he is, at least; I don't put her in the same class—he is a rich and powerful person. Perhaps his devotion to the church has given him a spirit of forgiveness. I sincerely believe that he feels that Gaul has expressed sincere remorse. I'm prepared to send him to one of our best treatment facilities as soon as all this is behind us. After all, they have known the man for years. Maybe they just want to forgive him and move on."

Malveaux seethed. He understood forgiveness very well as far as he was concerned. It was not easy to forgive, but it certainly wasn't something that was given automatically. And it wasn't something he had ever seen given so easily by parents to someone who had molested a child, let alone their own son. In fact, he couldn't ever remember two parents so willing to set aside such a vicious assault on their child. What was more, the parents were in the middle of an intense custody dispute and divorce. He had seen this before. Couples often fell apart after the loss of a child, or after a sexual assault on a child. He had seen parents pull together after these types of incidents and he had seen them fall apart. The Charlerois were definitely pulling apart, yet coming together over their common desire to see Gaul released. It didn't make sense to him that they were uniting over forgiving Gaul, and seeking leniency for him, but could not pull together over the well-being of their child. He would have expected Marissa Charleroi to use the assault as a bargaining chip in their divorce case in order to achieve a larger settlement. This move wouldn't help her at all in that regard.

Malveaux was well aware this was Charleroi's third marriage. If he remembered correctly, Charleroi had unceremoniously dumped the first wife as she was dying of cancer for the second wife. He dumped the second wife after a public fight over joint assets. He had been implicated in any number of ethical lapses but had always been cleared. While in Congress he was a regular on the tabloid pages, always at some party with a young staffer, always off on some trip when he should have been voting on legislation. Yet mysteriously, people loved Charleroi. He would admit that he was not the smartest man in the world, and people related to that, especially when he started talking about forgiveness, how awful it was that one sinner would throw stones at another.

All the forgiveness talk hadn't prompted Charleroi to forgive his wife, who was by all accounts a wholly unsympathetic mess. His investigators had confirmed, through separate interviews, that the couple was in the midst of a contentious battle that would be acrimonious until the end. Malveaux made a mental note to talk to the second wife and to also find out if any of Charleroi's other children, even though they were older, kept in touch with their younger half-sibling.

"I know that the archdiocese has an interest in getting these cases resolved and in moving forward, but really, Cardinal Lowell, I believe that Gaul belongs in jail."

Lowell did not immediately respond. Malveaux wanted to hear what he had to say. Didn't the man have a single sympathetic bone in his body?

"Listen to me, Malveaux," Cardinal Lowell hissed. "I don't give a damn what you believe. Your first duty is to the church, your client. The Charlerois are prepared to sign a release right now and we won't have to pay a dime. They're giving the money back to us. We can use that money to pay Gaul's legal bills. They're right, you know. Father Gaul has served a long time. I'm not going to just throw him away, particularly if I can see that he is acquitted."

Malveaux was speechless. Lowell continued, "You are a fine lawyer, and you have a fine team working with you. I know a thing or two about your obligations to your client, which happens to be the archdiocese."

"Look, Your Eminence, with all due respect, if this is about money..." Malveaux was sick and tired of the church putting money ahead its people.

"I expect you to zealously defend your client, Malveaux. That means you will do everything in your power to see that we pay out as little as possible on these cases. Furthermore, you will also make sure Father Gaul receives the best defense that can be provided, to make sure he is acquitted and out of jail as soon as possible, do you understand me?" Malveaux did not respond. "I accept your silence as assent. You are to come to my private study immediately. Hilda will meet you to show you in." Lowell hung up.

Malveaux threw down the phone and stomped out of the conference room. None of this made any sense. Malveaux was angry. He made his way to the cardinal's study and sat down across from Lowell, who sat at his desk, red-faced.

Lowell spoke first. "I had to change your flight reservations, Father Malveaux. I'll need the additional time with you to fully brief you on a change of duties for you—a temporary change, of course."

Malveaux was incensed. He knew that there was a small cadre of leaders who wanted to shut his investigations down. Some inside the church had complained about his work. This was truly unbelievable. Here he was, one of a few insiders willing to speak out against the pervasive abuse and the damage they were wreaking on the faithful. Just as he was making progress, he feared they had decided to remove him from the project and replace him with someone who had no regard for the innocent victims and their legacy of pain.

"I don't understand, Your Eminence. My investigations are at a crucial stage. We're just at the point where we're making real headway. I believe we're about to discover how far this thing goes. It must be stopped."

The cardinal pursed his lips. Malveaux noticed a slight trembling in the man's right hand. The first signs of Parkinson's disease, perhaps? Lowell spoke with conviction. "Yes, you are very good at what you do, Father. I'm sure that you will get to the truth in time. However, you know that our kingdom is not of this world. These times are so precarious. We must give people hope and draw their attention away from this train wreck to better, holier matters."

Malveaux grew angrier and angrier as Lowell continued. "I am convinced—I have been convinced for some time—that there is a desire in Rome to give all people examples of the faith to strengthen them in their daily lives." Lowell took another long sip of coffee. "I believe we must give people hope. I believe we must draw their attention to the true heroes of the faith. That's why this archdiocese has begun the process to seek canonization of father Jon Tomas Nũnes of St. Maarten. You see, Malveaux, we will give people of faith in this community a role model to take the despair from their hearts, and to help them heal with examples of holiness."

"Your Eminence, I think it's always important for the church to raise up these examples. But with all due respect, now is the time to address the child sex abuse scandal in the church and to remove the perpetrators from positions of power and influence. I've never heard of Father Jon Tomas, and I'm sure most people won't understand why you'd spend your time on such a campaign when there are children being abused by priests, of all people."

"Father Nũnes will inspire the people. I'm sure you know his story, you being from the Caribbean and all. Jon Tomas Nũnes sold himself into slavery for the express purpose of getting close to and ministering to other slaves. His is the perfect tale to draw the attention of the people of this town away from this mess."

"Let me get this straight." Malveaux was even more agitated. "You're going to tell a bunch of poor black and Hispanic families that you don't really care about their children being abused by priests, and you're going to give them a saint to look up to so they can forget their pain?" Malveaux raised his voice in anger. "This is the most patronizing and insulting thing I've ever heard. What makes it worse is that you are in multimillion-dollar settlement talks with the family of a white millionaire's son who was abused and you didn't even tell me about it. What you're offering to those poor black kids in southeast DC is an insult, and I won't be part of it." Malveaux jumped from his seat and paced to the other side of the room.

"Sit down," Lowell barked "You're perhaps the only one qualified enough for me to trust to take this on. It's not what you're thinking at all."

Lowell had his attention. Malveaux returned to his seat and crossed his legs angrily.

"I never said I wasn't going to offer those 'poor black kids' anything." Lowell imitated his voice so exactly that it sent an icy wave along Malveaux's spine. "We'll give them something. Although God knows what they would do with the money."

"That's about enough, Your Eminence. I guess you don't believe the pain these kids feel is real. You don't understand the damage done will affect each and every one of those kids for the rest of their lives. If we don't intervene, they will grow up, have their own children, and repeat the cycle of abuse. And we can make sure Gaul stays in jail. That's where he belongs."

Cardinal Lowell picked up his coffee cup and took another sip. "As I was saying, before I was so rudely interrupted, you need to get into the real world, Malveaux. You cannot underestimate the harm that Charleroi can do. If you think he's going to get treated better because of who he is, you would be right. For once."

Lowell slammed the cup onto the saucer. "It's much more complicated than you can understand. You see, I believe that demonic possession is involved."

Malveaux laughed. "You've got to be kidding me." He shook his head in disbelief. "Let me get this right. You expect me to go into court and say, 'Ladies and gentlemen of the jury, you cannot hold Father Gaul and the archdiocese responsible for the horrible things he's done.' Pedophilia is a disease, Your Eminence. It is a sickness. It is dangerous, and we're liable. It is harmful. It is criminal. It is evil." Malveaux stood, enraged.

"That is what I'm trying to tell you, Malveaux. It is evil in the deepest sense of the word. Now sit down!" bellowed Lowell. Malveaux returned to his seat and crossed his arms in angry defiance. A bowl of pale green apples sat on the coffee table between them. Lowell grabbed one and bit fiercely into the succulent fruit, spraying juice that crossed the expanse between them and landed on Malveaux's cheek.

Lowell produced a slender silver skeleton key from his pocket and unlocked the top drawer of his ornate antique desk. The wood inlays and handsome brass drawer pulls were accented by the highly polished cherry wood. An electronic keypad rose slowly from the drawer.

The cardinal methodically entered a long string of numbers. After the computer issued a series of musical notes, he entered another seemingly endless code.

A silk tapestry with a tree of life motif hung behind the desk. Malveaux guessed from quality of the work, style, and fabric that the piece was more than three hundred years old. Then the figures on the tapestry began to pulsate, as if a beating heart lay behind it in the wall.

The cardinal glanced over his shoulder. "Yes, I know you're wondering how old the tapestry is. Everyone asks that question." Lowell studied Malveaux, then returned his gaze to the tapestry. "Our records show that this piece originated in France. It was carbon-dated last year as an early thirteenth-century piece. That damage there on the bottom right corner occurred when the piece was rescued from a fire in an obscure convent near Chartres." Lowell gestured to a discolored section that Malveaux hadn't noticed before.

"Yes, it is too bad that Eve seduced Adam to eat of the fruit of the Tree of Knowledge," Lowell went on. "Had he been a little more… resolute, shall we say, we should not be in this mess today." He took another bite of the apple and chewed with amused satisfaction. "But we are only human. Who wouldn't want to know at least a little bit more about the mysteries of the universe?" Malveaux did not respond. Lowell droned on, almost philosophically, "I suppose Eve could not help but feel ready to take on more responsibility. I'm sure she thought she would be able to handle it." He looked sternly at Malveaux. "Eve couldn't handle the knowledge, Malveaux. I hope you can." He took another bite of his apple.

Malveaux let Lowell have his say. The cardinal's voice changed to a whisper. "What we are about to discuss is confidential."

"Cardinal Lowell, you understand that my prime responsibility is to the injured victims of the church. I cannot, I will not, keep any matter confidential if I believe it will harm innocent victims of the church's malfeasance."

The cardinal pointed to an Oriental rug under the coffee table. "Bob, I need you to stand up, and you are going to want to move that table off the rug."

Malveaux frowned. This was the first time he remembered the man calling him the name used by only his close friends. A strange mechanical noise sounded from the area beneath the table. He could see the rug rising slightly from the floor, and the table along with it.

"Hurry up now, grab that rug," ordered Lowell. Malveaux obliged by moving first the table, then the rug, to the area beneath the window. A steel plate rose from the floor to knee level, revealing another electronic keypad. Lowell kneeled and entered a series of codes into the keypad. "Stand back," he said. A series of warning signals sounded and the steel plate opened on a hinge, revealing a set of stairs descending into a quarried stone chamber. A slender wrought-iron railing was perceptible just below floor level.

Malveaux gazed at Lowell, who seemed accustomed to accessing this hidden chamber. "I know you want to know everything possible, Bob," the cardinal said quietly. "Don't you think you should know everything the church knows about these matters?"

Malveaux was speechless, wondering if they were both losing their minds. Cardinal Lowell continued, "I know you have asked me questions about these matters many times, and I have not been able to explain our reasons for silence. I know you want to do what is right and proper for these young victims. That is what we all want here." Lowell gazed at Malveaux with serious purpose. Then he rose and inserted the skeleton key into a keyhole in the side of the upturned steel plate, turning it gently three times. "This will keep the door open until we come back up. It's no good to be trapped down there when the lights go out." He removed the key and inserted it into his pocket. Almost simultaneously, the keypad retracted into the desk. Lowell proceeded into the newly exposed chamber. With each step, a soft light illuminated the stair ahead of him. Lowell looked at Malveaux and said, "Come, follow me. I am going to give you the chance to finally know what the hierarchy knows. Shouldn't you know what they know, if you're going to eradicate this menace from the church? Think of all the people you could help with this knowledge, Bob."

Each time Lowell called him Bob, Malveaux shuddered. Words his mother had spoken came to mind: "Son, do not engage in dialogue with the devil. Your pride will deceive you into thinking you can outmaneuver him." He also thought about what he taught his law students—to always look for the hidden explanation.

Malveaux shivered as he watched Lowell recede from view. When he called after him, his voice trembled. "Cardinal Lowell, with all due respect, I've asked you for information for the past eleven years—" he said, but Lowell was disappearing from sight. Malveaux followed to keep him in view. "I've asked you for information before these cases started appearing in the newspaper and before archdioceses all over the country began paying judgments through the nose and falling into bankruptcy because they wouldn't do the right thing for the victims until they got nailed to the cross by the lawyers. What possibly could you have to show me or tell me now that would make a difference?"

The cardinal looked at Malveaux and smiled. "Malveaux, don't play games with me. I know that you are out to enter the church leadership so that you can change things. Let me ask you this." Lowell paused at the bottom of the stairs, and the beginning of what Malveaux perceived to be a corridor. The hair on Malveaux's neck stood on end, the stale air suspended around him. Lowell stooped to tie his shoelace. "I know that you are as smart and as devoted as any of us. I suppose this American disease, this racism, has kept you from advancing."

Malveaux gazed at Lowell, almost uncertain of what he was hearing. When had the cardinal become a civil rights advocate? These thoughts had crossed his mind many, many times. He'd seen other, less capable priests rise through the ranks. He would certainly be lying to himself if he thought otherwise. He was always being assigned to hardscrabble neighborhoods in urban ghettos. He couldn't remember any black priests being assigned to plum positions, even for a period of respite.

"The church is an imperfect institution. I wouldn't even be here talking to you today if it wasn't." He wanted to get back to the reason he was here: discussing the continuing child abuse scandal.

Cardinal Lowell took another bite of his apple and chewed with satisfaction. Malveaux craved an apple for himself as he observed Lowell chew as if it was the most succulent, delicious fruit harvested since the dawn of time. He heard his mother's voice again: "Thou shall not want."

"Malveaux, I've talked with them about their racism so many times. I feel as if it is holding us all back. Don't you?" Malveaux nodded. "I'm just trying to help you here. I don't think they should have this unfair advantage any longer." He finished the apple and tossed the core into a wastebasket along the corridor. "I mean, really. They shouldn't deny you information because you are black."

Malveaux was confused. How had this visit turned into a study of racism in America? "Look, Your Eminence, I don't know what you're talking about. All I know is that I thought I was coming here to talk to you about the cases and you start talking to me about using a saint who ministered to slaves to take attention away from this priest abuse scandal in DC. And now here you are opening up a secret chamber beneath your office and all of a sudden you talk like you're Martin Luther King, and you're concerned about race relations. I just don't get it."

Lowell paused, Malveaux close behind. "I don't care what they say; I don't think you would cause harm with the information I want to share with you. You see, my son, they have never wanted to play on a level playing field with you. Not as far as this abuse scandal goes, or in any other thing. I just don't think it's fair, and I want you to have the knowledge they have. Francis Bacon said it best, didn't he? 'Knowledge is power.'" Lowell smiled, showing sharp, discolored teeth that made it look as if the cardinal had been eating a bloody steak rather than an apple. Malveaux looked away.

"They told me I didn't need to know anything more. They said there were mysteries and motives I could not appreciate, mysteries they were trying to protect."

"I know that's what you've been told," said Lowell as he continued along the corridor, "but I think you are just as capable and dependable and intelligent as they are to handle it all."

Malveaux paused, then followed. The bright November moonlight retreated as a dark gray cloud enveloped the moon. The light from the cardinal's office faded as they proceeded down the corridor. Malveaux hurried to keep up with Lowell, who walked with the determination and energy of a man half his age.

Lowell gestured to the stone walls around him. "These chambers hold the relics of over eight hundred Christian saints and martyrs." Black slabs of granite were adorned with names and dates. Malveaux's eyes adjusted to the dim light around him. "These walls also serve as the repository for a number of ancient documents, scrolls, and accounts of the apostles and early martyrs." They reached another stairwell and the area flooded with light as Lowell stepped onto the descending riser. The men walked determinedly through the hallway. Dimly lit display cases lined the wall. Malveaux glimpsed gold and silver chalices, crosses, rosaries, scrolls, and a number of books, documents, portraits, and photographs. Lowell paused and touched the glass display case to his left. The inside gradually flooded with soft yellow light.

"This is a Gutenberg Bible," Malveaux said, pausing to regard the treasure, but Lowell was already ahead of him, illuminating another portion of the display case.

"Here we have an early copy of Saint Augustine's *City of Joy*."

Malveaux marveled at the scrolls in the dimly lit case, but Lowell was off to the next treasure. "The light helps protect the documents from deterioration," the cardinal explained. He gestured next to a pair of ragged sandals. "These are believed to be the actual sandals of St. Cyprian." He barely paused and then walked toward another case on the right. "Here are four of the Qumran Scrolls; these particular scrolls were not canonized in the official Hebrew Bible."

Malveaux was astounded by the array of items in the seemingly endless display cases. Lowell gestured as he walked defiantly down the hall. "This section over here"—he pointed to the left—"is the restricted reliquary."

"I thought we already passed the reliquary," replied Malveaux. "It was on the first level upstairs." He observed the bronze plaques engraved with ornate script. "I had no idea that any of these things were here." He estimated that there were at least one hundred plaques on display.

"Yes, we did store some more common relics upstairs. These, however, are kept here because they are more valuable. Their authenticity is not in question. This reliquary is arranged in chronological order; the oldest relics are located farther along the corridor."

Malveaux recognized names: St. Jude, St. Thérèse de Lisieux. Lowell paused near the end of the passage. "These are the oldest relics here, the remains of the early Christian martyrs." He pointed to a row of plaques above his head. "There you can see we have some relics of Thaddeus, Bartholomew, St. Paul, and St. John. Of course it is extraordinary to have relics from the apostles. I know you are surprised. This vault was consecrated in the 1930s.The church decided to move a large number of artifacts here after the conclusion of World War I. You see, the Holy Father thought it would be prudent to move at least some of the relics to remote sites. We couldn't have these treasures falling into the hands of fascists and Nazis, could we?"

Lowell continued down the hallway. "Over here on the right are records, writings, and more artifacts." He paused and entered a code on a keypad in the center of the display case. For the first time, Malveaux noticed there were keypads located approximately every three yards along the corridor. As Lowell entered a log sting of numbers, the light illuminating the display case increased in intensity.

"We keep these lights yellow to protect the various documents and artifacts, as I said before, but they use a slightly different method because these artifacts contain traces of organic material. We hope to preserve any existing traces of DNA." He looked at Malveaux to gauge his reaction and pointed to gold cups decorated with script. "This chalice is believed to have been part of Solomon's treasury, part of the original temple. Were the Israeli government to learn of its existence, you can imagine the conflict we would face." Lowell smiled and his stained teeth seemed sharper, almost pointed.

Malveaux was speechless and at the same time aware that his "gift" began to take hold of him, flooding his senses with light. His heart began to beat erratically, seemingly so loudly that it filled the chamber with an organic drum solo. He gasped for breath and staggered away from Lowell. Something was here. Something fearful.

Lowell continued to speak, oblivious to Malveaux's heightened sensitivity. Malveaux saw Lowell's lips moving, but he could only discern the sound of his own beating heart. A parallel world opened around him, enveloping his feet. Malveaux startled. A giant red snake slithered up and created a pedestal around Lowell's feet. The serpent raised its ugly head and hissed at Malveaux, emitting a screech that was eerily human. This snake glistened as if perspiring. It circled and climbed Lowell's legs, leaving a trail of slime on his pants. Then it began to speak in Lowell's gravelly voice.

"Bob. Your mother and grandmére send their regards." The snake entered Lowell's open mouth and disappeared. Malveaux shivered. Then the vision retreated and Lowell's voice returned as if it were coming from deep inside him. He would have to be careful about whatever this man said or told him to do.

"Come, Bob. I need to sit down for a bit. I am so fatigued by all this."

Malveaux approached, but not too closely. He silently recited the Lord's Prayer through shallow breaths. Lowell's voice grew stronger and his face took on a pulsating, sweaty, ruddy hue. As Malveaux watched, the man's fingernails seemed to grow more pointed, like talons. Lowell's gait had abruptly changed. He seemed to glide along the corridor as if suddenly riding some moving sidewalk.

Lowell continued along the corridor and reached for another keypad. He entered a code and the display chamber to the right opened to reveal a stainless-steel room with a desk, two chairs, and a notepad. A rush of compressed air issued from the walls two times. As the men entered, the door closed behind them.

"This area is restricted." Lowell took the legal pad and wrote four series of numbers on it. "That steam was a disinfectant. We need to make sure this room remains as sterile as possible. Some of the organic material we are exposing is sensitive and may degrade with handling and exposure."

"You should commit these numbers to memory as soon as possible. The first set will allow you to access the corridor from my office; the second set allows you to enter the lower chamber; the third accesses this office; and the fourth gives you access to the Caine file, which can only be viewed in this room."

Malveaux sat down, looked at the paper, and folded it and placed it in his breast pocket. "No," said Lowell. "You need that code to access the file. You should try it."

Malveaux retrieved the paper, went to the wall, and entered the fourth in the series of codes. Two steel drawers emerged from an imperceptible section of the wall. Lowell walked toward the drawers and explained, "Each section of the Caine file has two drawers. Only one portion of the file may be accessed at a time. The left drawer always contains the original document, and the right side contains a translation and transcription of that document."

None of this made any sense. Malveaux was confused. "What does any of this have to do with the altar boy scandal? These documents are hundreds of years old. What's the connection here?"

Lowell returned to his chair and looked Malveaux squarely in the eye. "Malveaux, you know that this scandal is ruining the church. It is destroying many good men who have devoted their lives to God. It may well destroy me."

"With all due respect, I don't give a damn about a bunch of pedophiles being exposed or ruined. What you and the whole bureaucracy have lost sight of is of all the children, the innocent victims of this abuse."

Lowell put his head in his hands. "I hear what you're saying. I'm not trying to diminish the victims' pain."

Malveaux did not believe Lowell was being the least bit sincere, but he continued to listen. "You see, we thought if we elevated a saint from the Caribbean, we could focus some positive attention on what the church is doing, and buy some time to settle these abuse cases in a way that would not destroy everything we were working for." He looked up wearily. The older man seemed to have aged since they'd entered the chamber. "We decided upon the cause of Jon Tomas Núnes of St. Maarten. You said you didn't know him."

"No. I don't know anything about him."

"Jon Tomas was from prosperous Portuguese family. He entered the priesthood and traveled to the Caribbean. He was reportedly a 'seer,' one who had the ability to view the supernatural world around him. He was allegedly protected by angels. Does any of this ring a bell with you, Malveaux?"

"No, Cardinal Lowell. I don't know this story, only what you've told me so far. I grew up in New Jersey, remember." He took a seat opposite Lowell.

"I thought, with your Haitian background and all, you might know of him."

"I'm sorry, I don't know the story. Please continue."

Lowell looked even more exhausted as he continued. "Jon Tomas Nũnes was so troubled by the plight of slaves in St. Maarten that he sold himself as an indentured servant and used the proceeds to free a young couple who had been worked nearly to death and who were expecting a child. Then the young man died in a devastating hurricane, and the young woman died in childbirth."

"Nũnes raised the free child, who grew and joined him in ministering to the slaves. He named him Lemuel and said the boy shared his gift of sight, and they used this gift to work miracles we have been documenting in the investigation of his cause for sainthood."

Malveaux was captivated by the story. He listened intently.

"Several years ago, in the '80s, I was traveling extensively through the Soviet Union. I had the chance to meet an orthodox prelate at an ecumenical conference, and he offered me the opportunity to purchase several ancient manuscripts and texts that he claimed were of theological importance. Of course, I jumped at the chance. You know how I love ancient writings."

Malveaux nodded. Lowell's reputation as a bibliophile was well known. His staff routinely presented him with first-edition books or out-of-print manuscripts for his personal collection.

"As director of written acquisitions, I often traveled and purchased items 'off the books,' as they say. The man who sold me the books purloined them, I'm sure. I heard he purchased a dacha for his mistress with the funds. Anyway, the lot I purchased contained several diaries. Most were of no account, but one was significant. In fact, I did not realize its significance until my staff cataloged the lot and cross-referenced the contents as containing the writings of Jon Tomas of St. Maarten written in the actual hand of his ward, Lemuel, the child whose freedom Jon Tomas had secured." Lowell ran his hands through his thinning hair as if he were anxious or troubled.

Malveaux was confused. "I don't understand what this has to do with the Caine file. You said in your office that this had something to do with the Caine file. What's that?"

Lowell cradled his head in his hands. "It is a complicated story, Malveaux. The Caine file is a compendium or collection of sorts. It was accumulated over the lifetime of the Irish Benedictine monk, Seamus Caine of the Grave. The file contains accounts of demonic possession from the earliest times, dating back to Creation. Seamus Caine accumulated an exhaustive list of the names and occasions of demonic possession and exorcism. After his death, his order continued to research and record such incidents. In 1549 the, shall we say, 'cataloging' process was moved to the Vatican and continues to this day."

Malveaux was confused more than ever. He did not like where this story seemed to be going.

"We catalog demons according to the file," Lowell said. "We note the date of their first appearance, characteristics, name, et cetera. The file notes the date of exorcism and details related to the exorcist. The file is up to date. The most recent entries were recorded in 1993 in Turin, Italy."

Malveaux was listening but having difficulty processing the information. His head was throbbing, he was sweating, his heart thundered in his chest. He really would need to see his doctor about the pacemaker.

"Caine created an alphanumeric system to identify the evil tormentors as he called them. For example, alpha demons are those evil tormentors who appear in singular form, and who have been successfully exorcised, as evidenced by the fact that they do not reappear."

Malveaux was bewildered. What did any of this have to do with Jon Tomas or the altar boy scandal?

"As I was saying, the record is quite extensive, and although it dates back to the Creation, the eyewitness accounts go back to the time of apostles in the reign of Nero." Lowell rose again and retrieved a slender manila folder. "Let me show you this file as an example. This is the file of Case A-45. This demon is classified as an alpha because it manifested in AD 45 and was successfully exorcised. There has been no documented reoccurrence of the evil host in nearly two thousand years. The file contains all the usual information you'd expect. It gives the name of the demon, its host, its stated purpose, and the method and manner used to free the victim."

Lowell handed the folder to Malveaux, who started to peruse it. Several pages were typewritten. Lowell retrieved another file, a much thicker manila folder labeled B-416.

"This folder is a beta file. Beta files contain the histories of evil hosts that manifest but have not been successfully exorcised. B-416 first manifested in Constantinople in AD 416—if I my memory is correct—and has reappeared periodically. It's a confusing file, really. Caine had evidence that this particular evil host may have appeared as early as 3200 BC, based on records he reviewed that were reportedly part of the Library of Alexandria."

"I was taught that the library was burned and all the scrolls and papyri were destroyed. Countless ancient original manuscripts were lost."

Lowell smiled. "Yes, many texts were lost. But some were saved. Of course, that is not common knowledge. The Vatican library contains many controversial texts that are presumed to have been lost to antiquity."

Malveaux listened intently.

"B-416 may have appeared as many as four previous times. Unfortunately, the pattern is unpredictable. Manifestations occurred in 416, 1233, and 1769 in St. Maarten, if we are to believe the writings of Jon Tomas Nûnes."

"I really don't understand where all this is going," Malveaux interrupted. He looked at his watch. They had been in the underground chamber for nearly two hours.

"You see, Malveaux, in studying Jon Tomas's cause for sainthood, we became aware of an incident during which he and the boy Lemuel were asked to exorcise a demon that we now believe was B-416. Now understand, we update these files every two hundred years. If an evil host does not reappear in three hundred years, we presume the exorcism to have been successful." Lowell cleared his throat. "B-416 was reclassified as an alpha file in about 842, but reclassified again in 1236 after the 1233 manifestation. There was no doubt that the 1233 manifestation did not end in a successful exorcism, and the file was reclassified as a beta file. There was little activity associated with the file until recently."

"How was that?"

"Well, as we began to study the life of Jon Tomas and came across his diary, his testimony, we became convinced that his activities, and the account related by Lemuel in the diary, documented a clear interaction with B-416."

"What made you so sure that Jon Tomas was describing B-416?"

Lowell appeared tense. "There are many distinguishing characteristics of B-416. This demon has a practice of challenging extremely holy men and women. You will need to read the file yourself to discern its many characteristics. Yet I will say that this manifestation has on each occasion been apparent where there are purportedly cases of child sexual abuse."

Malveaux was irate. "I don't like where this is going. This is absurd. This is the twenty-first century. You think you're going to blame the child sex abuse scandal in the Catholic Church on some ancient demon? That is the most evil and perverted thing I have ever heard. If you thought I was going to buy into this and become a part of it, you are absolutely crazy."

"Believe me, Malveaux, no one intended to make this connection. You see, Jon Tomas's cause for sainthood may be affected if B-416 was not fully exorcised during his time in St. Maarten. Certainly there is some suggestion that Nũnes is not eligible for sainthood if he was not able to cast out this demon.

"Some pages are missing from the Nũnes diary, we know that. But things have become more complicated. A detail has arisen in the Charleroi case that seems to tie the two matters together."

Malveaux shook his head in disbelief. "These cases are about evil men, Cardinal Lowell. They are criminals. No doubt some of them have psychiatric disorders, but if you think for one minute you're going to mount a 'the devil made me do it' defense, I'm not going to buy it and I won't be any part of it." He stood, suddenly feeling claustrophobic. "I'm going back upstairs. I need to get out of here."

Lowell handed him another folder. "Look at this first. It's from the bedroom in the Charleroi case. Just take a look."

"I don't understand. You assured me that I had been given the entire Charleroi file. The file I was given didn't contain any photographs. This is outrageous. How am I supposed to do my job if you hold out on me?"

"Like I said, Bob, I want to make this a level playing field. They say that what you don't know can't hurt you, but this time I believe we need to come clean and let you know what you're dealing with. These pictures were taken at the time of the incident on November 5th I believe."

Malveaux opened the folder to a series of black-and-white photographs, some unremarkable. A staircase. An older colonial home. Trees. Fences. A green highway sign that read "Leesburg left, Point of Rocks, right." Several color photographs were labeled "Bedroom— Juvenile Subject." As Malveaux surveyed the crime scene photograph, he saw a bloodstained bed. A man in the corner of the photograph appeared to be Father Gaul. On the wall beside the bed, a message was scrawled in red. The words were written in archaic script but clear enough: "Jon Tomas B-416 encor." Malveaux closed the file and sat down, confused, "the gift" bringing troubling images to his mind.

Lowell walked to the nearby work table and he sat in an uncomfortable steel-backed chair. The atmosphere reminded Malveaux of a morgue. "There is some other information that was not provided to you," he said. "It is the DNA analysis of the blood from the wall of the crime scene."

"I don't understand."

"That's not paint, you know. That's blood on the wall. The blood type was the same as the young Charleroi boy's. We naturally assumed that he wrote this message himself in an altered state of consciousness. But recently we performed a DNA analysis. The blood does not match his. It does, however, match a sample from the diary of Jon Tomas Nũnes." Lowell paused. "A sample Nũnes says came from his encounter with the demon B-416."

Malveaux shook his head. None of this was making any sense. He too sat down at the table. Lowell looked at Malveaux carefully. "I have here all of the Caine file. This is the first occasion that the entire file, or in this case a copy of the file, has ever been in this hemisphere." He retrieved a thick file from the drawer and handed it to Malveaux. "Seamus Caine researched ancient accounts of demon possession using sources from around the globe. His access was unparalleled." Lowell sat and selected a remote control from the desk in front of him. "Caine traveled extensively over a fifteen-year period, visiting and consulting archives in Rhodes, Istanbul, Jerusalem, Amman, and later Timbuktu."

"Timbuktu?" exclaimed Malveaux, returning the file to the drawer and joining Lowell at the work table.

"It is not widely known, but for centuries ancient Islamic guardians have preserved texts dating from the time of Christ. Timbuktu is nearly inaccessible today. You can imagine how difficult it was for Seamus to make his journey hundreds of years ago."

A nearby television screen flickered on and a tape began to play. Lowell paused the film. "As I was saying, alpha entities are those demonic foes, pure evil, that are successfully ejected from their host through the rite of exorcism."

Malveaux laughed. "I see where this is going now, Cardinal." He shook his head, laughing so hard that tears streamed from his eyes. "You expect to blame the Charleroi case on a demon." Malveaux slapped his thighs, laughing so hard he began to choke. Cardinal Lowell arose and retrieved a bottle of spring water from a small stainless-steel refrigerator. Malveaux had not noticed it when they entered the room. He took the water and drank greedily until his coughing subsided.

"Cardinal Lowell. This whole exorcist thing was done to death in the '70s, don't you think? I mean, people don't believe that stuff anymore. I don't even know if I believe it, and I'm—excuse my language now—a fucking Catholic priest."

Lowell shifted in his chair, looking down at his hands while Malveaux continued. "Most of these cases of possession can be explained as manifestations of psychological disturbance. Epilepsy, schizophrenia, delusional syndromes, drug use, crack cocaine, acid, LSD—call it what you will, there's always a logical explanation."

Lowell looked sternly at Malveaux. "Then where is your faith? Even Jesus exorcised demons, didn't he? Are you saying our Lord was just some type of supercharged psychiatrist?"

Malveaux turned serious. "That's not what I'm saying at all. But we all know that from time to time horrible cases come to light of abuse where someone is trying to perform an exorcism and someone innocent is killed. I don't want to be any part of this."

"Well," the cardinal replied, "it sounds like your faith is not what it used to be."

Malveaux frowned. What was wrong with this man, and why couldn't he understand a word Malveaux was saying?

Lowell continued, "You need to let me finish. Seamus Caine went to Timbuktu and compiled a list of demons, their characteristics, historical facts associated with their appearances, and destructive powers. B-416 is unique, having first appeared as I said in A.D. 416. We have concluded that B-416 was responsible for the deaths of many early Christian martyrs. We believe this demonic entity instigated the burning alive of Christians as torches and provoked the murder of many innocent souls. B-416's manifestation at that time coincides with three deviant cultural phenomena: the sexual molestation of children, the appearance of subjects known to be dead, and involuntary servitude or slavery. Then there are other distinguishing characteristics: the human host has no mother. It leaves the skinned flesh of its victims behind as a freakish calling card. There are always suicides. It leaves puddles of water around. The pattern of death and destruction was reported without fail in each successive manifestation."

Exasperated, Malveaux exploded. "So what you're saying is that this demon that no one seems to be able to get rid of comes back every couple of hundred or thousand years, and now it's come to Washington, DC? We don't need demons here, Cardinal. We have Congress!" He shook his head at Lowell in disbelief. "It is so pitiful that you and the church would stoop to such a ridiculous story to clear the names of those shameful men. That is the only evil here. You should be ashamed of yourself."

Lowell punched a button on the remote control device. A grainy black-and-white film began to play. "I just want you to watch this. It's from the surveillance film at the Charleroi residence at the time of the incident." An image appeared on the screen. A young boy lay on a heavily padded bed, writhing, swearing, and convulsing. Malveaux watched intently, disturbed at what he saw. The film was horrifying. As he watched, a man and a woman entered the room, and then two more men, who battled with the boy to restrain him to the bed.

"Maybe I have misunderstood you, Cardinal. I assumed you were saying that Father Gaul was possessed by this B-416 when he molested the Charleroi boy. That's the boy in the film."

As Malveaux watched, the boy began to vomit, twisting his head from side to side and projecting the dark sputum toward a nearby wall with such force that it seemed to be emanating from a firehouse. As the boy struggled and continued to vomit, there was no mistake: the very message Malveaux had just seen in the still photograph materialized on the wall, drawn in stained vomit. "Jon Tomas B-416 encor." It hardly seemed possible.

"Play that back again," Malveaux said, and Lowell repeated the sequence. It was definitely the writing in the photograph. The tape continued. The boy, suddenly calm, looked directly at the camera and began singing in French. His eyes oozed blood and pus. "Tu, tu, tu, tu, tu," the boy sang over and over again as he threw his head back and cackled. "I'm waiting for you, tu, tu. Who has seen the wind, priest? Malveaux, Malveaux, what is the reply?"

Lowell stopped the tape. "I have shown this only to my most trusted colleagues in Rome. The others who were there discussed this incident with no one. No one really knows why he's asking about the wind."

Malveaux felt troubled and drained. His head began to throb. "It's asking me to play a game. My mother and I played it when I was a child. My mother would sing these songs to me, or recite poems. She's say one verse and then I would say the next one. In order to win the game you had to be the one who remembered the next phrase in the poem or line in the song. I haven't thought about it in years. It's asking for the reply to its question; 'Who has seen the wind?'" The room was suddenly awash with golden light. He took a piece of paper and a pen and wrote quickly in block letters. He turned the paper over and pushed it across the table toward Lowell.

"We played the sequence over and over again. I brought you here because the boy is asking for you. There's no way he could have known about you."

The cardinal pushed the play button and the tape continued. The monstrous boy-thing writhed and screamed. Malveaux could not be sure who it was, but one of the men looked in the direction of the camera. He knelt and prayed while the scene around him spiraled in confusion and disarray. Malveaux was sure he saw Gaul, who appeared to be restraining the boy. Other men, who wore blue blazers, came in to help, as did Marissa Charleroi and an older African American woman.

The boy now sang sweetly in heavily accented French. It was a woman's voice—*his mother's voice.* Malveaux froze. The boy abruptly switched to English and sang, "Neither you nor I." Then the thing smiled and abruptly switched to the voice of an old man. "There you have it, priest."

Lowell stopped the tape and reached for the paper. He turned it over and read aloud, "Neither you nor I."

Lowell, seeming as weak and drained as Malveaux felt, spoke in a faint whisper. "Deliver us from evil." Both men made the sign of the cross. Malveaux stared ahead, speechless.

CHAPTER
THIRTEEN

Leesburg, Virginia

Vaughn used the remote control to surf the channels and ended up watching an episode of *I Love Lucy* that he swore he'd never seen before. He fell asleep, but he wasn't sure for how long. When he awoke, he heard his mother singing in the kitchen while she washed dishes. Vaughn was lying in his regular place on the couch, listening to the familiar sounds. He rationalized that he was having a vivid dream.

His mother had been dead for three weeks now. She was all he'd had left, and he couldn't believe she was gone. It had happened so unexpectedly. He'd called Charleroi to let him know, but the man hadn't even had the decency to return his call. He didn't send flowers or a card, or even attend the funeral. He was just another asshole.

In his dream, his mother turned off the TV and whispered, "Good night, son," and made her way to her chair. Everything was so lifelike. He could remember her humming and the click and clack of her knitting needles. Vaughn drifted off to sleep again.

A noise roused him. It was trash collection day. Vaughn made his way to the bathroom, did his business, and returned to the kitchen. It was immaculate. The dishes and pans of the past few days were washed and in their appropriate places. Vaughn's heart raced. He walked to the living room. The TV was turned off. He remembered the dream and smiled. He crossed the room, passing his mother's chair.

Squish.

That was strange. The carpeting was wet, but only right in front of his mother's chair. He ran his hand over the seat. It was damp too. Vaughn looked up at the ceiling. There was no evidence of a leak. Vaughn grabbed a towel from the bathroom and pressed it into the carpet to absorb the dampness, then left the house to take a walk.

His stupid cousin would be back in an hour to help him get the house in order. He needed to get some exercise before he dealt with her again. She got on his nerves, but he was glad she did the dishes. Next time, though, she'd need to put them away. He wasn't doing that. That was a woman's job.

CHAPTER FOURTEEN

Marissa Charleroi knocked on the screen door and then stepped back. She could hear a man and woman shouting and cursing at each other inside, their angry words audible over loud music. She knew there was no possible way they could hear her. A tattered blue La-Z-Boy recliner was directly to her left. The well-worn headrest was shiny from much use. A lumpy pillow inside a faded yellow pillowcase sat waiting for its user. Marissa could imagine Mae Etta sitting there surveying the neighborhood on a warm summer day.

The woman screamed, "I don't care what you think. You're crazy and you've always been crazy. I haven't been here today and I sure as hell didn't wash your damn dishes. You need to clean up after your own damn self."

Where was Mae Etta? She had seemed so reliable. It didn't make sense that she would just stop coming to work, that she would leave her purse behind and not even pick up her paycheck. Marissa needed her back. Mae Etta had a calming influence on Sam. The episodes had practically stopped since she'd come to work there, except for that bad incident two weeks ago when the police came to the house and took away Gaul. Marissa couldn't figure it out. Mae Etta hadn't stopped coming after that crazy night. She'd come in every day, even on the weekend, until a few days ago, when they'd decided to readmit Sam to the hospital. Marissa reasoned that maybe Mae Etta misunderstood.

She could still come in and work, even if the boy was in the hospital. But Marissa needed her back so she could get some rest.

Marissa knocked insistently on the window directly behind the recliner. Damn it, she wasn't going to wait here all day. They had better come to the door. Marissa had felt bad enough looking in Mae Etta's purse to verify her address. The bag was not Marissa's style and not what she would carry herself. It was an old lady's bag. When she'd looked at Mae Etta's driver's license, she had been surprised to learn that Mae Etta was sixty-nine years old.

Marissa banged on the door again, this time using her fist as a hammer. The arguing stopped abruptly and the screen door swung open. A tall, brown-skinned man stood on the porch before her. Marissa instinctively straightened her back and pulled her hair behind her ears. A dark young woman with twisted hair peered from behind him, hands on her hips.

"Hello," whispered Marissa, suddenly losing her confidence. "I'm looking for Ms. Rock. I came to bring her purse and her paycheck. She left them at my house."

The man and woman looked at each other and stared like they didn't understand a word she'd said. The woman glared at Marissa.

"This is Ms. Rock's address, isn't it?" The man continued to stare at her. Marissa babbled on. "She started working for me about six weeks ago. She was so dependable. I knew something must have been wrong when she didn't show up again today. This morning I found her purse in the kitchen, and when she didn't come in or call or anything, I thought I'd come over and see what was wrong. She's been helping with my son. I'm Marissa Charleroi, Leon Charleroi's wife. From The Oaks."

The man and woman looked at each other again. The man cleared his throat. "Ma'am, I don't know what kind of joke this is, but it's not funny. You need to get on out of here."

Marissa frowned and became angry. "Look, I have her purse right here. She didn't show up again today and I want to see her."

The woman reached through the screen door and snatched the purse from Marissa's hands.

"Now wait a minute, bitch," Marissa said. "You don't snatch anything from me. If you don't get Ms. Rock out here this minute, I am going to call the police and tell them something is wrong here."

The man stood between Marissa and the angry cursing woman behind him. "Get out of here, lady. Go on. Get off my porch." He moved his arms to shoo her away like a stray cat.

"She's drunk!" yelled the woman.

Marissa held her ground. "I said I'm not leaving here until I see Ms. Rock, and I mean it."

"And *I* said go on now." The man moved off the porch and herded Marissa down the steps. Marissa pulled her cell phone from her bag and started to dial. "Lady, you can call the police all you want. My mother isn't here. She's dead."

Marissa looked up, not comprehending. "She's dead," he repeated. "Now go on."

"Oh my God," stammered Marissa, covering her hand with her mouth in disbelief. "I just talked to her."

"That can't be. Go." The man gestured for her to leave. "I'm going to call the police if you don't get out of here. They'll arrest you if they think you drove over here drunk."

The woman joined them on the porch. Her eyes bore into Marissa with anger and burning hatred.

"I'm Marissa Charleroi. Mae Etta worked for me. She told me that if she didn't show up, I needed to find Beta right away. Are you Beta?"

The man dropped the papers he was holding onto the ground. A swift wind whirled, sending the papers flying. Hi cousin ran to gather them.

Vaughn's mouth was, in an instant, totally and completely dry. His mind raced back to his mother's words, words she had spoken many times when he was a child. She'd said, "If anyone ever comes to you and tells you I asked them to go find Beta, you'll know there's trouble coming. You get them to Beta right away, you hear?"

Vaughn sat down, and Marissa stared as tears ran from his eyes. At last he looked up at her and said, "Let's go."

***

Marissa and Vaughn drove silently north on Route 15 until they reached I-70 in Frederick, Maryland, then headed east to Baltimore. Vaughn laughed to himself. He must be out of his mind to be driving up to Baltimore with this crazy alcoholic woman. She smelled like booze, although it was before noon. And even after his time in the military, he could honestly say he'd had never heard a woman curse as much as this one. She was not the kind of woman he would have expected Charleroi to marry. Even so, he had to go with her to speak to Beta.

Vaughn hadn't thought about Beta in years. He had never mentioned her to anyone—not to his wife, past girlfriends, not to anyone. His mother hadn't spoken of Beta her older sister for years either, come to think about it. Maybe they'd had a falling out.

When he was a boy, back in the summer of 1983, he'd accompanied his mother on three or maybe four visits to see "Aunt Beta" at the Oblate Sisters' residence in Catonsville, Maryland. At the time, it was the farthest he had ever traveled from home. Beta scared him. Even then she was big and wrinkled, like she'd had had a long life, and she was cloaked in one of those old-timey nun outfits. His mother called what Beta wore a "habit." He laughed as he remembered telling her that Beta needed to break that habit and fast.

They had laughed and laughed over that corny joke. That summer was a strange one. His mother had kept him home from summer day camp and in the house watching movies while she was at work. He didn't tell her he snuck out during the day to play with the other boys in the neighborhood. It was the first time he'd bonded with them. They had been teasing him for years, calling him "ginger boy," but that stopped after he fought them a few times. They had all been scared that summer because Marvin Talbot said a psycho killer was on the loose, someone worse than the Zodiac Killer who had stalked Northern California.

There was a new boy in the neighborhood. They'd played together a few times. It was the first time Vaughn had met a kid who looked like him. He remembered the boy smelled bad. None of the other kids knew him. But they had fun. Vaughn was sad when he stopped coming around.

Even after all these years, Vaughn remembered his way to the Oblate Sisters' House. He signed in with Marissa and was led through a narrow corridor to a first-floor room. He thought it was strange that Marissa didn't ask him any questions. She'd just gotten in his car with him to go see Beta like Beta lived right around the corner and was someone she'd met a thousand times. Marissa had fallen asleep on the way up to Baltimore. Vaughn was not really surprised because she seemed so drunk.

He opened the door to the narrow sitting room and there was Beta, just like she'd been waiting for him to come. Several tall bookshelves lined the walls of the simple, white washed room. The elderly woman greeted him with a familiar but aged voice. "Boy, I could feel you coming from miles away. It's in my bones—I could feel you."

Vaughn had not seen Beta in twenty years. There was no way she could have recognized him, as he bore absolutely no resemblance to the skinny, knobby-kneed, peanut-shaped-head boy he used to be. It was odd, he thought. Neither he nor Marissa Charleroi had called the Oblate Sisters to announce they were coming to visit Beta. He hadn't even known if Beta was still alive. But he didn't even need to Google the directions. Over the years he'd made many trips up Route 15 and then east on Route 70, where they'd join the Baltimore beltway to Catonsville. It was a simple trip.

Beta looked about the same to him. She had been an old woman when he was a child, and she was older still now, only more wrinkled, smaller, and thinner. Dark sunglasses shielded her eyes. Her breathing was labored, as she struggled for air. When they'd arrived minutes earlier, neither he nor Marissa had given their names to the lay volunteer who admitted them to the compound. The woman had said he was expected. How could she have known that?

"Why don't you all sit down?" Beta droned. "You and Lourdes need to talk to me about what is going on."

Marissa turned to look at Beta and frowned. Her jaw hardened. Color drained from her already tired face. Her hands shook as she grabbed Vaughn's forearm to steady herself into the chair, her lips pursed and tense. Vaughn saw her face drain of all color—no small feat for the olive-complexioned woman.

"Lourdes, you've been awfully quiet today. Know you've got a lot on your mind." Marissa looked at Vaughn, who turned his attention to the ancient woman before him. She smelled of urine, a sign of kidney failure.

"Hi, Beta, it's me, Vaughn, Mae Etta's son." Vaughn had the sensation that someone was watching him from behind. He turned to the left and to the right, but no one was there. "How did you know I was coming today? I haven't been here in years."

Beta coughed thick sputum into a white handkerchief, which she then secreted into a pouch in the left side of her habit. For the first time he noticed she was sitting in a wheelchair. She removed the dark glasses with her clawed hands and laid them on the desk beside her. Marissa gasped as Beta opened her eyes to reveal two enormous glistening cataracts cloaked in thick mucosa. Marissa looked down at her hands.

"Beta, what's going on with your eyes?" Vaughn asked. "You need to see a doctor. What's wrong with these folks?"

Beta wiped the mucus from her eyes onto the sleeves of her habit. Gray streaks clung to the fabric. "Boy, you still ask more questions than anyone I have ever known. You ain't changed one bit." She coughed violently.

Vaughn took a seat next to Marissa directly opposite Beta. "I've been meaning to come see you..."

"No, you ain't." Beta coughed again, more fiercely. Marissa looked away in disgust.

"Beta, how did you know I was coming to visit you?" Vaughn asked again. He stared into her vacant eyes, uncertain of whether she could see him or not.

Beta pulled her handkerchief from its secret place and coughed more intensely. "Why, boy," she whispered, "Alpha told me you were coming."

Vaughn's heart leapt wildly in his chest. Marissa looked at him quizzically. Vaughn raised his voice. "Look, Beta, that couldn't have happened. That can't be."

Beta responded with equal intensity. "We've been talking a lot lately these past few days." She turned slightly to address Marissa. "You got a mess on your hands, don't you, Lourdes?" She adjusted her small frame toward Marissa. "She told me I had to tell you and when the time came you'd know. Told me that yesterday. She said you'd come seek me out. I know you're scared. You got good reason to be."

Vaughn hadn't even thought to reach out to Beta about his mother's death. Of course, it was possible that someone else would have let her know. Maybe one of his cousins had. He simmered. "Why do you keep calling her that? That's not her name. You don't even know her name."

"You tell him, honey," Beta said with an intensity that exceeded her age and physical condition. "And you, Vaughn. Your mother has been trying to spoil and shelter you all these years any way she could. I told her you needed help, even when you were a small child, but she just protected you and sheltered you when she should have gotten you help. Lord knows I tried to help her."

Vaughn was puzzled. Beta continued, "I know what you were doing over there in Iraq. You need to pray to God to deliver you, boy."

Marissa looked at Vaughn but did not speak. Beta raised her arms and made the sign of the cross in the air. "Lord, help this boy and this woman. Deliver them from the clutches of evil." Her voice grew in intensity. "I know who you are and you need to be gone. I'm not afraid of you." Beta gesticulated wildly. The large mahogany bookshelf to her left shook violently, then tilted forward and crashed down beside her, narrowly missing her outstretched arms. Marissa and Vaughn jumped back as Beta threw out her arms and bellowed.

The door to the sitting room opened abruptly and an attendant rushed into the room. "What is going on in here, Sister Mary Claire? Are you all right, hon? What happened to the bookcase?" She looked accusingly at Marissa and Vaughn.

Beta retrieved her glasses from the table, shielding her eyes. She reached for a drinking glass sitting there and flung it at Vaughn. The glass shattered, narrowly missing his head but striking and cutting his right hand with a sharp crystal shard.

"Deliver us!" Beta screamed. "Deliver us from the evil one!" Beta pushed herself from her wheelchair to stand squarely before them. The diminutive woman threw her arms into the air, palms stretched in their direction, screaming, "Be gone, evil one. You have no place here! Be gone!" The bookcase to Beta's right hummed and vibrated. Marissa, Vaughn and the attendant stepped back away from it, running from the room. Books flew from their shelves with invisible ferocious energy striking Beta violently on the head, battering her and tossing her from left to right like a sad rag doll.

"Get out of here now," barked Vaughn, glaring at Marissa. He maneuvered behind the wheelchair, seeking to avoid the flying volumes, released the brakes, and struggled to wheel Beta from the narrow room.

Marissa stepped forward. Beta coughed violently as the books continued to batter her drawing blood with each vicious blow. Vaughn stopped, unable to dodge the tomes flying around her. The wheelchair was blocked by the books now littering the floor around them. Beta cried, "I tried. I tried Alpha! I tried! Father Robert will need to do it! It's too strong for me! He'll need to get rid of this evil one! He'll need help for it to work. God help us all!"

Marissa put her hand on the woman and looked into her unseeing eyes, assaulted by the whirlwind of books battering her now as well. "What about Father Robert, Beta?," she whispered. Beta coughed more violently than ever, this time spewing briny blood and thick mucus onto her clothing.

"We have to leave right now! We have to get her out of here! She's sick." Vaughn barked, as the books flew striking Beta again and again.

"I need to finish my conversation, man," countered Marissa, blocking their path.

Vaughn continued pushing the wheelchair over the books in his path until Marissa was forced to move out of the way. The plump attendant from Baltimore rushed into the room, screaming at the chaos. Every book in the room was now on the floor. "You're lucky I haven't called the police already," she said. "I could smell you were drunk the minute you came in here. You brought this upon us. Look at all the damage you've caused. This unholy mess came with you. If she hadn't said you were coming this morning and that she wanted to see you, I'd never have let you in. Get out of here; I'm calling security. You've made a mess and you've nearly killed her."

***

Vaughn and Marissa scrambled across the gravel pathway to the car. Neither spoke as Vaughn drove to a nearby Dunkin' Donuts. He purchased two black coffees and returned to find Marissa's gaze fixed on her hands in her lap. She bit her lip and turned to look at him, shaking her head.

"I need to go back to talk to her some more. I need to find out what she meant." In the bright sunlight Marissa looked haggard, aging years since he'd met her just a few hours earlier.

"Look," Vaughn replied, blowing on his coffee to cool it. "Are you kidding me? We can't go back. Something about Beta just ain't right. It's never been right. You saw those books flying around there!"

Marissa tasted her coffee, grimaced, and placed it into the cup holder, shaking as she spoke "I need you to tell me about what she was talking about in there. Who is Alpha?"

Vaughn took another sip and returned her gaze. "The way I see it, you're the one who needs to answer some questions here. You come to my house and tell me my mother has been working for you for the past two weeks, but I know that's impossible because she's been dead almost that entire time." He wiped his mouth with a napkin. The tension rose in his voice. "Then you tell me my mother told you that you needed to talk to Beta, whom I haven't seen or talked to for twenty years." Vaughn finished the coffee and threw the cup into the backseat. "And to top it off, she keeps calling you Lourdes. Maybe you decided to pull a scam after you found my mother's purse. Maybe you're the reason your son can't sleep at night. I think all this has to do with you."

"Shut the fuck up," Marissa hissed. "If I'm so crazy, then why did you drive me up here? Who in the hell are you? You're probably some drug hustler. You hear Beta's name and the next thing I know you're driving me to see some lunatic. You don't understand what we're dealing with here. This is the kind of shit I'm dealing with every night. And she just fucking called me by my real name, and no one—not my husband, not my family, not my friends—no one alive knows that."

Vaughn stared at her, a sickening feeling growing in his stomach. "I had a sister," Marissa went on. "She died when she was eleven. Her name was Marissa and I was named Lourdes." She took a hand-rolled cigarette from her purse and turned to look out the window. She took a deep drag of the cigarette and continued. "I don't know why I'm telling you this. I just met you. My husband doesn't even know." She paused and took several puffs. Vaughn swore he could smell chemicals in the smoke: marijuana, tobacco and the tell-tale traces of PCP. "When I was in my country, I was a wild girl. I got into trouble and I got sent to jail. I sold drugs, sold my body for money. I drank. I stole. I did what I needed to do to survive."

Vaughn listened intently, turning on the car to warm him. He was very cold, but the aromas from her joint were warming him up.

"I had a pimp. He used to beat me and take my money." She sipped her coffee between puffs. "One day he beat me so bad I thought I was going to die." Marissa opened the window and flicked the ashes into the parking lot. Vaughn waited for her to continue.

"He beat the shit out of me, and I knew he would kill me next time. When he passed out later, I got a knife and I put a chair by the bed. I took that knife by the handle with both hands, and then I jumped off that chair and plunged the knife into him and twisted it and he began to scream. I grabbed a pillow and I held it down over his face with every bit of strength I had while he struggled to get the knife out of his chest." She took another sip of coffee. "I hated that knife. He used it to line up his coke. He used it to cut his food and toenails and everything. I got this scar on my arm when he cut me with it once." She rolled up her sleeve to show him the deep scar on her left forearm. She grew animated. "I was so high. For a while, I didn't even believe I had actually killed him, but I did. I ran. I took his money, but it was my money anyway. I went to the vital records office and got my sister's birth certificate, and I guess I just became her. I got some new ID and I made my way across the border. I've never told anyone. I said I came from Cuba and no one even questioned that."

Vaughn breathed deeply. He thought she would say more if he waited.

"I don't know how that old bitch knew my name. There's no way anyone could have told her." Marissa threw the cigarette out the window and pulled another one from her bag. She lit it, hand shaking, and took another long drag. She blew the chemical smoke into Vaughn's direction. "Did he put you up to this?" she demanded.

"I don't know what you're talking about." Vaughn stared at her. He wanted her out of his car, but he liked being around her just the same.

"Now you have something to tell me." She took another hit and looked out the window, then back at Vaughn. "Who the hell is Alpha? Maybe you and your mother are the scam artists." All the trust and confidence of her confession evaporated, and her tone betrayed her regret at telling him anything at all about herself.

Vaughn looked into Marissa's angry eyes and did not speak. His heart beat faster and faster. The cigarette smoke choked him as he opened the car door and jumped out, slamming it behind him. He strode down the sidewalk away from Dunkin' Donuts in the direction of some nameless Catonsville neighborhood.

He heard the passenger door slam behind him but he did not look back. He could hear Marissa or Lourdes or whatever her name was screaming obscenities.

"Motherfucker, don't you run away from me when I'm talking to you!" Vaughn kept walking. He could hear that she was about to catch up to him. Then she grabbed his arm and spun him around to face her. "Look, motherfucker, I don't know what game you're trying to pull here. For all I know, you and your mother or whatever she is are after my money. But let me tell you this you, asshole." She was screaming now, but Vaughn showed no emotion. An old man leaving the drugstore across the street looked in their direction but then walked away, minding his own business. Marissa lowered her voice.

"I don't have any money," she said. "Everything I have belongs to my cock-sucking husband, who's divorcing me right now. I am going to lose everything I have—my home, my son, everything. I'll probably even get deported, and that would be OK with me. Really it would just be fine." Tears were streaming down her cheeks. "I just can't deal with what has been happening. I am scared shitless. I can't sleep in my own bed, and I'm afraid to hold my own damn kid. I'm so scared." She smeared her tears away with the back of her hand. "Your mother was the only reason I was able to get any rest for the past few weeks. She told me she knew how to deal with it and she did."

"All I know is that your husband said you needed a housekeeper and for someone to keep an eye on your kid. I don't know anything more than that. Charleroi has known my family for years. My mom used to work at The Oaks. She was born there and grew up there. My mother hardly mentioned you. She didn't talk about her job, just told me she hadn't expected it would be at night. Charleroi told me it would be at night, but I didn't' tell her that. I felt bad. She really needed the money. I was too ashamed to tell her that it was night work. How do you think I felt having to send my mom at to work at night at her age? And I told you, she's been dead for the past ten days. So if anyone is shitting anyone, it's you, bitch."

Marissa covered her mouth with her hand and turned to walk away. She took several steps and stopped sobbing. Vaughn followed her. He pulled several napkins from his pocket and gave them to her. She blew her nose.

"Let's go back to the car," he said, wrapping his arm around her shoulder. "I have this. Look at this. I was going to the bank this morning to close out her account when you came by." He reached into the breast pocket of his jacket and pulled out a folded sheet of paper. "You need to read this. It's my mother's death certificate."

Marissa looked at him and took the paper. "She died November first," Vaughn said. "You can see the cause of death was a car accident. She died on Route 15, headed north. A car crossed over the center line and killed her instantly." Vaughn was crying now.

Marissa read the document and handed it back to him as they continued to walk toward the car. "Let me show you something." She pulled her cell phone from her pocket. "Watch this and look at the date." She handed the device to Vaughn. A video began to play. "You can see the date there in the corner. It's November fourth. That's three days after you said Mae Etta died. It was a Wednesday."

Vaughn looked at the video. He saw a preteen boy and a portly man wearing a suit coat that was too small for him. Mae Etta was humming and stirring something vigorously in a bowl. She smiled at the camera and said, "Ms. Marissa, you're going to love these biscuits. They'll make you want to eat." She laughed. A flat-screen TV was visible in the background. Katie Couric was discussing the special, off-year election results to fill the seat of a deceased congressman and the surprise win of a conservative Republican candidate in Massachusetts, which had stunned the entire country. This was news that had not happened until November 4.

The camera focused on his mother, who was hard at work stirring the biscuit dough. Then video showed the fat man again and the boy, who looked tired.

"Who's that man?" Vaughn knew many of the employees who had worked for Charleroi over the years, but this man was new to him.

"That fat shit is the security detail. He took off after that night. I don't know what happened to him. I can't blame him, though, because that night was the worst."

Neither spoke again until they reached the car. As Marissa opened her door, she looked at Vaughn and seemed years older than she had when they'd set off in the morning. Her skin was sallow and blotchy. "You never said who Alpha is. Who is Alpha, Vaughn?"

Vaughn opened the door and sat down. He looked at Marissa and then back at his hands on the steering wheel.

"Alpha is my mom. It's her nickname. The only one who ever called her that was Beta. Alpha and Beta."

Marissa looked straight ahead. "We need to go back," Vaughn said. "But before we do, I need you to tell me something."

Marissa looked at Vaughn now, a vulnerable, scared shell of a woman. "You see, your mom—she was helping me with my son. She was just supposed to watch him while I was out at night. I haven't been able to sleep for weeks. There are these sounds in the house. Weird shit. I hear my son calling me and he sounds like my sister. He's calling me in my sister's voice."

Vaughn thought of the tapes Charleroi had given him. He hadn't reviewed them yet. He'd told Charleroi his mom would help out weeks ago.

"In the spring, I didn't want to be there. There were noises in the wall. Everyone heard them, it wasn't just me. I was out and I brought these guys home and this woman. I'd never met them before. I met them at Nathan's in Georgetown and they said they could help me. We did some Troll and we drank some. They were cool. I mean, they were cool until we got back to the house. Then one of the guys disappeared and ended up throwing up all over my dining room."

They reached the convent. Vaughn parked. It was two thirty p.m. He figured after about a half hour or so they would try to go back in.

"The cops came and took them and I was high, but I just wanted them out of there. I mean, I even thought they might arrest me too. The next day I got a call that all three of them were dead at the Leesburg jail. They hung themselves, the girl and the guy. The other one, they found…"

"He was skinned, right?"

"How did you know that? I had to pay to get that information from one of the deputies. That's not public information."

Vaughn laughed. "Yes, it is. All you have to do is talk to somebody who works there and they'll tell you. Everybody in town knows it's like that murder that happened in the '80s. No, let me tell you—your son got sick and started acting strange, talking in foreign languages, using foul language. He had a stench in his urine. The furniture in his room shook and he spoke in voices that sounded like they came from hell and not from him." His voice did not betray his wildly beating heart.

"You've seen it before, haven't you?" she asked, looking back at him intensely.

Vaughn laughed softly to himself. "Girl, stop playing. That was a movie. All those devil movies are the same." He lowered his voice. "I had a sister too. Trina. She was older than me. I was just a baby when she died. I was always afraid Trina was coming back to take me. I was so scared when I was a child, I couldn't even close my eyes to sleep. I've always felt these voices whispering all around me. It gets better for a while and then sometimes it starts up again, so I know what you mean when you say you just want to stop hearing stuff. Sometimes I drink to dull the noise.

"In the army they had me talk to a psychologist, and they gave me some pills. He said I had PSTD and was just reacting to all the shit around me." He looked away. "I've never seen what you're talking about before, but I don't believe in any of that voodoo devil stuff. Oh, now, my mom did. Believe you me, she believed in all that stuff, but if you ask me, I think you should go see a doctor. You've got money and you probably have really good insurance too. There's enough evil in the world without having it come from another dimension. Trust me. Just get a prescription. That will take care of it better than anything. That's what I'm going to keep doing. Stuff like that's just not real".

"She told me that day that I hired her, the first day I met her, that she would help me close the door and would get Beta to help. I didn't know what she was talking about. I thought Beta would help with the babysitting or something. I thought she was talking about closing the doors to the house—it's drafty sometimes—but she couldn't have been. I think she was talking about something else. I don't' see how Beta could possibly help, not after seeing what happened in there. My only chance is that maybe whatever this thing is, it followed us here and maybe it will just stay here with Beta. That's my only hope."

Marissa and Vaughn left the car then and walked back toward the convent. An ambulance, passenger van, and fire truck were parked outside the front door. As they approached the main gate, Vaughn could see the paramedics packing up and leaving without sirens or apparent urgency. A man watched them walk in but did not speak. The fat attendant from Baltimore was there, red-faced and crying. She approached them aggressively.

"You killed her, you know." The people around stopped what they were doing and turned to look in her direction. "She was sick and you got her all worked up. She wasn't strong enough to fight anymore. You brought it with you and you killed her. You took the last strength she had and she died because of you."

Marissa and Vaughn looked at each other, then turned around and went back to the car. As they settled into their seats, Marissa reached across the front seat and kissed him deeply.

They stopped at Motel 6 just outside Baltimore and stayed there for hours.

***

Vaughn returned to his mother's house. He'd traded cell phone numbers with Marissa and headed inside, declining her offer to continue their party at the Days Inn in Leesburg.

He locked the door behind him and made his way to the dining room, where he'd left the videotapes Leon Charleroi had given him to watch several weeks ago. By his count, there were eight films to watch. If he put his mind to it, he could probably finish them by the morning.

The tapes were grainy, but Vaughn was able to make them out. Even though he was nursing a buzz from all the drinks he'd had earlier. Several showed the boy, Sam, playing with some other kid outside the mansion. The kid seemed familiar. Vaughn was surprised at how little the private security officers did. They usually walked around the house once an hour, but mostly they sat around reading the paper and eating.

The tape of the dining room and parlor caused him to go back and focus on an area that was difficult to see. There was something dull in the corner. Vaughn zoomed in, losing some resolution as he did so. But there—in the dining room was a tall hooded figure with its back to the camera. Vaughn pushed away from his viewer screen. The Bone Man was in the room, his smiling face reflected in the mirror on the wall.

Vaughn bolted from the room. He had to call Marissa. Everyone at The Oaks was in danger.

CHAPTER FIFTEEN

Washington, DC

Malveaux returned to his room after a game of cards with Geraldine. It was good to catch up with her and the others in the clerical residence. He changed from his work clothes into sweats and propped himself up in bed with his glasses, notepad, and pen, ready to take notes. He would get a head start on reading this Caine file before he had to go to tomorrow's court hearing.

St. Maarten

The Year of our Lord 1792

Grace and peace be unto you from our Lord and Savior Jesus Christ! Lo, how I wish I had the strength and fortitude to write these words in my own hand. Lemuel, who has been with me these many years, asked me to do this so often, but I put the task aside, and wisely so, to follow the pursuits God has given me over these years. I do so now only because the bishop has ordered me to give an account, for in doing so I may help others should the menace return.

Lemuel is a good and patient scribe and I am grateful for his relative youth, now that my hand and body no longer submit their functions to my will. Mercifully, I was able to write the majority of this text in my unsteady hand. I hope that Lemuel has accurately recounted this record. He read me the portions I dictated to him, for I cannot see the faint letters: my eyes have failed me. Yet I am ready to leave this life, for I know that my Redeemer lives and that in this state we cannot possibly understand our condition and the condition of our fellow man, who, although made in His image, suffers impossibly here. Suffers so impossibly.

I have been here some forty-three years, longer than any other white man. Certainly longer than any other slave. The bishop has never understood how I, a white man and a priest, sold myself to become a slave and to serve the Africans who are captured and brought here to die in this cruel and inhumane place. As a servant of the living God, what other choice could I make? And in this choice I have found freedom and love and an understanding that I am utterly dependent on God for all things. I did not begin with this understanding, however. I should explain how I came to this place, as I was once like the bishop himself. But, much like the apostle Paul, I was knocked off my bearings on my journey when I encountered the living God at Fort São Jorge da Mina de Ouro, during that time when I traveled to the Atlantic coast in Africa to attend to my father's shipping business.

Lemuel has heard these tales for a very long time indeed. I have known him for as long as I have been here. At first he could not believe that I lived as I had. But on this blessed day I can truthfully state that I am not the man I once was. Truly, it is impossible that I could ever have become what I am today had I not endured the suffering and afflictions these many years. Lemuel cannot believe I was a wild and unpredictable youth, full of vigor and abandon. I am so old and broken now, with but three teeth and bad eyes. I have not had a woman or strong drink for these forty-three-odd years, but there was a time when I did enjoy the pleasures of life to the fullest. When I think of those days, it is as if I am looking at the life of another man. And that would be true: I was another man, in another place and time.

I was the seventh child of my father, Luis Estevan Nũnes Carneiro, and the second child of my mother, his third cousin once removed, Isabel Beatriz Gaspar Goncalves. My father was a wealthy man, born into the noble line of the Nũnes family through his mother. Since the beginning of the kingdom of Portugal in 1139, my ancestors served the kings and queens, making vast fortunes which we kept close through marriage with only our most wealthy cousins and distant relations.

The Nûnes estates were sizeable. Our olive groves dated from Roman times. Their oil and fruit were light and tart and were prized throughout the continent of Europe. Our vineyards too dated to ancient times and produced robust, aromatic, and luxurious ambrosia, rich in flavor and medicinal benefits. Our shipping fleet was large—not larger than that of our cousins in Brasil, but charmed, because they returned time and time again to port. No Nûnes sailing vessel had been lost, plundered, or destroyed during the lifetime of my father or even my grandfather.

My father's first wife was my close relation and aunt, having been the younger sister of my mother, Isabel. She was Leonor Catalina Gaspar Goncalves, and I have seen her portrait. She was a beautiful woman with dark eyes and raven hair. Leonor died young while giving birth to the fifth of her children, my half-brother Symao, who lived his life with guilt poured upon him. When my father would drink and cry with fits of bottomless melancholy, he would blame Symao for the death of his beloved wife, and he would beat anyone—servants, children, or family, anyone in his path. In this manner he caused the near death of Dom Manuel Tristam Caro Sanches, grandson of the Duke of Trancoso, when I was four. I was, of course, not present for the event, but heard Ana Paula and the other servants whisper about it. To truly understand, you must know that all who knew him loved Dom Manuel. He was strong, decisive, and a beloved leader of the men around him. His older brother and heir to the duchy of Trancoso, Dom Francisco Diego Caro Sanches, was also loved. Dom Francisco and Dom Manuel were closer than most brothers. Their relationship was so rare. I have heard about the never-ending political scrabbles in many noble families, but there was no such disorder in the house of Trancoso.

On that fateful day, Dom Manuel was indisposed. Only two weeks earlier he had narrowly escaped death when an avalanche of falling rock from the hillsides overcame the caravan and particular carriage in which he was riding. The startled horses bolted, stepping off the steep cliffside road into a steep ravine, breaking the axle of the carriage and sending it over the side of the hill. Lord Bernaldo, his trusted advisor, was fatally injured, having his skull split and brains dashed on the rock. *I heard them tell that he remained conscious for the better part of an hour, talking as if nothing was amiss, until he expired.*

Dom Manuel, who found himself pinned under the twitching body of a caramel-colored steed, cried for assistance, but was answered only by the moaning of the coachmen. But God is good. Members of the royal military guard descended the ravine and through their labor extracted Dom Manuel, who had lost consciousness from the pain of his broken lower extremity. As fate would have it, our estate was closest in proximity, and within some time the guards arrived, pulling Dom Manuel on a litter behind a gentle horse to our doorstep, where he would recuperate for a fortnight.

It was during this sojourn that Ana Paula established a liaison with the lesser of the four guards who arrived that night. To hear Ana Paula talk, she was the object of every man's desire. (To be sure, her son Rey, my one-time playmate, dates his conception to the time of that visit.) She made it sound as though one could not have believed the spectacle caused by bringing members of court to our rural estate that very night as Dom Manuel's accoutrements and all manner of finery made their way to our home, having been recovered from the carriage. Ana Paula said his servants came with fine feather beds draped with the most exquisite silks from the Orient. I did not know whether to believe her or not. The beds were so soft, she said, they could only be compared to what the angels must feel in heaven, lounging on clouds as they glorified the Father.

I remember the excitement and the colors more vividly than those I now see before me, although I was so young, I sometimes wonder how much I truly remember and how much was told to me. Massive casks of wine and golden goblets, encrusted with jewels and gold from the New World, encircled Dom Manuel's special goblet. Ana Paula described for me the sky-blue stones of turquoise, the lapis lazuli and emeralds swirling in a sea of color as they made their way to his parched lips. And the food! Ah, well. We were comfortable and did not miss meals even in times of great hardship, but nothing the likes of this had ever been seen at our table. Each night was an exotic feast of roast fowl and the tenderest morsels of venison cooked to perfection. With him dined his guards and his companions, and of course my father, who was hospitable and hardworking until he began his descent into drink.

Each night began the same. After sunset Dom Manuel would be carried into our great room, where we were asked to entertain him. My mother would sing and some of my older sisters would dance. We had a yard man who was an accomplished juggler, and also a dwarf who performed for him. Dom Manuel would drink and drink so as to dull the pain of his broken leg, leaving him and his guests in a stupor, so that all manner of lasciviousness occurred among the servants and his companions. Even Graca, our cook, told me she found Dom Manuel's own confessor in my dear mother's apartments with one of the maids. I hear he screamed at her to get back and tell no one. Nevertheless Graca whispered everywhere, telling all who would hear of the confessor's infirmity. Our servants dared not look at him lest they be reminded of his small member, which Graca described as no bigger than an acorn.

It was during this time that Dom Frederico returned from his travels in North Africa and came to retrieve his brother and see him home. Ana Paula tells that he arrived at our estate with much speed to see to his brother's welfare, brushing past all in the drunken orgy to see his dear brother.

It is then, I hear, and have heard many times, that my father, who lounged nearby in a great stupor, saw Dom Frederico approach Dom Manuel, looking much agitated and wearing the traveling clothes of the merchants with whom he rode. It is then that my father took the great oak crutch near Dom Manuel and beat Dom Frederico over the head as he bowed to be near his brother's side. A great scuffle and melee ensued in which many people were injured. My mother, who was pregnant, was struck in the abdomen and run over by Dom Frederico's companions. Her ankle was crushed, and although she recovered she walked with a limp from that day forward.

Ana Paula told that my father was seized and awoke the next morning, groggy and in leg irons, in the dungeon of the duchy. Dom Frederico was left no more than a simpleton, repeating over and over his favorite childhood poem. He died some four years later. In retribution, some of his men set fire to our home, and many of our olive groves were *destroyed. A few trees survived, a miracle from the Lord and a merciful blessing.*

I did not see my father again for many years, and when at last I did, I mistook him for a vagrant as he was bent over and filthy in rags, looking at the ground. I was twenty and a man, and our fortune, once grand, was diminished to but two vessels, several hectares of olive groves, and the present estate. We did not starve, but things were not as they had been in those glorious days. Indeed, our sister Paola and brother Juan were lost to sickness. Perhaps they would have survived if there had been more or better food in those days. I survived by emulating Ana Paula, who knew the herbs and roots of the land, which gave me strength and fortitude. The babe my mother carried in her womb at the time of my father's arrest was born and was likened to him in the manner of his face and build. Yet this child, Christovao, was not like other children. A mute, he did not speak, and as he grew, clung to my mother's skirts and spent endless days sitting on the hearth, legs akimbo, rocking back and forth and humming as if transported to some distant land. He would let no one touch him save our dear mother and was given to fits and rants that terrified me in their intensity and duration.

It was in this manner that I became the man of the house when I was barely four years old. I must say, however, that I never felt like a child in those years. Ana Paula said I was destined to be a blessed saint and a man of God. She swore to me that these things had been revealed to her while I was carried in my mother's womb. She avowed that I alone would ensure the survival of our family during this difficult period. I dismissed her country ways as mere fantasy.

✳✳✳

The healings...I do not remember the first time they happened. I do recall the first time one was pointed out to me. I was a boy of six, no more or less. During that time we were forced to sell many of our father's prized horses, as we could no longer afford to keep and care for them. The sale of the prized beasts would bring gold to secure us in the upcoming years. I was charged to assist in cleaning and grooming the animals, and to brush their luxurious manes and flowing tails.

I have not mentioned Pero. He had lived on our estates his entire life. Nearly sixty years of age, he served as a blacksmith and cared for the horses and draft animals. That day was unusual in that even in the early hours, the air was thick and warm, making certain promise that the noontime sun would become unbearable. I resolved to do my chores as early as possible, and I greeted Pero in the stable as he wheeled a barrel of horse manure to the olive grove nearest our home.

That morning it was as if we were the only two persons alive in the world. All was silent. There was no noise in the far distance from the house, no gathering of kindling by Ana Paula, no calling out chores by our mother. I cannot explain how it was that the bull was not in his pen. I had just begun to gently pet and groom the mane of the gray horse when Pero's cries reached me.

I ran from the stable as fast as I could, surveying the fields until I found Pero prone and the great bull thrashing his horns and throwing Pero into the air like he was nothing more than a lifeless doll. My immediate reaction to this horrific scene was to run to the house for help, but I could not, as the bull was between the house and Pero. I was frozen in fear and dropped the grooming brush. I have heard that animals sense fear. This massive beast must have sensed my own helplessness and anxiety. I heard Pero's cries and I whimpered a prayer, short and direct. "God preserve me," I breathed inaudibly as the bull charged toward me.

I cannot explain what happened next. I have never spoken of it to anyone. As the bull charged with a speed and power that would surely end my brief life, I closed my eyes and fell to the ground, unable to witness my certain fate. I heard the charging bull racing closer and closer, and then suddenly it stopped. I could not bear to look. I was so afraid that I urinated right there.

When I lifted my eyes, I saw them. A sight like none other—three, perhaps four luminescent warriors, tall and shining brilliantly. And the bull saw them at that very instant and halted in his tracks as if restrained by an invisible force. The massive creature then put his head down and the luminescent beings led him to the pen and secured it firmly in place. I could not stand but remained in the most abject fear, for I knew what I now witnessing was not a natural sight. I could not take my eyes off them. They looked at me, raised their hands in saluta-tion, and then they were gone.

Fear and anxiety and wonderment all consumed me at that moment. At the same time I felt certain that God had heard my prayer and delivered me for his service. I stood and looked frantically about me, but the luminescent ones were gone. As I came back to my senses, I heard the gurgling cries of Pero, who suffered from vicious wounds. I ran to him, leaving a pool of urine in the dust.

As I approached Pero I was afraid. He was grievously wounded. Why of all mornings was no one else awake but me? I did not know what I would do. As I approached I saw his lower bowel exposed. The blood and tissue gave Pero the appearance of a newly slaughtered calf. As I approached, he grabbed my right hand and placed it on what remained of his abdomen. The hot blood, sticky to my touch, pulsated and I felt as if I had touched a hot brick on the hearth of our fireplace. The indignity and gruesomeness of it all was too much for my sensibili-ties, causing me to recoil and vomit. I grabbed my hand from his grasp and turned to run to the house for help.

As I ran I could see Ana Paula running in my direction. She scooped down to grab me and looked in my eyes and rubbed the blood from my cheeks. As our eyes locked, I knew that she had seen them too. From then on she treated me with the same love but with a reverence and respect usually reserved for the most elderly or distinguished persons.

I do not know how much time passed; it could have been an instant or it could have been hours. It was as if time had stopped at that moment. Then Ana Paula took my hand and we turned back toward Pero, who was reclined on his elbow, conscious and smiling as if he had stopped to pick mushrooms rather than having been gored by a bull. As we approached he wept with joy, his tattered clothes and face covered with blood, sweat, and dirt. I tried to hide behind Ana Paula, for I could not bear to look upon his wounds again. But Pero grabbed me with his iron grip, once again taking my hand as I squirmed to get away. He bowed his head and brought my hand to his lips, kissing it with great reverence. "I am healed!" he laughed, and as I looked at his abdomen with astonishment, his wounds were gone. Only the blood remained.

Ana Paula turned to me and we looked at each other. She grabbed me by the shoulders and whispered, "Say nothing to anyone about these things, my little one. You are blessed."

I was perhaps in some kind of trance. I do not remember how I got from the yard that morning into the house. Nor do I remember anything else that happened that day. But I felt the most overwhelming sense of joy. A sense that I was not alone in the world and that there was a greater power guiding me and keeping me safe.

The next day Ana Paula sat with my mother and Pero in the kitchen by the fire as Ana Paula told of the events of the previous day. I recall my mother staring straight ahead as if she did not believe it.

"Ana Paula, you know it is foolish to say such things in front of a mere boy. You will bring the wrath of the church upon us all." She stood bravely and brushed the dirt from her apron as if to end the conversation.

In those days, the church brutally burned and stoned heretics of all [illegible]. In my heart I believe that these men and women were innocent souls, sacrificed to the bloodlust of evil men. But I did not question my mother's wisdom in these things because I knew that our family could not bear the scrutiny of the church into our daily lives. We were fortunate to have escaped death and imprisonment because of our father's actions.

My brother Christovao wakened then, entered the room, and raced to my mother, clinging to her knees, rocking back and forth, and mumbling. "See?" my mother said as she reached out to comfort him. "You have awoken Christovao, and now I will not get the chance to make our bread this day in peace." She gently lifted the boy from the floor and seated him on a bench near the table where the baking would begin. Christovao began to rock again and flailed his arms about so that the wooden bowl and ladle sitting there were knocked to the floor at my mother's feet. I dropped to my knees and collected them.

Angela Ciccolo

I cannot explain what happened next. It was as if the pain in her ankle called out to me for comfort. At this moment I was seized with an impulse that was not my own. I grasped her bare foot and joint with my two hands, bowing my forehead to the ground. Ana Paula told me later that all manner of words and sounds came from my lips as if originating from someplace outside of my body. A tremendous wave of energy rocked me and my mother fell forward as if some powerful force had pushed her from behind. In the confusion Ana Paula and Pero rose to assist her and to seat her upon the bench next to Christovao, who seemed transfixed. I too collapsed and rose to steady myself by placing a hand on the bench, but instead I touched Christovao's leg. Ana Paula looked at me as if she could see what I was feeling. I can only describe it as this: it was as if a great fire shot from my hands and consumed Christovao, who began to convulse and flail about, tipping over the bench, my mother, and myself and landing across the room as if some unseen force had placed him there.

I rose and helped my mother to her feet as Pero and Ana Paula ran to Christovao, who lay on the floor weeping and saying over and over, "My God. My God. My God." My mother looked at me and then ran to him. It was only later that she realized her action was effortless and her ankle had been healed.

I too went to Christovao. You must remember well that he was my brother, and for these early years of his life he had lived behind a veil of sorts that separated him from joining fully with all of us. He was with us, but never really part of us. Yes, he ate and drank and threw the fits that scared me, but we never communicated. He lived in a distant place where I could not go. But when I looked into his eyes that morning, I can only say that it was the first time he had ever looked back at me as if we were in the same place and time.

Tears of joy streamed from his eyes. He cried, "Mama, Mama," over and over as my mother rocked him in her arms. Pero and Ana Paula stood nearby, praising God and crying for joy. I felt drained somehow and ready to sleep again. I addressed each of them, begging them to tell no one what had happened lest we all face persecution. At such time I went to my chamber and slept well past midday.

The Caine File

How our father returned to our lives

It was some fourteen years later that I saw my father again. He arrived at our gates in autumn, late November and close to winter. Our fields were active, as this is the best time to harvest olives because the ground begins to frost and the nights become brisk and festive. My companion, Lemuel, does not understand this concept of cold, having lived his entire life in the heat of the Caribbean. The cold is bracing and the winter wind cuts through the night air like a fast-moving horseman.

I was in the fields that day with my mother and my brothers, sisters, and a few faithful servants who did not desert us. Ana Paula was there. She helped us to survive those starving years. The sky was beginning to darken; the days were growing shorter and shorter. Perhaps another half hour of light remained. It was crucial that we retrieve every olive from the groves. Our survival depended on pressing the oil and selling it, and preserving as many olives as possible. We used the olive oil to trade for things we could not produce on our own. The olives themselves provided nourishment and life. We ate pickled olives, olive paste, olive bread, and anything else you can possibly think of made from olives. And so it was during that evening that I had just climbed down from the upper branches of one of the trees near the edge of the grove closest to our estate when I saw an elderly man shuffling and limping along the path to our estate. My brother Pedro saw him too and scurried down from the branches before me. Pedro was older and suspicious of this late-evening traveler with no belongings. My brother Christovao, who had been recalled to life, helped by carrying the bushels of ripe fruit to the olive press. In those days we could barely feed ourselves, yet our mother always prevailed on us to be kind to everyone and share what meager food we had with the poor. As the man grew closer, we could see that his pant legs were in tatters. Our old dog, Rafael, who could barely see and was nearly as old as I was, lifted his head and looked in the direction of the vagrant. Then, as if propelled by some outside force, Raphael stood on his arthritic legs and trotted out to the man, not barking to warn or guard us, but to greet the man.

It was most curious. The vagrant dropped to his knees as if an unseen hand had pushed him to the ground, and Raphael barked for

167

joy and licked his face. My mother and sisters and Ana Paula now were leaving the grove as it grew dark, and their chattering stopped when they saw the man on his knees, crying softly and, most strangely, calling the dog by its given name. As we slowly approached, my mother broke free and ran, her words hushed: "It is your father. He has returned."

I confess to you now, I did not feel great love or relief or any kind of emotion at that moment. It is strange. I have thought back on that moment many times and still do not know why I could not join the others as they raced to embrace him. It seemed I was not free to join them. In the years since my father had left, all manner of living had been difficult for those he left behind. I had spent many hours talking with Ana Paula, who told me of my father's legendary temper and lack of self-control. I identified his lack of temperance as the reason for our misfortune and the cause of much suffering. Too I say that there was something about him that repelled me, and I had good reason when I learned his plans.

A changed plan for me

Yes, I did not remember my father, and this man who returned to our lives was strange to me. My mother and others encouraged me to befriend him and to welcome him back into our lives, but somehow I could not. The years of confinement and deprivation had not changed him much. He drank much wine and beat my mother fiercely. During the night hours I could hear her weeping and running from her bed-chamber to hide from him, while he called out to her in the shadowy corridors to come back.

After a period of some weeks past the harvest time, he did begin to settle down. He ordered my mother and Ana Paula to retrieve clothing we had stored for him under the floor where we secured our few remaining valuables. These consisted of my mother's wedding ring, a pair of earrings that had belonged to her mother, and some books. The servants were instructed to clean and to mend the clothes, for he was planning a trip on which I and my two brothers were to accompany him.

Christovao and Pedro were excited and had fallen under our father's spell. They would have followed him anywhere. He explained to my mother that we would travel to a port city to reclaim our remaining ships. At this time only two remained in our fleet, and they had been leased to pay my father's many debts. The others were lost at sea during the dark years of my father's imprisonment. We were to travel with a cargo of virgin olive oil to the coast of Africa to a place called El Mina, where we would pick up our next cargo.

We set forth within a fortnight and had an uneventful journey. Christovao, Pedro, and I marveled at the sights and huge number of people we saw. I could not help but stare at two young men of perhaps my age and stature who carried an awning over a noblewoman to shield her from the rays of the sun. Their color was of the same ebony richness as the olives we grew. My father explained that these were slaves and less than I. I discounted by father's words because when I smiled at the young men, one looked my way and smiled back.

This scene would haunt me for the remainder of my life. I can still see them when I close my eyes, and they are as real to me as this dreadful heat. These were not animal eyes staring back at me, or property, as my father reasoned. I knew these were men like me. I did not thereafter feel the same lightheartedness I had known before. Yes, I visited the vast cathedral and ate with my father in all manner of taverns with amusements I am too modest to reveal, but my father and brothers noticed my change in demeanor. They did not address it with me, however, due to their preoccupation with the pleasures at hand.

My father and brothers and I met with the two captains who had maintained our vessels over the years. Each had been modestly successful in trading and remained loyal to my father. Both seemed truly gratified to see he had survived his ordeal. These seafaring men had wisely invested our share of the proceeds and presented a bank draft which my father used to redeem a modest sum of gold coin and plate. A deal was struck wherein my father agreed to sell one of the two vessels, the Zhorig, to a venture company formed between him and the two captains. By this manner he acquired another sum of gold and plate which he deposited in the bank, half being for the benefit of my mother and the other half for the benefit of his male children upon his death.

At this time I inquired as to provision for our two dear sisters, who had not married due to the absence of a dowry and the shame of our father's action. His reply was callous and so vile that I cannot repeat it here. I vowed then that some portion of my inheritance should go to their happiness so that they could marry and enjoy full lives.

After three weeks' time, we prepared our ship for its next journey by bringing on a store of provisions and all manner of lead chains and iron pens, which my father claimed were for exotic beasts. Our new captain, Smyth, did not ease my concerns, as he and my father had become acquainted during a time each spent in the royal prison. Smyth was an Englishman whom I took to be of low breeding due to his speech, which was filled with all manner of invectives and curses. The first time I saw this man he was cursing loudly and holding a young boy no older than seven or eight years by the hair with one hand while he beat him with the other. He glared at me and I turned away from him and he retreated. Christovao, who was with me at the time, said, "He will not bother you, brother. Who in his right mind would bother a man with angels by his side?"

I looked at Christovao with much skepticism. It had been some years since he had been returned to life. In this time I had never discussed his healing with him or anyone else. Christovao had such a childlike, innocent quality. He was so pure. He turned to me and smiled. "I can see them. I have always seen them. They are always with you. You should not fear." He left me and I watched him fade into the crowd. I did not have the opportunity to raise this topic with him again, as our journey began the following dawn.

Our cargo

I spent some weeks below deck, stricken by a fever and sickness too dreadful to recall. I fell in and out of consciousness and was able neither to eat nor drink much for nearly three days' time, whereupon I recovered and made my way to the top deck, somewhat unsteady but ready to breathe the sea air and take some porridge. The climate was warm and a scorching sun took its place high in the western sky. In the far distance I spied a shoreline and a great fortress atop high cliffs.

One by one my father, brothers, and I, along with the captain and a number of the crew, were lowered into the water in small boats which took us along a sturdy pier shrouded in dense fog. Every forty yards or so there was a torch on the shore, and any number of objects drifted by our boat. Mercifully, I could not positively identify any of them, for in my heart of hearts I am sure that a human torso and head floated past on my right. These sights caused me to place my head in my lap, where I could feel my heart beating as if to escape my chest. As I left our small craft and walked, unsteadily at first, on the land, I spied along the road any number of miserable men and women who appeared to be in a stupor, as if incapacitated by drink or some strange paralyzing plague. And then there was the smell, which was faint but nauseating.

Christovao and I walked near the rear of the party. I was fatigued and still recovering from my illness. I could not hear the conversation between my father and the captain and the strange man who guided them. I could not see his face or hear their words, but as we proceeded up a steep hill, I felt fear and trepidation. As we continued to walk, I became increasingly aware of a low and sorrowful moaning. I removed a handkerchief from my pocket to cover my mouth and nose, for the stench would surely overcome me. Truly, as long as I live, I will never forget the mournful sound. Even to this day I hear it in my sleep. I confess I was terrified then. I could not imagine what manner of animal could make such a cry that was so human and yet inhuman.

By this time we had walked for the better part of an hour. A lush tropical jungle with all manner of plants and trees I had never seen before lined our way, and there was an eerie silence except for the mournful cries, which became more intense as we drew near them. Our only source of light was the two torches, one to the front and the other to the rear of our party, each carried by members of our crew. I recall the moon was present but shrouded by the dense fog.

In my small world I could not imagine what manner of cargo we would find here. What strange mineral or plant valuable for trade would we find in this place? I fell back from the party to relieve myself quickly along the side of the road at a clearing. At that moment, and just for a moment, the fog lifted and the moon appeared as if God had once again separated the light from the darkness. What I saw was unmistakable. It was a sight I shall never forget, one that haunts me to this very day. A large wildcat scurried across the clearing and headed in my direction, carrying prey that it momentarily dropped to gain a better grip. Then I was able to clearly see this proud cat's trophy, which was unmistakably the delicate forearm of a child. The cat peered at me with crazed eyes, seemingly terrified, then grabbed its prey and retreated. I secured my breeches and ran with all my might to the path to rejoin my party, and I did not look back.

As I hurried, I was haunted by the images that were now burned into my memory. It has been so many years since these sights were first seared onto my mind and soul, but I knew even then that I could not and would not forget the revulsion and fear I experienced that night.

As I joined the group, my senses were once again assaulted by an odor that caused me to vomit alongside the trail. Each of the men, including my father, my brothers, and our guide, covered their faces with kerchiefs to mask the stench. I can only describe the smell as completely nauseating, a combination of death, vomit, blood, urine, feces, and whatever vile combination your imagination could concoct. My stomach could not control its function and I gagged and regurgitated what seemed to be everything I had eaten over the course of the journey. This behavior on my part was not well received by my father, who removed his kerchief to scold me, and then he too began to vomit, causing the party to stop for him. Our guide pulled a flask from his pouch and handed it to my father, but he waved it way. I sat with my back against a tree, still vomiting. The guide assured us that the smell would improve as we traveled up the hill and that this was the worst we could expect to endure.

Christovao could not contain himself and demanded to know the nature of the inhuman stench. Our guide laughed, demonstrating his vile lack of humanity, yet in replying he did not remove the kerchief from his face. Raising the torch and gesturing to us behind the tree line, he bade us to look to the west.

There in the dimly lit night, by his torch and the barest glint of moonlight, we received a glimpse of what can only be described as an incomprehensible sight. Piled in mounds along the side of the road just behind the tree line were piles of corpses. All were men, women, and children of the African race. I could not comprehend what I was seeing. It did not immediately register with me that this tangle of legs, arms, hands, and feet, so many that they could not be counted or distinguished one from the other, could be human beings.

I then began to weep such as I have never done before, and I ran along the path to escape this nightmare. Christovao ran after me, panting and heaving as if his breath would never stay in his body, also crying the bitterest of tears. We embraced and cried for some time, whereupon we were joined by my father and the others in the party, who assisted him on account of his having fainted at the sight and being unable to continue for some time.

We proceeded up the hill to a fortress of some sort, where we were greeted by a number of weary-looking soldiers bearing arms. As the great gate opened to envelop us, we entered into a courtyard where appeared a number of captives in chains, heads down and surrounded by guards. I stood not three yards away, speechless at this horrific sight, assaulted by their nakedness and repulsed at the urine and feces on which they were forced to remain.

Let me now stop here and say that it had not occurred to me until that moment the nature of our cargo. Surely I knew there was trade in slaves, but it seemed to me as foreign as tales I had heard of giant animals in the east, of the lizards Ana Paula used to tell me as a child. I knew that this was a cursed place and that we as a people would certainly be cursed, generation upon generation, for our participation in this outrage against humanity and against God.

I have never made this confession, but I do so now freely because I am surely near my end and the Holy Father has demanded this account of me. You see, now I think with reflection and maturity, and I understand things I did not know and could not appreciate in my youth. I suppose that Lemuel and I share this trait, as we are oft stubborn men, at times full of pride and regret, and our flesh is weak in the face of fear. I suppose that despite the training, strength, and faith I now have by the will of God, all men including myself are apt to revert to our own

*impulses and abandon our faith when we are afraid. For first impulse
was to run in the face of this sight, to do nothing and let evil prevail.
It was as if all time had stopped for me and I was left to confront God
and my conscience. Much like the apostle who denied our Lord three
times before the cock did crow, I believed that there could be no God,
because surely he was not in this place. For if he were, how could he let
this suffering occur?*

*Surely these events would curse all who benefited from this evil
trade, generation upon generation, until redemption at some price did
occur.*

*Yes, at that moment, I felt as if the Lord had abandoned me, had
forsaken us all. Why would he let this happen? Where was his ven-
geance? Why did he close a blind eye to these men and women made in
his image?*

*All my life I have had a special relationship with our Lord and
with His Father and with the Holy Spirit, who has been my true protec-
tor all these years. I cried out to ask him how we would ever gain his
forgiveness for this horrible transgression against our brother. For all
men are our brothers and we must at all costs ever endeavor to love and
to serve them all. As horrifying as it all was, I could not look away. I
made my way to a nearby wall, where I put my head to my knees and
began to sob until I fell asleep.*

*When I awoke the next morning, shivering in the light morning
mist, I saw that the captives had slept chained in the courtyard, exposed
to the elements and shivering in their own excrement. That night many
things were clarified for me. As I awoke, I knew that by the work of the
Holy Spirit I had come to understand that my purpose as an instru-
ment of our Lord was to serve this lot. I had no more fear, revulsion, or
anxiety, for as assuredly as He died for our sins, I understood that He
had already borne my sins for this hideous act, and I knew that I must
serve Him by serving them, the least of my brethren, by teaching them of
His grace and mercy no matter what our circumstances, be they death
or bondage. What a wondrous God we serve! Even the lowliest of men,
free or slave, can serve Him and find freedom, mercy, and goodness
for all time. Surely I would meet these brothers in paradise. They who*

had done no wrong and were serving a sentence of living death, of hell on earth, would praise God forever in their mansions and live in the resurrection as new creatures side by side with me someday, all brothers in Christ.

I awoke stiff and sore. I stood and relieved myself on the wall where I had slept. "Boy, come here," a voice called out to me in strongly accented Portuguese. In the foreground was a portly man wearing a ragged hat, dirty, sweaty clothing, and a patch over his left eye. "Come here, boy, and help me." I approached cautiously. "Take this pail and follow me. Don't get too close now, they'll kill you." He thrust a crude wooden bucket into my hands and I followed him as he approached the captives in the courtyard.

I remember the feel of the bucket in my hand, as I was in great pain for some days after as the splintered wood eased its way into the flesh of my palms. I followed the portly man. Each man and woman chained there appeared to be awake, seemingly in shock and much distress. The bucket I held contained a coarse gruel that appeared to be made of millet and some oats. In the center of this sad group there appeared some type of shallow trough, not unlike the kind we had on our farms for feeding livestock. My portly overseer pulled the bucket from my hands and poured its contents into the trough without comment, then proceeded to kick a woman as he passed in a very cruel manner and with such harshness that her leg did begin to bleed profusely. She screamed out in pain as the shackles around her ankle rubbed against the raw flesh of the open wound. The others did pay no heed to her distress and proceeded to claw at the sustenance with their hands as if they had not been nourished in many days.

One man chained there in the midst of this sorry group examined me and focused on my own eyes. He was a mature man, certainly much older than the others, strong and regal in appearance, with skin so dark it seemed blue to me. He continued to watch me and I looked him in the eye. We stared at each other for some time, well after the portly man had walked away, leaving the bucket for me to retrieve. When I did so, I passed near the injured woman and bent near her as she continued to cry out. I determined that she was grievously injured. Clearly the *portly man had kicked this unfortunate soul on many occasions and with purely evil hatred. I believed no one was watching me, for the portly man and the captives were the only souls present on that morning. Without hesitation, I stooped to her and called out to my Savior and asked the Holy Spirit for comfort as I began that day. I placed my hands upon her and healed her wounds. She said words that I could not understand as I retreated far from the watch of the regal man who bore an interest in me that day.*

My days fell into a predictable routine. I kept out of my father's eye, and with Christovao I played all manner of sport and undertook exploration around the fortress. This structure was built on a massive hill in view of the bay and ocean, but seemed carved out of the granite hill through some natural process of erosion. The dungeon they called the holding pen, as it was in this area that the captives were held in such utter distress and chaos it is a wonder they did not lose all sensibility in such crowded conditions of stench and filth.

The pens were now empty on account of an epidemic of some sort that had swept through the area the fortnight before our arrival, thus accounting for the horrific mountain of corpses we encountered on our first night. I learned thereafter that the captives in the courtyard were the only survivors of this dreadful disease and were being kept in open air lest they be re-exposed to the source and expire themselves. Our guide explained this as part of his desire to protect our investment.

Some days passed when soldiers arrived bearing new captives, tethered by chains about their necks and feet, which caused me to recall my vow to serve them.

I regret to say that this sojourn did not improve my opinion of my father and his companions. I suppose that in some ways I had idealized him when he was absent from our home. Truly, when he first returned I aspired to live as a family and recover the lost years. Yet when he returned I felt myself reserved and unable to spend time with him, either in conversation or activity.

The incident with Dom Manuel, which laid bare my father's raucous inability to master the drink, was not some temporary aberration or lapse of thought, but rather his pattern and habitual manner of societal intercourse. His cruelty knew no bounds and we were spared his wrath only after the strong drink claimed him in sleep and gave us a respite from his tyranny. I can speak no more on this subject, which causes me much bitterness and is the true reason I found myself bound aboard the ship with the captives.

For nearly six days, Christovao and I carried wood and left it near the pier. At times the captain pressed me to deliver foodstuffs and grain sacks. During this time the numbers of our captives grew exponentially, and they were forced most cruelly into a cell unfit for any beast, let alone any man. The stench and their cries have haunted me through my life. There is no way to describe the mournful sounds of their begging for release, crying out, and questioning the Creator why such ordeal should befall the innocent. As a servant of the most high God, I can but relate their suffering to that which Lord and Savior did suffer for our sins.

I did not witness the captives being forced onto the ship and into the bowels of the vessel, crowded like animals, beaten and crying, wounded and rebelling. None were old; all were young, except for the mature one, exclaiming with all their power and pleading with every breath for release. At that moment a great darkness fell over the port and lightning struck as if a fast-moving swell was approaching and would swallow us in a furious tempest. We sat terrified as the ground around us shook fiercely, knocking several men in our party flat onto their backs.

At this sight the crew secured the ship, anchor, and ropes, and the storm surged, rocking the waves and the ship. We ran, wet and furious, for cover in the fort, which was perhaps one mile inland and located on the side of a high hill. As I turned to look at the sea, a fearful sight, I shall never forget what impressed me. It was high tide, yet the sea was retreating into itself, exposing the belly of the ship, the sand, and all manner of debris on the seabed.

I do not remember after these long years how long we huddled in darkness as the tempest raged around us all. The windows of the structure where we sought refuge were shattered, and the animals we had brought with us—sheep, some cows, and goats—cowered and

paced frantically. In my life I have not witnessed such rain and light-
ning strikes. And in the intermittent flashes of light, I spied the surf
advancing on our refuge as if the sea would swallow us whole. The
fast-approaching water did cause us to retreat from the rear of the struc-
ture to higher ground. The animals scattered ahead of us as the water
blew horizontally with tremendous force and energy. It was impossible
to stand, and we clung to each the other and made our way over the
uprooted trees, vines, and rocks. The landscape had changed but we
did not know it. We ran, following the animals, whose instinct directed
them into the hills. It was clear that the sea was no longer contained
and would swallow us if we did not continue our advance. Ernesto,
the water bearer, was lost that evening when he stopped to rest on an
outcropping of rock. I looked back and saw him breathing heavily,
exhausted, as the wind blew around him. I called for him to come until
Christovao pulled me to follow. That is the last time I saw Ernesto in
this life, as he did perish soon after, with many scores of others.

We huddled there some days and nights in the hills without shel-
ter, food, or water until the ocean did retreat and we made our way
through the disaster and back through a new landscape, a new land
that bore no resemblance to the one we had abandoned days before. In
the distance, I could see that the shoreline was greatly altered, and the
outbuildings were simply gone. The fort and the holding cells were dam-
aged, though standing and salvageable.

The captain and my father found new energy and made their way
in the direction of the shore, swinging machetes to clear the way, as any
path not obstructed by trees, rock, and debris seemed to be the natural
one. We encountered the bloated bodies of men and beasts and a reeking
stench that I will never forget until the day I go to meet our Lord and
Savior.

Although my father never said so, nor did the captain, I surmised
their urgency in reaching the shore was due to a desire to assess the dam-
age to the investment of captives, whom I had most shamefully forgotten
in my efforts to spare my own life. My father and the captain raced to
the shore single-mindedly, as if mad. I sensed that we would be ruined
financially; certainly there was no possibility for the ship to have been

spared in such a violent and destructive tempest. I raced behind them with Christovao, where my breath was taken away by the sight before us, which we viewed from a newly formed but hardly stable cliff.

The ship was no longer in the water but was repositioned perhaps a furlong away on the westernmost shore. The deck lay vertical to the beach but intact, resting on the port side and held together by the skeleton of the ship itself, as the hull was gone. It resembled the remains of giant sea creature. My father and the captain and several men (I confess I do not remember which ones) approached the wreck in tears. We made our way around the anchor, which had imbedded itself upright in the sand as if it were a monument to man's foolish belief that he is in control of his fate.

Everything inside the ship was gone or destroyed. Sadly, the captives had perished in their chains, men and women and the smallest of children, all drowned and now bloated and bursting from exposure to the salt water and the sun. I turned and vomited, as did the others, sickened by the stench. My father made his way alone toward the aft, which was raised some twenty feet in the air, and to the bodies suspended there. It was so horrible I began to cry, and he came and slapped my face and shouted me down until I dropped to my knees in tears, surrounded by the dead, where I stayed some time while the men surveyed the damage. Then most suddenly a man called Juan cried out to God that by some miracle a number of captives had survived, and were now cowering and jabbering insanely. Juan and the captain went to free them. There were, by God's grace, seven of them, and Juan and the captain assisted them down from the precipice to the land. Then the captives, badly injured and weak, looked back at Juan and the captain in the knowledge they were free. They walked, supporting each other, and as they passed I recognized the mature one, the survivor of the early plague and witness to my healing. He looked directly at me where I knelt, crying, but he did not hesitate and continued on his course with the six other helpless souls.

An altercation there ensued as my father, now hysterical and screaming, cried, "What are you doing? What are you doing? Don't let them leave!"

Those around were most assuredly ashamed at the thought of returning these souls to imprisonment, their ordeal most truthfully more unimaginable than anything we had sustained in the tempest. I had always attributed my father's erratic and unpardonable behavior to the drink. This situation caused me to reassess this belief, however, as he certainly had had none in all the days we endured the tempest. His behavior now was shameful. He cursed the men for not regaining the captives and ran—on what basis of strength I do not know—until he reached one of the women and seized her arm. She pulled away, crying out in disbelief, and spit upon him, then hit him squarely across the face with a staff she was using to support her unstable frame. My father looked shocked and then grabbed the woman and began to beat her. This caused a melee as the remaining captives seized my father and beat him, only to be joined by the remainder of our party in a most pernicious fight to the death.

After a time our party did subdue the captives save one whose skull was crushed by a rock catapulted from some distance. From my position I viewed her life force and blood ebb onto the saturated sands as her legs twitched for some time until they stopped and moved no more.

Here I must confess that I did not once consider going to her and laying my hands upon her. Indeed, death seemed a blessing from Almighty God, for the alternative was life in this cruel and unbearable state of bondage. Truly, I hear the cries in my dreams to this very day, even though I am certainly near my death. Of the seven who survived, three remained. And yet,

For most of my life I have believed this cursed thing and demon was brought about by the ranting of the man who assumed leadership over the band. In later days he performed a silent ritual dance and spoke words in a language I did not know, but I immediately understood them to be curses directed at my father.

I have come to the certain realization that the origin of this thing lay in my own father, whom I discovered, to my horror, engaged in sexual sin with the captive boy who was no more than eight years of age, and whose task is was to bring small items to various members of the crew at their command. When I found my father thus, I fought him away. He was evil to me and to Christovao, who was an innocent as a lamb.

I am sorry that I must confess these horrors. They are unimaginable. But I trust this is enough detail on the subject even for the Holy Father, who seeks to determine the origin of this pathogen.

My father's behavior intensified in the period following the tempest. During this laying over the men replenished their stock of captives, while my brother and I replenished the foodstuffs and waited for our other ship, the Zhorig, to come, if it had not been destroyed.

After some months, two vessels arrived with news of the horrific events that, by all accounts, were felt across the sea, even in our native land. The Zhorig had been preserved.

Each evening for a fortnight, my father met and discussed certain rumors of the New World colonies and grew enamored with the idea of settling there and making his fortune anew. There was no word of my mother, sisters, remaining family, or servants, and to this day, I do not know their fate or whether they faced some catastrophe. My father made no mention of them and made no provision to gather them with us in a new land. This caused me to openly grieve. The events that followed are less certain in my mind. We continued to restock our provisions and to prepare for some journey, which I earnestly hoped would lead me home. Each day was a battle, for as we reclaimed the land from the sea, many corpses and bloated sea creatures and animals were exposed as the water receded. Disease became a constant friend, and many were struck down and buried there, like Pedro our brother. I have wondered many times in reexamining this phase why I did not turn to my God to heal and restore those around me. I did not know the gravity of his situation and regret that in my own illness and preoccupation with others that I did not act to help him. I cannot say with any certainty, but only recall that I was preoccupied with the tasks around me and perhaps inclined to let nature run its course wherever it might take me.

It was during this time that I too was stricken with illness. I vaguely recall being attended by Christovao and others, perhaps even my father. I do recall an unpleasant odor and darkness, and being jostled in a bed. When I awoke from my delirium, I discovered we had been some days at sea on the Zhorig, *that had come to our aid some months past. My confusion was intensified, I think, by the rum and beer, for fresh water was not available at sea, and the alcohol subdued us and sustained us.*

I passed from consciousness to delirium and back. Many did not survive the strenuous journey and were tossed unshrouded into the abyss. I came to recognize that many captives were held in chains below the deck in a state so inhumane and barbaric, one could not rightly conceive that man could treat his brothers this way. I saw many corpses carried past the place on the aft side where they had laid me to recover. The bodies were tossed overboard to much consternation from my father, who cursed them, each one, for dying and destroying his "investment."

The crew was generally occupied during the voyage. In their free time they rolled dice for coins and played cards. Some told tales of other voyages. Juan cried that we were cursed on account of the captives and that the tempest was a sure sign from God that this enterprise would not succeed. All agreed that the voyage was difficult, clouded with sickness and death—a cursed passage. The matter was made worse by an incident occurring after three captives broke free and flung themselves into the sea. I witnessed only part of the event but heard it in great detail from Christovao, who heard the commotion and observed that two men and one woman had broken free and were holding the coxswain as hostage as they made their way on deck, pushing him aside before rushing toward me. Instinctively I grabbed the leg of the woman to keep her from what I feared they did contemplate, but, weakened from my illness, I could not hold her. How I prayed they would live and not do this horrible thing I sensed was at hand! But before there was an opportunity to stop them, they jumped over the railing to certain death. Christovao was much troubled as he ran to the rail with others and saw their smiling, upturned faces as they plunged, shackled, to their death.

This event did cause all witnesses to commiserate with the captives and their impossible conditions. I do confess that in these many years I have seen them many times. I see them in my mind, am haunted by my dreams—but this is not what I am saying. I have continued to see the with my natural eyes.. I hear their footfalls in the night in my abode, and I smell the stench of death and captivity. In the looking glass I have spied the true spirit of the woman standing behind me and smelled the fetid decay of her perspiration and heard her garbled, watery struggle more times than I can count. But these visions have never hurt me; only the impure and evil spirits have tried to pry the life from my body. In my visions, I stand on the battleground between the forces of good and those demon spirits intent on the certain destruction of those around. This kind is only destroyed when the remedy and ritual of ancient prayer are performed to cast them out

We sighted land not long thereafter, and we thanked God Almighty for bringing us safely to land and to St. Maarten, a beautiful sanctuary. Those originating the journey were some four hundred sixteen captives and thirty-nine crew. Those disembarking at St. Maarten numbered some ninety-two captives and eighteen crew, in whose number I count myself, Christovao, and my father, who was by this time not to be controlled. Of the captives who survived the tempest, I counted three: the mature man whose curse was multiplied by the active sins of my father, us, the one who had lost his left eye in the melee, and one young woman. As a memento of my illness, I found I had acquired a weakness in my left leg, which caused me to limp, first slightly, but more markedly as I aged.

Our first foray onto the island began badly, with my father while in a drunken stupor, mightily insulted the kindest woman, the wife of the provincial governor. How in the span of several hours of our arrival he could molest this woman and defile her as if possessed by some unholy force, I do not know. Before the sun had set, his fate was sealed. He was hanged by the neck and his assets taken by a Frenchman who had a longstanding legal dispute with the executioner, a Dutchman there. He argued that no Dutchman had the right to decide the manner of death for those who lived and died in that part of St. Maarten and the bystanders all agreed. The Frenchman took what little my father had in satisfaction of the Dutchman's debt who felt ill prepared to protest due to the governor's absence due to his voyage back to Amsterdam. Our father did not give any last words or fear death and or seek repentance.

He swung from the gallows spewing invectives that only ceased when his bloated body dropped through the scaffold.

Christovao and I, terrified, slept in a barn. Only I awoke the next morning. When I turned to rouse my brother, he did not respond and was cold to the touch. I realized he had passed on during the night, whereupon I removed his body and wept. I buried him on the edge of the seaport village, the name of which I do not know. I tried to find his grave in the years after, but I could not find the place I had laid him.

For as much as a fortnight, I wondered near the edge of all civilization in shock and tears. Native fruits and roots sustained me. I slept beneath the trees in a crudely constructed lean-to. Then a kind woman took pity on me in my affliction and took me in, letting me sleep in her barn and do chores around her homestead. This arrangement sadly came to a conclusion upon the return of her son and husband, who had journeyed to the remote western perimeter of the island. I was banished again, dependent on the benevolence of any who would have me.

During the course of my travels I had the opportunity to observe many great plantations established by the Dutch and occasionally by a Frenchman. These enterprises were successful due to the forced labor of the Africans, although on two or more occasions a red Indian captive came to my attention. I learned that they were not favored for this type of work as it required fortitude and discipline, though I can truly say from my discourse with representatives of this race that they are also a people full of grace and beauty, and that their perceived weakness was due to disease that decimated their existence, incidental with the arrival of the European peoples.

I do not know how I was sustained, but in my travels I preached the word of God to all I met. Through His providence I lived on for some time. I made it my goal to make the Lord known to each captive. All time ran into one continuous stream. I ate as I could and worked as hard as the captives, but not under the same restrictions, for I could come and go as I wished.

I made the acquaintance of two priests, but thought them immoral. They did not celebrate a formal Mass or give alms. These

*men generally did not leave the parish house and did not tend to
the needs of the poor, but did selfishly indulge themselves in food
and drink. In my fourth year on the island, I resolved to live as a
captive and sold myself as an indentured servant to the Carpathian
Trading Company. As I had no way to make a living and no bene-
factors, this opportunity gave me the chance to use my gifts and
preach God's word. Many were saved, and I know I will meet them
in eternity.*

*I labored for seven years preaching the Gospel, and that is when I
met Lemuel's parents and assumed his care after they perished. After my
indenture was complete, I was told my freedom awaited me. I resolved to
take Lemuel away and educate him properly. This was of some concern
to the trading company, for they held his name in inventory as a valuable servant. Thus I labored seven additional years to earn his freedom.
And while he has told me on many occasions of his gratitude, it is I
who am grateful for the occasion to win more souls to Christ during
that period of time.*

*In the final year of my second indenture (Lemuel could have been
no more than eight or nine years of age), word spread of strange manifestations and possession at the home of a Frenchman whom I can
identify as X.* [N.b.: The surname of the family was [illegible
stricken from this record at the request of the Bishop, due
to the family's prominence and relationship to the church.]
*There were discovered strange and gruesome signs on the X homestead.
Cats, birds, and two male slaves were murdered, disemboweled, and
found with their entrails stuffed into their mouths and nostrils. Four
of the house slaves ran and abandoned the property. They were found
some time later. I witnessed each pleading not to be returned. They were
beaten savagely. Each told of a demon that had come to rest on X's son,
of unspeakable curses,* [illegible] *levitation by the possessed soul, and
the ability of the possessed to speak in the captives' native language,
describing in great detail their prior existences as free men and women
in the village of their birth. This was of particular concern as the slaves
had come from a remote village, and had met no one during their captivity who spoke their tongue.*

It was reported that there was screaming at night and crashing of furniture. Too, I observed strange lights and sounds that were not human in origin.

This period coincided with a number of murders throughout the township, executed in every manner conceivable—drowning, beheading, throat slashing, and other methods which are not particularly relevant except that they occurred near the time of X's possession and spread in an eastward pattern to the capital. In each instance the immaculate and bloodless skin of each victim was left in a barn, shed or other structure. Understandably, much focus was directed at the home of X and the disturbing events occurring therein. The number of dead increased, and four slaves from that place did expire. They were said to have leapt from the cliffs rather than return to that house.

It was at this time that the bishop sent the humble servant of the Lord, Monsignor Louis Raynaud, to assist in the spiritual cleansing of the home of the demon. As Raynaud was my acquaintance, I could not turn him away when he begged my assistance after his first attempt to free X's son had failed. Let me say that in my long life, I have come to know what evil is and its many different forms. In some ways it is a cunning temptress that eats away the good in man's soul, chipping away until nothing but the shavings of a man are left. There are other manifestations of the kind of evil that consumes and drains a soul of its very humanity. This demon was in league with Satan himself, and it took grave offense at our arrival.

No man or woman greeted us at the gate to the X plantation. The road leading to the main house sorrowed me. The once-meticulous fields were in disarray, unkempt. We passed several dependencies on the way, all abandoned. Weeds encompassed the thresholds, and insects, hornets, bees, and wasps had consumed several of the buildings. This once-proud and immaculately maintained farm was now consumed with decay.

A solitary African woman sat along the edge of the road, weeping and rocking back and forth on her haunches. She did not acknowledge us and seemed quite impervious to the gentle rain that began to fall from the darkening skies. I moved to ask her what was the source of her trouble, but she jumped away, startling me by opening large, cataract-shrouded eyes, and she continued to rock and wail.

As we proceeded, a child wearing a tattered grain sack for clothing raced by. I was much more mobile in those days and was able to catch his left arm. He was a small child, and I bent down to greet him face to face. His eyes were red, infected, and encrusted with pus. He gestured excitedly as he spoke to me. He laughed and spoke words I can never forget, words that were to save my life and the lives of my companions. "You must cross them, priest. They are of the spirit world and of the water, but they cannot cross the threshold unless you bid them come in. They will give chase at night. They occupy the darkness. You must cast them out. You must [illegible]. They have no natural mother, priest. You must get them out." With that, he ran off across the field, not in a straight line but in a circuitous fashion as if to avoid something that none of us could see. His words troubled my countenance. At once I regretted bringing Lemuel along with me. It seems strange that we have not once discussed those days. I had supposed he was frightened and kept it inside. It is a mercy if he does not remember it, having blocked it from his mind as if it did not occur. We approached the house with trepidation. It was a rectangular, two-story structure with a broad, long porch separated by broad columns that held the structure in place. It was a common design, like many structures of that time. On the upper level, one solitary shutter had broken free and dangled precipitously, banging against the porch more loudly and fiercely than the gentle wind would seem to allow.

The stairs leading to the front porch were upswept, and soft mud left a path to the front door, which was ajar. Lazy flies flitted nearby but did not enter. Strangely, there were no birds in the sky. Each story had four windows on either side of the front door. Although the season for wind and rainstorms had passed, all the windows were secured as if some powerful whirlwind was anticipated.

As we climbed the few stairs, Monsieur X appeared, unshaven, disheveled, and dirty, hair uncombed. He did not greet us. Perhaps he did not need to. His face was swollen with fatigue, dark circles rimmed his eyes, and his hands were marked with any number of scratches and abrasions as if he had battled a great and fierce cat. His clothing, once impressive, was tattered and streaked with blood, some fresh, some old. He reeked of vomit and sulfur.

Our visit coincided with the arrival of a fast-moving swell that came up behind us and now seemed positioned over the house itself. As we entered, the oncoming storm and shuttered windows gave the impression that we were arriving past midnight.

Monsieur X did not speak but led us into the parlor, which had once been a grand room but now gave the appearance of having been ransacked. The great mirror above the mantelpiece was shattered. The once-proud chandelier lay in the center of the room. In several areas the plastered walls were rendered bare, revealing the studs and framework of the house itself. I could not tell if something had broken out of the wall.

I looked at Raynaud as if to ask why no one had bothered to clean up the glass. Indeed, I kept Lemuel from this area to avoid his stepping on a sliver of glass, which would have been difficult to remove under the circumstances.

Livestock ambled through the downstairs room, including several goats, swine, and chickens. They appeared hypersensitive, preferring to stay where we waited for the other family members, who had gone to secure libation and lamps for the prayers. These animals seemed unusually calmed by our presence.

Some other members of the household came to join us, two women and their young grandsons, one being the young man in the sackcloth with the pus-filled eyes. The other boy held his face close to her and attempted to remove the scales from his eyes. We sat together around waiting for the family of Monsieur X to return with the boy. The women carried in glasses of ale, some bitter tea, several biscuits, and some salted fish that had been gently smoked for preservation. Raynaud inquired after Madame X, the mother of our subject. Monsieur X did not reply, but the older woman pulled me aside and related that Madame—Claire—had not remained to endure this trial. On the agreement of all involved, she had been transported under a doctor's care to Monsieur X's younger brother, who had established a farm and commercial interests in West

Africa. The other siblings had been dispatched as well. Those from his first marriage to a woman called Isabella were dispatched to their relatives in Brazil. The children of Claire, save the subject, had been dispatched to the North American colony of Virginia.

It was difficult to see. I could not understand why the windows remained shuttered, the storm season having clearly passed. On closer inspection I saw that much of the window glass had been shattered, with an odd pane here or there remaining. I also posited that the closed shutters would keep the vermin and bugs out, although it struck me as odd that the place was devoid of those creatures presently.

I inquired of Monsieur X over the condition of his fields and their apparent abandonment. Raynaud meanwhile began to remove items from his knapsack, including vestments, a Bible, crucifix, and holy water. Monsieur X then related that some months ago, perhaps six months past, there had been some sort of tremor that left a gaping hole in the earth. In retrospect he noted that his son X had become withdrawn and odd in that period. He further described the strange noises emanating from within the walls, as of a great scratching. In great frustration he laid his ax on the wall to open it, but to his disappointment found nothing there. He further related that as night drew near, he would be forced to bind his son to prevent the young man, who by all accounts slept and seemed normal by daylight, from engaging in vile behavior, including murder of the slaves and anyone he could catch. I was horrified that this young man was apparently to blame for the maniacal rage that had engulfed the region, yet I understood that this was no mortal murderer, the method of death being so gruesome and vile.

I perceived that Monsieur X's great love for his son was tinged with fatigue and fear. He further described the bloodlust, which is too horrific for me to relate here; suffice it to say he indicated that the boy spoke in languages he did not understand, languages that were entirely foreign, and that the furniture in his vicinity moved and shook spontaneously without provocation. Monsieur described several instances in which X, though bound to his bedpost, had risen with the bed and thrashed against the very ceiling, yelling and cursing vile oaths.

Angela Ciccolo

At this time Monsieur X led us up the stairs and displayed the bedroom for our observation. The room itself had been stripped to a bare minimum, with only a washstand, bed, and two chairs. The windows were secured tightly with shutters. Some daylight was visible, and in it Monsieur X gestured toward the ceiling. We gasped at the blood-smeared display. When I inquired as to X's whereabouts, Monsieur stated that for the most part, during the daylight hours, X sat in the garden, walked, read, and conversed, though fatigued. He had no memory of these night fits, but the dark circles under his eyes and scratches on his arms and body betrayed the violent and sudden nature of the fits.

Based on my discussion with Monsieur X, it became clear that the ramblings of the boy I'd met earlier were indeed correct. I did not begin to understand what he meant when he said we needed to cast it out. I regret that Monsignor Raynaud seemed terrified, and I earnestly prayed he was up to the task.

There was no disturbance on that first night, and we all fell asleep when the daylight began to break. It was some time past mid-day when I arose. Lemuel was fast asleep on a pallet on the floor near my chair. I was stiff and sore and somewhat disoriented by my late-night watch. I sensed that I was being observed but saw no one. Then, as I turned slightly toward the back of the house, certain that I must relieve myself but still too tired to move, I saw the boy standing there watching silently. I bade him to come close and he did. He was a handsome young man of perhaps fourteen years. He wore a nightshirt that was most foul and dirty, and he reeked of urine and feces and blood. Dark circles ringed his eyes, and he appeared to be missing the fingernails on his left hand, which was crusted with stained blood. He stared at me and I smiled gently, a smile that he returned.

"Let's change you out of these garments," I offered. I rose and he followed me to the kitchen, where I had one of the women pour a bath. Together we bathed him, and it was in removing his clothes that I saw the welts and scratches covering his body, as if he had been beaten for unspeakable crimes. The boy did not utter a word during this time, but complied with all my commands. In this way we were able to bathe and feed him. Thereafter I led him to the small garden and showed him the

names of several plant specimens that were still identifiable despite the overgrowth. I resolved to clean this area, and I collected some tools and began to instruct him in basic horticulture. In this way he was most useful, until he grew tired, whereupon I instructed him to lie on the grass for rest while I continued to work and to make myself useful.

This pattern of quiet nights continued for four days. The boy, although not speaking, enjoyed the garden work and restful naps and nourishment. Monsieur X was quite pleased, as was the entire household, for this was their first respite. Monsignor offered to say a Mass of thanksgiving in honor of a saint whose name now escapes me. We retired to the chapel, which was a short distance from the house, but the boy was nowhere to be found in the early morning hours.

As Monsignor began to recite the Mass and to bless us in the name of the Father, Son, and Holy Spirit, we were startled by a sudden rush of darkness, which could not be explained by a sudden storm or swell, as there were no clouds in the sky that day. Monsieur X, Lemuel, and I, were present when an exchange of words occurred in the rear of the chapel. There outside the threshold stood the boy in the open door, ranting as if one thousand voices emanated from deep within him. Raynaud looked grave when the boy began to revile the priest in a language I did not know, although I guessed it to be Latin. This exchange was so disturbing to the monsignor that he disturbed the Communion chalice and stepped backward, falling and knocking himself unconscious. We ran to comfort him, only to see the boy urinating full stream into the rear of the chapel and laughing maniacally. It was clear to me that the demon had returned and would present a formidable challenge.

Monsignor Raynaud awoke, somewhat disoriented. He instructed the others to leave the room then and there and to find the boy. At this time Raynaud made his confession to me, which I cannot relate in explicit detail, but I can say that he told me the boy had spoken to him in an obscure dialect familiar to him. It was the one his long-dead grandmother, who had immigrated to Spain from a faraway land, had used to speak to him as a boy. He further related that the boy had described an embarrassing event from his youth known only to him and to his grandmother, an event he had never confessed to anyone before now. I will not share details of this event, but suffice to say that from this point forward, Monsignor Raynaud was of limited assistance to me due to what I can only describe as fear.

Monsieur X was beside himself with anxiety, for he related that these events had never occurred in the daylight hours, but were always confined to the darkness. We found the boy on the roof of the main house, screaming. With the help of three other men, we were able to restrain and bring him down as the demon boldly threatened that he would kill the boy.

Regrettably, the monsignor was of no more assistance, having been demoralized by the secret revelation from his youth. I continued in prayer and fasting and witnessed many unspeakable horrors. There were scratches and marks on the boy's body, and he released unrestrained, fetid streams of seemingly endless urine. On one occasion he drank the contents of the chamber pot. He rose off the bed several times and remained in a suspended state until we were able to wrestle him down and tie him to the bedposts. I truly feared that if others witnessed what we were seeing, that the boy would be seized and killed in violence. I believed him wholly innocent and under the control of an unholy, sadistic master.

During the daylight hours, for most of my observation, the boy appeared normal and attentive yet unrealistically exhausted. There were several instances when he escaped from my care and was discovered, always in the early morning hours, bloody and covered with scratches. These escapes coincided with brutal murders throughout the island. Of these nights

Malveaux looked for additional pages but found none in the folder. The journal's abrupt ending left him disappointed and worried that he would be of little use in the battle against the thing that called to him in his mother's voice on the videotape. He would go down the hall and brush his teeth before going to bed. Hopefully he would be able to sleep.

CHAPTER SIXTEEN

Malveaux returned to his room and dropped the file folder on his bedside table. He wished the journal had continued. It was frustrating that there were missing pages. He felt a kinship with Jon Tomas and wanted to know more about him and how he exorcised the demon. He was unclear at this point if Nũnes had been successful. His chest throbbed. "Must get my pills. Too much for one day." He reached for his briefcase and then paused as a subtle scratching noise caught his attention. When he looked up, the sound stopped abruptly. He looked at his bag and frowned. A puddle of water lay on the floor near his bureau. He went to the bathroom, grabbed a towel, and threw it on the puddle. He would talk to housekeeping about that. As he focused his attention again on his briefcase the sound reappeared. *Scratch. Scratch. Scratch.*

There was no mistake. The noise originated from the armoire near his door. Malveaux stood upright and proceeded to the armoire which dwarfed him in its immense size. He paused and listened. A mouse, perhaps? A rat? This was Washington, DC, after all, which was famous for its rats. He proceeded to the armoire and shouted, "Hush!" The scratching immediately stopped, as if whatever lay inside had obeyed his command. Satisfied, Malveaux returned to his briefcase, retrieved a pill, placed it under this tongue, and sat down on the side of his bed.

The sound was barely perceptible at first but then intensified. *Scratch. Scratch. Scratch.* "Cut it out, for God's sake, will you?" Malveaux pleaded. He was tired and nervous because of what he'd just read. The scratching stopped.

Hundreds of thoughts ran through his mind. The film he had seen today. The pictures. The sound of his long-dead mother's voice playing the game they had played so many times until she became sick and died. Malveaux wracked his brain. No one knew about that game. He and his brother and mother were the only ones who had ever played it. How could this monstrous thing speak to him with words only he would recognize, words that resonated deep in his soul? He felt like a feather whirling through the sky on a windy day.

Malveaux looked out the window. The overcast skies had been replaced with a steady gray rain. A raw night. Good for sleep and not much else. The scratching continued. A bolt of lightning flashed in the distance. The hum of electricity receded, causing the lights to blink on and off and throwing the room into darkness. He looked around the room. It was simple—bare, really. A white bedspread covered the twin-size mattress. A crucifix hung above the bed. The curtains looked as if they'd hung there for decades. A maroon wingback chair with worn arms was positioned next to the bed. *Too cheap to upgrade the electricity, I suppose,* he thought.

He turned the light switch off and then on again to see if the lights would come back on. *Scratch. Scratch. Scratch.* Malveaux turned to look at the armoire, heart pounding. *Scratch. Scratch, scratch.* More intensely now, louder and louder.

"Stop it," Malveaux commanded. This time the scratching did not stop. His heart drummed in his chest. The lights flickered on and then off again. The scratching intensified, and the armoire began to shake as if something inside wanted to escape but did not know how.

Malveaux considered how he might cross the room without approaching the armoire. The lights flickered. The scratching and rocking were almost more than he could bear. He would go down the hallway, sit in the parlor, see or talk to someone. He was panicked. Someone had to be here in the residence. He could not be alone. Not now.

He approached the armoire. The scratching continued. His heart pounded so loudly, it was surely audible. A puddle he had not noticed before was beside the armoire. Malveaux shook his head. He'd have to take it up with the maintenance staff. Later. But something had changed. The scratching abruptly stopped. The lights flickered as the thunder crashed outside, this time closer. Closer. The armoire began to shake as if whatever was inside would now break free. Malveaux froze. The piece rocked from side to side, no longer flush with the wall. The mahogany giant shook and pivoted toward him like an over-loaded washing machine.

"In the name of God, I command you to stop!" Sweat beaded on his forehead. *Thump. Thump, thump.* The armoire continued to shake.

He'd had enough. He strode toward the armoire and threw both doors open with a terrified scream. He flung his arms up to protect his face as the wild thing inside sprang toward him, snarling.

"Oh, God!" Malveaux cried as he pushed the thing away, his heart ready to explode from his chest.

"Boo, priest! I scared you!"

It was Geraldine. Malveaux sank to the bed, wiping the sweat from his brow as she cackled.

"Geraldine, what is wrong with you?" He looked up at the laughing woman, shaking his head and now laughing nervously himself. "You nearly scared me to death!"

The woman laughed hysterically. "I got you. I got you. I slipped in when you went to the bathroom about a half hour ago." She clapped her hands, clearly amused that she had caused such a reaction. "I scared you, didn't I? Didn't I? I got you. I scared you. I got you." She ran from the room. Malveaux followed her down the hall.

"Geraldine," he called after her, "at least the next time you come to my room to clean, you should make sure you do a thorough job!"

"I was in there all the time, and you didn't even know!"

How could he have forgotten Geraldine and her juvenile practical jokes? Malveaux laughed, more relieved that she would ever know. He returned to the room and locked the door behind him. The lights were on now, shining brightly. He got a towel from the bathroom to clean the water from the floor so he wouldn't slip. He went to the armoire. But the puddle wasn't there. It was gone.

CHAPTER

SEVENTEEN

Washington, DC

Malveaux made his way to the court house for Father's Gaul's hearing. He felt lucky to have missed running into Cardinal Lowell. He rode the elevator up several floors and strode through the corridor. The courtroom was filled with eager, cynical attorneys. Family members—mostly elderly women, grandparents and aunts of several of the defendants—were scattered along the public benches. There were a few men in the crowd, but it was mostly women who waited.

Judge Fred Friendly was nothing like his name. Most attorneys felt the jurist went out of his way to screw their clients. Friendly had taken over the calendar and cases of Judge Lomax, who'd suffered a stroke more than three weeks ago and was not expected to resume his duties anytime soon.

Malveaux sat next to the archdiocese's local, outside counsel, Amber West. West was a relatively new attorney. Her job was to listen to the outcome of the status hearing and analyze how it might impact the civil case that would likely be filed by the Charlerois and the parents of the altar boy case victims at the conclusion of these criminal proceedings. Her boss, Ian Doyle, would be there too, but later. A conviction in the criminal case would significantly strengthen the families' bargaining position.

After a few minutes the bailiff made an announcement. "Folks, looks like we'll be starting a little late this morning, by at least thirty minutes. If you've already checked in for your case, you can leave the courtroom and come back in about half an hour."

The bystanders and lawyers left the room, as did Malveaux. He'd rather walk in the hallway than sit and wait.

Outside the courtroom, Malveaux looked for the docket sheet. He expected to find it posted outside the courtroom door. Things were more advanced than when he'd started practicing law. There was an electronic board displaying the motions calendar for Judge Friendly. Their case was fourth on the roster. There would be time for him to go back over his notes on the Caine file while he was waiting.

"Excuse me," someone said. Malveaux turned. An elderly man wearing a black overcoat approached. He was thin, with steel-gray hair. Deep wrinkles lined his face. The man seemed familiar but Malveaux couldn't quite place him. The man extended his right hand.

"I'm Father Darien Reese. Cardinal Lowell told me I could find you here this morning."

Malveaux shook the man's hand, which seemed frail. Reese's clerical collar was visible as his scarf loosed around his neck.

"Yes, of course." Malveaux glanced down the hall and was caught off guard. Cardinal Lowell had mentioned that Ian Doyle, the attorney from the law firm, would certainly be there with Amber, but who was Reese? He could see Doyle across the corridor, laughing with a group of other lawyers. He waved to Malveaux but continued his conversation. They had plenty of time. The calendar would not be called for another fifteen minutes or so.

"Could we speak over there?" Reese asked, gesturing toward an empty corner down the hallway.

"Sure." Malveaux followed Reese, clutching his briefcase.

When they had a bit of privacy, Reese said, "I wanted to speak to you about the Charleroi matter."

Malveaux's ears perked up. As far as he knew, only a few people knew about the Charlerois—Cardinal Lowell and himself, maybe

Hennigan. The Charlerois themselves, of course, and maybe some of his staff. But perhaps Reese had been involved in making the settlement offer to them.

"Lowell called me in to see if I could assist them with their son."

Reese was not the kind he would have expected to be working with Lowell. There was nothing lurid about him. He radiated genuine sincerity. He had a kind face, someone Malveaux would feel comfortable with in confession. Malveaux liked him immediately. Yet it occurred to him that Reese was the same man he had seen at morning Mass, and as he thought about it more carefully, he thought Reese could be the man in the video the cardinal had shown him.

Malveaux had read all the most available literature on molesters. They shared a common trait in that all ceased to pray and turned away from a life of faith and community. This man didn't fit the bill from what he'd seen. Malveaux decided to let Reese talk as much as he wanted. Maybe he would find out something.

Reese sighed. From the corner of his eye, Malveaux saw Doyle approaching.

"This kind of work has been my specialty for a long time." For the first time, Malveaux noticed the man had a slight accent. Malveaux had served in many positions across the United States and the Caribbean during the course of his career, yet he'd never met Reese.

The man seemed to read his thoughts. "I spent much of my career in Rome. Occasionally, as the need arose, I was asked to take on assignments."

Malveaux met Reese's steady gaze, hypnotized by his words. "How did you become involved with case, Father Reese?" Malveaux was slightly irritated—not at Reese, but at Lowell. He was not being forthright about anything.

Reese looked at his watch. "The hearing should get started soon."

Malveaux nodded. "Cardinal Lowell didn't mention that you'd be meeting me here this morning. I didn't see him this morning of course, but he's never mentioned you. I hope you don't think I'm being rude, but I feel that I can be direct with you. It would help me a great deal if you could explain what role you're playing in the investigation. We might be able to help each other. If you were involved in making the offer based on the Charlerois' settlement demand, it would help me move things along. I can't really understand their position."

Reese smiled. "Father Malveaux, I can't provide you with any information on the settlement front."

Ian Doyle was entering the courtroom with his colleagues. He caught Malveaux's eye and nodded. Malveaux was expected to follow.

Reese followed Malveaux into the courtroom. Malveaux turned to him to continue their discussion. "Are you one of the Vatican lawyers here to weigh in on these cases?" Maybe a blunter approach would cause Reese to open up.

Reese smiled again. "Heavens, no. That's not my field at all. I don't know Cardinal Lowell well. I really just met him a few weeks ago. I expect he hasn't told you all of the information you'll need to be effective in this matter."

The men entered the courtroom and took seats on the left side of the room, near the court reporter's station. The courtroom clerk and bailiff were chatting, readying the room for Judge Friendly's arrival.

"I expect he'll show you the Caine file, which is very interesting from its historic perspective," Reese said. "I'm sure you noticed that the text ends rather abruptly. I was able to track some of the missing pages down. I brought them for you—well, a copy, anyway."

Malveaux wondered if there were additional case files Lowell had failed to disclose. Getting Lowell to share information was driving Malveaux to anger and frustration. "You see," Reese continued, "I haven't had the opportunity to address this particular issue since 1943 in the matter of Harold Gamble."

Great, more names to remember. Malveaux pulled an index card out of his left breast pocket and wrote the name "Gamble."

"The onset of the war prevented me from traveling to Virginia when the first report came to Rome," Reese said. "I arrived just as the police became involved." He handed Malveaux a thin manila folder labeled HAROLD GAMBLE in block letters. "Perhaps this file is the simplest way for me to explain this to you."

Two attorneys chatted with the courtroom clerk. Malveaux heard one ask to be placed near the end of the docket because his client was nearby but not yet present in the courtroom.

Reese continued, "We didn't get to finish with Harold Gamble, which certainly contributed to the incident in 1983."

Malveaux was growing concerned. Perhaps these present cases—the altar boy cases—were related to an older series of cases of which he was unaware. If word got out that the recent cases were in a line of historic cover-ups, the effects on the church's ability to pay claims would be even more seriously impaired. More significant, however, was the damage to the faith and trust of the young men and women who had suffered abuse, possibly for centuries, all carefully guarded from civil authorities. Blind obedience to the church might have been the rule in other countries, but in America, such behavior would not be tolerated.

Malveaux sighed. This was not the church he had joined and pledged his life to preserve. He thought of the "What Would Jesus Do" bracelets that many were wearing these days. He knew exactly what Jesus would do. He would take out his whip and beat the abusers, the molesters, and the enablers from the church. Some days Malveaux just wanted to quit. To go somewhere and do something else. A man his age could start over. People reinvented themselves all the time, after all. He shuddered. Perhaps Reese was part of the cover-up. The reports from the Charleroi house filed by the private security officers on the scene indicated that the boy, Sam, claimed the priest was abusing him. Malveaux thought it strange that Lowell had never mentioned Reese as a possible suspect. His mind raced. The report noted that two clergymen were present at the Charlerois' house on the date of the incident report, which, amazingly, did not identify the two men. One certainly was Father Gaul, whose hearing they were now attending regarding the DC altar boy cases. But in the confusion, the agent had failed to get the second man's name. None of the other witnesses, Mae Etta Rock, or Marissa Charleroi seemed to have been questioned on this point.

"Reese." Malveaux turned slightly to address him. "Tell me, do you have any information on Father Michael Gaul, or is it just the Charleroi case that you want to talk about?"

Reese looked into his eyes. "I wanted to talk to you about the Charleroi case." He sighed. "I know Gaul has done this kind of thing before. He's been moved in and out of treatment in New Mexico. No one wants him. He should have been kicked out years ago."

This was all news to Malveaux, and more evidence that information was being withheld from him. Yet, as he listened to Reese his "gift" told him with certainty that this man was not like Gaul and that he might be able to work with him to get help.

"All rise." The courtroom clerk announced Judge Friendly's arrival.

"Father Gaul was helping me in Leesburg," Reese whispered. "He's not a good man and was not the right man for the job. I didn't get to finish with Harold Gamble."

Malveaux turned his attention to what Judge Friendly was saying. But Reese's whisper became urgent. "Listen, Father Malveaux, I need to finish. You need to help me finish. You have permission to help. The letters in the folder give you permission. You're the one who needs to get it done."

This at last gave Malveaux a missing piece of the puzzle. The reports of the private security agents indicated two priests were visiting the Charleroi house on the night of the incident. Father Gaul had been a regular visitor since Charleroi had been elected to Congress. Gaul and Charleroi had attended prep school together in New Orleans. He had officiated at Charleroi's first marriage and baptized each of Charleroi's children from that marriage. Malveaux wracked his brain to remember the details of the agents' report. The interview with Marissa Charleroi indicated she did not remember the name of the second priest, and no one seemed to have asked Ms. Rock the identity of anyone present that night. The security agents referred the Leesburg's sheriff's office to the official sign-in sheet. For some reason, neither one of the agents had inspected the log, and the entry beneath Father Gaul's name was illegible.

"I need your help," Reese said. "You see, Father Gaul...he wasn't the right one to assist."

Malveaux had no idea what Reese was talking about. Reese looked down. "I'm older now," he said. "I haven't been well. But, you should know this. I've tried to help every way I could. When I was able, I even made sure your reports got leaked to the media. The cover up about these cases is entirely wrong. Cardinal Lowell knew I was coming. I notified him. That's what I was required to do."

Judge Friendly called the first case on the docket. Attorneys representing the District of Columbia and a middle-aged female defendant approached counsel's table.

Reese continued, "You see, the Caine file led Rome to believe that Case B-416 was closed in approximately 1769."

The defense attorney was arguing a motion to dismiss his client's case. Malveaux continued to listen to Reese, gratified to know that at least someone in the church believed he was right about these cases and wanted to help him.

"It wasn't until the 1940s that we found evidence that caused the case to be reopened," Reese said. Malveaux tilted his head to the left to hear better.

"In the 1930s the Roosevelt administration, through the Works Progress Administration, undertook several projects to document various folk art practices and to gather other historic information. One project was designed to document the lives of ex-slaves."

Reese became excited and spoke quickly in clipped tones. "Today, with computers, we would have picked up the reference years earlier. You know, you do a search and then voilà, you have hundreds of records. The reference really was uncovered by coincidence. A novice visiting Rome brought some early copies of the WPA narrative regarding religious practices of ex-slaves in Virginia and shared the information with our predecessors who had traveled to the Caribbean and were interested in the narratives." He looked left and right as if someone might be listening.

"An elderly man in Loudoun County, Virginia, known as Absalom Henry, recounted a story told to him by his grandmother, who came from an island. The man said the *Zhorig* came haunting."

Malveaux listened but stared attentively at Judge Friendly, who was dressing down the attorney for the defendant. "Absalom Henry and the others were asked by the interviewer to tell their life stories, to discuss their religion and faith," Reese went on. "Most subjects told about their hope for freedom. Some told of lost parents or escapes during the night." Malveaux put his finger to his lips, signaling to Reese to whisper. He didn't want to attract the attention of the courtroom clerk and get reprimanded like the poor lawyer taking a berating from Judge Friendly. "Some of the former slaves told of extraordinary meteorological events and sang spirituals they'd learned as children. Absalom Henry was different. He told the researchers about a haunting. The WPA studied the language he used and tried to draw etymological links to Africa."

The clerk called the next case, but when no one came forward, Judge Friendly dismissed it. The next case was called and the litigants made their way to the counsel tables.

"The interviewers didn't think Absalom's story made sense and asked him whether he'd ever seen the *Zhorig*. They really didn't know what he was talking about but knew it sounded supernatural in nature. Ab—that's what he called himself—told them he had seen a *Zhorig*, during the Great War. That reference led Rome to send a team to Virginia to determine if any records might be located to address old Ab's story."

The bailiff's booming voice interrupted. "All rise. The court is in recess." Judge Friendly rose and left the courtroom. Malveaux could overhear the clerk saying the judge needed to take an emergency call.

Malveaux turned his full attention to Reese, but before Reese could continue, Doyle tapped him on the shoulder. "Father, I'm going out to make a couple of calls. Sit tight. They should be getting to our case soon."

Malveaux nodded and noticed several police officers out of the corner of his eye. Several other courtroom observers and a few lawyers left the room. Malveaux wanted to make sure Doyle was gone.

"Look, Father Reese, this is a little confusing for me. I read the B-416 file Lowell gave me. I think I read something about the *Zhorig* but I can't say I remember."

Reese cleared his throat. "The *Zhorig* was a vessel, a sailing ship. It was one of two ships believed to have survived a tsunami in the Caribbean in 1757. The vessel was one of the last slave ships to leave Africa that year. Accounts tell that during the course of the voyage, at least three of the captives, maybe more, made their way to the upper deck in chains and jumped into the ocean to their death.

"In his narrative, Old Absalom noted that a few of the remaining captives made their way to an island of San Marten sometime after the great storm struck."

Malveaux listened intently. "The interesting thing about Absalom's narrative is that it was so accurate," Reese said. "His description of the storm, as well as his account of the suicides, matches what was noted in other contemporaneous sources. We can date that event with precision to 1757. The date also coincides with the year the *Zhorig* sailed for the last time from the coast of Africa.

"The brutality of the crew was unimaginable. After the three captives left the ship, in order to instill fear in those remaining, the crew took three other captives and skinned them alive. Only a few of the crew survived the voyage, and those who returned to Europe told of strange happenings. A haunting. Each swore that they still saw the captives years later passing near them, their images always reflected in a nearby mirror, looking glass or pond.

"These appearances—of the walking ghosts, the suicide victims, the skinning—and possession by a demon have recurred since the beginning of what we know as the modern era. In other words, these spirits commandeer a human vessel, often a child or young person, in order to complete their journey. They seek revenge and retribution for the harm done to them."

Reese did not seem irrational or delusional. His strange words did not cause Malveaux to question the man's sanity based on what he'd read and seen during the past two days. Reese continued. "This particular manifestation is known as B-416. Its first recorded appearance was in 416 BCE in Mesopotamia, or modern-day Iraq."

Malveaux interrupted, "Cardinal Lowell said that it manifested in Constantinople in 416 AD. You're saying it's older, and it started elsewhere."

Reese cleared his throat again. Malveaux handed him a cough drop from his pocket. The judge would return in a minute or two and he wanted to hear the rest of the story.

"I'm sure that most of what Lowell told you was hearsay and just plain wrong. He hasn't studied this like I have. Lowell's mind isn't that sharp these days. You may have noticed. Anyway, you've heard all those stories about the early martyrs walking for miles through the hot sun carrying their own decapitated heads in their hands, or saints who didn't eat or drink food for twelve or more years, haven't you?" Malveaux nodded and chuckled. "Those are likely just stories," Reese said. "There are no eyewitnesses, no credibility. Some of what is in the Caine file is like that—just stories. I've pieced through the file to identify those manifestations that have some evidentiary credibility. The most detailed record of the manifestation is from the diary of Blessed Jon Tomas Núñes of St. Maarten."

Malveaux blurted excitedly. "Lowell is nominating Jon Tomas for sainthood. He wants to use Jon Tomas to draw attention from the altar boy claims."

"Yes. Jon Tomas of St. Maarten was reported to be a mystic with healing powers. He ministered to the impoverished and indentured himself to preach the gospel and although he couldn't free the enslaved men and women around him in St. Maarten, he worked without ceasing to bring them closer to God. He appears to have been a passenger of the *Zhorig* and worked his entire life to right the wrong perpetrated by his own father, who was part owner of the vessel. Some feel the pathology rested in the father. He was by all accounts a terrible man."

"I started reading the file last night. I've read some of what you're telling me."

"There are always the same signs, you know, Father," Reese whispered. "Always the suicides, the ghosts, and the vessel—that is, the person possessed and the skin. And there is the water, of course."

"The molestations are only a tangential aspect of the evil we are dealing with. The possession itself must be addressed. It was believed that Jon Tomas of St. Maarten destroyed the B-416 pathogen by a successful exorcism." Malveaux stared at Reese, listening and trying to absorb the implications of what he was saying. "When Lowell opened up the case for Jon Tomas of St. Maarten, quite a bit of research was undertaken, as you can imagine. Absalom Henry's narrative suggested that Jon Tomas was not successful and that the demon was still present and walking the earth—at least in Virginia."

The bailiff chatted with the courtroom clerk and took a phone call. Reese continued undeterred. "A team came to search for records to verify the occurrence at the time of the First World War."

"What kind of records?"

"Church records, police records, newspaper accounts…anything that told of a series of suicides or other strange occurrence."

"What did they find?" Malveaux's curiosity was piqued.

"Unfortunately…" Reese began to cough. Malveaux handed him another cough drop. Reese covered his mouth with a handkerchief and breathed deeply. Several of the cops across the courtroom turned to look in their direction. Malveaux nodded at them and smiled.

Reese spoke again, this time much more softly, as if the words were an effort for him. "They didn't find much. Suicides were not uncommon during wartime. The Spanish flu pandemic left so many dead that there were many cases of desperate people who'd lost loved ones and decided they could not go on.

"I became involved in 1943 when I was a seminarian in Rome. World War II made it difficult to travel. The church itself was in turmoil." Reese looked down and chuckled. "I was very low on the totem pole then. Still am. Some felt the church made compromises with the powers of evil—with the Nazis." He coughed some more. "When I finished my additional training, I was dispatched with two others to Washington, DC, for a period of time."

"What additional training?"

"I'll save that for another time, if you don't mind."

Malveaux nodded as if he understood. In reality, everything Reese was saying made sense. There was just something about him that made what he was saying seem so reliable. "During my visit, Father Malveaux, I had regular pastoral duties. In the fall of 1943, however, a telegram arrived and I was sent with two other priests to Loudoun County, near Leesburg. It seems a local pastor had written to his bishop, seeking advice on particular events that had occurred there that he considered to be satanic in nature. That letter made its way to the Vatican and then to us."

"What kind of events?"

Before Reese could go on, the bailiff interrupted. "Court will be in recess for at least another half hour, folks. Judge is tied up."

Malveaux spotted two female attorneys for the District of Columbia. The lead attorney was in deep discussion with another young woman he did not recognize. The attorney handed the other woman a large file. He heard her say, "I'll be back," and then she left the courtroom.

Reese continued. "There was a report of a spirit, a haunting by what they called a bone man. The thing was seen in the area, and there were several gruesome suicides. Then there was the telltale sign."

"You said something about water. What was it?"

Reese looked down. "A young boy drowned. We didn't find his body in the pond, just his skin folded nearby. His name was Harold Gamble. He had been skinned alive. Two young African American girls said they saw the Bone Man take Harold. The folder I gave you contains their interviews. You may need them."

"Did you interview them yourself?"

"No, my colleagues did. I saw them, though. Harold never really did well in school. His mother seemed to keep him with her a lot.

She was very overprotective. The girls said Harold started acting wild and had to be tied up at night. They said he made strange noises. Fear made the hair on their arms stand up. They all lived on the dependencies of The Oaks, as household servants and sharecroppers, I believe."

"In the 1940s?" Malveaux was astounded.

Reese laughed softly. "Virginia was still very much the capital of the Confederacy then. It was not a progressive place. The girls said Harold was enraged, screaming in a language they did not know, but that he said one word over and over again. '*Sorig.*' I think they were saying *Zhorig.*

"We arrived and tried to evaluate the boy, and we spent several nights with him." Reese looked directly at Malveaux. "I saw and heard him during those nights. There were things I cannot explain and do not understand." Malveaux did not respond. Reese said, "Before we could finish our work, he was found dead in a pond at the rear of the property. The girls said the Bone Man took him."

"What did the police do?"

"Well..." Reese paused. "They came, interviewed people. Took some pictures. Not much more. Police really didn't care much about the murder of a black child back then. They kept it very quiet. Claimed they didn't want to scare anybody. It was awful, really. Their prejudice kept them from searching for justice. I was interviewed. Everyone was. Nothing came of it. I returned to DC and then to Rome. We didn't hear any more for almost forty years. Then in the 1980s there was another occurrence. This time the victim was a John Doe. I was living in Pittsburgh at the time and was called in after the murder."

"Who was the victim?"

"The body was found in a garage in Leesburg. The victim was not identified. The police investigated but the trail was cold. There were many reports of satanic occurrences, but it was happening when an exorcism horror movie was showing in theaters. A local Baptist church held a revival, and some of the parishioners said the devil was walking in Leesburg because two young people had disappeared and were never located. That's about it."

Before Reese could continue, Judge Friendly breezed back into the courtroom with a flourish and called several cases. At last they reached Gaul's case. Ian Doyle went to counsel's table and prepared to make his arguments. The brief Doyle had filed was a motion to dismiss the District of Columbia's case. The attorney for the District was absent. Judge Friendly asked one of the other attorneys for the DC attorney general's office to come up to counsel's table and to represent the city.

Then Judge Friendly started his tirade. "Where's Ellen Campbell?"

The substitute attorney looked shaken. No one liked being dressed down in front of their peers, especially by Judge Friendly. He'd thrown lawyers into jail for contempt of court, and had a reputation for throwing items at them from the bench.

"Your Honor, she's handing a status hearing at the US District Court. She asked me to stand in for her."

Judge Friendly sneered with disapproval. "Well, Mr. Doyle, what's your pleasure?" He peered over his glasses, waiting for Doyle's response. "I've told the District a million times, I want counsel for record here for these motion hearings—not a replacement, not a second chair, and not a stand-in." Friendly was outraged.

Malveaux was astonished. Friendly sounded like he was about to dismiss the case against Gaul outright. *How could there ever be justice for these victims?* None of it made sense. It seemed like Gaul would go free in this DC case. The prosecuting attorney couldn't get her act together. The Charleroi case had parents who didn't want to testify against a man who had allegedly abused their child, and who wanted to use the settlement to help the perpetrator. The court system had no interest in justice. The cardinal had the audacity to try to shield church assets against another abuse scandal by trying to draw the attention of the community onto Jon Tomas Núñes's cause for sainthood. accusing the victim of demonic possession. Mr. Doyle cleared his throat and smiled at the court reporter as if he couldn't believe his good fortune. Then he calmly asked for the dismissal of all charges against Father Gaul.

Judge Friendly paused and pursed his lips. He began in a strong voice. "I am dismissing the case *DC v. Father Michael Gaul.* After having examined the pleadings of the District, I believe there is insufficient evidence to proceed. Several prominent persons have testified that Gaul was not in the District of Columbia at the time of the incidents. These prominent people, including members of the church hierarchy and former members of Congress, are quite credible. The evidence presented by the District of Columbia on behalf of the victims, on the other hand, can only be characterized as sparse and is barely circumstantial. The witnesses aren't specific at all and when I weigh what they have to say about Father Gaul's alibi, I must find in his favor. Moreover, the charging documents are a sloppy mess and lack the appropriate statutory basis to sustain grounds for prosecution. I looked up the statutes myself. It makes no sense that the District would charge the defendant with loitering and receiving stolen property. Clearly, someone just cut and pasted these pleadings together in a very sloppy manner. They're a mess regardless of the defendant's alibi."

Judge Friendly paused long enough for the court reporter to catch up. "I am very sympathetic in particular to the Gates family because the slipshod work presented on behalf of the prosecutors means that Father Gaul must go free today. It is clear that this is not the first criminal complaint against Father Gaul. From his record, I can see that approximately twenty-four years ago, he was charged in the District with assault of a minor. He received probation for misdemeanor assault. The other charges in the late 1980s, let's see…" He leafed through the file. "Yes, 1981 and 1987 were not prosecuted. Both charges involved alleged indecency with a minor."

The clerk continued to sip her Starbucks drink and took notes as the judge spoke.

"In both instances the victims refused to testify." Judge Friendly looked at the defense table and pointed directly at Father Gaul. "Apparently these issues with you just keep coming up. It's not enough, however, to put together a sloppy case here in the District and expect me to let this case proceed. I should have you sanctioned, madam, because I think the District filed these papers in an effort to keep Gaul off the streets while it tried to get its act together.

"I am acutely aware, Father Gaul, that your name continues to be associated with other claims in this city that will likely be consolidated into what the newspapers are calling 'the altar boy cases.'"

The courtroom spectators looked at Gaul, who gazed ahead, expressionless.

"Father Gaul, there isn't enough to hold you today, but I want you to know that if I ever see you in my courtroom again, I'm going to make sure that all parties are prepared to proceed so that justice can be served. But for now, you're free to go. I'm dismissing the case without prejudice. That means that when the District finally gets its act together it can re-file these charges."

Judge Friendly stood abruptly. "All rise," bellowed the bailiff as the judge exited the courtroom.

Malveaux pushed past Reese and hurried to join Doyle and Amber West as they were leaving. Ellen Campbell, the lead attorney for the District was coming in the door as they were exiting.

"What just happened?" she asked, looking scared.

Amber smiled. "He dismissed it," she said and kept walking.

None of their party spoke. As they made their way to the escalator, Malveaux could see clerks, lawyers, and defendants milling around the floor below. Having the criminal case dismissed would save the church money in the civil claims filed in the altar boy cases which were set to go to trial the following year. Another injustice, he concluded as they made their way past security onto Indiana Avenue. Gaul followed closely behind Ian Doyle but did not look up and did not speak to him. He maintained a silent, steely gaze as Doyle explained that the case might be refiled, but only under very strict circumstances.

A middle-aged African American man wearing an overcoat called out to them as they passed the low concrete barrier circling the courthouse. Several men and women sat on the barrier, smoking cigarettes and talking on cell phones.

"Father Gaul." The man stood up, tears streaming down his cheeks. His words captured the attention of those nearby, who directed their collective gaze on the man. "Julius Gates is my son and nobody hurts my boy!" he screamed.

Malveaux could see what was happening but could not react. The man pulled a sawed-off shotgun from his overcoat. Malveaux quickly grabbed Amber West and threw her to the ground as Ian Doyle ran in the direction of D Street.

The intensity of the gun blast scattered the crowd in all directions. As Malveaux tackled Amber to the ground, he saw Gaul's head blown back and felt hot blood splash onto his cheeks. "Forgive me, Lord," the shooter said, and then placed the shotgun under his chin and pulled the trigger, pulverizing his skull and raining blood and bone fragments onto Malveaux's shoulder and Amber West's trench coat. Silence surrounded him. He could see people screaming, women and men and a police officer covering their mouths in horror, he just couldn't seem to hear clearly.

Several minutes passed and at last the silence was broken. An ambulance materialized and police officers cordoned off the area with yellow tape. A voice on the courthouse's public address system announced that the building was on lockdown until further notice. Malveaux could see Doyle sat in the back of an ambulance, giving an interview to a frazzled-looking police officer. Doyle's expression was a mix of anger, fear, confusion, and rage. He was crying and gesturing and shaking his head as if he didn't know what had happened.

Gaul's body lay on the sidewalk, his face unrecognizable. His jaw-bone rested several feet behind him. It was being photographed by a forensics crew. The shooter was also unrecognizable. His body was covered by a sheet that was being blown by a gentle wind, giving the eerie impression that the shooter wanted to get right up and go on about his business.

A local news crew stood twenty feet to his right, and behind him was David Levin of *The Secret*. A middle-aged officer helped Malveaux up from the ground. That was all he remembered. A policewoman comforted the hysterical Amber West, whose face was streaked with blood not her own.

***

Police officers shuttled Reese away from the others being interviewed at the crime scene.

"Darrien Reese?" asked one officer, an older white man.

"Yes, how can I help you?"

The other officer, younger and Hispanic, responded, "You are under arrest, Mr. Reese. Please turn around. You have the right to remain silent. Anything you say can and will be used against you in a court of law. You have the right to an attorney. If you cannot afford an attorney, one will be appointed for you."

Reese was speechless as the white officer handcuffed his wrists and walked him to the squad car. "We have a warrant for your arrest and you will be remanded to the custody of the Loudoun County sheriff."

CHAPTER
EIGHTEEN

A black Lincoln Town Car pulled up beside the curb. A man emerged, undaunted by the overwhelming police presence. Malveaux recognized him from the rectory. The man searched the crowd until his gaze fell on Malveaux. He approached and held out his hand. "Father Malveaux, I hope you're all right."

Malveaux stared, unable to understand what the man was saying. The man raised his voice. "Cardinal Lowell wants me to bring you back to the rectory."

Malveaux nodded, holding tight to his briefcase. It had never left his hands during the ordeal. He followed the man into the back of the Lincoln, where he wept gently.

They returned to the rectory without incident. As they reached their destination, Malveaux could hear the radio reporting that a shooting had occurred minutes earlier at the DC Superior Court, and noted the victim and shooter were both dead.

The next thing he knew he was sitting in Cardinal Lowell's study, waiting for him to finish dictating a statement to the press—something about not taking the law into one's own hands and letting the justice system work. Then there was something about God's grace and forgiveness and his ultimate judgment in all things. The aide taking the dictation did not look at Malveaux, but promised Lowell he'd have a draft back right away for his review.

Lowell turned to Malveaux and looked at him intently. Malveaux realized his hands were trembling as he poured a glass of water for himself from the pitcher on the side table near Lowell's desk.

Lowell was angry. "What happened? I can't believe Gaul is dead. Is it true? I have just spoken to Mr. and Mrs. Charleroi. They are beside themselves. They are going to be lost without him."

Malveaux took a pill from his breast pocket, popped it into his mouth, and washed in down with the rest of his water. His hearing had not fully returned, and he hoped he had not heard Lowell correctly. He remembered Father Reese walking off with two officers. What had happened to him? Why hadn't he ridden back with him to the rectory?

"I suppose I have to tell you the rest now, Malveaux. I need to come totally clean." Lowell sipped from his glass, and a trickle of fluid ran from the corner of his mouth. "I have something to show you, but first I have something to tell you." Lowell stood and walked to a nearby window as he spoke. "Father Gaul was a problem for many years. We did move him around. We got him counseling. We tried to keep him away from young people. This practice preceded my arrival at the archdiocese. As a student, Gaul's spiritual gifts never became clear. He did not teach or work in a parish like we did. I suppose Gaul's friendship with Charleroi helped him gain access to those parishes in DC. I suppose when there was trouble with his son, Charleroi probably thought Gaul would be able to help, and that he'd get some more insight on what was going on in the house since he was living apart from his wife. He'd known Gaul for most of his life, you know."

Malveaux took another sip of water, his tremor more noticeable this time. "You see, Malveaux, when Gaul went to The Oaks, Marissa Charleroi asked him to perform an exorcism on her son."

Malveaux stared ahead, his eyes fixed on the tapestry. There were so many charges against Gaul wherever he went. How was it that Charleroi hadn't known about them? Why hadn't Lowell told him about the exorcism? Was this what Reese was trying to tell him?

Lowell made his way back to his desk chair. "I know it is hard to understand. Charleroi thought all those charges against Gaul were fabricated. He used his influence, at Gaul's request, to get the charges dismissed." The cardinal sat and rested his head on the back of his chair. He closed his eyes and continued talking. "Gaul was performing an exorcism on the Charlerois' son, Sam, at the time these charges were leveled. Charleroi encouraged Marissa to let Gaul come out to their house and Gaul at some point they must have decided to let him perform the rite of exorcism, as they were convinced the boy was possessed. Gaul let some of his friends in on what he was doing. He was reprimanded, of course, and was highly unsuitable for this work due to his background. He was, by all accounts, a very sick individual. There was child pornography involved. A real network of very sick and scary people is involved."

Lowell drank from his water glass and shook his head in exasperation. "I suppose some of this is my fault too. I wanted to be close to Leon Charleroi. I thought he might be able to make some significant donations and that he would introduce me to some of his wealthy friends. I thought having Gaul around would help convince Charleroi to give a large donation to the church." He stood and faced Malveaux. "It's even worse…perhaps I should have told you. The idea about Jon Tomas Nūnes…it came from Gaul. I didn't think it was a bad idea to focus attention elsewhere. His friend J.D. Hunt, who's also Charleroi's lawyer, thought it was a brilliant idea. When we put his cause forward, the church began its investigation but ran into a roadblock from Reese, who became convinced that B-416 had reemerged from time to time, and therefore Jon Tomas had not accomplished his mission. I still think he's saint material because of all the enslaved people he helped. His work really has a valid message for the oppressed. That's when Reese came over from Rome and I sent him out to help Gaul. Reese has been chasing this thing for years, but it didn't want to deal with him. For some reason, it wanted you."

Malveaux remembered "B-416" from the haunting video he'd watched with Lowell and from the papers he'd examined from the archdiocese. Reese had also mentioned it.

"Sam was a classic host, or vessel, in the truest sense of the word," Lowell said. "He grew up unbaptized. We know a christening was scheduled shortly after his birth, but it did not occur due to a blizzard. It was never rescheduled."

Malveaux watched Lowell closely, trying to read his lips. He looked down at his pant legs and saw streaks of blood from the afternoon's massacre.

"We knew he did not have a mother in the truest sense of the word," the cardinal went on. "I'll have someone else explain it to you because I don't really understand the biology of it all, but we looked at Marissa's records, pulled them from the hospital files the same day you got here. Sam Charleroi was in close proximity to the direct summoning of the demon because of those lunatics his mother picked up at that bar. They didn't know what they were dealing with. They all died at the jail in Leesburg. Murder and suicides. The demon's presence was confirmed by a woman with psychic ability. She was seen on the premises both before and after her death, as were all of the walking ghosts associated with the phenomena."

Malveaux tried to make out Lowell's words. He had faith, but did it extend this far? Was his concept of a devil really an explanation for man's own inhumanity to man? Wasn't demon possession easily explained by other diagnoses? Wasn't it just another name for mental illness, mental personality disorder, seizures, or an idiot savant's gift of language?

The cardinal spoke, "I've just gotten off the phone with Hennigan from your office."

"Hennigan?" Malveaux was confused.

"I've asked him to send your files. You know—the files you've been working on. I've asked my assistant to help you for the next few weeks. You're going to need help."

Malveaux did not understand. "Look, Cardinal, you're treating all this like a game. I thought I was coming out here to talk about these cases. I thought you wanted to talk to me in detail before you began settlement discussions on the altar boy cases. I just don't know what to say."

Lowell looked at Malveaux sternly and did not smile. He closed his eyes and rubbed his temples as he spoke. "Yes, I fully intend to work on these files with you while you are here. Maybe they can be all settled quickly now that the criminal cases against Gaul will be closed. They can't put a dead man on trial. However, the matter of B-416 will also require considerable attention on our part for at least the next several days."

Malveaux was exasperated. "Several days?" Things were becoming more confusing the more Lowell spoke. "I don't understand. I have a flight back to Minneapolis. It was already moved forward a day to tomorrow night."

Lowell retrieved an apple with his left hand and continued to stroke his hair with his right hand. He did not look at Malveaux but closed his eyes with heavy fatigue as he spoke.

"Your official work, to any and all who ask, is related to the investigation and settlement of the altar boy cases. Indeed, I have arranged a number of meetings with our lawyers. There will be an expedited pretrial conference and a series of mediation talks with the magistrate judge assigned to the case. We can get these cases settled Malveaux."

Lowell did not open his eyes. Malveaux could not gauge his response. "Cardinal Lowell, you just sent me the details of the Charleroi case a few weeks ago. I expected that I'd talk to you about it when I came here. But since I've been here I've learned the case is in a really different posture. You've already made a settlement offer on the case without even telling me about it." Malveaux raised his voice. "You know I'm not well. In the past two days I've had an angina attack. They say I probably need a pacemaker. I narrowly missed being shot to death at the courthouse, and I had Father Gaul's brains blown out all over my pants. Gaul's dead, but you're right the civil cases, the cases that are all about the money and the damages will go on. I didn't get the chance to interview Gaul. He never even underwent the independent competency exams requested by the court. We aren't going to be able to make a defense in those cases. How do you think I can have all this ready in a few days?"

Smoky, defiant anger seeped from the corners of Lowell's eyes. "You're not stupid. You knew the Charleroi case would never go to trial, Malveaux. Political reasons would have kept that from ever happening. Charleroi is a powerful man. He would never want this story about his son and his occultist wife to get out. That wouldn't go over very well with his conservative Christian supporters and investors now, would it?" Lowell bit in to the apple with great satisfaction. "In fact, I was close to moving the Jon Tomas Núnes case forward for beatification until the church investigation team got the DNA results back from the lab."

Malveaux screamed back, exasperated, "I don't understand!"

Lowell leaned back in his seat. "Charleroi wants to settle his civil case. That frees up the money you would have spent on your defense of Gaul to help settle all the altar boy claims now." He leaned forward and whispered, "Perhaps the appearance of B-416 is a coincidence. I don't know. But I know that we must stop it."

"We?" exclaimed Malveaux. "What do you mean by we? And besides that. The money you saved on the Charleroi case won't come close to paying the claims for the altar boy cases. You know that!" A range of emotions flooded his mind. Malveaux's head throbbed. He needed to lie down.

"What I'm trying to tell you is that you need to prepare yourself for what is ahead. You will be spending the next few days exorcising this demon, and that's not a lot of time, I tell you."

"Cardinal Lowell, I don't have any idea what you're talking about or what kind of games you're playing with my head right now. I don't want any part of it." He stood, shaking, and prepared to leave.

Lowell stood in response, raising his voice in anger. "Look, Malveaux, whether you like it or not, that thing is asking for you. It has selected you—not me, not anyone else—as its challenger. In calling you by name, it has followed the pattern of selecting its challenger. This has been the pattern for thousands of years. And I know you just got here and you're upset and maybe even ill, but that's just too damn bad. All of us have to catch up on the learning curve on this thing and right now."

Lowell slammed his palm on the desk, causing a pen to fall to the floor. "I've read some of the file," he said. "I know that B-416 is an aquatic, nonluminary, recurrent host that has appeared in the past when prurient behavior has been recorded. I know that the demon manifests and seeks a vessel, or host, and that this means it has not been successfully exorcised. I know that it calls for its challenger and that it has called you. I know that each challenger has been a man of great holiness, insight, and faith, and I know that you fit that bill." Lowell grew red in the face. Veins bulged at the side of his neck and temple. A thin trickle of blood drained from his right nostril.

"I also know that we've lost two days here fucking around trying to learn what's going on out there, and that we can't waste any more time because if we do, this thing will escape into the world. That, Malveaux, will make your altar boy cases look like an afternoon at Disney World." Lowell grew pale now, wiping the blood that had trickled down to his upper lip. "You need to pick up where Gaul and Reese left off. You need to finish reading the damn file and get busy. You need to do it now."

"Let Reese do it. You didn't even tell me about him, he just showed up at the courthouse. Let him do it!" Malveaux raged.

"He can't do it. He can't help you. He was arrested this afternoon and transferred to the custody by those idiots out there in Leesburg. They put him in a holding cell. Can you believe doing that to a man his age? We've gotten him bailed out and he's in the hospital out there. He got beaten up pretty badly in jail. He can't do much of anything right now. It's got to be you. You have to do it. Don't you get it?" The cardinal stormed from the room, leaving Malveaux even more alone and afraid.

CHAPTER

NINETEEN

Leesburg, Virginia

Luby returned to his office from the city council executive session on the earthquake and the murder/suicides at the jail that had occurred earlier in the year. The meeting had been brief. Luby reported that the matter was still under investigation and that a report on the earthquake was forthcoming from the National Geologic Survey. After promising to provide a full report in the future, he returned to his office, where the intern was waiting.

"OK, Sheriff, I finished your assignment."

Luby looked at her squarely. This woman had sat in his office with him half a dozen times. Even so, he would have been hard pressed to describe her to anyone else. He still could not seem to get her name straight. He hadn't given her any other assignments because she hadn't finished the one important one he'd given her.

"I ran the prints from the Gamble file against the national fingerprint database. They aren't the greatest prints, and they didn't match anything in the database, but the analyst I spoke to said he'd try to enhance them and run them again." The girl smiled. "The fingerprint tech and his wife had quadruplets believe it or not. He's been on family medical leave for months. He had so many messages from me that he ran those prints I sent as soon as he got back to work. You'll like this, though. The unidentified prints in the Gamble file did match a set of prints found at the John Doe site. Those prints were lifted off the side of the station wagon in the garage. They didn't match the victim or known family members. It also matches an unidentified print from the Charleroi house."

Luby's ears perked up. Two sets of identical prints, forty years apart. "Were you able to identify the prints? Did you run them to see if we can get a match?"

Kristine or Krissy or whatever-her-name-was continued. "I thought it was interesting about the Gamble case."

"What was interesting?" Luby asked. Why couldn't this girl just get right to the point?

"There was a witness, a girl, who said she saw Gamble go off with someone she called the Bone Man."

"Was she ever identified?" Luby probed. "Who was she?"

The girl did not look up but traced her finger over her notes. "It looks like she was just a kid. I don't think the investigators took what she had to say seriously."

"What was her name?"

"From what I can tell, her name was Mae Etta Turner."

Luby did the best he could to drag the information out of the intern. "How old was she in 1943?"

"She was nine."

"What happened to her?" Luby felt like he was pulling teeth to get answers out of this girl.

"Well, Sheriff, she's also referenced in the John Doe file."

"In what way?" Luby remembered the name from the 1983 case. Mae Etta had been a neighbor, a middle-aged black woman who had been interviewed but hadn't seen or heard anything.

"What makes you think they're the same witness?"

The girl looked up. "Just a hunch. They both had the same first name, a pretty unusual one. How many people do you know named Mae Etta?"

Luby stood up and walked to the window. It was starting to get dark. Days were so short in the fall. It made him feel like he came to work in the middle of the night and left work in the middle of the night.

"They also had the same birthday."

Liz knocked on his door and entered, interrupting the discussion. "Sheriff Luby, Charleroi's assistant just called. He said Charleroi can see you if you're able to get over there in in about two hours."

Luby grabbed his jacket from the coat rack and barked, "Tell Snyder to meet me in the parking lot." He turned back to the intern. "What was the address of that Mae Etta woman?"

Kristy wrote the address on a sheet of paper and handed it to Luby, who grabbed it and made his way out of the office. The address was close by. He could see her first and then visit Charleroi.

***

Luby and his deputy met at the squad car. According to the telephone directory, Ms. Rock's house was two or three blocks from the station. Luby figured they probably could have walked there as quickly as it took them to drive to her house. As they approached, he saw a La-Z-Boy recliner on the front porch. According to his records, Ms. Mae Etta Rock was almost seventy years old. He'd likely find her at home midafternoon, watching Oprah or Judge Judy.

He knocked and knocked again. No one answered the door. Luby slid his business card into the frame of the screen. He'd try to talk to one of the other witnesses, Darrel Hawk, who lived in Ashburn, before he headed back to meet Charleroi. He could swing back by Ms. Rock's place tomorrow.

***

Luby and his deputy approached the house on Garden Gate Circle. A hefty man who looked to be in his forties was using a leaf blower to collect fall foliage into a large tarp in the middle of the yard.

"Hawk?" Luby and Snyder walked closer. The man turned off the blower and looked at them. His eyes were rimmed with dark circles. He did not smile.

Snyder pulled his badge from his pocket and presented his credentials. "Mr. Hawk, we only need a few minutes of your time. I called your command center and they said you were on medical leave. I thought I'd be able to catch you here."

Hawk looked at them and then at the ground. "That's right."

"How're you doing?" Luby inquired. He turned to Snyder, "I know Hawk from way back."

Hawk looked at Snyder and then at Luby. "I just need some time to get my head together." Hawk looked down again and then up at Luby. "My wife's at work. We can go in the kitchen and talk."

Hawk was jumpy. His face was puffy. Every other minute he looked over his shoulder, as if he feared someone was watching him from behind. They entered the kitchen through a side door. Hawk poured coffee into matching mugs, offered cream and sugar, and sat down with Luby and Snyder at the kitchen table. No one spoke for several minutes.

"Look, I know why you're here," Hawk said.

Luby drank from his mug. The coffee was pretty good. Hawk looked like coffee was the last thing he needed, though.

"I haven't been back to work since that night, the night Gaul was arrested. I heard some big ass lawyer friend of Charleroi's flew up on his private jet up here and had him out on bail within a few hours," Hawk said. Luby nodded and listened. "I had been on leave the week before everything went down. I took about a week. That was my first night back on duty. It had been really stressful working there with all that was happening. My nerves were shot, just like all the other guys. The company was giving us extra leave to keep us motivated."

Hawk began to tremble as he spoke. "When I went to the room that night, I just..." Tears leaked from his eyes. Hawk was one of the biggest men Luby had ever seen. He was enormous really, huge, like a night club bouncer. He wasn't the type to be crying in a coffee mug at his kitchen table during the middle of the day. Luby had known him as a rookie officer at the police academy. Hawk had transferred to the Secret Service and then later to a private security outfit. Luby had known him for years and considered him solid. Now here Hawk was, sitting at his kitchen table and crying like a little kid. It was like a switch had been thrown and the tears just got turned on.

"When I went upstairs that night, there were sounds and things like I'd never heard before. Just unnatural." Hawk put his coffee down and placed his head in his hands. His voice dropped to a whisper.

"I opened the door and that's when I saw Ms. Rock helping pull Marissa and Gaul away from the boy. I passed out. They said I was talking nonsense when I came to."

Luby took another sip of coffee. "What kind on nonsense?"

"There was a thing in the room, Sheriff. I put it all in my statement and they tore it up."

Snyder spoke up for the first time. "What kind of thing?"

Hawk looked Luby in the eyes. "I've known you for a long time, Luby. If I tell you, you're going to think I'm nuts."

"Go on, Hawk. What did you see in there?"

Hawk paused several minutes then spoke, "I saw this weird skeleton man, a devil thing. It was on the boy, like it was coming out of him. I can't even explain it."

Snyder looked at Luby but did not speak. Hawk continued, "And then Ms. Rock was there, but she couldn't have been."

"What do you mean?"

Hawk was shaking now. His hands and voice trembled. "When I left my shift on the morning of the first—that was my last workday before my vacation—Route 15 was backed up because on an accident, a fatal crash. I got out of my car and walked up to the scene to see if I could help." Tears streamed from his eyes.

"Go on, Hawk."

Hawk paused again. "I saw the rescue squad pull Ms. Rock out of the car. They used the Jaws of Life to get her out. There was so much blood...she was crushed all on her left side. When I called The Oaks,

I didn't get an answer. The answering machine was full and I didn't even get to leave a message to see if they knew. The next day the accident was all over the papers, but no name was released. They were trying to get in touch with her son. He was in Delaware visiting his ex-wife and kids. I sent a sympathy card to the family because I liked her. I knew her and she was a nice lady."

Hawk trembled, "So you see, when I went back to The Oaks and saw her there that night, it just didn't make sense, you know?" He looked up, pleading. "You were there that night, Luby. You probably saw her too."

Luby did remember. One of his deputies had pointed Ms. Rock out to him. She was sitting at the kitchen table. She'd asked to give her statement later, and the deputy asked Luby if that was OK. Luby had said it was fine because it was so late, and that was the last he'd thought about it. He'd been tied up with campaigning for the election that week. He knew the elderly victim of the Route 15 crash had not been identified at the scene, as she had no purse or identification on her. When she was identified, her name wasn't released for several days, pending notification of kin. He remembered that the woman's son lived with her but was away in Delaware at the time of the accident. Luby had been so busy, he never found out the victim's name. The report was still sitting in his inbox. He'd never even looked at it.

"So you know, I hit my head when I passed out," Hawk said. "My supervisor said it was better not to file my statement about the devil thing and Ms. Rock because it would keep me off the job."

Snyder nodded. He clearly believed Hawk was ready for an extended inpatient stay at the psychiatric hospital. Luby's mouth was dry. He drank more coffee as Hawk continued speaking. "I've been on short-term disability leave. My counselor says that when I hit my head, I must have suffered some type of concussion and that my 'delusions'"—he made air quotations—"are most likely related to the injury."

"That sounds reasonable to me," Luby said. He stood and extended his hand. "You get better now." Snyder nodded.

"You know me, man," Hawk stammered. "I'm ashamed to even talk about it."

Luby nodded in agreement and left the kitchen with Snyder. The two men made their way back to the police department. Snyder was talking nonstop about Hawk's statement, but Luby didn't hear or say a thing. When they reached Luby's office, Luby made a beeline for his inbox. He found the accident report near the bottom of his pile. He read the document and threw it down on the desk. The crash victim had died at the scene on November 1. She was positively identified by her pastor as Mae Etta Rock, age sixty-nine, of Leesburg.

CHAPTER TWENTY

Luby went to the Charleroi residence. Leon Charleroi was waiting for him in the formal parlor. A twelve ounce glass of amber liquid sat within reach of his right hand. As Luby approached and greeted the former Congressman with a firm handshake, he confirmed that Charleroi was drinking whisky. An aide sat on a chair near the bookcase.

"Ross, you're free to go," Charleroi said. "I'll call you back in when I need you." The aide nodded and left the room by a rear door.

Luby sat down across from Charleroi. "Kinda early for whisky, isn't it, Mr. Charleroi?"

Charleroi took another sip, grabbed a second, smaller glass, and slid it across the table to Luby. "Sheriff, get yourself a drink. You're probably going to need it." He laughed and chugged the rest of his drink in one long gulp. Then he reached in his desk, pulled out a bottle of whisky, and poured himself another drink. Luby didn't blame Charleroi for drinking whisky at in the afternoon. He'd probably have a drink too if he were in the same position.

"Sir, I need some information from you."

Charleroi looked down. His confidence, bravado, and self-assurance were gone. The man looked like hell. Like he hadn't slept for days. He was weeping and distraught, barely able to get his words out. "Don't you get it? Gaul is dead. Father Gaul is dead."

Luby was taken aback. That would bring his investigation of Gaul to an end. There would be no need to gather evidence against someone who would never go to trial. But there was more at stake here. More that did not add up. "When?"

"Late this morning in DC at the courthouse. It's all over the news. "Charleroi continued, slurring his speech, "I can't tell you anything. You need to talk to my wife."

Luby pressed forward, undeterred. "My men took some information from the sign-in sheets at your house the night of the incident. I need for you to tell me all you know about the other priest who was here that night with Father Gaul. He left before we could talk to him. I need to know what you know about him."

Charleroi was evasive. "She's not here. You need to talk to Marissa. Have you been able to talk to Sam at all?"

"We'll get the opportunity to interview him when he's doing better. He's probably sedated."

Charleroi looked up. "Well, that's probably best under the circumstances."

"Mr. Charleroi, there are welts and cuts and bruises all over that boy's body. Do you want to tell me what's going on here? I'm about ready to bring you and your wife in."

Charleroi took another long drink, and then refilled his glass. "Well, Sheriff, if you interview the staff and the security men, they'll tell you this is the first time I've been here in several weeks."

Luby tried not to betray surprise. Charleroi continued, "My wife and I are separated. I've been staying at my condo in DC for some time. We'll be divorced as soon as I can establish we've lived apart for a year." Charleroi sloshed his drink onto the desk and onto his shirt. "I asked those damned security guys to keep me informed about everything. The night when this thing went down, my man made a report to Social Services. I asked him to."

Charleroi started crying again. "Every time I see my boy, he's got welts on him. I thought she was hurting him to get back at me, just because she's an evil, dirty bitch." He rubbed his mouth on his sleeve. "Gaul was helping. He was going to make it better and now he's dead and I can't find the other guy who was helping him."

Charleroi's comments about the divorce made sense. Luby had learned from the hospital staff that the wife and husband had both visited the hospital in the past forty-eight hours, but never together. Luby had seen Mrs. Charleroi there and she was not what he had expected. She looked like a drinker. He noticed several of her teeth were broken, reminding him of the meth addicts he'd arrested dozens of times. She seemed anxious but slept long hours in the chair next to her son's bed during her daytime visits.

Luby pressed further. "I also need to ask you some questions about Mrs. Rock, and what she was doing here and I need to know what Gaul and the other priest were doing here." He did not inquire further about Charleroi's marriage; it was not his business, after all.

Charleroi took another long drink and belched loudly. "Ms. Rock lives in Leesburg. Her boy, Vaughn, has been doing some work for me on the security system. I've known her for years. Ross can get you the address. She hasn't been here for about a week. Just stopped showing up for work. The priests are Father Gaul, whom I've known for years—he's from DC, or was—and the other is Father Reese, from Rome. He's here working out of the Washington Archdiocese."

Luby waited as Charleroi took another long drink. "Ms. Rock is dead you know. Killed in a car crash. What were they doing here that night?"

Charleroi took another drink and burst into hysterical sobs. "All they were trying to do was help. I wasn't here, you know."

"What kind of help?"

Charleroi met Luby's gaze but didn't answer. "I said, what kind of help were they giving your son?" Luby asked again.

"Spiritual help," Charleroi said finally.

Luby was puzzled. "Spiritual?"

Charleroi nodded. "That's what I said, spiritual." The man took another drink and did not elaborate.

"Thank you. I'll get that information from Reese. I will need a number where I can reach you by phone. I expect you'll be hearing from Social Services about the boy."

Charleroi took a sheet from the engraved memo pad on his desk and scribbled a few numbers. "You can reach me here at either one of these numbers."

Luby closed his notebook and prepared to leave. "Where's your wife? Is she at the hospital?"

Charleroi belched loudly, "How the hell should I know?"

Luby nodded and thanked him, folded the paper and placed it in his front breast pocket, and then left to see if he could talk to the boy or his mother at the hospital.

Luby checked his Blackberry as he sat in his squad car. There was a message from Liz telling him to listen to his voice mail. He punched in his code and listened as Deputy Westin spoke excitedly.

"Sheriff, the fingerprint tech did it. We got a positive match on those prints. They belong to Darien Jason Reese. I couldn't get a hold of you so I asked the DA to get a warrant for his arrest as a suspect in the 1983 cold case. You aren't going to believe this. We lucked out. The guy traveled into the country about two weeks ago from Rome. We got his prints when he entered the country. He was taken into custody by the DC police about an hour ago and our deputies are heading out to pick him up. and listen to this Gaul's been shot. Shot and killed at the DC courthouse."

Luby reminded himself. He needed to listen to his messages more frequently.

***

Luby drove to Loudoun County Hospital. He was used to the old hospital in Leesburg. The new hospital was modern and full of conveniences, with a nearby professional medical building. But it just didn't hold any memories for him like the old hospital did. He heard the plan was to tear the old building down.

The sheriff made his way to the second floor, turned right, and proceeded through the ICU to Room 536. An orderly was mopping the hallway. Luby navigated around two yellow "Wet Floor" signs. He peeked into the room but the boy was gone. An elderly woman lay in the bed.

"Sheriff?"

Luby turned to face a portly nurse with bright red hair. "He was moved to the fourth floor," she said. Then she whispered, "He's on the psychiatric ward."

Luby did not respond, hoping she'd say more.

"He was out of control. I've never seen anything like it." He noticed the woman was wearing a stethoscope around her neck. Her name badge read "Anne." She looked around.

"What do you mean? What happened?" Luby found himself whispering even though there was no good reason to do so.

Anne shook her head. "I don't know. All I can tell you is that he was the only one in there. His mother had gone to get something to eat and probably to have a smoke. It sounded like a hundred people were fighting in his room."

The hair on Luby's neck rose. The woman looked around again to see if anyone was listening. "Dr. Cohen ran in with me and Katherine Rodriguez, who was making the meal delivery. We found him sitting in the corner with his hands and arms over his head." She pulled Luby by the arm into a corner and whispered, "Every piece of furniture was upside down and stacked up in a corner. I took a picture with my cell phone. See?"

Anne pulled out her phone and showed the picture to Luby. Every single piece of furniture in the room—the chairs, hospital bed, IV stand, trash cans, everything—was stacked in the northwest corner of the room. "I don't see how he did it," she went on. "He's a puny thing. I had just been in there two minutes earlier to check his vital signs. I even looked at the security tape. No one went in or out after me. Now I'm just waiting for my shift relief so I can go home. Something isn't right. I just know it doesn't feel right."

Luby gestured to the cell phone. "Can you send me that photo?"

"Here. There's a video too. I don't have time to show it to you now." Anne handed it to him. Luby entered his work e-mail and home address and forwarded the picture and video to himself for the file. Then his own phone vibrated. It was his deputy, Snyder.

"Yeah, what's going on?" Luby asked. "I got your message about Reese. Did our guys pick up him up yet from DC? I want to speak to him if you have."

Snyder coughed. "Sheriff, DCPD picked him up and transferred him to us pretty quickly. I sent two officers to get him, and they found he'd been beaten up pretty badly by one of the other inmates in the holding cell. He kicked in the groin area and has some cracked ribs."

"What?" exclaimed Luby.

"We brought him right over to the hospital; he's there now being treated. Had a broken nose, and the dude who did this tried to bite off his face. He was beaten up pretty bad. He's an old guy."

"My God. What room is he in?"

"Liz says she sent you a text. He's in Room 845. Are you still over there?"

"Yeah, I am. I'd better go and check in on him."

"They said they'll be keeping him for at least a couple of days. The ER doctor said something about sewing his lower lip back on."

Luby gulped hard. The thought of a torn lip made him queasy.

"You need to come back over to the office, Sheriff. We've got the mayor here making a scene, demanding to see you. We got a heads up that the Justice Department has asked for a federal civil rights investigation of the jail suicides. Some advocacy group said we didn't do enough to assess their mental condition before we locked them up."

Luby was speechless. He'd never known the Justice Department to move so quickly. He bet it all had to do with Charleroi and all his bullshit. He looked down at his Blackberry. It didn't have a charge. He would need to go back to his car and charge his phone for a bit. He was sure he was going to need his phone.

***

After charging his phone for about 20 minutes, Luby made his way from the parking lot back into the county hospital. From the messages he was getting it looked like Reese was a tough old bastard and was improving. Luby walked down the ramp of the parking garage to ground level. An exhausted-looking man passed him carrying several Mylar balloons welcoming a new baby girl into the world. Luby exited the garage and walked to the entrance, bypassing the information desk and moving directly to the stairwell. Liz's message on his Blackberry indicated that Reese was in room 845.

Snyder texted him that Reese might be able to talk. He said that Reese currently had a visitor—another priest, Robert Malveaux. The deputy on duty texted that Malveaux had wandered down to the cafeteria. Luby decided to go down to the basement and see if he could find him there. It was early, near the shift change; the day shift was winding down.

Luby hated hospitals. They reminded him of his mother's long struggle with cancer. He surveyed the cafeteria and didn't see anyone fitting Malveaux's description. He followed the hallway back to the elevator to the second floor. He breezed past the nurse's station and a young lab technician. The brightness of the florescent lighting hurt his eyes. The door to Room 845 was slightly ajar. As he moved to push the door open, a voice startled him.

"May I help you? Visiting hours are suspended when we administer our afternoon meds and serve meals."

Luby turned to survey the overweight nurse whose territory he had invaded. He pulled his badge from his breast pocket and showed her his credentials. "I'm Sheriff Roger Luby. I need to talk to the patient, ma'am."

The woman examined his credentials and returned them. "I'll have to ask the doctor. The patient already has a visitor from the archdiocese. He is in a very groggy state. He's elderly. I can't believe you had him arrested like that."

Luby ignored her. It would make sense for the archdiocese to send one of their own to look after Reese. "Ma'am, this is a matter of police business. I really need to see if I can get information from Reese before…"

"Before something else happens to him?" she interjected.

"That's right, before something else happens. He's a murder suspect, ma'am."

The woman looked at Luby and to the door, seeming to change her mind about how she felt about her elderly patient. "Go ahead, but I didn't see you. It might take me a little while to reach the doctor anyway."

A deputy waited in the area immediately inside the room. A curtain surrounded an area concealing Reese's bed. The deputy rose to greet Luby.

"Sheriff, he's asleep."

Luby grimaced. "Is his visitor here?"

"Yeah," he whispered. Here's his card. He said something about going to the cafeteria to get some coffee in case Reese woke up before he had to head back to DC. He asked me to page him if Reese woke up. He just came back up here a few minutes ago. He's been in there reading."

Luby took the card and read it. *Robert Malveaux, Attorney, Archdiocese of Minnesota.* Then he nodded and gently pushed the curtain aside. The room was unremarkable. A single hospital bed filled the center of the room, surrounded by machinery. An oxygen mask covered a bruised and bloodied head swollen to the size of a small watermelon. A middle-aged African American man wearing clerical garb was sitting in one of the two chairs. He looked up as Luby opened the curtain. A briefcase was at his side and a number of file folders were stacked neatly in a pile on the laundry hamper nearby.

Luby reached out and shook the man's hand. "I'm Roger Luby. Loudoun County sheriff."

The man nodded. "Father Robert Malveaux." He looked into Luby's eyes and spoke in hushed tones. "He's gone in and out of consciousness since they sewed his lip back on. He lost a lot of blood and had stitches to close the wounds. He has two cracked ribs and his right wrist is fractured in two places."

"Has he said anything to you?" Luby inquired, pulling out a pad to take notes.

Malveaux shook his head. "No. Don't think he'll be able to. The nurse told me his attacker also tried bite off his face and chew off his tongue but cut his lips instead. The doctors sewed them back on the best they could."

Luby put his notepad down and did not speak. Two nurses entered the room and were startled to see the visitors.

"Gentlemen, you'll have to leave for at least the next forty minutes or so. We need to change the patient, administer his meds, and get him fed and settled."

Luby nodded. Malveaux collected his briefcase and files and met Luby in the corridor. "I'm going back down to the cafeteria," he said. "You can join me if you wish."

Luby nodded and followed Malveaux silently into the elevator. In the cafeteria, each purchased a large coffee and sat down opposite each other at a table near the back. Luby examined Malveaux, who looked every bit as tired as Luby felt.

Luby sensed he could trust Malveaux and decided he did not have time to beat around the bush. One witness he had hoped to talk to, Mae Etta Rock, was recently deceased. At age sixty-nine, she would hardly have been considered a suspect anyway. The other witness, Reese, was nearly eighty-four, from the data Luby had been able to collect, was doing well, but he had to consider the possibility he might not survive. There was every indication he'd been at The Oaks in 1943 when Harold Gamble drowned. His fingerprints, previously classified as unidentified in the 1983 incident, matched those recently recovered from the Harold Gamble file and from the Charleroi case. He had to consider him a suspect.

"So did the archdiocese send you to give the sacraments to Father Reese?"

Malveaux looked up from his coffee to meet Luby's gaze. "Are you Catholic, Sheriff Luby?"

Luby paused. He was not a man to think about such matters. He had attended Sacred Heart Parish School until fourth grade, when his mother died. Then his father had pulled him out. Said he didn't believe in all that stuff. Now that Luby thought about it, that year was the last time he'd attended Mass or church of any kind. His father had retreated into himself, and Luby and his brothers and sister were left to raise themselves.

"I suppose. My mother was. She died when I was a kid. I'm not a churchgoer, if you know what I mean."

Malveaux nodded. "My mom died when I was a kid too. I ended up with the nuns.

Do you believe in God then, Sheriff?"

Luby took a sip of his coffee. He hadn't thought about God in a very long time. In his entire life, no one had ever asked him that question. He didn't want to offend Malveaux. If he said yes, the priest might feel more comfortable talking to him. If he said no, he might lose the chance to learn more about Reese. Before he could respond, Malveaux spoke for him.

"You want to say yes, Sheriff, because you think I'll be more forthright with what I know about Father Reese. The truth is, you've been mad at God for a very long time—since your mother died—and you haven't really thought much about religion since."

An awkward silence ensured. Malveaux had read him like a book. Luby continued to drink his coffee. He cleared his throat. "I guess you would be right. Don't think about things like that much. Seen too much evil, I guess."

Malveaux turned to the chair next to him and retrieved a file from his briefcase. "Sheriff, I'm not Reese's confessor, if that's what you think. I'm probably here for the same reason you are. I pulled up the story about your jail. I know you had the suicides there and that one of the victims was found—now how should I put this?—skinned."

Luby would have to take a chance. The fact that suicides had recently occurred at his jail had been reported in the press. The fact about the skinned victim had not. Malveaux obviously knew something, maybe something that would help.

"I'm talking to you off the record now," Luby responded.

"And so am I. It was easy to find out about the skinned victim. I just had to ask. It seems a lot of people are talking about it. They're afraid and rightly so."

Luby took another long sip of coffee. "What I have here, Father, is a number of very gruesome deaths, going all the way back to the

1940s. Fingerprints were found at the scene of two deaths, the one from the '80s and the other one from 1943. We also found prints in Sam Charleroi's bedroom. Those fingerprints match Father Reese's. I wanted to talk to him. I had him picked up and sent to the detention center. I really don't know if he's a suspect or a witness or what. I had hoped to get to talk to him tomorrow. I got bogged down today. Next thing I know, I get a call from the detention center that he was attacked and over here at the hospital."

Malveaux shot back. "And what I have, Sheriff, is a number of very gruesome deaths going back twenty-five hundred years. I have more than one hundred cases of child sexual abuse by members of the clergy. One involves a prominent Virginia family. And yesterday, when I was at the courthouse to hear allegations concerning the suspect, Father Reese here introduced himself and told me an unbelievable story. Then the suspect, Father Gaul, got released on a technicality, and just happened to get shot in the head. Then, when I went to find Reese, I found out he'd been beaten up in your jail."

"I want to ask you about Father Gaul, Father Malveaux."

Malveaux smiled. "I knew you would ask me about Gaul. I'm an attorney by trade, Sheriff Luby. I represent the archdiocese. I can't discuss Gaul. You know that would violate attorney-client privilege."

Luby smiled back. "Well then, I'll do the talking. We charged Gaul in the Charleroi case. I was there that night, you know. I can't really explain it. It's something supernatural. Something evil. I just know it. It's just bad. Really terrible. Unbelievable, but real."

Luby suddenly felt as if he was in confession. He'd been to confession exactly one time—before his First Communion, the year before his mother died. She had been well enough to attend. He remembered her smiling.

"I know what you mean. None of this has felt right. Tell me what you remember."

Luby went on. "It was strange. The mother...she was out of control. Like she was on speed or something." He shook his head as if trying to forget the scene. "The father was nowhere to be found. The boy was running through the corridor screaming. There was blood, and there were welts all over his body. He had on a pair of briefs. That's all. I could see the welts on his back. The sounds coming from him—they were guttural. They were coming from inside him but the voice was distorted, like it was being piped into him and projected through his mouth, almost like he was a ventriloquist's dummy."

"Why wasn't any of this information in your report?" Malveaux asked. "You know you're required to turn over this type of information to the defense."

"The kid was running from room to room, jumping on tables and shit like that. One of my deputies caught up with him and was able to corner him in the bedroom."

Luby's voice began to tremble. "The mother was there, and the housekeeper. Ms. Rock was there. So was Gaul, and another priest. I assume it was Reese. It's kind of hard to tell from looking at him now. But I did get fingerprints. Just one print, really, but that's enough to know he was in the room." He was sweating now. "The kid was vomiting on the walls, spewing what looked like words and pictures. There were feces all over the room. It smelled just awful. It was hot and cold and humid and dry all at the same time. It's not what you would expect from a family like them. Not that kind of filth."

"Ms. Rock was saying the Lord's Prayer and Gaul and the deputies were grabbing at the boy. He was swearing, screaming about how Gaul was molesting him. But that wasn't the words he used. The language was foul, vile. I'd never expect it from a kid. I've never even heard grown men use that kind of language. Gaul was screaming, 'Tell me your name' over and over, which didn't make sense, because he was there in the house with the family. He had to know the kid's name. We asked Gaul to leave the room. We took him into the hallway. One of the security officers had passed out. The other one was helping but he had these burns on his palms."

Malveaux took notes. "After the deputies removed Gaul, we got restraints on the boy," Luby went on. "The paramedics sedated him and the deputies took in him in a squad car to the hospital."

"Why didn't you call an ambulance?"

"The father called. Said he didn't want any details about his son's appearance in the report. His badass lawyer called too. Threatened to sue if we called an ambulance." Luby felt ashamed. "Look, I called Child Protective Services. That's what I'm supposed to do. The father was pissed. Said I'd interfered. But I should have put it in the report. I haven't been able to sleep well since that night. I've got an election coming. If Charleroi came down on me, I would lose for sure.

"Father Malveaux, I haven't been able to talk to anybody about this. They would think I'm crazy."

"Why would anyone think that that?"

Luby finished his coffee and dropped his napkin into the now-empty cup. "I've been reading. I think the boy is possessed. I'm convinced they were doing an exorcism. I took that out of my report. If I say what I think was happening, then Charleroi will ruin me for sure. I can't tell anyone what I think. No one would believe it." Malveaux's expression did not change. "And Ms. Rock, Father. She was there, I saw her and I talked to her, but she couldn't have been there. See, I went to interview her again, to ask her some questions. She wasn't home."

"So did you get to talk to her?"

Luby stared into Malveaux's eyes and reduced his voice to a whisper. "She was dead. She'd been dead for almost three or four days when she was there in that room. I saw her. The deputies saw her. The mother said she was working for her. We all saw her."

"There must be some mistake, Sheriff. You must have the wrong date, that's all."

"I checked the death records. She died November first as the result of a head-on collision on Route 15. Her funeral was November 5. Almost her entire church went to her funeral. That night, though, she was there with us in the room. She's on the videotape. The security people interacted with her; so did the mother, so did I, and so did my deputies."

Malveaux stared at Luby. Several nurses entered the cafeteria wearing scrubs and laughing loudly about a pregnant woman who had delivered a baby in the elevator.

"And I need to show you this." Luby handed his phone across the table. Malveaux tilted the screen to get a better view of the images.

"What's this?"

Luby looked around the room. He didn't want anyone to hear what he was about to say. "One of the nurses gave it to me. It's the boy's room here at the hospital. The nurse left the room to get a change of sheets and to call housekeeping. When she came back, she found that the boy had urinated all over the bed and the floor. She said it was unnatural—almost an inch of urine was pooled on the floor under the bed."

"What's all this furniture?"

Luby took the phone and swiped the screen with his fingers to zoom in. "Take a look at this."

There in the corner of the photo was the boy, balanced on the pinnacle of the furniture pile. His mouth foamed and dripped saliva. Luby hit another button and a short video began. The boy howled like a hyena in the bush. At the same time, female screams erupted from his mouth as his body convulsed and he thrashed atop the pile.

"Where is he now?" asked Malveaux. "Is he still here in the hospital?"

Luby pursed his lips and shook his head. "I asked. My office just emailed me. The hospital told the family they weren't equipped to handle this kind of problem. One of the nurses told me that he was still here as late as this afternoon, but his mother had him sedated and sent home. The family hired a visiting nurse to keep him medicated."

"What?" exclaimed Malveaux.

"I'm going to find out what is going on here. I need to talk to him and to Reese."

"And so am I, but I can tell you this: Reese is no killer, and I don't think he's a child abuser, either."

Luby looked sternly back at him. "I'm going back to let Reese rest tonight. I'm going back to The Oaks to talk to Marissa Charleroi. I need to know if I'm right about what Reese was doing."

"I've been through enough here," Malveaux said quietly. "I'm not up to any more stress. It's killing me. All I can do now is pray for him to recover. That's what you need to do too."

CHAPTER
TWENTY ONE

Leesburg, Virginia

The doorbell rang when Vaughn was in the bathroom. He wasn't expecting any visitors. He pulled the curtain back just in time to see the mailman opening the gate to continue his deliveries. Vaughn rushed outside to retrieve the mail from the box attached to the side of the house. Then he took his keys from his pocket and locked the door behind him.

He noticed through the door that the picture his mother kept on the piano of his sister, Trina, had fallen over again. Trina had died a long time ago, when Vaughn was a child. He barely remembered her. He'd often wondered what it had been like for his parents, having two children nearly sixteen years apart. He was lucky to have been born at all. He was all they had after Trina died. For the past week that picture just kept falling over. It wouldn't stay in place. Maybe it was a sign. Maybe his mother was trying to tell him something.

He got into his car and threw the mail onto the passenger seat. He turned on the car and looked behind him to back out of the driveway. He could see the mailman in his rearview mirror, waving from across the street. Virgil had delivered their mail for most of his Vaughn's life. Now Virgil made his way over to the car. Vaughn rolled down the window.

"I rang your bell. I was going to leave this package for you, but it needs a signature," Virgil said. He must have been in his late sixties, Vaughn thought, but he looked fit and energetic. "I realized the signature card was missing. If you hold on, I'll go check and see if it came off in my truck. Just hold on, I'll be back."

The large brown envelope was addressed to him, James Vaughn Rock Jr. The return address was Catonsville, Maryland. Inside he found an old Bible with some papers inside and an envelope, also addressed to James Vaughn Rock Jr. Vaughn placed the Bible on the seat next to him and opened the envelope. He was named after his dad, but no one ever called him James. He'd always been Vaughn. Inside the smaller envelope was a letter dated November 24.

> *Dear Mr. Rock:*
>
> *I regret to inform you that your aunt, Sister Mary Claire St. Bartholomew, went to her eternal rest on November 22, 2003. It was her desire that her possessions be sent to you. Enclosed please find her rosary and Bible, which were her most treasured belongings. During the performance of last rites, Sister Mary Claire gave her confession and expressly asked that a message be conveyed to you. This message was given to her by your mother on November 5 in each of its three parts.*
>
> *Sister Mary Bartholomew asked that I convey the following message to you exactly. She also made her confessor promise to do so.*
>
> *First, she said that I was to tell you that there is a key in your mother's purse that opens a safe deposit box at the First Bank of Leesburg. You need to visit her box and examine its contents.*
>
> *The second part of her message was confusing and the confessor asked her to repeat it. She asked that you seek spiritual guidance and said that you should cease all discourse with that boy, whom she called a vessel, but she would not tell us what boy or where to find him.*
>
> *Third, she said your mother would give further direction to Robert Malveaux when she sees him about what needs to be done. She said Robert Malveaux would understand. She said to make sure you knew that God's word would cover your every need.*

I sincerely hope that these words prove some comfort at this time of loss. We will keep you and your family in our prayers.
Yours in Christ,
Mother Helena

Vaughn tucked the letter into the Bible and retrieved the crucifix from the bottom of the envelope. It was worn and unremarkable. He placed it back inside. His hands shook as he placed his key into the ignition. His mother was the only one who had ever called him by his given name, James, and she only called him that when she meant business. The letter didn't make any sense. His mother had died on the first of November. There is no way she could have spoken to Beta on the fifth. And he didn't know a Robert Malveaux.

The mailman returned, out of breath. "I knew it. It was on the floor of the truck. I knew it was there." He handed Vaughn a pen and a card to sign and was on his way.

Vaughn needed to talk to Marissa, if she'd see him.

CHAPTER TWENTY TWO

Malveaux proceeded up the long driveway. The house and vicinity were quiet. It was barely six p.m., but the fall brought darkness down around him like a heavy velvet curtain. He'd spent the entire day attending meetings on the altar boy cases and trying to convince his superiors that Gaul's death didn't help them because the civil cases still had to be settled. It had taken more than an hour to drive out from D.C. He regretted not being able to stop and see Reese again this evening. He'd spent most of the night there the evening before with Luby and thought it would be best to just let Reese rest.

A full moon provided light, making it easy for him to see the way from his car to the front door. He noted a side door and outlying security booth. He changed his direction slightly and made his way to the side door. He noted that the booth was vacant. The side door, which opened directly into a spacious and well-appointed kitchen, was ajar.

Malveaux carefully pushed open the door to a dimly lit room. "Hello?" he called in his deep baritone. Why was it so dark?

He made his way into the room. Suddenly the door closed behind him. He jumped at the sight of a solitary figure of an elderly black woman. Something was wrong. "You need to keep these doors shut. And you need to get his name before you cast him out," she said in a dry, cracked voice.

Malveaux broke into a cold sweat. This could not be happening. It was the woman from the video, and she couldn't be here because she was dead.

His attention was diverted to footsteps running in the hallway outside the kitchen. The light footsteps of a child. A cackling scream arose from the hallway and the shadow of a figure ran past the kitchen through the corridor. Two beefy men lifted the still-struggling boy from the floor and moved past Malveaux to the stairway at the other end of the long hallway. Apparently for the first time, the remaining members of the group each turned and stared at Malveaux for some time without speaking.

Leon Charleroi sat with his back against a wall but did not rise from the floor. He looked at Malveaux. "How did you get in the house? We locked all the doors to keep Sam in."

All eyes turned to Malveaux, who turned to point at the woman who was now gone. "I came in through the kitchen door and a woman let me in."

Marissa Charleroi looked frantically at her husband and the others. "What did she say?"

"Something about the door, about keeping the door shut. She was just here." Malveaux looked wildly around the room for her. Where was she? His heart beat violently in his chest.

"What did she look like?" Sheriff Luby wiped the sweat from his brow. He was wearing the same shirt he'd been wearing the night before at the hospital when he and Malveaux had coffee together.

Before Malveaux could answer, Marissa Charleroi crossed the room and handed him her cell phone. A video image showed an elderly African American woman in the kitchen, stirring the contents of a large ceramic bowl.

"That's her. That's the woman who let me in."

The group exchanged knowing stares but did not speak. Marissa Charleroi's lower lip trembled. "What else did she say?"

An African American man who appeared to be in his thirties stepped forward. His voice was calm. "Think hard. What exactly did she say to you?"

Malveaux closed his eyes and tried to visualize the conversation, which had lasted only a matter of seconds. "I told you. She told me to keep the door shut."

"What else? What else? There must have been something else!" Marissa Charleroi looked frantic.

"Luby, what's going on here?" asked Malveaux.

Luby had taken a napkin and wrapped it around his hand to stanch the bleeding. "Malveaux, you know exactly what is going on here."

Marissa Charleroi approached Malveaux. "Gaul was trying to help us," she said. Even in the dim light she appeared haggard. Her arms were scratched and bleeding.

Charleroi stood to join them. "Reese was helping. He's the specialist. He's dealt with this kind of thing before." He turned to Luby, enraged. "And now, thanks to you, Sheriff, he's in the hospital because you got the bright idea to arrest him." Charleroi's anger burned bright. "I can't have this getting out. We were going to handle this!" He turned and pointed accusingly at Luby. Charleroi threw himself at the sheriff and pushed him hard against the wall. "That's right, Mr. Bright Ass. We were making progress when you came and arrested the wrong man and then hauled my kid off to the psychiatric ward."

"Don't forget your part in this," Luby shot back. "You're the one who had your man call Social Services to report abuse before I did. Then you tried to back track. You were trying to get the advantage in your divorce case. You didn't even care your kid was being shredded at night by a bunch of pedophiles."

Malveaux stepped in to pull Charleroi from Luby, who was swinging his fists wildly. The lights flickered and returned to normal. Luby turned to Malveaux, pleading, "You're supposed to be here, Malveaux, and you know it."

Marissa panted hysterically, jumping between Malveaux and Luby. She grabbed Malveaux by the arms so that he faced her squarely. "When my husband and I met you in the lawyer's office, we weren't supposed to see you. Our appointment was with Kevin Delmonte. He was supposed to give us a settlement release, we were supposed to sign it and that was supposed to be it."

Malveaux considered her words. He had indeed been surprised to learn about the Charleroi case at the last minute. Cardinal Lowell had sent the file to him, or at least parts of it. He'd insisted Malveaux come to Washington right away, but it had never made any sense. The case had already been settled, for all intents and purposes. That became clear to Malveaux during their interview. He couldn't understand why Lowell had insisted he meet with the Charlerois when the events were so recent. In his experience, these cases often took years to settle. He had assumed it was because they were powerful and didn't want a media circus. During the interview, they had never addressed him by name.

"Beta said you would come," Marissa said. "It's going to be all right. Now that you're here, it's going to be all right." Despite her positive assertions, she continued to cry and shake uncontrollably.

Charleroi pointed at Luby, screaming, "You're finished Luby. I'll see that you're never elected in this county." He grabbed at Luby and the men swung wildly at each other.

Vaughn approached and extended his trembling hand, ignoring the chaos around him. "I'm Vaughn Rock. My mother is the one who let you in. You are supposed to be here. Beta said you'd be here."

Malveaux ran his hand over his head.

"But since you're here, I suppose you already understand that my mother couldn't have let you in, since she passed away two weeks ago."

Malveaux did not respond. Marissa and Leon Charleroi approached. Vaughn's jaw was rigid from exhaustion. "We've been here trying to do our best to get rid of this thing. It said you would come here today, and here you are."

Malveaux shook his head. "I don't know what you're talking about."

Marissa Charleroi grabbed his arm and spun him to face her. "Then why did you come?"

Malveaux pulled his arm away, irritated. "I know what you think is happening here. I know you think this boy is possessed, and I'm not saying that I disagree with that, but right now I think you're all acting like you're crazy. I don't even know why I decided to drive out here this evening. I suppose I felt I had to. To get the settlement papers signed, and because Lowell insisted I come." He looked at each one of them individually and tried to appeal to their logic and rationality, "Luby, I can't believe you're a part of this. We talked. You know that boy needs help. He needs a good psychiatrist. That's the best I can offer here and maybe some prayer. I don't think I have the skills to do what you're asking me to. I think it would be a mistake to engage this thing. Especially right now. Look at yourselves. You're all hysterical."

Marissa slapped Malveaux hard across the face, drawing blood. "Shut up!" she shrieked. "You don't know the first thing about hysteria."

A high-pitched scream pierced the air. "Let's go!" Luby cried. "The sedatives have worn off." He looked from Malveaux to the Charlerois and then back. "You know what you need to do here."

Malveaux's mouth was dry. He recalled his meeting with Reese at the courthouse, which now seemed years ago. During their conversation, Reese had mentioned several times that Malveaux "had permission." His thoughts raced back to his days as a seminarian nearly thirty years ago, when, as part of the curriculum, there was a one-hour lecture on the rite of exorcism. All he remembered was that demonic possession was evidenced by unnatural signs and manifestations. Certainly some of what he had witnessed this evening qualified. He also remembered that the exorcist was not supposed to engage the demon in conversation except for one purpose: to discern its name. Finally, he remembered the exorcist needed permission from church authorities to conduct the rite.

Something dropped hard on the ceiling above them, causing them each to jump and look above their heads. Luby broke free and bounded up the stairs, followed by the group. The home nurse was nowhere to be seen. The bedroom was empty. That meant the boy was loose in the house.

Their attention was diverted to footsteps racing toward them. Unfettered by restraints, the boy lunged, grabbing Charleroi with fury and throwing him head first down the stairs with a screaming rant.

Luby grabbed the boy, who now seemed taller, stronger, and faster, only to be scratched with maniacal intensity across the face with the boy's free hand. Marissa clung behind Vaughn, unmoving and terrified. The boy ran straight for Malveaux, laughed demonically, and then arched his back and levitated off the floor. Malveaux made the sign of the cross before him, pulled a vial of holy water from his pocket, and flung the contents at the boy. The child was thrust to the ground with extreme force, writhing in pain. Red, blistering welts rose from every area the water had touched.

As the boy breathed heavily, his size began to shrink and he collapsed as if the very life force within him had vanished. Marissa pushed Vaughn aside and screamed, "You did it!" Charleroi clung to the banister. Malveaux barely noticed that he was making his way back up the stairs. "Quick, let's get him back into the restraints."

Vaughn nodded and lifted the boy into his arms. The boy breathed deeply as if in a drug-induced coma, a stark contrast to his behavior only moments earlier. Charleroi, Marissa, and Luby worked quickly to secure the boy's restraints on the hospital bed located in the center of the bedroom.

Frantic tapping came from the closet. They looked at each other as Malveaux made his way to open the closet door. Winston and Stroder, the two private security guards bolted from the closet, hysterical.

"We couldn't get out, the door wouldn't budge!" The men looked frantically at the group and ran down the stairs from the house like frightened children, slamming the front door behind them. Malveaux could hear their cars start within seconds and careen down the gravel road away from The Oaks.

Malveaux turned to the remaining group. "The closet door wasn't locked. It wasn't even stuck."

They went down the broad hall and up the stairway. The nurse was back now and called anxiously. She said, "It's started again. He's calling for someone named Robert."

A thin, greasy fog crept from beneath the door. Malveaux could hear a young boy weeping, and then his voice changed. Now it was a woman's voice that called from within the room—the voice of a Creole French–speaking Haitian woman.

"Entrez, Robert. C'est Maman."

Malveaux's head throbbed. A cold sweat drenched his forehead. His chest heaved as he breathed in the sulfuric fog. He reached nervously into his breast pocket, retrieved a pill case, selected a small blue tablet, and popped it under his tongue.

The voice changed again, now a deep baritone so loud that the door vibrated on its hinges. "She's here with me, Robert. Why won't you come in and say hello?"

Malveaux placed his hand over his mouth, which was now dry with fear. "How many people are in this room, Mr. Charleroi?" he asked.

"Two. My son and the nurse. She's highly trained. She's a psychiatric nurse and has a martial arts background. My son is in restraints so he doesn't hurt anyone." Charleroi placed his hand on Malveaux's shoulder. "That's your mother's voice, isn't it?" Malveaux did not answer. "It said your mother would call you here."

Vaughn chimed in, "It said we would be defeated because you do not believe."

Malveaux moved to open the bedroom door. A large bed lay in the middle of the room, surrounded by several blue foam gymnastic pads. The windows were covered with plywood. The boy lay there perfectly still as if asleep. As Malveaux drew closer, the bed began to shake of its own volition. The boy did not move. A water pitcher and glass rose from their place on the nightstand in the corner by the window, flew high into the air, and then propelled themselves across the room, striking the opposite wall and crashing into pieces on the floor.

Marissa Charleroi was sobbing in the hallway. "Mom!" the boy cried, turning his head toward them. "Please, Mom, let me loose. It hurts. Please help me."

Marissa pushed them aside and approached the bed. In an instant the boy's demeanor changed; his face contorted and pulsated as if some force beneath the skin sought escape. A steady stream of urine rose from the bed to the ceiling, spraying them and causing them to move away. The boy's head moved from side to side again, this time relaxing and calling out in the woman's voice.

"Son, I am so sorry I did not get to raise you. Those nuns messed you up. I had to come here instead."

Malveaux froze. It was indeed the voice of his mother, dead nearly forty-five years and yet so familiar. His mind flew back to when she had died. Her death had bothered him for his entire life. He had a fear of being alone. He'd felt alone since the day she'd died and yet he'd never discussed it with anyone—not his brother, not a friend, not under any circumstance. If he had pursued grief counseling as an adult, he was sure he would have learned that his entering the priesthood was his attempt to avoid the pain close personal attachments had brought him. He'd been hiding for a long time, but the circumstances that brought him here this night meant he couldn't hide anymore.

The "gift" resonated inside him. He had to resist conversing with this thing. His heart wanted him to talk to his mother, to learn the mysteries of the other side, but his faith told him not to engage the thing. "Son, I need to talk to you. I need you to get me out of here," the voice pleaded, crying. "It's so hot here." The bed continued to shake, and the voice grew louder and stronger. "I know there's so much you need to ask me, Robert. Ask me before I have to go." The boy's body convulsed, contorted, chest heaving, arms struggling, and the bed continued to shake harder and harder. "Ask me. Ask me!"

Suddenly all movement ceased. The woman's voice continued, but now another voice came from the boy in unison with the woman, the baritone again, this time in Latin. The voices rose louder and louder, leaving Malveaux unable to comprehend the words. He knew that he couldn't engage the monstrous thing in dialogue of any kind. That would be a mistake. It would also be a mistake to proceed without a plan. That's what had happened before, leading to this disaster. Those who'd come before him, Núnes and those who'd confronted it had all been seduced by its words. He'd have to get them to hold off until they were ready. He believed, but was not ready. He was seeing with his eyes and feeling with all his senses an inexplicable evil, ancient as the world itself. He would fight it, but only after rest, after achieving clarity of thought, and after girding himself spiritually.

Luby grabbed Malveaux and spun him around to face him. "Now, Malveaux, are you going to tell me he just needs a psychiatrist?"

The nurse moved in close with a syringe, but Charleroi waved her away. "Too soon. We need to wait at least four hours between doses."

The woman nodded and retreated, along with Malveaux and the others. The group made its way down the stairs and to the dining room, where they sat in silence as the threatening voices called out to them through the night. When the voices stopped, they made their way across the house to the family room. Dazed, they slept until awakened by the late morning sun.

CHAPTER
TWENTY THREE

Charleroi woke and found his wife and Luby sleeping on couches across from each other in the formal parlor, or family room. It was Monday morning and he judged the time to be somewhere between ten thirty and eleven. He made his way into the kitchen. Malveaux was seated on a high stool at the kitchen island, papers laid in various stacks before him.

The floor creaked beneath Charleroi's weight. Malveaux looked up, startled, as Charleroi and Vaughn came into the kitchen. Vaughn opened the door to the refrigerator and located a gallon of orange juice. "Where do you keep the glasses?" he asked. Charleroi nodded toward the cabinet near the kitchen sink. Vaughn removed three glasses and poured juice for each of the men.

Malveaux was the first to speak. "I'm reading some information the cardinal gave me when I arrived. I haven't had a chance to study it in any detail before now."

Vaughn sat at a chair opposite Malveaux and drank his juice. Charleroi leaned against the wall. "Who am I supposed to talk to about any of this?" Charleroi asked. "I have a major meeting this afternoon with my board of directors. Aspirion Sector has special products in development. How am I going to go there with scratches all over my hands and looking like hell? I'm not even ready." Charleroi was angry. He hadn't planned to be up all night, let alone wake up in this condition.

"Why don't you call your assistant to see if she can move your meeting?" Malveaux suggested. "Maybe they could put you on the agenda last, right before the meeting adjourns. You need to be here. Your son is seriously ill."

"Yeah, and tell them your cat went off on you when your power went out," Vaughn added.

"I fucking hate cats. I'll be back," Charleroi said. He went to his study to call his assistant.

Malveaux and Vaughn stared at each other. Vaughn broke the silence. "My mother was born here, you know. She knew this place like you wouldn't believe."

Malveaux nodded. "She's in several of the videos."

Luby entered and updated them on his interview with Agent Hawk, now disabled by what he had witnessed. He asked Vaughn, "Have you seen your mother since she passed?"

He thought for what seemed like minutes before he answered. At last he shook his head. "I haven't seen her, but I've felt that she was around, you know. I did notice some things at home that gave me the creeps. I've been finding these puddles of water in odd places—the kitchen floor, the table. I found one puddle on her dresser. The only other thing I've noticed is the front and back doors being left open, and things being moved around. I thought my cousin had come over to pack away some of Mom's stuff and that she'd washed the dishes. We got into a fight because I told her to make sure she locked the doors when she left. She was angry because she said she hadn't been there and hadn't washed any dishes.

"Your mother let me in here last night," Malveaux said. "She told me to shut the door and said something about getting its name before I threw it out. I think she said 'cast it out.' I thought it was odd to find the door ajar when I got here last night. I thought she just meant for me to close the door behind me. I mean, come on. It was not an average night here by any means. I came in and it was dark, and you were here."

Luby leafed through a stack of papers on the kitchen island. "What are you reading?"

"Reese gave me some papers and so did the cardinal. I'm just starting to make my way through them." He turned to Vaughn. "Son, did your mother ever talk to you about this kind of thing? You know, did she ever tell you any ghost stories? Anything you remember?"

Vaughn shook his head and went to get more juice. "I can tell you what I know. I'm going to make some eggs, though."

Malveaux looked at Luby closely for the first time. His face was puffy. The scratches on his forehead looked red and infected. Charleroi returned and offered Luby some Tylenol and some medicated ointment from a cabinet. Luby splashed water on his face from the sink and applied the ointment, guided by a small mirror on the refrigerator.

Vaughn beat the eggs into a frenzy, adding salt, pepper, and cheese to a buttery skillet. Charleroi made toast. After they were all seated, Vaughn began.

"One night when I was little, my dad and I were sitting on the front porch. We were talking about scary things. You know, ghosts and spirits. There were some other people there, and some of them were older. They started talking about Harold Gamble and how peculiar he'd acted before he died. He'd changed. They said he was a nice boy and that his mother babied him."

"You know, I went to your house the other day," Luby said. "I wanted to talk to your mom about that case. She was a witness when she was a girl."

Vaughn ate his eggs hungrily. "The kid started killing small animals, dogs and cats and stuff, before they found him in the pond. Not his body, just his skin."

Vaughn took a bite of toast and a long drink of juice before he continued. "I was scared. Then Momma came out of the house with some drinks. She was mad about what they were saying."

Marissa entered the room. Vaughn scooped some eggs onto a plate for her. She wolfed them down as he continued. "Later, when she was putting me to bed, she told me that there was more to this world than what I could see. She told me never to tempt the dead, and that if I heard a spirit talk, I should ignore it. She told me I was not to talk back to it ever. I was scared. And she told me that if I ever saw the Bone Man, I should run away."

Vaughn ate the rest of his toast. "I was so scared of Harold Gamble, I couldn't sleep at all that week. Momma said that if a boy named Harold Gamble ever came to play with me, I was to close the door, say the Lord's Prayer, and come find her or Aunt Beta. I didn't know why she would tell me a story like that and try to scare me."

"Sam has a friend named Harold Gamble," Marissa offered. "Sam told me he's been playing with him. I was happy he had made a friend in the neighborhood. Sam said they usually play outside, and since it's getting cold, I told him that when Harold came over he should invite him in." Marissa paused. "Vaughn probably told you. We went to see Beta. She said you'd get rid of it. That thing followed us out there," she looked to Malveaux, pleadingly.

Charleroi turned to Malveaux. "You're a priest, you've seen this kind of thing before."

Malveaux was speechless. Charleroi seemed close to tears. "I'm a businessman for God's sake," Charleroi said. "I don't know anything about this stuff." He pointed at Marissa angrily. "It's all your fault, you bitch."

He lunged at her but was restrained by Luby and Vaughn. "Just stop—you're feeding it!' Malveaux yelled. "All your anger is feeding it, making it stronger."

Charleroi seethed. "I need to get dressed to go to my office. I'll be back later." He looked at Malveaux. "Look. That guy Reese and Father Gaul, they knew about this stuff. You're a priest. You must know something."

Malveaux stared. "I have this manuscript, Reese's notes, and Luby has his old files here. The cardinal told me the thing is something called B-416, but I didn't talk with him about how to get rid of it. I guess Reese was supposed to help me with that." He stood to leave but turned back to Charleroi. "We need to work through this. I need a whiteboard and a copier."

"The copier is in a cabinet in my office. The whiteboard too. I'll help when I get back."

Malveaux copied the B-416 folder from the Caine file along with Reese's notes and brought a set of each to Luby and Vaughn, who were drinking coffee in the kitchen. Sam was there now too, chatting with his mother. He bore no resemblance to the troubled boy from the previous evening. He was thin, tired, and anemically pale. Marissa offered him eggs and toast, and he seemed content to watch the *Today* show on the wall-mounted flat-screen television. The men read while she cleaned up.

Marissa picked up the remote control and wandered through the channels until she reached the cartoon network. The boy watched the program and ate quietly, seemingly unaware that he was being watched with fear by the grown men sitting there, and being looked after by his mother who both feared and loved him at the same time.

Malveaux decided to break the silence. "Sam, your mother tells us that you have a friend named Harold, is that right?"

The boy looked at them and nodded, then returned to the television program.

"What kinds of things do you do with Harold?" Malveaux probed gently.

Sam paused and then responded quietly, "We play. You know, we play in the barn sometimes." He turned his attention back to the television screen.

"What does Harold like to do, Sam?" Malveaux pressed. The boy did not respond. "Does he ride bikes? Play video games? Play basketball? Does he like to swim?"

Sam turned, now interested. He looked at Malveaux directly in the eyes. "He doesn't like the water. He won't go near it, especially the pond."

At the mention of the pond, all turned their eyes toward Sam, who munched on his toast. "He scared me. I told him to stop. He said there were ghosts that walk near the water there and that they curse."

"They curse?" asked Vaughn.

Sam nodded. "Yes, they curse."

Malveaux maneuvered to the table where Sam was sitting. "I need you to think carefully. Tell me what he said exactly. Did he say 'they curse'?"

Vaughn became agitated. He walked over to Sam and gazed into the boy's tired eyes. "You mean they say curse words, don't you?"

The boy shook his head. "No. Harold talks kind of funny. Sometimes he's hard to understand. He said they lay a curse."

"Tell me again," Malveaux probed. "What did they say?"

"They lay a curse to open doors and then they come in."

"Open doors?" Marissa asked.

"Then what?" Vaughn prodded.

"Then they come in." The boy returned his attention to the cartoons, ignoring the adults surrounding him.

"Son?" Malveaux took the remote control and muted the sound to get the boy's full attention. "Did Harold tell you how to get rid of the ghosts? Did he talk to you about that?"

The boy nodded. "He said you have to close the door."

Marissa took the boy's chin in her hand. "Honey, how do you close the door?"

Sam looked annoyed. "He said that only certain doors will open. The ghosts keep trying until they find one. He said somebody named Robert would need to get Michael. He said only Michael can close the door."

Malveaux nodded. "And what about the curse, son, what about that?"

"I don't know. Mom, can I go play now?"

Marissa nodded. "You can play in the living room. Sheriff Luby will keep an eye on you."

The boy and Luby left the room. Vaughn asked, "Well, what does it mean, Father?"

Malveaux retrieved his eyeglasses and the manuscript from the kitchen island. "According to what I've read, and all I've seen, I'm inclined to believe the boy is possessed. I am concerned about his dialogue with this boy, Harold. I'm convinced Harold is very real and very dangerous. I also think there is a strong possibility that Sam suffers from very severe paranoid and schizophrenic delusions. He probably needs to go back into a psychiatric facility for evaluation. I'm not a psychiatrist, I'm a lawyer. But I'm also a priest. I think he should be baptized. I take it that he hasn't been. I would like to baptize him."

Marissa nodded. "That's right, he hasn't been." She looked nervous. "He said Robert needs to call Michael. I know you're Robert, but who's Michael? He said something about Michael needing to shut the door."

Vaughn moved away from the others and looked out the window at the pond. "Michael the Archangel. He defends the world against demons."

Malveaux sat down at the kitchen island. "That's right. Michael the Archangel has historically been seen as a defender of souls."

Marissa joined Malveaux at the kitchen island. Malveaux wished she would calm down. She was so skittish, continually running her fingers through her hair and looking around the room. It made him ill at ease.

The men looked at her, aware there was something wrong. Marissa stared back. "What are you all looking at?"

"Can't you just sit still? What's wrong with you?" Vaughn said. Her twitching and constant motions were clearly getting on his nerves too.

Marissa snarled back, "Look, I haven't had a drink in two days, and I haven't had a cigarette. It's harder than you think, so don't fucking look at me. I'm trying to make changes, OK?"

"Well, if you don't stop shaking and moving, I'm going to have to give you some pills or something because you're driving us all crazy."

Charleroi returned to the room, dressed for work. A computer bag was thrown over his left shoulder. He sneered at her. "Why don't you just be honest, Marissa? Why don't you tell them you haven't had any meth or cocaine over the past two days?" He looked at Malveaux. "I'm headed in to do this presentation. I should be back by five or so. I asked my assistant Travis to come by to help out. He should get here in about forty-five minutes."

"Did you tell him what's going on here?"

Charleroi shook his head. "I told him I needed him for a project that would require his utmost discretion, and that he could never discuss it with anyone outside the people he would meet when he got here."

Luby returned to the kitchen. "Karen just showed up, but she says she's quitting. She said she'll watch Sam until the tutor gets here and then she's leaving."

Malveaux cleared his throat. "Look, Mr. Charleroi, you need to get back here as soon as you can. Your boy told us that we've got some serious work to do here, serious spiritual work."

"I have an initial public offering of my stock in the next several weeks. You know I have a business to run. I could be financially ruined if this doesn't go through."

Vaughn stood. "I need to get out of here for a while too. I've got to run some errands. I need to go to the bank."

Charleroi addressed Vaughn more gently than he'd addressed any of the others. "I'm headed that way. I could give you a ride if you want."

Vaughn shook his head. "No, thanks, I don't know how long I'll be."

Charleroi put his hand on Vaughn's shoulder. "I know it was hard losing your mother, and I know there is no reasonable explanation for what is going on here. I didn't even know she died. No one gave me the message." He glared at Marissa. "I'm sorry I wasn't there for you, Vaughn."

Malveaux stood up. "I'm going to stay here and keep reading, but I suggest that while you're about your business today, each one of you examines your conscience." Marissa looked down at the floor and exhaled hard. Luby stared out the window, averting Malveaux's gaze. "If we have to make amends, we'll each have to look at our own lives and try to right any wrongs. According to the manuscript, that's what Jon Tomas of St. Maarten did."

*****

Sam sat in the parlor playing a handheld video game. His Play Station was upstairs and Karen wouldn't let him go upstairs alone.

His tutor would be coming soon. The room was quiet, punctuated only by the sounds of his game. Then he heard heavy breathing behind him.

Sam turned. He could see his friend outside the window. Harold always wore the same ragged shirt and pants. He looked angry. Sam didn't like it when his friend was angry. His hands were balled into tight fists at his sides. He could hear him speaking and breathing just like he was right there in the room with him.

"Why did you tell them?"

"Tell them what?" Sam asked, rising to cross the room to the window.

"You told them about the ghosts. They're mad, Sam. The ghosts are very angry."

Sam stepped back, conscious of his friend's simmering temper.

"They hurt people when they're angry." Harold breathed deeply, almost hyperventilating. A puddle of water pooled at Sam's feet.

"Sam, what's going on in here? Who are you talking to?"

Sam turned as Karen entered the room. Alice Blandis, the tutor, followed close behind. He turned quickly back to the window, but Harold was gone. Only a glistening pool of water remained on the floor.

***

At the First Bank of Leesburg, Vaughn presented his identification to the bank manager and followed her to the vault to retrieve Box 31. The manager laughed. "This box has been with us for a long time—since 1974. From the access card, it looks like no one's visited it since 1989." She giggled nervously as she pulled the box from the wall and set it on the table. "I'll leave you here. Just ring this buzzer when you're done." She gestured at an old-fashioned door buzzer mounted on the door frame.

Vaughn inserted the key into the narrow metal box and lifted the lid to reveal its contents. Inside there were several envelopes. His mother's will. Newspaper accounts of his sister's death in 1974. He looked at Trina's photo and examined her features. He thought he resembled her, certainly around the eyes and forehead. His nose was different, sharper, and his coloring was lighter. Some light-skinned ancestor must have jumped across the generations to give him his burnished-honey complexion.

He found a yellowed sealed envelope addressed to him. He turned it over. The words "Do not open until after my death" were written across the flap in his mother's steady handwriting. Vaughn opened the envelope and removed a folded document—a birth certificate. The mother was listed as Trina Rock. His sister. Mother's place of birth, Leesburg, Virginia; mother's age, sixteen. Father unknown. Father's place of birth unknown. Child male, six pounds, thirteen ounces. Born May 21, 1974, in Winchester, Virginia. James Vaughn Rock Jr.

Vaughn sat down on the solitary chair in the vault. There were other papers in the envelope. A court order granting adoption of James Vaughn Rock Jr. by his next of kin, his grandmother, Mae Etta Rock. There were newspaper clippings. According to these papers, his sister was his mother, and his mother was his grandmother. Why hadn't anyone told him?

Hot tears streamed down his cheeks. Vaughn collected the items from the box and rang the bell to leave.

***

Karen and Mrs. Blandis were nowhere to be found. Luby heard Malveaux breathing deeply from the settee, where he lay in a deep sleep. Luby paced the room, his heels tapping on the plank floors. The boy was in a sleeping bag behind the two couches, also asleep. A Lego village lay to his right and a video console to his left.

Luby went to the kitchen for a drink and a snack and a chance to decompress by reading the newspaper. It was good Malveaux and the boy were getting an afternoon nap. It was nearly four thirty p.m. and getting dark. There would be no pretty sunset this evening, no pink clouds decorating a fading sky.

***

Charleroi returned to the house. Malveaux was reading, taking notes in the kitchen. Sheriff Luby was gone. According to Mrs. Blandis, he'd gone to his office to sign some paperwork and get some sleep but would be back later. Vaughn's car was gone. Apparently he was still out. Charleroi peeked in on Sam, who was going over math problems.

As he walked down the hallway, he noticed the door to the chapel was open. Marissa was sweeping debris from the floor. Charleroi noted that the stained glass windows had been covered with plywood sheets. The few narrow pews were dusty. He sat down on one near the rear. It was an uncomfortable seat. He cleared his throat to get her attention and she jumped. "Sorry," he said. "I didn't mean to scare you."

Marissa put down the broom and dustpan and sat down in the pew in front of his. She looked into his tired eyes.

"You know, I just want to get Sam through this," Charleroi said.

Marissa nodded. "Me too. I thought I would clean up in here and that we could baptize him in here."

"This isn't going to change anything between us. I made a big mistake when I started seeing you."

Marissa's expression was hard. "I shouldn't have left my family," Charleroi went on. "My wife was a good person. She didn't deserve what I did to her, and neither did my kids."

"You knew what you were doing, and you liked it as far as I could tell. From what I remember, there wasn't a line of cocaine you ever said no to either."

"And you never met anybody you didn't open your legs for. You're a disgrace. It's over. I'm done."

"We'll see how done you are," she retorted. "I have pictures, remember? And that sex tape of you with—what was it, two women or three? Oh—I'm sorry." She laughed. "One was a woman, the other one was a sixteen-year-old girl. I don't think you'd want that to come out and ruin your precious stock offering."

Charleroi remained calm. "And I don't think you'd like to find yourself back in Cuba facing life in prison for the murder of—what was his name?" He pulled a handkerchief from his pocket and calmly blew his nose. "All this dust makes me sneeze. But you wouldn't' be going back to Cuba because that was a lie too Marissa—or should I call you something else, since that's not even your name?"

Marissa's anger left her and she began to shake. She glared at Charleroi. He continued, "My investigator actually found out quite a bit about you. Unless you want to end up in prison, you're going to cooperate with our divorce, leave Sam with me, and go back to that hellhole you came out of."

"He told you! That son of a bitch Vaughn told you, didn't he?" She was furious.

"He didn't have to. I've been able to hear everything. I put a remote listening device in his car the day I met with him. I knew you'd meet up somehow when I asked him to get his mother over here. I know you've slept with him too. I hope he didn't catch anything from you."

A tear slid down Marissa's cheek. "I'm going to turn my life around."

Charleroi's response was direct and unemotional. "I am too. I'm going to right all the things I've done wrong, and that means you won't be any part of my life."

"You can't take my son away from me." Marissa was crying, shaking.

"Oh, no." Charleroi remained calm. "You see, Marissa, you're going to receive a visit from some nice agents from the FBI's Washington field office. There is a federal warrant out for your arrest. Some of those druggie friends of yours have some not-so-nice friends—you know, terrorist, money-laundering types. All your drug dealing has put you right at the center of their activities. The money they've been giving you that you've been sending out of the country—that's a federal offense. And seeing how you lied to get into this country anyway…well, it doesn't look good for you. And don't think you can pretend you're not a user. The track marks on your arms are a dead giveaway."

"And how are you going to stay clear in all this? I'll just say you were part of it," she spat.

Charleroi calmly wiped her saliva from his jacket. "You're so stupid, Marissa. I've been an informant for almost a year since I asked for an investigation. That's when I moved out of here. Everything they've told me about you just reinforced my own conclusions. I gave them the

OK to tap my phone and keep you under surveillance. Those cameras aren't security cameras. They're to watch you."

The doorbell rang. It was probably Luby, who'd said he would return around this time.

"And Vaughn," Charleroi said. "You confessed everything to him in the car, and we have it all on tape. You're done."

"But how did Beta know? How did that old hag know? She couldn't have been in on it."

Charleroi laughed. "Like I said, you're stupid. My people briefed her. She was in on it."

"You don't understand, it was there with us when we went to see her. It attacked her." Marissa looked down. "I know this doesn't mean anything to you, but I am sorry. You don't know how sorry I am. I'm sorry for every bad thing I've ever done. Just let me get out of here. I'll get my stuff and go." She began to sob.

"I think that's a good idea." Charleroi stood and left her crying there.

CHAPTER
TWENTY FOUR

Vaughn awoke from his nap. He looked up at the ceiling but did not move. So much had happened in the past seventy-two hours that he could not keep his thoughts clear. He was forgetting things. He felt like he was back in Iraq. The nightmares, the screaming, the wandering down the town road with no memory of how he'd gotten there. That's how they told him he'd been injured by the IED—wandering through the village like he was sleepwalking. Then there had been all those civilians brutally murdered, then skinned. The government had successfully kept the details out of the press. And there was that strange Iraqi boy who'd spoken English. Vaughn had shared his cigarettes and sweets with the kid. He couldn't remember his name, and in his heart of hearts he knew something was wrong because he swore he'd seen that same boy talking to Sam on the surveillance tapes. The boy reminded Vaughn of a boy he had known and played with sometimes at The Oaks when he was a child.

Maybe this was all part of the post-traumatic stress he had been reading about. His mind was playing tricks again. And the whole thing with his mother. His sister, Trina, was his real mother. But there was no further explanation, nothing. Who was his father?

All of his family was gone now. Mother gone, grandmother gone, father unknown, grandfather gone, Beta gone. Strangely, the safety deposit box told him something he'd always known. He didn't really look like Mae Etta or Jimmy, although he did have some of Trina's features. He was light. They said it happened sometimes that light and dark features expressed themselves through children's hair and honey-colored skin tones across generations.

Sonny his mother's second cousin, was still in town after retiring from his work at The Oaks. Vaughn would talk to him, and he would talk to Charleroi. Charleroi would know. Charleroi had always been there with an odd job, a bicycle on his sixth birthday, extra money in envelopes. There was the call he'd made to Notre Dame Academy, securing Vaughn's admission to the exclusive secondary school. The connections with the local network when Vaughn decided to focus his studies on sound engineering and communications. Charleroi had made each of these connections possible for him. Lots of focus from the distant man. Charleroi had tried to pull strings to keep Vaughn in the States when his reserve unit was sent to Iraq, but Vaughn had refused. He wished he had let Charleroi help. If he had, Vaughn might not be in the mess he was in today.

He remembered a few times as a child when he'd come home and found Charleroi in the kitchen talking with his parents—actually his grandparents, he knew now. His mother had always told him that if he was ever in trouble, he should go to Charleroi. That's what he would do now.

He rose and went to the bathroom to shower. He removed his shirt. There in the mirror he could see deep scratches along his abdomen and chest.

***

Malveaux and Luby sat across from each other at the kitchen table, reading documents and comparing notes. "I've read this file and the diary over several times now," Malveaux exclaimed, exasperated. "I understand that we're looking for a child whose mother is not exactly that."

Luby nodded. "I was able to finish reading the files that Reese left with you."

"Tell me what they say." Malveaux was exhausted.

"I think it's best if you read it yourself."

Luby pushed the manila folder across the table to Malveaux. The tired priest pushed his other reading aside and opened the mimeographed sheets. A faded image at the top right corner of the document bore the Vatican seal. The document was five single-spaced pages. Two pages stapled to the back appeared to be a photocopy of some more ancient document which seemed to be written in Latin.

Testimony

I make this declaration in my own hand as the final confessor of Jon Tomas Nūnes of St. Maarten, who preached here to the enslaved population, seeking reparation for the evil done on behalf of commerce and the inhumanity shown toward our fellow man.

At our first meeting, Father Nūnes bade me destroy several pages of his testimony that he ripped from the writing even in his feeble state. He said this writing was best left uncommunicated, as it contained his own confession between him and God. I did not commit these pages to the fire but instead secreted them away. I have forwarded them to you in a secure packet. Hopefully they will have reached you by now.

As requested, I have provided with this testimony, the writings of Jon Tomas. They were dictated to the boy Lemuel, but some were written in his own hand according to Father Nūnes. I must confess that this in and of itself alerted me to his confused sensibilities and dementia in his last days, as the events he recounted in his recollection had occurred some fifty years earlier. When I arrived, I inquired about the boy, who had certainly grown to manhood during that time. I was assured by all I encountered that Father Nūnes had lived alone in his last years, unattended except by the poor and enslaved people to whom he had ministered these many years. Two servants from the nearby plantation, an elderly woman and a young stable hand, did however offer that on occasions over the years, a young mulatto boy had been spotted near Father Nūnes's door. The woman, a laundress, said she had never approached the boy or spoken to him because she thought him strange. The stable hand was more explicit, calling the boy a "haunt" or "spirit," as his clothes and appearance did not change with the passage of time. The boy related that in earlier years, his friends had played with this same boy and met no good end, drowning in a pool behind the plantation's rear gates. He bade me to steer clear of this boy should I encounter him.

Father Nũnes related that during this tribulation, Monsieur X freed a number of slaves whom he had fathered by natural relations, and made Nũnes promise to baptize each one. They were baptized by him and invested into the faith, and, having accepted Christ, were given a generous stipend to start their life anew. Father Nũnes indicated that after these baptisms and many prayers, he was able to gain release from the evil there and that all in the vicinity were henceforth able to live in peace once more.

We did not immediately discuss the X heir, who by all account was released of possession through Father Nũnes's work. Feeling I must make an account of the heir, I did ask his whereabouts to determine for myself his condition these many years later. Father Nũnes informed me, and it was confirmed by the laundress, that the X heir had many years past made his way to the colonies in America to join his siblings. They had frequent communication with him by letter and through the father, who remained in St. Maarten. There was no indication whatsoever that the tribulation had returned to him. The boy was now by all accounts a devout and pious man and a defender of the Catholic faith in [censored].

And as you requested, I did inquire the name of the evil spirit, but Father Nũnes said he had not discovered it.

***

Charleroi's cell phone rang. He recognized the number as belonging to J.D. Hunt. By the time he picked up the phone, the call had gone to voice mail. Charleroi dialed in his pass code and listened to his old friend.

"Hey, buddy. I hope you're doing well there. I wanted to get back to you about that thing in Catonsville. I sent my guy over there to visit with that nun and they wouldn't let him see her. They said she was in the infirmary or something. I went back myself two days later to see if she was any better. We never got to talk to her. She passed away on November twenty-second. Anyway, let me know when you can get together. I want to update you on the US attorney's request."

Charleroi's blood ran cold.

***

Vaughn drove through the woods to The Oaks. Luby's police car was back, as were two other cars he did not recognize. Malveaux's rental car was parked there, along with one vehicle from the private security company.

Vaughn parked his car and popped the trunk to retrieve his briefcase. He tucked the Bible Beta had sent him into the glove compartment. He needed to talk to Marissa. He needed to warn them all. He shut the trunk and threw the bag over his shoulder. As he walked toward the house, movement to his left caught his attention. Vaughn stopped in his tracks. Walking along the left side to the rear of the house was the boy, the one he had known and befriended in Iraq. He was wearing the same shirt and ragged pants.

"Hey!" Vaughn called. "Hey, stop." He ran to catch the boy, who paid him no attention. Vaughn pulled his cell phone from his jacket and clicked to photograph the boy from the rear. The picture was fuzzy, but he was certain that he had his digital image. Vaughn ran to catch him. He was barely ten yards away when the boy made a sharp right turn behind the house. Vaughn sprinted after him and turned sharply to the right, calling to the boy. But when he turned the corner, there was no one there.

***

"How did you get in here?" Sam asked, looking up from his video game. Harold was standing by the sofa.

"There are all kinds of passages in this house." Harold bounced a small rubber ball rhythmically on the wooden floor.

"Will you show me?" Sam asked eagerly. "That is so cool."

"I'll show you, but you have to promise to keep it a secret."

Sam nodded.

***

Vaughn found Malveaux and Luby in the kitchen, deeply engrossed in what sounded like a theological discussion. Both men turned to look at Vaughn.

"What's wrong with you?" Luby asked, putting his arms squarely on Vaughn's shoulders. He looked intently into Vaughn's eyes and then back at Malveaux. Vaughn shook uncontrollably. Malveaux pushed a glass of brandy into Vaughn's hands, urging him to drink deeply. He pulled out a chair and he and Luby guided Vaughn to the seat.

"You need to tell us what's going on," Luby said. "It might be important. We might not have much time."

"When I was in Iraq, there was this boy. A local kid. I used to see him when I was out on patrol. That day my squad members were killed, I saw him right before the IED exploded. I know something is wrong here because I just saw him."

"Where?" asked Luby.

"He ran behind the house."

Mrs. Blandis burst into the kitchen. "Is Sam in here?" she asked anxiously.

Malveaux stood abruptly, reflexively rubbing the back of his neck with his right hand. It was wet. Blood dripped from behind his ears onto his white collar. There was demonical laughter behind him. All turned to see Sam laughing behind Malveaux. He cried out in an inhuman voice, too deep and dark to come from a child his age, "I'm going to kill you, you motherfucker!"

The boy lunged at Malveaux, who threw up his arms to fend off the attack. Luby grabbed for the boy but missed, leaving him free to attach himself to the hysterical tutor, striking her in the leg and side as she tried to get away. Luby circled back and snatched the boy, who lifted him like a rag doll and threw him across the kitchen island, knocking the pans from the rack above it. The boy would not be subdued as he crashed into the nurse, pummeling, scratching her, and knocking her to the floor, breaking the ceramic tiles where she fell. The suddenness and ferocity of the attack was astounding.

Malveaux lay incapacitated by his wounds, and the nurse lay unconscious. Blood dripped from the boy's frenzied mouth as he foamed and frothed, running toward the tutor and screaming. He threw the woman to the ground as she screamed and tried to defend herself from the attack. Luby scrambled up and seized the boy's hands in an effort to release his chokehold from around the woman's throat. Charleroi and Marissa joined him to grab the boy and pry him from the woman. She lay gasping for air and crying, hysterically.

The boy ran toward the door, throwing it open and running faster than seemed possible down the gravel path toward the woods. All but the tutor followed, watching him flee the house as if in flight; his legs did not touch the ground. As he reached the woods, he stopped and turned toward them, displaying a hideous monstrous visage. In the cool dusk air, his breath emanated from his nostrils with great intensity, like a steam engine. His shoulders hunched forward and he bellowed and growled, the sounds deep, animalistic and unintelligible. He pawed at the ground with his feet like a bull ready to charge. His face, mangled by an uncontrolled and venomous spirit, was unrecognizable, and his arms, back, and legs swelled with muscle beyond his years.

"Excuse me. I knocked but no one answered; someone left the door open, so I let myself in."

The group startled and turned to see Reese entering the kitchen holding his arm in a sling and supporting himself with a cane. A satchel was slung over his left shoulder.

"You scared the shit out of us, Reese!" Malveaux cried. "What are you doing here?"

Reese hobbled toward them. "I checked myself out of the hospital—against orders, of course." He chuckled and looked pale. "I didn't really check myself out. I just left. I've waited my entire career for this. I had to make it here. Where is the boy?" He looked at the tutor, who was crying on the floor with her back braced against the kitchen cabinets.

Vaughn answered without taking his eyes off Sam, who continued to rant and pace. "He's out there. He's saying something, but we can't make it out."

Reese hobbled forward and gently pushed Vaughn aside to gain a better view. On seeing Reese, the boy raged at the sky with great intensity.

"He is speaking an ancient language used at the time of Agamemnon, a derivative of early Greek," Reese said calmly. "It is manifesting itself and preparing for battle. He wants you to leave the house, to follow him. He hopes to disable you all one by one. And by the looks of it, he's done a pretty good job."

Malveaux held a wad of dirty paper towels to his neck, working to stop the bleeding. Reese turned to Marissa. "Make yourself useful. Go get some alcohol and bandages and try to clean out his wounds. Do the same for the sheriff. I am going to need everyone's help."

"What's Sam saying?" Charleroi asked anxiously.

"Well..." Reese stopped to listen. "There's something about all of you." He looked at each one. "Marissa, he keeps calling you Lourdes and says he'll see you in hell because you are a murderer and a thief and one of his own." He turned to Charleroi. "He says you are a guilty adulterer and a womanizer and that you deny your own son."

Charleroi looked furtively at Vaughn, who glared at Charleroi and turned away. Reese looked at Malveaux. "He says you started the fire and it's your fault all those people died."

Malveaux froze, seized by fear and the revelation of another hidden episode from his past. He grabbed a pill from the container in his breast pocket and forced a blue tablet under his tongue. He wept bitterly as he thought of the burns suffered by his brother on his account. No one knew that he'd been lighting matches and throwing them into a waste bin at the rear of his apartment building that day, unaware of the oil-soaked cleaning rags just around the corner. The rags had ignited and the flames spread to engulf his brother, who was coming around the corner to look for him.

Reese turned to Luby. "He says you're nothing. You think your faith will save you." Finally he turned to Vaughn. "He says he knows you from Iraq and that you're a coward like your father. He also says your grandmother says hello."

Vaughn banged his fist on the countertop and paced near the door. "What's he saying about you, then?"

Reese shook his head. "Lots of vile words. He says I'll never catch him."

The boy shifted his language to French, then Hindi, then Spanish. Maniacal twin voices warbled a frenetic duet that emanated deep from within the boy.

"How does it know those things?" Marissa cried.

Reese removed his satchel and set in on the kitchen table. "You would be surprised at the knowledge in the spirit world. Things that have been witnessed. Things that have been seen by forces beyond our comprehension."

Malveaux stood beside Marissa who shook terrified. He recited the Lord's Prayer under his breath.

The thing continued to rant, this time at Mrs. Blandis, who continued to cry hysterically, her head in her hands. "It says you were molested by your uncle and you liked it," Reese said. The woman did not respond. The others tried to ignore her sobs.

The nurse rose to her knees in a stupor. "I'm getting the hell out of here." She stumbled toward the door and into the yard, running as best she could toward her car. Marissa rushed to slam the door behind her.

Luby, Vaughn, and Charleroi remained. "What happens now?" Luby asked.

Reese pulled up a stool and sat down at the kitchen island. "It should be obvious to you all by now. The boy is possessed by a strong demon, an ancient force." The trio watched him silently. "I gave Malveaux my files and I tried to tell him to prepare himself."

"We read the file and couldn't make much sense of it," Luby said.

Reese ran his left hand across his face with a handkerchief dripping with sweat. He did not look well. Vaughn went to the refrigerator and grabbed a carton of orange juice. He poured a tall glass and handed it to Reese.

"Thank you," Reese said, and drank it down while outside the ranting continued unabated. "We—the church—have tracked this beast for a long time. This demon is always associated with a young boy of indeterminate race. There are always references to this boy, but he's usually only seen by one person."

Luby was excited. "Jon Tomas Nũnes repeatedly refers to the boy in his narrative. In fact, he says he dictated the text to him."

Reese nodded. "It also said the boy remained unchanged in all the forty years Jon Tomas preached in St. Maarten."

"And that no one else saw him," Charleroi added excitedly.

Marissa interjected, "Sam has a friend, Harold. I've never seen him. I've told Sam to ask him in. Sam seems to like him, but Harold has never been inside."

"Is his name Harold Gamble?" Vaughn asked.

Marissa nodded. "Yes, how did you know?"

"My mother told me about him. He died when she was a child."

"No, that's ridiculous," Marissa protested. "It's a coincidence."

"He died here at The Oaks in 1943," Luby said. "Reese, your prints were found at the scene. How do we know it's not you? Maybe you brought it here."

"I was there. That's right. I was here in 1983 too. I've been trying to get rid of this thing for decades." He pointed at the Charlerois. "You called in Father Gaul to help you. That was a mistake. Gaul didn't have the moral or spiritual fiber to attack such evil. He probably made it worse. I know what we're dealing with here and it's a demonic force. How else do you explain the deaths at the jail?" Luby ran his hands through his hair nervously. "I can't explain it. They were all in individual cells. No weapons were recovered, no knives or anything. The surveillance film...I saw it. It looks like a tornado swept into the cell, and within seconds they were all dead. Just like that."

"And then there are the ghosts who manifest," Reese said.

Marissa grew frantic. "That guy Reggie who was here. He said a presence was in the house. He said he saw it. All those people who died saw it. They saw it and then they died. We're going to die too."

The lights in the kitchen began to flicker. "You're missing the obvious!" Charleroi shouted. "Ms. Rock was here too."

"She was definitely here after her accident," Marissa agreed, shaking. "She's on videotape and everything."

Malveaux chimed in. "She apparently even let me in last night."

"Yes," Reese said. "And we have the other who is not a mother."

All turned to look at Marissa, sensing she was the least maternal of woman who'd ever lived. Charleroi remained silent, remembering what John Hunt had told him about her genetic condition. Sam was not her son.

"What's wrong with you?" Malveaux lashed out at Charleroi as the lights flickered. "The lights are always going out in this place. Don't you have a backup generator or some candles or something?"

The lights went out, leaving the house eerily dark. There was no sound from outside.

Reese spoke calmly. "You must follow my lead. We do not know what we may see or hear. Do not ask it any questions no matter what evil lies you hear. My job is to learn its true name so we can be rid of it. No one has yet discovered its name."

"I'm going out there," Vaughn said. "Maybe I can lure him in."

Reese shook his head. "No, that's not a good idea. It's not safe."

"How else are we going to get him back in here?" Luby asked, exasperated.

Marissa trembled. "I don't want him back inside."

Charleroi slapped Marissa hard across the face. "You ungrateful bitch! He's our son. He's sick. He needs help. What is wrong with all of you? Sam needs to come in here so we can baptize him and then call a doctor."

Marissa lunged back, scratching Charleroi across the face. "Look!" Vaughn shouted. "Something's wrong. He's not moving."

Charleroi and Marissa suspended their fighting to look out the window. While they fought, the boy had dropped to the ground in a heap. Slowly he got to his knees and began crawling toward the house.

"I'm going out there," Vaughn said. "We can't leave him out there. It's getting dark. It's November, for God's sake. He'll freeze." He moved toward the door.

"Call an ambulance!" screamed Charleroi. "We've got to do something!"

Malveaux looked nervously at Reese. "What do we do now?"

Reese shook his head. "You can't bring him in. If you invite it in, it will kill us all. It's not safe." Reese motioned each one of them closer and traced the sign of the cross over himself and over Luby, Marissa and Charleroi. He braced himself against the counter, using his good hand to retrieve a glass vial of holy water from his breast pocket. Malveaux took the vial from him and sprinkled them liberally while reciting a quiet prayer.

The boy neared the kitchen door. Tears streamed down his face as he howled. "Help me! Please, Mommy, Daddy, please help me. Please." He moved closer and closer along the path. His ears and face were bright red with cold.

"I'm going out there." Vaughn pushed past Luby and ran to the boy, dropping to the ground to scoop him up. The boy kept moving determinedly along the gravel path to the kitchen door.

Reese pushed Marissa aside, slamming the door and turning the deadbolt lock simultaneously. "You can't let them in."

"You're crazy, Reese!" Charleroi cried. "I'm not leaving my son out there!"

"I'm going to call fire and rescue and get them over here," Luby said.

Outside, Vaughn held the boy in his arms. He reached for the doorknob with his free hand and said, "Let me in."

"This is my house, damn it!" Charleroi yelled at Reese. "Who do you think you are, locking him out like this?" As he reached to unlock the deadbolt, Reese slapped his cane down hard across Charleroi's hand, causing the man to leap away in pain. Chaos erupted as

Reese, weakened, wrestled with Charleroi. Luby moved to open the door but was tackled by Marissa, who bit ravenously into his shoulder. Malveaux stood back, dizzy and paralyzed, watching the battle around him.

Vaughn jammed his elbow through the windowpane and reached inside with his free hand to unlock the deadbolt. Reese lay breathing heavily in the corner. Malveaux leapt forward to help Vaughn with the boy.

"You people are all crazy," Vaughn panted. He laid the boy on the kitchen island, sweeping objects sitting there onto the floor.

The child began to convulse. Malveaux ran to keep him from falling to the floor as Reese prayed loudly from the corner. All eyes were on the boy. Malveaux's gaze was turned to Vaughn who held his neck at an odd angle. Face contorted, Vaughn began to wheeze. and spun coughing, contaminated by the invisible vector of possession. Before they could react he grabbed a kitchen knife and lunged at Marissa, stabbing her repeatedly.

He turned stabbing Charleroi in the stomach; hollered, turning to the tutor, slashing her, his arm swinging in fast motion plunging the knife into her again and again. He leapt wildly across the room and then slashed Malveaux across the back before he ran toward Luby. The men struggled on the floor, rolling and crushing the broken glass beneath then. Reese continued to pray frantically, rocking back and forth frantically in tandem with Vaughn's frenzied attack and the convulsions of the boy on the kitchen island.

Luby and Vaughn struggled as a putrid stench rose in the room. Voices of men and women called out from deeply within the boy. Unintelligible screams and a chorus of baritone voices rang forth. The men struggled for Luby's gun.

In the distance, the wail of a siren came closer and closer. The ambulance would reach them soon. Luby screamed, "Someone let the ambulance crew in!"

The boy still lay on his back on the kitchen island, convulsing wildly as Vaughn rampaged through the kitchen, stabbing at Reese as the priest prayed loudly with all his strength in an effort to exorcise the demon. "Tell me your name! Tell me your name!"

As Vaughn raged, Reese began quietly reciting the Litany of the saints. "Holy Mother of God. Holy Virgin of virgins. St. Michael. St. Gabriel. St. Raphael. All holy angels and archangels. All holy orders of blessed spirits. St. John the Baptist, St. Joseph. All holy patriarchs and prophets."

Malveaux responded to each invocation with fervor. "Pray for us." Reese continued the Litany as the turmoil in the kitchen escalated. Malveaux synced with Reese. "Deliver us, O Lord."

The demon swirled, larger now, giving Malveaux the opportunity to view the beast in its demonic glory. It screeched, speaking to him in curdled tones. "You'll never defeat the pedophiles of the church. Your mother killed herself because of you and your brother. You will fail here."

The demon turned its attention to Reese, taunting him. "You will never conquer us, you want to be like us; to feel the power of the ancients, but I tell you this: I will greet you at the gates of Hades this very day!"

The voice switched now, mimicking the gentle whisper of a child. "Woman, you call yourself her name, but we both know who you really are." The voice, now altered, called out in a booming baritone. "Woman. I'll see you in hell in just 2 years, on October 13th." Marissa screamed uncontrollably covering her ears at the fearful words.

Reese slouched down, weakening. "Don't listen to him. Everyone. Listen to me. Tune him out. Keep praying. Don't stop praying no matter what it says or does. Don't listen to it."

Malveaux began the Lord's Prayer. "Our Father who art in heaven, hallowed be thy name; thy kingdom come; thy will be done on earth as it is in heaven. Give us this day our daily bread; and forgive us our trespasses as we forgive those who trespass against us; and lead us not into temptation, But deliver us from evil."

At the word evil, Vaughn rushed Malveaux, knocking him down and then pouncing onto Reese like a rabid, feral cat, expelling nauseating greasy smoke from his nostrils. Reese raised his good hand and placed it on Vaughn's forehead, unassailable as he directed the hideous beast.

"I command you, unclean spirit, whoever you are, along with all your minions now attacking this servant of God, by the mysteries of the incarnation, passion, resurrection, and ascension of our Lord Jesus Christ, by the descent of the Holy Spirit, by the coming of our Lord for judgment, that you tell me by some sign your name, and the day and hour of your departure. I command you, moreover, to obey me to the letter, I who am a minister of God despite my unworthiness; nor shall you be emboldened to harm in any way this creature of God, or the bystanders, or any of their possessions."

Vaughn froze, now poised over Reese, mesmerized by the rhythm of his steady words. Luby, conscious, but wounded moved in to subdue their attacker, crawling around the lifeless body of Ms. Blandis and grabbing Vaughn as Reese continued to pray. As Luby held Vaughn in his grip, Malveaux could see Sam's form rising from the kitchen island; writhing and transforming, transparent now revealing a glowing inner skeleton. The boy's flesh then materialized. Blue flames thundered forth from every orifice, scorching his mouth, nose and anus. Maggots rained about them, bursting onto the floor as mature flies which raced in unison to devour Marissa who swatted them madly away from her.

Vaughn rose above them now, suspended by the power of an invisible hand. An ancient, primeval shriek ricocheted around the room. "One of us will leave you in this very hour."

Reese screamed. "We're close. We are close. Keep praying. Only a few minutes more."

Malveaux stretched wide his arms directing one palm toward Vaughn and the other in the boy's direction. He plunged deep into the recesses of his memory to that place where all rote memories were stored. Surging past all logical recollections, the words surged to his lips allowing him to pronounce the command he learned decades ago, while in seminary. Using all remaining strength he recited the powerful directive while genuflecting with all his might:

"I cast you out, unclean spirit, along with every Satanic power of the enemy, every specter from hell, and all your fell companions; in the name of our Lord Jesus Christ. Be gone and stay far from this creature of God. For it is He who commands you, He who flung you headlong from the heights of heaven into the depths of hell. It is He who commands you, He who once stilled the sea and the wind and the storm. Hearken, therefore, and tremble in fear, Satan, you enemy of the faith, you foe of the human race, you begetter of death, you robber of life, you corrupter of justice, you root of all evil and vice; seducer of men, betrayer of the nations, instigator of envy, font of avarice, fomenter of discord, author of pain and sorrow. Why, then, do you stand and resist, knowing as you must that Christ the Lord brings your plans to nothing? Fear Him, who in Isaac was offered in sacrifice, in Joseph sold into bondage, slain as the paschal lamb, crucified as man, yet triumphed over the powers of hell. Be gone, then, in the name of the Father, and of the Son, and of the Holy Spirit. Give place to the Holy Spirit by this sign of the holy cross of our Lord Jesus Christ, who lives and reigns with the Father and the Holy Spirit, God, forever and ever."

Reese shouted a mighty amen, picking up where Malveaux left off; perfectly reciting the Roman ritual he had delivered many times in the past. Luby struggled to hold Vaughn still as Reese's words poured forth.

"I adjure you, ancient serpent, by the judge of the living and the dead, by your Creator, by the Creator of the whole universe, by Him who has the power to consign you to hell, to depart forthwith in fear, along with your savage minions, from this servant of God, who seeks refuge in the fold of the Church. I adjure you again," Reese made the sign of the cross on Vaughn's forehead. "Not by my weakness but by the might of the Holy Spirit, to depart from this servant of God, whom almighty God has made in His image."

Malveaux marveled at Reese's strength in the midst of grievous injury. The elderly injured priest, propped his back against the cabinets raising this hand and making the sign of the cross in the air as he spoke.

"Therefore, I adjure you every unclean spirit, every specter from hell, every satanic power, in the name of Jesus Christ of Nazareth, who was led into the desert after His baptism by John to vanquish you in your citadel, to cease your assaults against the creature whom He has, formed from the slime of the earth for His own honor and glory; to quail before wretched man, seeing in him the image of almighty God, rather than his state of human frailty. Yield then to God, who by His servant, Moses, cast you and your malice, in the person of Pharaoh and his army, into the depths of the sea. Yield to God, who, by the singing of holy canticles on the part of David, His faithful servant, banished you from the heart of King Saul. Yield to God, who condemned you in the person of Judas Iscariot, the traitor. For He now flails you with His divine scourges; He in whose sight you and your legions once cried out: "What have we to do with you, Jesus, Son of the Most High God? Have you come to torture us before the time?" Now He is driving you back into the everlasting fire, He who at the end of time will say to the wicked: "Depart from me, you accursed, into the everlasting fire which has been prepared for the devil and his angels." For you, evil one, and for your followers there will be worms that never die. An unquenchable fire stands ready for you and for your minions, you prince of accursed murderers, father of lechery, instigator of sacrileges, model of vileness, promoter of heresies, inventor of every obscenity."

Vaughn, wrestled with Luby, hurling him aside. He seized Reese, clawing at his tattered flesh. Malveaux could hear the sirens of the fire department now upon them. Reese struggled pronouncing his words now with difficulty as he fought with his last ounce of strength. Coughing blood and sputum, his tattered lower lip dangled from his face dancing with each word.

"Depart, then, impious one, depart, accursed one, depart with all your deceits, for God has willed that man should be His temple. Why do you still linger here? Give honor to God the Father almighty, before whom every knee must bow. Give place to the Lord Jesus Christ, who shed His most precious blood for man. Give place to the Holy Spirit, who by His blessed apostle Peter openly struck you down in the person of Simon Magus; who cursed your lies in Annas and Saphira; who smote you in King Herod because he had not given honor to God; who by His apostle Paul afflicted you with the night of blindness in the magician Elyma, and by the mouth of the same apostle bade you to go out of Pythonissa, the soothsayer. Be gone, now! Be gone, seducer! Your place is in solitude; your abode is in the nest of serpents; get down and crawl with them. This matter brooks no delay; for see, the Lord, the ruler comes quickly, kindling fire before Him, and it will run on ahead of Him and encompass His enemies in flames. You might delude man, but God you cannot mock. It is He who casts you out, from whose sight nothing is hidden. It is He who repels you, to whose might all things are subject. It is He who expels you, He who has prepared everlasting hellfire for you and your angels, from whose mouth shall come a sharp sword, who is coming to judge both the living and the dead and the world by fire."

Sam's body descended to the surface of the kitchen island. Malveaux watched the boy's body convulse. Bolts of electricity pulsated beneath him. The boy cried out; his words thundering from him like a tidal wave. "We are the minions of Bael. We have roamed the earth from the day we were cast out of heaven."

Malveaux moved in closer, praying feverishly aloud with all his strength. "I command you. Tell me your name!"

Sam cried out, now frantic. "Help me. Don't let me die! They won't let me go. Don't let them take me!"

The demon wheezed. "Priest of God. My name is Deceit! I will depart now, but I am taking these souls with me and am leaving my twin with you!" A sonic wave reverberated from the boy's body throwing Malveaux in a heap across the room. Sam collapsed, his body motionless on the kitchen island.

As Malveaux drifted from consciousness, he could hear Reese whispering a prayer of deliverance and he could see Vaughn hunting

Marissa who ran from the room, tripping over the rug in the hall way. Instantly the beast was upon her, clawing and biting at her chest.

Malveaux could hear the firefighters inside the house now.

"Grab him." Luby shouted. The firefighters threw themselves upon Vaughn pulling him by the shoulders and waist, prying him from Marissa who lay gurgling beneath them, passing into unconsciousness.

Epilogue

Dr. Greenhill of the Loudoun County medical examiner's office seemed relaxed as he testified before the grand jury. He had been with the office only a week at the time of the incident, but his experience testifying as the deputy medical examiner in St. Louis had prepared him well. He had been testifying without a break for past ninety minutes, relaying his office's findings in the deaths that had occurred several weeks before at The Oaks, an old plantation just outside Leesburg.

He had described the death of Mrs. Alice Blandis, who had served as a tutor for the Charleroi family. Her cause of death was lacerations to the femoral artery secondary to blunt-force trauma. She suffered more than 136 secondary wounds to her throat and upper torso. Nearly 70 percent of the knife wounds were on her hands. In his years as a forensic pathologist and medical examiner, Greenhill had never seen hands that were essentially filleted as they fought for life. Blandis's husband was in the process of filing a multimillion-dollar wrongful death suit.

Summarizing Mr. Charleroi's death had taken thirty-two minutes. The former congressman had suffered a number of wounds to the upper back, but the cause of death was a cerebral hematoma caused by a severe blow to the head. Mr. Charleroi had been transported from the scene of the carnage to the trauma unit at the Inova Fairfax Hospital, where he lingered in a coma for eight days until his death. His ex-wife Agnes and grown children were at his bedside at the time of death.

Darien Reese, the visiting priest from Rome, had been beaten and stabbed with such physical force that he was rendered unrecognizable.

A colleague from the Vatican who had been visiting New York was summoned to identify the body after the members of the Washington Archdiocese with whom Reese had been consulting were unable to do so. Reese was ultimately identified by his fingerprints. He left no living relatives. Reese's belonging were boxed and retuned to Rome, where a memorial Mass was held and well attended by members of his order.

After a recess which turned into a lunch break, Greenhill started his testimony on the death of the juvenile decedent, Samuel Vincent Charleroi. Greenhill testified to the number of welts and scratches on the boy's body, circulating photographs that brought tears to the eyes of several grand jury members. Greenhill testified that his review of the medical records from the boy's recent hospitalization, combined with the pending police investigation, were consistent with child abuse.

As for the cause of death, although the boy's body showed a number of scratches, lacerations, and burn marks, none were contributing factors to his death. When asked about the cause of death, Greenhill looked into the prosecutor's eyes and stated in a loud voice, "The cause of death was drowning."

Greenhill calmly described his findings but provided no explanation of how the drowning had occurred. The prosecutor spent nearly ten minutes asking questions about the medical examiner's other significant findings, including the numerous scorch marks on the boy's back, buttocks, and rear calves. Greenhill testified that the marks were consistent with some type of conflagration beneath the boy. The ambulance technicians who first reported to the scene, and the members of the Fairfax County forensics unit and the FBI liaison who arrived later, all testified that a large amount of ash was found under the boy.

Testimony from Sheriff Luby and Father Malveaux, who had survived, indicated that on the day of the incident, they had been reviewing written files and records that were photocopies of original records provided by Father Reese. But officers testified that no records were found among Reese's personal effects, either in his room at the rectory or on his body. Malveaux described the records as historical and religious in nature but could not be precise regarding their content. Luby only offered that he had reviewed a mimeographed copy of an ancient diary. He noted that some pages had been missing and the narrative had been especially difficult to read as the translation was written in longhand.

Both men were empathic that at the time of the incident, no candles or incendiary devices were in use in the kitchen area. Neither had witnessed abusive behavior during their interaction with the family, although both said that their involvement with the Charlerois was directly related to their investigation of the molestation allegations lodged against Father Gaul. Luby and Malveaux agreed that the lights seemed to work unevenly in the house. They had requested lights or flashlights at some point, but neither remembered using or seeing candles. The court ordered their comments about an exorcism stricken from the record as there was no evidence that Sam Charleroi was the object of such a ritual at the time of his death.

Marissa Charleroi did not testify but gave sworn videotaped testimony from the Kelburton Psychiatric Hospital in Richmond, Virginia. After hearing her testimony, the judge asked the jury *sua sponte* to disregard the evidence because he questioned her competency. Grand jury members were further instructed to disregard her references to Satan, the devil, and the demon. Jurors were further instructed that no evidence had been presented to verify the existence of ghosts or poltergeists.

Upon motion by the defense, the judge allowed a truncated portion of Mrs. Charleroi's testimony to be read, wherein she stated that she and friends had tried witchcraft after binging on methamphetamines, cocaine, and alcohol in order to help her communicate with her deceased sister. The court accepted the prosecution's argument that Mrs. Charleroi's use of witchcraft may have been an alternate explanation for the abuse of the juvenile decedent, which they argued resulted from occult practices rather than from the defendant's actions.

After Mrs. Charleroi's treatment for her injuries, she was tried and convicted of racketeering, drug charges, money laundering, felony child abuse, conspiracy to commit murder, attempted murder, heroin possession, and illegal entry into the United States. She was sentenced to life imprisonment and sent to the women's prison in Red Onion,

Virginia. She died two years later on October 13th of indeterminate causes.

Neither the prosecution nor defense was able to locate a minor witness who was identified as John Doe in the record because of his age. The investigating officers and paramedics testified that a young boy had been found hiding in the pantry at the time of the incident. Identified only as Harold, the boy was described by witnesses as being soaking wet at the time he was discovered in the kitchen at The Oaks. Richard Newton, corporal with the Loudoun County Volunteer Fire Department, testified that he and others told the boy to stay put so they could ask him some questions and contact his family. Corporal Newton said he and his colleagues were concerned for the boy, who appeared to be unbathed and wore ragged clothing. Newton confirmed that he and others lost track of the boy as the injured were taken from the scene, and that he could not be located later that evening. The Loudoun County sheriff's office confirmed that a canvass of the neighborhood and schools in the area failed to locate the minor witness.

Vaughn Rock was charged with murder in the first degree in the deaths of Mrs. Blandis, the private tutor for Samuel Charleroi; Napoleon Etienne Charleroi; and Father Darien Reese of Rome. Further charges against him included the attempted murders of Marissa Charleroi, Father Robert Malveaux, and Loudoun County sheriff Roger Luby; mayhem; false imprisonment; conspiracy to commit murder; assault with a deadly weapon; and endangerment of a minor. To further support its case, the prosecution offered evidence in the form of letters and other documents found in a Bible in Mr. Rock's car. The letters confirmed that Leon Charleroi was the natural father of Vaughn Rock and documented an exchange of payments over the years to Mr. Rock's grandmother for his general support and care. The prosecution argued that Vaughn Rock sought to murder Samuel Charleroi in revenge for parental rejection. His purported affair with Marissa Charleroi was offered as further evidence of Mr. Rock's scheme to get back at the father who rejected him. Mr. Rock was ordered held without bond at a secure psychiatric facility in Richmond, where he was prescribed a series of psychotropic drugs and therapy. After two years he was judged unfit to stand trial due to his mental state and committed for further treatment until such time as he was fit and able to stand trial. Doctors testified that Mr. Rock displayed textbook signs of paranoid schizophrenia, with auditory and visual hallucinations.

The diagnosis was corroborated by army psychiatrist Edmund V. Anderson, who had served as a member of Mr. Rock's platoon in Iraq. Dr. Anderson testified that Mr. Rock's medical discharge from the Virginia National Guard was initiated after he was observed on multiple occasions to be talking to imaginary subjects. Shortly after the diagnosis, Mr. Rock was wounded by an IED, accelerating his medical discharge and dispatch back to the States. Dr. Anderson testified that Mr. Rock had not participated in any psychiatric therapy during his rehabilitation at the Walter Reed Army Medical Center because his psychiatric records had not reached the staff at Walter Reed during his hospitalization. Treatment at Walter Reed was focused on Mr. Rock's physical injuries only. Dr. Anderson further testified that Mr. Rock's medical records had been located only recently, before trial, after being found misfiled with the records of a solider named Rocco Preeti of Patterson, New Jersey.

At the hospital in Richmond, staff generally avoided care of J. Vaughn Rock Jr., claiming that strange phenomena in the form of temperature changes occurred in his presence. Staff reported that he told them things about themselves– personal things that no one else knew. After two suicides among the staff, Mr. Rock was transferred to the Clifton T. Perkins Hospital for the Criminally Insane in Baltimore. He remained on lockdown status and was allowed one hour of exercise per day. Therapy and psychiatric treatments failed to yield positive results. Periodic medical reports to the court reflected the serious and persistent nature of Mr. Rock's psychiatric disorder.

Visits to Mr. Rock by members of the public were curtailed after members of a paranormal church called The Gate led to a bizarre attempt to liberate Mr. Rock from confinement, ending in a near riot and a four-day lockdown of the hospital. Mrs. Charleroi's connection to The Gate and the members of the cult who died in the Leesburg

Angela Ciccolo

jail bolstered the prosecution's contention that Mrs. Charleroi and Mr. Rock had conspired to abuse and murder Samuel Charleroi in an effort to secure Leon Charleroi's personal property and business assets. Visitation to Mr. Rock was subsequently limited to family members. His ex-wife and children declined to comment when the press asked about him after the riot.

Father Malveaux spent four months in convalescence and then resigned from the priesthood to work as an attorney for several small nonprofit organizations in Chicago. After a short courtship, he married a volunteer worker, Shirley Banks. They moved to Chicago's South Side to a house Ms. Banks inherited from her father. From time to time Malveaux receives letters from his order asking him to return to the priesthood. He takes joy in burning the letters in the living room fireplace. He sees his brother once a year and attends Mass daily. Malveaux continues to suffer from unremitting night terrors.

Malveaux retrieved the contents of a safe deposit box belonging to his friend Donald O'Reilly after O'Reilly's death from secondary infections related to AIDS. Malveaux copied and forwarded the contents of the box to reporter David Levin of *The Secret*.

O'Reilly's documents led to the indictment of an elderly, Father Charles. On account of the man's dementia and health condition, prosecutors declined to proceed to trial.

Cardinal Lowell and the Archdiocese of Washington settled the altar boy claims for an undisclosed sum in the spring of 2007 after a series of articles published by David Levin in *The Secret* disclosed internal memoranda describing the church hierarchy's efforts to destroy evidence related to the DC altar boy claims. Levin received a Pulitzer Prize for investigative journalism. His new book, *Vatican: Shattering the Code of Silence*, was one of the bestselling nonfiction books of 2006.

Cardinal Lowell abandoned his efforts to beatify Jon Tomas Nûnes of St. Maarten. When asked about his efforts to win sainthood for the priest who served the slave population, Cardinal Lowell was quoted as saying, "The matter remains under investigation."

An articulate and passionate group of lay leaders founded an advocacy organization to agitate for reforms in church leadership. The group continues to grow in the United States and internationally and has assisted thousands of victims with counseling, rehabilitation and with their legal claims.

Roger Luby was reelected in his run for Loudoun County sheriff. Two weeks after the Rock trial, Luby announced his decision to retire from office and made plans to move near his brother's home in Santa Clara, California. He was killed four weeks later in a three-car accident on his way to Dulles Airport when a tractor trailer jackknifed and slammed into vehicles on eastbound Route 28. He was the only fatality.

In 2007 six handwritten pages purported to be from the original journal of Jon Tomas Nũnes were purchased as part of a private sale to the Vatican archives by an obscure art dealer in Moscow. An unidentified source confirmed the pages were authenticated and filed in the archives with other material related to the Caine file.

In 2013 the Virginia Court of Appeals held a hearing on the matter of the conviction of James Vaughn Rock Jr. The defense charged that the prosecution had withheld DNA evidence and other material evidence that could have cleared their client. The appellant offered film obtained from Aspirion that had not been available at the time of trial. At the time of his death, Mr. Charleroi had been wearing a Cybervisionwear suit jacket he used during his board of directors meeting. The jacket remained activated throughout the attack. In an *in camera* hearing, the court was able to view the attack in great detail. Experts from Aspirion testified that the jacket had been returned to the company by one of Charleroi's aides, who had come to the scene recognized the jacket as the Cyberisionwear prototype, important company property. Aspirion's custodian of records testified regarding the company's possession of the jacket, which it produced for examination after it received a summons from the appellant requesting "any and all transmissions projected from the jacket at the time of Charleroi's death." The company representative testified the film had not been edited or altered. An expert witness for the commonwealth agreed.

The evidence showed the Cybervisionwear jacket was activated at 4:15 p.m. by Leon Charleroi during a demonstration at the company's board meeting on the afternoon of his death. The suit had not been deactivated and remained live at the time of the incident. The transmission was played for the court in chambers, though the judge described it privately as "unhelpful because all [he] could see was a tornado in the room." The defense team argued that the transmission conclusively demonstrated Vaughn Rock was not in the kitchen at the time of the attack. Of particular consequence were frames 11315 to 11998 of the transmission, which showed Mr. Rock visible outside the kitchen door and in the backyard of the mansion at the time the attacks were taking place.

The defendants further asserted that no DNA evidence from Vaughn Rock was found at the crime scene, and that with the injuries he'd suffered and allegedly caused, it would have been impossible for him to have left no traces of DNA at the scene. The court ruled the DNA evidence inconclusive and accepted the prosecution's argument that the number of people in the home at the time of the incident and the actions of first responders contributed to the contamination of the crime scene.

The prosecution, which hoped to uphold the conviction, relied on evidence presented at trial in the form of several security cassette tapes found pursuant to a search order of the Rock family home after the incident. The tapes showed various views of The Oaks, including several of Samuel Charleroi playing in his yard with an unknown child. Other scenes revealed multiple images of Vaughn Rock inside the property, generally in the evening and night hours, walking through the mansion or sitting in the kitchen, parlor, or bedrooms. The court rejected the defense's argument that the presence of a skeleton figure walking along the corridors of the mansion with Mr. Rock conclusively demonstrated the films had been altered. The court rejected this evidence, relying on expert witness testimony, to a reasonable degree of scientific certainty, that the images were defects in the film from the factory. The court ruled, that in its opinion, the videotape evidence reinforced the charges of conspiracy to commit murder between Marissa Charleroi and Vaughn Rock. The court further accepted the prosecution's argument that Mr. Rock's reflection in the kitchen window may have given the appearance that he was outside the kitchen at the time of the attack, but that the evidence presented by the fire-fighters on the scene could lead a reasonable juror to find that Mr. Rock was indeed inside the house at the time of the crime beyond a reasonable doubt.

The court upheld the conviction of Marissa Charleroi and James Vaughn Rock Jr. on all charges, including criminal conspiracy to defraud and murder Leon Charleroi. Despite the serious evidence against him, the court sustained its finding that Vaughn Rock suffered from severe mental illness, and it remanded the case to the lower court for a determination of whether a sentence of not guilty by reason of insanity was appropriate. The lower court agreed with the determination and returned Mr. Rock to treatment at an undisclosed medical hospital in southwest Virginia. After several years of aggressive and purportedly successful treatment, James Vaughn Rock Jr. petitioned for release from custody, seeking a return to society. Mr. Rock's petition was denied. During a visit to the hospital dental clinic for an abscessed tooth in December 2013, Vaughn Rock slipped away from his attendants and left custody. His current whereabouts are unknown.